JUNO

MW00846843

KING OF STORMS AND FEATHERS

King of Storms and Feathers

Book 1: Courts of the Star Fae Realms

Copyright © Juno Heart 2023

All rights reserved.

Cover design by saintjupit3rgr4phic

Special Fae King Edition paperback design by Orina Kafe

Character art paperback & hardcover illustration by Xena Fay

Edited by The Word Faery

Ebook: ISBN: 978-0-6456242-6-7

Paperback: ISBN: 978-0-6456242-7-4

Special Edition Color Hardcover ISBN: 978-0-6456242-8-1

Special Fae King Edition Paperback ISBN: 978-0-6458956-0-5

V231209

Author's Note

This series contains dark, steamy elements and is suitable for mature readers. Although all major plot elements are wrapped up in this book, there's a **juicy cliffhanger** with **a scream-out-loud plot twist** that won't get resolved until book two.
So mind the cliff and the hero with morals approximately the color of a raven's wing.

For detailed information on content warnings, please visit Juno Heart's website.

To the brave souls sallying forth, welcome to the **dark side** where the villain will break your heart, then piece it back together in better shape than ever... **eventually**.

*For the lost leaves that were blown far from home.
If you've been stomped on and broken, bide your time
and rebuild your strength... what has been forgotten will be
remembered.*

Zali O.

Chapter 1

THE GIRL

R ough voices woke me. I wrapped my fingers around rusty bars, blinking and focusing my gaze through swollen eyelids.

An awful taste soured my mouth, and my head pounded as if I'd been unconscious for a week.

Where the hell was I?

The sun burned my skin as I stared down at three hooded figures who stood in a cloud of red dust below me, their boots planted wide and arms folded across their chests.

I moaned, dropping my forehead against the bars and rearranging my sweaty limbs. The space was tiny, sticky with blood, and I hated to think what else. Nausea swept over me as cold horror dawned—I was trapped inside a cage.

"Get her out," said the tall, hooded male in the middle of the group, his deep voice sounding rough with disuse.

A shock of dark gold hair trailed down the front of his shoulder, and his partly opened cloak revealed a black shirt and muddy leathers. When my gaze landed on the water pouch hanging from his lean hips, a shudder of longing rolled over me.

If I could, I'd stab my own eye out in exchange for a drink.

"Her?" asked the slavemaster, reaching into the cage and tugging on the chain that linked my wrists together. "She's too scrawny for hard labor."

Anger boiled my blood. I wished I had the energy to spit on him.

Gold-hair lifted his chin. "If that's the case, your price must reflect her condition. Do you wish to lecture me or make a sale?"

The man was fae, I was sure of it. No other species spoke with such casual arrogance.

Where was this place? The light was too bright, too harsh to be the Earth Realm, which meant I was far from home and probably fucked. I swallowed bile and took deep breaths, trying to slow my hammering heart.

Steel shuddered, locks clicked, then the slaver's calloused fingers dragged me from the cage.

The movement amplified the hunger gnawing at my innards, and the filthy shift I wore fell farther down my shoulders. It gave no protection from the bite of the midday sun or the harsh glares of the fae.

I blinked at my bare feet—a mess of bruised flesh and badly healing sores—and rolled my wrists. Rubbing my head, my fingers ran over a painful bump, and I hissed out a curse.

The ground tilted, and I listed sideways. The bearded slavemaster shook me, a warning not to ruin his sale. As the three fae stepped closer to inspect me, I reeled away from the glow of their supernatural eyes.

Gold-hair's silver gaze burned bright, more merciless than the desert sun. The fae on his right, a female with blue hair and eyes to match, glared at me as if she'd never seen anything so repulsive.

Long dark hair fell into the other male's syrup-brown eyes, tiny lines crinkling around them. The laugh lines suggested that he was the kindest of the three. But more likely his laughter came at the price of another's pain.

I had no idea where or even who I was, but I remembered something important about the fae as a species. They were bastards. Every damn one of them.

With a greasy thumb, the slavemaster peeled apart my cracked lips, displaying my teeth for their inspection. I raised my head and glared at the tall golden-haired fae—the one who appeared to be in charge. He stared back with an unflinching silver gaze.

"How much?" he asked.

"Twelve feathers," the slaver replied.

Dark-hair snorted. "Twelve! Arrow, that's high robbery. We should slit his throat for the offense."

"He's new. Doesn't know who we are," the gruff Arrow replied. "What's her name?"

"None listed," said the slaver. "You can call her whatever you want."

"A gold eater?" the fae asked.

The slaver shrugged. "Who knows. But since she's human, more than likely."

A golden brow rose. "Here's what I'm willing to pay. Take it or leave it." He gave the master three gold filigree feathers the length of my palm. "Hand her over. I'm in a hurry."

A tiny wound festering in the crease of my elbow itched. I scratched it, and the slaver slapped my hand away. "Do you want to take the clothes she was wearing when I got her?"

"No. Just show them to me," said Arrow.

The slaver disappeared, then returned carrying a small bundle. He held up a ripped tunic of woven wool and linen pants. If they were mine, I didn't recognize them.

Arrow stared at the tattered items, his lips compressing in a look of distaste. "These clothes aren't from the Light Realm. Where did you find her?"

"Port of Tears docks when I passed through a week ago. A merchant found her unconscious in a gutter, then a tavern owner sent him my way."

"It was your lucky day, then. Did you shave one side of her hair?"

"No. It was like that. Strangest thing I've ever seen."

"I doubt that," my new owner muttered.

The slaver gave the blue-haired fae the keys to my wrist shackles, and Arrow stepped onto the platform, crowding me with his large body. An act of intimidation. "Give me your name."

My name... I shook my pounding head.

What in the realms was my name?

I didn't know.

A wave of nausea crashed over me, and I swallowed to avoid splattering his boots with bile.

"I don't know it." Clearing my throat, I straightened my spine. "And even if I did, I wouldn't tell *you*."

One side of his mouth twitched. "Very well. You'll change your mind. I guarantee it."

He was wrong, but I admired his confidence.

"Esen, give her water," he told the female as he stepped off the platform onto the dusty ground and scanned the crowded outdoor market.

Scowling, the blue girl unhitched a water skin from her belt and lifted it to my lips. I drank greedily, then vomited it back up on the ground between us. She snarled as she led me down the steps.

"Where are we?" I croaked, stumbling.

"Be quiet." Esen shoved me into motion. "Get a move on."

The haughty Arrow swept his eyes over me, then strode ahead. Dark-hair ran to catch up with him, leaving Esen to tug me along behind them, the stink of resentment seeping from her pores.

Breathing slowly through my nose, conserving energy, I inspected their clothes. Tight leathers beneath black cloaks, Arrow's embroidered with gold feathers. Then I checked the positions of their weapons; knives and swords everywhere, many of them easily accessible.

I didn't know who I was, but I was certain I knew how to handle a blade.

As I stumbled on a stone, memories rushed through my mind—an overgrown forest, a sword flashing in front of me as I gripped the hilt in my fist, and a green-eyed opponent smiling back at me. Warmth, instead of fear, flooded my chest.

Home. It had to be.

We neared the Farron Gilt Market sign that hung over copper-colored gates, and a fight broke out between a gold vendor and a customer at a stall to the left. A crowd gathered to watch, creating a perfect distraction.

I pretended to trip and fall, snatched a knife from Esen's boot, stabbed her outer thigh, then ran as fast as I could, ducking and weaving through sweat-scented bodies. I passed slave cages and tables packed with scales, vials, fabric, and mouth-watering food piled high on golden trays.

Behind me, the shouts of my new owners echoed, the girl's sounding vicious and brown-eyes' voice frantic. I heard no sound from Arrow, but I felt him gaining on me like a wall of wildfire, relentless, I knew he'd never stop.

As I dodged and ran, I felt no pain. Dust flicked up, coating my throat. I slid under a table, my palms burning as they scraped the ground. Then I crawled between stacked barrels, my sights fixed on a sandstone building that looked like a tavern.

If I could make it through the low wooden door on the building's side that I hoped led to a cellar, I could take refuge with the roaches and rats. I'd bide my time, then make my escape under the cover of night.

Where I would go after that, I had no idea, but running was better than being trapped.

Panting hard, I waited until the foot traffic worked to my advantage—not too heavy, not too light, perfect for weaving about twenty paces through to get to the cellar door. I found my opening and bolted from between the barrels, my teeth clenched and fists pumping as hard as they could with the chain rattling between them as I ran.

Nearly there... The corner of the building was a mere arm's length away. I would make it, even if it killed me. Then *bang*, I slammed into a wall of leather-wrapped muscle. Cruel fingers gripped my shoulders. I looked up.

Fucking *Arrow*.

"Where do you think you're going, gold eater?"

Shaking with rage, I took ragged breaths through my nose. "I'm not a gold eater."

"How do you know? I thought you had no memories. Amnesia, the slaver said."

"Do you usually believe what every idiot you meet tells you?" I asked.

"Not as a habit, but I'm inclined to believe a slaver over a serum-sucking human." He slung a heavy arm across my shoulders, pressed a knife into my side, and walked us back toward the market sign.

"I'm surprised I'm not dead already," I said, baffled why he hadn't killed me yet.

"There are plenty of hours left in the day to deal with the likes of you."

I shot him a surprised look, my gaze slipping along his square jaw and strong chin.

"Don't look so shocked, gold eater," he said. "If I were you, I would have run, too. But I'll warn you; if you do it again, I won't hesitate to slit your grimy throat."

I longed to ask what use he had for a half-dead slave but decided for morale's sake, it would be best for now not to know the answer.

"What place do you come from?" he asked, his deep voice vibrating low in my stomach.

Too tired to speak, I shrugged a shoulder. I wished I knew. It was one of the many questions currently wracking my brain.

Who was I? How did I end up in that shit-stained cage? And why the hell couldn't I remember?

We exited the market and strode through a yard toward dirt-flecked horses and a large, covered carriage, a red mountain range visible in the distance and gold dust swirling through the foreground.

Pitiless silver eyes bored into me. "Farron is a desert market town on the border of the Light Realm and the Sun Realm, if that helps to loosen any memories."

"I don't recall hearing the name of the market before," I said. "Tell me where you're taking me. Perhaps I'll know of the place."

"A little bossy for a captive, aren't you? It's in that direction." Halting, he pointed at the mountains and the storm clouds broiling above them. "The City of Coridon in the Light Realm of Storms and Feathers."

"Never heard of it," I lied. Of course I knew of the desert city of gold and the fae who lived there and maintained ruthless control of the most valuable commodity in the five realms.

They were cruel savages and rich enough to indulge in every disgusting whim and desire imaginable.

We approached Esen and the dark-haired fae. With their arms crossed, they stood frowning in front of a black, grime-covered carriage. By its size and severe boxy lines, it appeared designed for swift travel and defense. Four muscular horses stamped the surrounding ground, raising more of the throat-clogging, red-tinged dust.

Over her dark leathers, a cloth bandage wrapped Esen's thigh, but her weight seemed equally spread between each booted foot. Other than her bruised pride, she didn't appear to be suffering much from the knife wound I'd inflicted, which was a shame.

"What took you so long?" asked the male, his eyes crinkling with a grin.

Arrow pushed me toward the scowling girl, then sheathed his knife. "Given her shocking physical state, this one had a surprising amount of life left in her. Make sure you feed her something when she wakes, Esen."

"Wakes? What do you mean?" Esen asked.

Arrow grimaced at me. "She's about to pass out."

The hood slipped to his shoulders, revealing more of his strong, handsome features and ears like blades parting his tousled hair. He was too beautiful to ever be mistaken for a human.

I wanted to stare, to commit to memory the brutal face of my enemy, but my vision blurred, and I canted sideways, darkness engulfing me.

When I came to, I was on a padded bench seat inside the carriage, and Esen sat across from me, glaring out of the window as she fiddled with the bandage wrapped tightly around her leg.

She glanced at me, then down at her thigh. "Don't worry, human, fae heal fast."

"If it's any consolation," I turned my badly grazed palms up, the chain clinking between them, "my hands are absolutely killing me."

Esen snorted. "Good."

The sound of jingling tack and murmured voices outside told me that Arrow and the other fae were mounting their horses. I kept my eyes closed, pretending to sleep again, and my ears pricked for useful information.

In a gruff voice, too low to decipher, Arrow gave the driver instructions. Then the dark-haired one asked, "Where do you think she's from?"

"I'm not certain, Raiden. Most likely she's a gold chaser who's made her way from the Earth Realm. Probably a forest dweller from the ruins of the human cities."

The forest...

Images assaulted me—the ruins of a stone building covered in vines and fallen leaves. Trees towered around me, the dark, delicious scent of damp earth and decay teasing my senses.

In a lucid dream, I walked through the verdant landscape, the sound of insects drowning out the words of the boy I followed. Dark, wavy hair tumbled around his head. He turned and smiled over his shoulder, bright green eyes flashing back at me, filled with humor.

Outside the carriage, the fae called Raiden laughed at something his arrogant boss muttered.

"The slaver had no idea who we were," Raiden said.

"More fool him," Arrow rasped. "When we return, check the gilt market's trade agreements. If you find any lapsed licenses, shut the vendors down immediately."

A thump sounded on Esen's side of the carriage. Arrow stuck his golden head through the window as she opened it. "We're taking the low pass through the mountains," he said. "I want to be back before dark."

Esen groaned. "Must we? The storms are so disruptive. Fucks with my magic."

"It's faster," Arrow said. "I'll do my best to control them without depleting too much of my energy."

Esen's sneer flicked over me. "Storms knows why you wanted this one. What were you thinking buying such a weakling?"

A beat of silence passed, then he said, "Feed her. She's awake."

My eyes were closed, my muscles held loose and soft, my breathing slow and languid. How could he tell I wasn't asleep?

"Fine," she said. "How would you feel if Raiden swapped places with me? This girl stinks, and *his* stomach is a lot stronger than mine."

"We'll throw her in the river soon enough." Arrow reined his stamping horse in. "Are you a soldier or a delicate high lady?"

Esen sighed and flopped backward, thumping the back of her head against the leather bench seat.

As the carriage jolted into motion, Arrow shot me a parting glare, a cloud of dust swallowing his silver horse.

Smoothing my dirty shift over my thighs, I watched Esen rifle through a satchel on the floor from which she produced flat bread, hard cheese, and a yellow apple. She sliced the cheese and fruit and passed me a serving on a waxed cloth.

Without a word of thanks, I gobbled the food like a half-starved wolf, then licked crumbs from my fingers. "Got any more?" I asked, my stomach growling.

"Later. You'll be sick again if you eat too much at once."

I grunted in reply. "When we arrive at this Coridon place, what will you do with me?" I dragged my dirty hair over my shoulder, finger combing it, then braiding it into a single rope.

"What makes you think we're going to Coridon?"

"Arrow said so."

She glared at me. "*Arrow?*"

"That's his name, isn't it?" I rubbed the clipped right side of my head, the short hair growing in soft and fluffy. "What do the fae of Coridon do with their slaves?"

Lips set in a grim shape, she looked out the window at the undulating landscape haloed in red and gold dirt. "Birds who chirp too much have their throats slit. That's one possible fate you might suffer."

"Not a desirable one," I replied.

Then I shut my mouth and waited for her to doze off, planning to inspect the weapons she wore and decide which one I could steal without waking her.

But instead of resting, Esen stared back, her blue eyes glowing as she drew on magic and juggled tiny bolts of lightning between her palms, her lips pursed in a smug line.

Like all female fae, she had the body and face of a queen, but her sour nature sullied her beauty, turning it into an over-ripe, disturbing thing.

After a while, I gave up waiting, shut my eyes, and let my aching muscles relax. I couldn't remember the last time I'd had a comfortable sleep—nor if I'd ever had one.

Then again, I barely remembered anything other than two undeniable things: I was human, and I hated the fae. Especially the self-satisfied Arrow, who had not only bought me, but caught me after I'd managed to flee.

Out of the three of them, he was the one I would target.

Chapter 2

ARROW

For the first few hours of the journey through the desert, I felt Raiden brooding beside me. When we reached the widest part of the Auric River, where it ran northward through the valley toward the Aureen Mountain pass, he finally broke his silence.

"What storm-cursed fit of insanity made you buy another mine worker? The reavers aren't due a new batch until next month. Why add a half-starved human to our overcrowded cells?"

"Why not?" I said, shrugging a shoulder. "Once they get regular meals in their bellies, the previously starved ones tend to work the hardest."

"Didn't you notice the way she looked at you during the sale? That one would sooner stab you in the eye than follow an order."

I grunted. "Perfect temperament for the gold mines. She might even last longer than a couple of weeks."

Raiden shot me a wary look.

"What?"

"It's not like you to act on impulse."

"And it's not like you to care," I replied, steering my stallion, Yanar, around a rock some idiot had left in the middle of the road.

A thump sounded on the carriage roof, then Esen's head appeared in the open window. "Arrow, she needs to pee."

"Tell her she can wait," Raiden answered.

"Exchange places with me, and you can tell her yourself," said Esen.

"Pull in near the riverbank," I told the driver as I scanned the low bushes along the river.

Esen climbed out of the carriage, pulling the weak-limbed girl along after her. They disappeared into the scrub, and Raiden and I dismounted, then cooled and watered the horses.

Golden vortexes of dust eddied across the plains, tiny black-winged sprites tumbling inside them. At the speed they traveled, the little shits would arrive at Coridon hours before we did.

I crouched over the water and filled my pouch, squinting at the bushes that Esen and the girl had disappeared into. What the fuck was taking them so long?

"Something's wrong," I said, rising and wiping dust from my eyes.

Esen appeared, her fingers pressed on her forehead, blood dripping between them.

"Arrow, I swear I only looked away for a second, and the damned gold eater struck me with a rock."

Violence swirled in her sky-blue eyes. Esen couldn't stand being bested. If she found the girl before I did, she'd kill her without hesitation.

"Both of you stay here," I said, taking off at a run and following footprints through the scrub until the bushes thinned out and revealed a clear view of the mountains.

Where would a desperate gold eater hide?

I scanned the land, my senses tuning in to nearby sounds—buzzing insects, the scratchings of desert rats, then rapid heartbeats coming from behind a patch of golden cactus plants.

There was my quarry.

Sword drawn, I stalked forward until I was five steps away from where she was hiding. A twig cracked, and the human sprang up and ran, her arms pumping and brown braid lashing the air behind her like a whip. She was surprisingly fast. But unfortunately for her, I was faster.

"I'm beginning to think you enjoy this," I said as I caught her from behind, scooped her up, and tossed her over my shoulder in one smooth movement.

"You promised to slit my throat if I ran again," she huffed out, her chain hitting the backs of my legs. "Maybe I'm testing your mettle."

"Did I? Thanks for the reminder. But maybe I really like chasing things and you've just made yourself more interesting alive than dead."

Silent, she bucked against me like an unbroken horse. I walked in the direction of the carriage, and then slid her onto her feet by the river's edge.

I gripped her shoulders. "Run again and I'll be forced to decide whether I should crush your skull or keep you alive and fuck some sense into you."

Her throat bobbed as she stared at my boots.

"Look at me."

She obeyed, her green eyes unblinking.

"Understand?"

No response.

Pinching her chin between my fingers, I wrapped my other hand around her throat and squeezed. "Test me and find out."

"Yes," she spat, her eyes aflame with murderous intent. "I understand all too clearly what a lowlife bully you are."

Lowlife. I bit back a laugh. If only she knew how wrong she was.

Nobody had ever spoken to me with such unbridled hate before. I should kill her, but I hesitated, recognizing something in her gaze that gave me pause. The same icy bitterness that flowed through me, lit by a need for vengeance, cooled and heated her veins, too.

It was mesmerizing to see it mirrored in her narrowed green irises.

Raiden arrived beside me. "Arrow, give the girl to me. I'll watch over her while—"

"No," I growled, my attention fixed on those leaf-green eyes. "It's time you bathed, gold eater."

My fingers hooked into the neck of her shift. One simple tug and the garment tore in two. She crossed an arm over her scrawny body, shivering under the glare of the afternoon sun.

Gritting her teeth, she clasped her chained hands and whipped them toward my face. Before the blow landed, I seized her wrists, and Raiden drew his sword.

She snarled at him like a rabid dog.

"Leave her," I said, walking forward, forcing her to inch backward to the very edge of the riverbank. "She's nothing," I lied.

Truth: she was too gloriously fucking mad to kill.

I bent my head and whispered in her ear. "Time to get clean."

One little shove and she fell into the river, disappearing from view. Four slow heartbeats later, and she still hadn't surfaced. Perhaps she'd hit her stupid head on a rock and knocked herself out.

I crouched on the river's edge, watching the surface closely, muscles firing, ready to leap in and retrieve her.

Another two heartbeats and she surfaced, her braid a slick rope running down the middle of her breasts, the chain a loose curve between her raised fists.

"Wash the filth off," I said. "Or I'll come in and do it for you."

Without a word, she plunged under the water to her neck and began scrubbing her body with a smooth rock.

Esen's footsteps scraped the stones behind us. She elbowed me and sighed roughly. "You should drown the rat," she said, chewing on a stalk of dry grass. "She's trouble. The reavers won't get much work out of her before she provokes them into killing her."

Ignoring Esen, I looked at the human. "Get out."

Slowly, the girl rose. Water cascaded over her angular body as her chin lifted, eyes as green as the spring grass in the Sun Realm staring back at me, unflinching and defiant.

At a slow, insufferable pace, she climbed out of the river. As she walked toward me, the chain hitting her thighs with each sinuous step, she didn't once glance away.

The look in her eyes was nothing less than a challenge to engage in battle.

This girl had a death wish.

She stopped in front of me, close enough that I could rip her throat out with ease, and I made a slow appraisal of her body, inspecting everything on display.

The earthy scent of sun-warmed human teased my senses, and my gut tightened instantly. Not with murderous intent. With something far more dangerous.

Lust.

Furious, I whipped my cloak off and wrapped it around her shoulders so I wouldn't have to endure the sight of her, wet and naked and hating me with the same intensity I hated myself. "If you remove that cloak, I'll throw you in the river again."

"Does your commander know about your abuse of his slaves?" she asked.

I nodded. "Yes. He does. Now get in the carriage."

"As you wish, *Master.*"

Hissed out like a poisonous incantation, her words meant something closer to *fuck you, asshole*, and she didn't move a muscle or obey my order.

"As *you* wish, *slave.*" Throwing her over my shoulder, I stomped toward the carriage, fighting the urge to smack her skinny ass.

The backs of her legs were slippery beneath my hands, and the sensation made me hard. I bit out a shocked curse and tossed her inside the vehicle, while Esen stared at me like I'd grown two extra heads.

"Get in the carriage with her," I said, tipping my chin toward the human.

Esen blinked back at me.

"Storms, what the fuck's wrong with everybody today? Do I have to tell you when to scratch your own asses? And try to remember that she's only one tiny human. How much trouble can she cause us, for fuck's sake?"

"A lot, it seems," said Raiden, mounting his horse.

The carriage driver, a silver-haired goblin who I'd never heard speak a word in any of the realms' many languages, settled in his seat above the horses.

Esen's boot hit the step as she prepared to climb aboard, a cold smirk flickering at the edges of her mouth.

I grabbed her arm. "Esen." The hood of her cloak fell back. "It isn't your responsibility to punish the human for the injuries she's given you. That's my task. And if you rob me of it, you will pay. Don't doubt it."

She inclined her head, and then took a seat opposite the girl.

Through the window, I saw the slave jolt forward, her mouth opening as if she wished to give an opinion on the matter. I shook my head and held my finger to my lips, warning her to keep silent.

While everyone was busy looking at my face, I adjusted my leathers, willing my body's urges into a comatose state, which was basically how they'd been since my family's death three years ago, almost non-existent.

I connected to the energy of the smallest storm cloud above the mountains, drew its power within me, then blasted a lightning bolt into the metal panel above the human's head.

"Next time, I'll aim for your heart," I said, turning to mount my horse.

Wisely, the girl clamped her lips shut. One more squeak and she'd be dead before she got to see the gates of Coridon rising up from the desert sand, like golden portals to another world.

I was sick of the grating tone of her accent. The sweet, cloying scent of her blood. And most of all, the flat planes of her aggravating human face.

But unfortunately, it seemed I was not yet tired of her reckless defiance.

Chapter 3

THE GIRL

A sickle moon hung in the sky as we pulled into a large stable complex within the walls of Coridon City.

Esen prodded my shoulder, then ushered me down the carriage steps. I rubbed sleep from my eyes and blinked at the room's bright gold accents flashing in the light of the candelabras swaying under high bronze beams.

Rows of gleaming carriages were tucked into alcoves lining the walls, and grooms rushed from the shadows to tend to our sweat-glazed horses, issuing instructions to each other in hushed voices.

While I stared open-mouthed at my surroundings, Esen checked the chains on my wrists, creating new bruises in the process.

Despite the warm air, my whole body trembled, the shock of the past few hours, or possibly days or weeks, finally catching up with me. I longed to collapse in a boneless heap on the floor, but instead, forced one bare foot in front of the other and followed the fae out of the stables.

Thunder growled in the distance, and I shuddered, recalling the violent lightning that battered the carriage as we'd traveled through the mountain pass not far from the city.

I didn't think I was afraid of storms, but the wild, unbridled energy that was connected to Arrow's magic had unnerved me. And I was relieved when Coridon's golden domes and turrets finally emerged from the darkness.

So far, the Kingdom of Storms and Feathers was living up to its name. How predictable.

I wrapped the fae prick's cloak tightly around my chest as Esen bundled me along a series of covered causeways lined with tall palm trees, the vanilla scent of night jasmine thick in the air.

My new owner walked ahead with Raiden, his muscled torso and arms on display as he strode toward an unknown destination. Cloakless because of me, his burnished hair fell in loose waves over the plates of gold armor covering his shoulders.

My head pounded as I recalled his warm skin on mine at the river—his hand on my throat and the mercurial burn of his eyes after he'd torn my dress off and thrown me in the water.

I wished I could stop thinking about it... about *him*. But images of the curved feather glyphs that curled up his neck, decorated his left cheek, and the points of his ears, glowing gold as I defied him, assailed me.

He had wanted to kill me then. Probably still did—*and would*—if his commander allowed it.

A bell tolled somewhere in the darkness, and the screeches of unseen birds filled the air. Blinding pain struck my temples. Images exploded in my mind, ripping my consciousness from my march through the moonlit city with the fae and dropping me in the middle of a forest.

Torrential rain poured over me, and my blade hacked a path through pendulous leaves and thick tangled vines. Green eyes glanced back as I struggled to follow the boy, his crooked smirk urging me onward.

Memories of my life prior to the gilt market cage—they had to be.

"Hurry up," said Esen with a hard shove to my shoulder blade, jolting me back to Coridon and the disturbing present.

Hatred filled me. Hate for her and for Arrow and his damned silver eyes that had fixed on me as I walked from the river earlier today, red-faced with shame and fury.

He was an asshole.

If I had the strength, I would wrestle a knife from Esen and embed it in Arrow's unprotected neck, killing him without regret. Although I was thin and starved, my muscles held memories of strength and agility. And I wondered, not for the first time since I woke in that market cage, if I was a bad person—someone accustomed to anger and violence.

Perhaps in my past life I had been an assassin.

Or a traitor to my people—whoever *they* were.

While in the carriage, I'd overheard Raiden say amnesia was a temporary condition, not permanent, and that one day soon, I would remember everything. Well, I was counting on it.

In the meantime, somehow I knew without a doubt that I possessed the skills to kill this Arrow with a single blow. My ability to fight was the only thing I was certain of. I wasn't a stranger to pain, receiving it or giving it.

Esen clipped me over the ear. "I said hurry."

Light flashed over the backs of my eyelids, and I stumbled. Then darkness swallowed me, and I was trapped in the past again.

The entire world rocked and swayed as my fingernails scratched down the inside of a wooden barrel. I screamed my throat raw to get out, but no one came to help me. I felt sure I was traveling over a wild sea in a ship's hold.

I shook my head, then my vision changed, and I was on the back of a truck surrounded by tiny cages crammed with men and women, their moans prickling my spine.

My thoughts tumbled and raced between the past and the present as Esen pushed me, urging me to walk faster. I dug my fingers into my outer thigh and tried to bring back the visions, desperate to rewind them to the beginning of my story to find out who I was and who had wronged me.

Arrow glanced over his shoulder, his silver gaze raking over me once before he turned back and resumed his conversation with the brawny Raiden, the cruel twist of his mouth indicating he was still contemplating killing me slowly.

We entered the palace via a narrow side doorway at the end of a long courtyard. Once inside the building, we marched along deserted hallways, gold glinting off the walls lit by gilded sconces and candelabras.

Golden cages lined the walls at regular intervals, filled with raven-sized birds who rustled their gold and black feathers and peered at us with beady, bright-red eyes.

"What are they?" I asked Esen.

"Birds, obviously. They are called the auron kanara."

"Is that the name of their species?" I asked, frowning.

Esen shot me a glare. "Of course."

"Why are there so many of them?"

She snorted. "This is nothing. In some areas of the kingdom, entire streets and houses are crammed with their cages. But don't fret about it, human. Where you're going, you don't need to understand *anything*."

After a time, the corridors veered downward, below ground level, where nothing good was ever housed. Visions of dank dungeons gripped me, scenes of filth, degradation, and torture.

At the end of a hallway, two men in gold-accented black armor guarded narrow barred doors.

A guard stepped forward, bowed, and gestured toward me with a gold-tipped spear. "My King," he said, "where shall we take her?"

My stomach dropped to my feet. Had I heard right? The gruff, dust-covered Arrow was a king?

Brilliant. I had made an enemy of the ruler of the most powerful kingdom in the realms. I stared at him, struggling to view him in this new lofty role. I supposed he was arrogant enough for the job.

But why would a powerful king gallivant across the land, visit a dusty gilt market in an unmarked carriage, and buy a rebellious slave?

"Take her to the mine cells," said Esen.

"No." Arrow shot her a glare, then paused to contemplate me. "Take her Underfloor, but put her in the testing cells. Let the Sayeeda decide what she's fit for, if anything. If she makes one wrong move, slit her throat and feed her to the fires, dead or alive."

Swallowing a lump in my throat, I resolved that no matter how badly I wanted to scratch Arrow's eyes from his head, I would be on my best behavior from that moment forward.

I had to survive and return to the forest, find the green-eyed boy from my visions.

Esen's jaw hung slack. The guard hauled me through the ornate doors he'd been guarding and into the tiny chamber.

I gaped around at its strangeness. "What is this?" I asked as metal doors slid closed and the other guard stabbed a blunt finger at a gold button on the wall.

"An elevator," said Arrow, his smirk blurring as the chamber plunged downwards.

I yelped, then gritted my teeth, praying that would be the last I ever saw of him.

Intermittent moans and manic laughter echoed in the distance as the guard shoved me out of the astonishing contraption approximately two floors below where we had entered the palace, the doors clanging shut behind us.

Underfloor was a long dark tunnel, lined with overcrowded cells occupied by humans and a scattering of fae. I wondered if they were Light Realm fae and if so, what crimes they had committed to be forsaken by their own people.

Water dripped down stone walls from pipes secured at the back of each cell, forming crude drinking fountains. The stench of unwashed bodies, piss, and shit made me gag, and if I had more food in my belly, it would've erupted, landing on the guards' boots.

They marched me past the side cells and stopped in front of the largest one at the end of the tunnel. I squinted through the bars at the group of ragged people inside.

There were approximately twenty, most of them crouched low, a few standing and swaying on their bare feet, and one or two asleep, their bodies pressed against the walls.

Conditions in this cell looked somewhat better than the others, with less prisoners crammed inside it, most of them appearing in better shape.

The guard unlocked the door and pushed me through it. I whipped around and gripped the bars. "Please, wait..."

He glanced up, hitching his keys to a metal belt around his waist. "Going to offer your services for a chance to escape, pet? Don't bother. You're not worth losing my balls over."

"Why am I in *this* cell and not one of the others?"

He snorted, spat on the stone floor at my feet, then marched back along the tunnel, heading for the elevator that would carry him up to the light-filled halls above Underfloor and the irritating noise of the caged auron kanara birds.

Something prodded my shoulder, and I shoved away from the bars, my chained fists clenched and raised, ready to ram them into the man who stood before me.

The human male chuckled, flashing a near-toothless smile. I lowered my fists. He looked harmless enough, weak and starved, with brown pants hanging off bony hips and deep hollows between his bare, mud-streaked ribs.

"Nice cloak," he said, fingering the material wrapped around me. "Where'd you get it?"

"I stole it," I lied.

"It bears the king's crest."

"Does it?" I asked, glancing down at the embroidered golden feathers that glinted in the dark.

"Where did you steal it from?"

"The Farron Gilt Market. Found it on the ground when I ran from the fae who purchased me."

"Sure you did." He snorted. "And when this fae caught you, he or she didn't take it off you?"

I shook my head. "As you can see, they didn't."

"Interesting tale. I'm Davy." His gray brow rose, a signal for me to give my name.

I said nothing.

"And you are?" he asked when he grew tired of waiting.

I shrugged. "I've lost my memory."

"Convenient." He swept his palm toward the back wall. "There's water over there if you're thirsty."

A man and a woman sat beneath the water pipe, drinking like babes at a teat, their lips and teeth clashing. It didn't look very hygienic.

"No, thanks. I'm fine."

He pulled me toward the left wall, away from the other prisoners whose eyes were carefully averted, which struck me as strange. Perhaps Davy ran the show down here and had first claim to the fresh meat.

"Sit down. It'll be a while before they throw us our dinner."

Closing my eyes, I slid to the floor and wrapped the cloak around my knees, hugging them to my chest. I sighed. "Have you been here long? What is this place? What are they going to do with us?"

"So many questions," he said.

"With no memories of my own, questions are all I have."

Davy grunted. "Do you remember anything at all?"

I shrugged again. "Being locked in a cage at the gilt market. Prior to that, maybe an ocean journey trapped in a barrel, and before that, ruins in a forest that I figure must be my home."

"Sounds like you're from the Earth Realm of Dust and Stones. I'm a gold chaser from the Ice Realm. I got caught running a black-market operation, moving gold from port to port. Been here three days."

"Will they kill us?"

"Not until they've passed judgment. The guy who ran this cell before me said they choose docile, fit slaves to work in the palace. The fit but troublesome ones get sent to the gold mines. The weakest go straight to the fires."

I bit my lip. "The fire option isn't ideal."

"No. You look like a troublemaker to me. You'd better work on fixing that."

Glancing at him, I smiled. "Who decides?"

"A gold reaver elf called the Sayeeda who appears once a week. She's in charge of the slaves and the palace kitchens. Apparently, she's a big deal at court and close to the king, serves his food and everything. She's due to make her selections tomorrow."

I picked at a loose thread on the cloak, the gold glowing as if imbued with magic. "What's a gold reaver elf?"

"You don't know? An elven species of fae. Their blood feeds the mines, grows the gold. Somehow, they're connected to the birds upstairs. That knowledge won't do you any good, though."

He was wrong. Knowledge was power and could be exploited. I intended to gather every scrap of information I could, escape my chains, and shove a blade through the king's heart before I left the city.

Davy fumbled in his pocket, then passed me a piece of dried bread.

My lip curled at its sour smell, but I took it with a nod of thanks. "Why are you helping me? Everyone else in here is afraid of you."

He grinned. "You're a survivor. We might be of use to each other."

"Fair enough." I gnawed an edge of the hard bread, ignoring the grit between my teeth.

Davy stared at me, his dark eyes simmering with emotions I recognized all too clearly—desperation and determination to survive no matter what.

"Listen, if you make it to the kitchen and act the obedient slave, rumor has it your conditions won't be too bad. You might even get out of Coridon one day."

One day. I couldn't wait for some distant hypothetical day. It had to be soon.

Dropping my forehead onto my knees, my thoughts grew drowsy, exhaustion finally getting the better of me.

Survive, I told myself on repeat, digging my nails into my calves to sear the message into my flesh. *You must survive.*

I would learn the rules of the Kingdom of Storms and Feathers and pray that my memory returned soon. I would sacrifice my dignity to gain the means to escape and return to the green-eyed boy who waited for me in the forest.

For him, I had to survive.

There was no other choice.

Chapter 4

THE GIRL

E very shade of green, from lightest sage to darkest emerald, surrounded and embraced me. Even the stone ruins beneath my feet were covered in the black-green slime of decaying moss and vines.

Then sounds engulfed me—parrot calls coming from nearby trees, the rustle of creatures and snakes moving through the undergrowth. Damp heat coated my limbs as I ran, sweat beading my brow.

This was where I belonged, in the forest—with *him*.

My breath panted out in hard gusts as I ducked around a gigantic tree trunk, then came to a sliding stop in his arms.

"Got you, little Sapling," he said, wrapping his arms around me.

"Ash," I murmured, my palm thumping his shoulder. "I hate that stupid nickname. You're not that much taller than me."

A grin stretched over his handsome face, familiar green eyes crinkling as he pinched my cheek affectionately. I laughed, and his face blurred and morphed into a different person's features, the mood darkening. As I closed my eyes, a warm palm tickled the inside of my thigh and heated my belly.

Calloused fingers stroked higher, drawing moisture from my core as I flushed with pleasure and guilt. My muscles melted against his body, and with a loud moan, I looked up.

"You!" I said, staring into the King of Storms and Feathers' silver gaze. "Stop that."

"Why should I when you're so obviously enjoying it?" he rasped against my ear. "Don't deny it, little human. The evidence coats my fingers."

My head fell back against a rough tree trunk, another moan parting my lips. I gasped, first in pleasure, then in shock as water splashed my body.

Spluttering, I jolted awake to the grim sight of the Underfloor cell.

It was a dream. Only a dream.

Outside the bars, a guard tossed an empty bucket aside. An incredible woman stood beside him, the golden aura that shimmered around her body illuminating the darkened Underfloor passage. "Get your hands off the girl," she said in a low voice that brooked no argument.

My head swung toward the hunched form of Davy, bent over me with his rigid length in one hand and his fingers shoved between my legs. Two quick pumps of his wrist and liquid jetted on the stone floor between us.

Growling, I wrapped my fingers around his throat, squeezing hard. The gold tip of a spear pricked my shoulder, and I let my hands drop away from my assaulter. The spear lowered, and then the guard unlocked the cell.

"Line up for the Sayeeda, the bonded servant of King Arrowyn and his Mistress of Slaves and Spices," said a second guard, cracking a barbed whip on the floor near my toes.

With a grunt, I scrambled to my feet, choking on embarrassment and the desire to crush Davy's windpipe with my bare hands. Fury making me dizzy, I clenched my teeth and stood next to him at the end of the front line.

As the guard and the Sayeeda worked their way along the prisoners, I kept my gaze fixed on the corridor ahead and the hands that reached through the bars of the cells, clutching at nothing, their voices begging the Sayeeda to reassess them.

I hoped I didn't end up in their company.

In a calm voice, the slave mistress made her decisions, issuing commands as she inspected eyes, teeth, and limbs, casting us to our fates as if we were insignificant, worthless, less than animals.

"Fires. Mines. Fires. Mines," she said as she moved closer, the light from her clothing a golden glow at the side of my vision.

I longed to inspect this fae who held my fate in her hands, but a sense of self-preservation kept my eyes averted, my muscles frozen as I waited for her judgment.

An older woman destined for the flames screamed in protest, and the guard stepped back, flexing his gold-barbed whip and bringing it down on her body without mercy. She learned fast to swallow her cries of agony.

Then the Sayeeda's glow intensified as she prized Davy's mouth open beside me. "Extend your arms," she commanded. He held them out, and she pushed against them. "Mines."

Shadows swallowed all but the Sayeeda as she stepped in front of me. First, she tested my arms, then my legs. I kept my eyes lowered, breathing slowly while she made her assessment.

A firm finger hooked into my lower lip. "Open."

I relaxed my jaw, and she lifted my chin. I gazed into eyes of molten gold set in a serene face of glimmering beauty. Sharp fae ears. Angular cheekbones. And swathes of metallic cloth wrapped her body, a perfect match for her skin and shimmering unbound hair that curled to her shoulders, like lacquered threads of gold.

In what sort of world would an enchanting, ethereal creature hold such a terrible position?

She should sit upon a throne. Sing from a sparkling dais. Entertain. Enamor. Not be jailer and judge in a hellish fae prison.

For what seemed like an eternity, she stared into my eyes, calmly evaluating me. I saw the spark of curiosity extinguish.

"Mines," she said, and the guard pushed me backward, my cloak flapping upward with the movement.

Her head turned to me. "Wait. Where did you steal the cloak from, girl?"

"It wasn't stolen. The man who bought me from the gilt market wrapped me in it after he stripped me and threw me in the river in a rage."

A golden eyebrow flickered. "Do you have knowledge of food and spices?"

I nodded, my heart pounding like a drum. I had no idea if I could cook, but I would learn fast enough.

"Will you swear obedience to me on pain of death?"

My back teeth ground together. "Yes."

"The kitchens for this one," she said to the guard.

The guard ushered me toward the left wall. My breath released in short rasps as my shoulders scraped cold stone while I waited, relief warming my blood.

By the time the Sayeeda was done, only one other woman had joined me, also destined for the kitchens, and the rest of the prisoners were steered into the other Underfloor cells to await their fates.

"They'll stay there until the trucks come for them," the middle-aged woman whispered from the side of her mouth, silver-streaked dark hair curtaining her wrinkled face. "Could be a while until there's another slave shipment going to the mines."

"How do you know?" I asked.

"I've a cousin who was captured last year, a gold runner, who worked in the mines for a month before a trader helped him escape to one of the black-market cities hidden in the Realm of Dust and Stones."

"The human realm?" I asked, watching the Sayeeda glide along the tunnel toward the elevator at the end, seemingly unruffled by her unsavory duties.

"Yes, the Earth Realm. My name's Grendal—"

"Enough talk," barked the guard, cracking his whip on the floor.

He and another grim-faced guard trundled us out of the cell, through a doorway nestled in the stone wall, then along another sloping, claustrophobic passage that came out inside a torch-lit cavern with a steaming mineral pool at its center.

The steamy vapors wrinkled my nose, and I sneezed.

"Allergic to hygiene, are you?" said the tallest guard, pushing us into the water.

When I surfaced, thankful my chain didn't drown me, a cake of soap hit my shoulder.

"Wash," he barked. "And throw your rags out."

"What does he mean?" I said, looking at Grendal.

She lifted a thin brown tunic over her head. "Take your clothes off and toss them out. Are you deaf?"

"No, I'd just prefer not to get naked in front of them," I hissed.

She laughed. "In case you haven't noticed, your preferences don't matter anymore."

The king's cloak was far from a rag, but I slid it off my body and placed it on the rocky edge of the water. The shorter guard gathered it up and held it out for his friend to view, their eyebrows disappearing under the visors of their black helmets.

"Where did you get this?" he asked.

"None of your business," I said, scrubbing the rough soap over my skin.

The guards huddled in the corner, studying the cloak. When they moved apart, they watched me with suspicion but didn't bother me with further questions.

"What's your name?" Grendal asked as I passed her the soap.

"I don't know. I've lost my memory."

"How did that happen?"

I crossed my arms, hiding my chest from the guards' view. "I have a large bump on my head, so I suppose that could be the cause."

Her eyes softened, and she smiled. "You need a name. I'll call you Green for your bright eyes."

Before I could reply, the guards dragged us out, our naked bodies dripping water on the stones.

"The Sayeeda must be desperate for help if these two scrawny hags were the strongest of the females," a guard said.

Leering at my apparently deficient body, the fae grabbed my wrist, Arrow's cloak slung over his spear arm, and marched me along the tunnel and into the elevator. The other guard followed behind with Grendal.

The elevator took us up one level, then we exited into a wider hallway lined with gold and more auron kanara cages. Grendal and I walked side by side, a guard in front and one behind as we passed rows of narrow black doors set between the cages.

"Must be the servants' rooms," said Grendal, stopping and peering through the small rectangular window in one of the doors. "Where we'll live while we work in the kitchen."

"Get a move on," said a guard, shoving Grendal's shoulder and knocking her to her knees.

"Hey!" I scowled at him as I helped Grendal rise. "Injuring her isn't going to make her move any faster."

Grendal rubbed her knee, and the guard scoffed.

"Are you all right?" I asked.

"It's just bruised," she said, limping forward.

"Lean on me." I tucked my arm around her waist, and we continued down the hallway.

A few fae servants passed us, males and females dressed in sleeveless, knee-length tunics made of thin gold material. Their eyes raked briefly over us, but their faces remained impassive, as if we were dressed just like them, rather than walking along the hall stark naked.

"I wish those damn birds would stop fluttering and squawking," I said, my headache intensifying.

"They'll quieten soon enough," she said. "They only carry on like that when they're hungry."

"Then why doesn't someone feed them?"

"They will. They're waiting on the lightning weavers."

"The who?"

"The fae who conjure storms and can draw the force through bricks and stone, even gold, then direct it out of their bodies. That's what the auron kanara eat, the lightning created by the weavers. When the gong sounds throughout the city, it means they're taking up the feeding positions."

Shivering, I rubbed my arms. "There's something repulsive about that. Those birds disturb me."

Grendal laughed. "Perhaps they don't like you either."

At the top of the hall, the guards guided us through one of the black doors and into a windowless room, dimly lit with four opaque balls about the size of my head fixed to each wall. Forks that looked like lightning flickered inside them. More Storm Court magic, I guessed.

"The Sayeeda will visit soon," a guard said, throwing Arrow's cloak onto a bed. He closed the door, then locked it.

Grendal waved her hand in front of a globe, and the light disappeared. She grinned. Another wave of her hand and the globe lit up. "Lightning magic," she said over her shoulder.

"Where are you from?" I asked as I scanned the room's minimal furniture, two narrow beds and a lone wardrobe. And tucked behind a door in the rear wall, I found a plumbed toilet and a basin made of reddish, shiny copper.

"I lived in a gold runner encampment," Grendal said, rubbing her knee. "One of the human camps hidden in the mountains to the far north of the realm. Not very well-hidden, mind. We were always on the move and doing deals with traders and rogue fae to evade capture."

"Do you need treatment for your knee?" I asked.

She laughed. "No. It's fine. I was playing it up for sympathy."

"Devious," I replied, grinning back at her.

Opening the wardrobe, I found a row of gold tunics, similar to the ones the servants in the hall had worn, hanging on a bar. I threw one to Grendal, then tried to struggle into another, the chain between my wrists making it impossible.

"I'd prefer not to be an exhibitionist," she said with a grin, "but I think we're going to have to wait for the Sayeeda's help."

As she poked her head into the bathroom, I tried out a bed, surprised by the comfort of the mattress and the soft woven blankets covering it.

"Tell me honestly, is it really true that you have no idea where you came from or even who you are?" Grendal asked.

I nodded.

Sighing, she flopped on the other bed, bouncing her hips to test the mattress. "Well, I've never seen you before. So I can tell you with certainty that you're not a gold chaser from the north."

"When I eavesdropped on the fae who brought me here, I remembered quite a few of the things that they mentioned. Most things so far in the palace make sense, not elevators, though, which probably confirms that I lived a basic life, perhaps in a forest. But nothing the fae said sparked any significant memories."

I took a breath and swallowed. I wasn't sure why, but I knew I shouldn't tell Grendal that the Storm King himself had bought me from the gilt market. At this point, no one needed to know that little detail but me. And of course, Raiden and Esen and several guards who had seen me with him.

The door swung open, revealing the Sayeeda on the threshold, her face a solemn, golden mask. Over her pointed ears, she wore elegant cuffs with bony ridges, as if they'd been cast from the vertebrae of a small animal—perhaps a winged desert rat or a bat.

"Get up." She made an impatient hand gesture.

Snapping a golden bracelet around Grendal's bicep, she said, "You both look reasonably intelligent, so you'll begin work tonight scrubbing the dinner pots. I hope you will make the most of the opportunity and not try anything foolish."

"Of course, Sayeeda," said Grendal, bowing slightly, while I stared at the wall ahead.

"And you," the Sayeeda continued, enclosing my arm in a bracelet, "if you blink so much as an eyelid without my permission, it will be the fires for you or worse."

I rubbed my arm as the bracelet's inner teeth pricked my flesh, the feeling like being pierced by scores of tiny needles.

"Underfloor, you swore allegiance to me. If you meant what you said, now is the time to prove it. Both of you."

"I do swear to obey you, Sayeeda," I said, forcing myself to hold her golden glare.

After Grendal promised the same, the Sayeeda nodded, then unlocked the shackles and removed the chains from our wrists.

"Good. And should you break your vows, know this... those bracelets are topped up daily and release small doses of gold serum, keeping you subdued, addicted, if you will. In the unlikely event you escape Coridon's walls, your supply will be cut off, and your bodies will suffer horrific cravings for the gold. Not a pleasant fate, I promise you. Now get dressed."

Grendal's eyes widened as realization set in. She was trapped. We both were.

Scratching the red skin around my bracelet, I wondered when I would begin to feel its effects. Other than the initial pain when it embedded in my flesh, I felt nothing. Nothing at all.

The Sayeeda's mouth curved as she collected Arrow's cloak from my bed, fondly inspecting a tear in the material, then she turned toward the door. "Follow me. There is much work to be done."

We slid the tunics over our heads and hurried after her.

Chapter 5

THE GIRL

"**G**ods, I'm bored," said Grendal as she dumped dirty platters in the sink beside me.

"It could be a lot worse," I replied, stretching my back and thinking of the unfortunate slaves the Sayeeda sent to the fires on the day I arrived.

My roommate shrugged and marched to the other side of the white-washed kitchen and began cleaning one of the cavernous ovens.

Each day was the same. We peeled, sliced, and diced, then helped scrub the kitchen clean before falling into our beds in the middle of the night, our muscles cramped and aching.

For four whole days, I had played the role of an obedient servant, but I was growing increasingly frustrated. My movements were limited to the kitchen complex and the servants' hallway, which made it difficult to learn about the city's layout and security.

To compensate, I made sure every conversation, no matter how brief, with any palace worker who crossed my path, was a productive one. I collected every snippet, every tiny detail that might help me piece together a picture of the City of Coridon and the fae who lived here.

The arm cuff's effect on Grendal and the other servants—a mix of species where humans outnumbered fae ten to one—fascinated me. At regular intervals, their eyes glazed over, their movements slowing as they laughed at nothing in particular.

But the serum had absolutely no effect on me, and I assumed I was immune to it. So feeling mildly foolish, I slowed my limbs and softened my gaze at random times throughout the day, emulating what the drug did to my companions.

I wondered if any other servants were immune and if this was a key to my identity. I would watch closely. Ask subtle questions. And if there were others like me at Coridon, I would find them.

Either way, I was certain my life depended upon keeping my immunity a secret, especially from the palace guards. They roamed the corridors dressed in black and gold armor, the enormous golden feathers on their helmets making them easy to pick out in a crowd of servants.

Every waking moment, I paid close attention to my surroundings. In the hallway, I frequently passed guards discussing the schedules of the trucks that went back and forth between Coridon and the mountains, transporting slaves and bags of auron kanara feathers to the mines. What the miners needed the feathers for, I couldn't guess. But I planned to find out soon.

As long as we obeyed the emotionless Sayeeda, the guards didn't bother us, and since I aimed to be the best behaved, most trustworthy servant she'd ever had, I followed her orders without question. Until the day came when I wouldn't.

For four days, I'd done nothing but sleep and work hard, and take any opportunity to study the auron kanara. Because I was certain there was power in understanding them.

Watching the lightning weavers feed the birds was an addictive torture. I found any excuse to linger in the servants' hallway while they worked, my skin prickling as magical breezes swept the corridor, raking through my hair.

I closed my eyes and pretended I was traveling on horseback or running through the forest on a windy day, and for a few stolen moments, forgot that I was as much a prisoner as those poor, stupid birds were.

Other than the kanara feedings, my only escapes from kitchen drudgery were the intermittent visions that struck me from out of nowhere. Flashes of white, followed by flickering colors that morphed into scenes of the forest and the boy's vibrant green eyes. Eyes that were so similar to mine.

Tonight, as I scrubbed the dinner pots, I tried to recall everything I'd learned about the boy and the forest, committing each detail to memory. I pondered where we might have slept, what we ate, and attempted to recreate pictures of the happy life we'd led together.

I prayed to the gods the visions were real and not just something my damaged mind had fabricated to help me cope with my new life as a prisoner.

Indulging in these fantasies hurt my heart, but it made the time go faster and distracted me from my sore joints and muscles as I worked.

"Girl," said the Sayeeda, jolting me out of my thoughts.

She sat on a high stool between a line of stoves and the door that led down to the cellars, repairing a garment. Between graceful arcs of her needle, she stroked the black and gold cloak on her lap as if it was a favorite pet, not an item of clothing.

"Get a move on. We haven't got all night."

"Yes, Sayeeda," I said, scouring the pan faster.

I gave no excuse for my lethargy, since I'd learned that none were necessary. The serum caused regular lapses in attention, and the Sayeeda had to frequently wake servants from wide-eyed bewildered dazes.

Loud laughter boomed from the stairwell that the servers used during dinner to carry food between the kitchen and the Grand Hall. A moment later, a servant shrieked, and pottery rolled down the stairs. More laughter followed, and drunken male voices echoed into the kitchen.

Cloths and broom handles froze in mid-air as the king and Raiden appeared at the bottom of the stairs, brushing liquid from their clothes and grinning like wine-addled fools. Try as I might, I couldn't tear my gaze from them. Or rather from *him*. The arrogant king.

Since the night I went Underfloor, my only company consisted of servants and guards, so the arrival of Arrow and his friend was a startling event, and I wasn't the only one staring.

As if shaken from a dream, two servants rushed forward to sweep up the broken ceramic, and Arrow and Raiden stepped around them, as though they were invisible.

For no good reason, my heart pounded as they swaggered down the length of the room, ignoring me laboring over a sink as they passed, and stopping in front of the Sayeeda.

"Greetings, Ari," said the king in his deep, spine-tingling voice. "Is my cloak ready?"

Interesting. He'd called her Ari, not the Sayeeda as everyone else did. Perhaps it was her birth name.

With a rare smile, she raised the needle and gold thread, showing him her work. "Almost, King Arrowyn, only a few more tears to fix. I told you I would bring it to your chambers this evening. Do you require it sooner?"

Arrow leaned a shoulder against the wall beside her. "There's no hurry. I'm pleased it survived the mineral baths. I came to congratulate you on tonight's meal. Raiden here thought the stew was particularly tasty, and I agreed."

The Sayeeda gave him an odd look, as if he didn't often visit the kitchen to compliment the dishes she oversaw.

"I take no credit for the meal," she said. "Your thanks, if you insist on giving them, are owed to our new kitchen worker who suggested the combination of dill with barley, beef, and lemon, a meal she remembered from her home. Apparently."

The king's silver gaze landed on me, raking my body in a languid motion. "This girl?"

The Sayeeda nodded. "Yes. The one that nearly ruined your favorite cloak."

The shrew. Was she trying to get me killed? It wasn't *my* fault the guard forgot to take the king's cloak off me before he pushed me into the water.

"Perhaps the king might consider not wearing his favorite clothes while inspecting filthy gilt markets," Raiden said with a teasing grin.

Arrow's lips curved as he crossed gold-banded arms over the breastplate of golden feathers covering his broad chest. The rest of his torso was bare, revealing the dormant, pale-red feather glyphs that marked him as king. They circled his arms and trailed over his stomach before disappearing beneath dark leather pants that hung low on his hips.

My gaze lingered on the feather on his left cheek. Tiny sparks of gold moved along the beautiful filigree pattern, as if it was coming alive under my inspection.

According to Grendal, on the day of an old king's death, the Light Realm heirs inherited their glyphs along with their crowns. Blood magic, she'd said, the skin marking a painful process that laid the new kings low for days, if not longer.

I imagined Arrow writhing in pain on the day he was crowned, the Sayeeda wiping his sweat-soaked brow with her golden hand, and tried to remove my gaze from his aggravating form. But it was nearly impossible to look away from all that tanned skin on display.

For dust's sake, he was the king, not a court entertainer. Why couldn't he wear clothes that befitted his station? Or at least wear a few more of them?

Warmth curled in my stomach, a feeling that seemed to increase the longer I perused the Storm King's muscled body and the alluring curve of his lips. My mind raced, desperate to recall any carnal experiences I might have had with men in the past.

All I could remember was witnessing the coupling between a mare and a stallion and the intense energy that had infused the air before the act. Although the memory was mildly fascinating, it gave me no real insights into the frequency or quality of my own mating adventures.

If I even had any.

Either way, I was furious with my body for responding like an animal to the Storm King's unfortunate masculine beauty.

I felt certain that a special type of magic must have oozed from his pores, designed to make him irresistible and garner him an unfair number of potential mates. Which was cheating.

Someone uttered the name that the servants had given me—Green—for the color of my eyes.

"Sorry," I said, turning to the Sayeeda. "What did you say?"

"Not me. The king asked you a question."

Damn. I took a breath and met his inscrutable gaze.

"Correct me if I'm wrong, but you want us to believe that you somehow remembered a meal you once ate," he said, "but can't recall the name of the city you lived in. Is that right? Seems strange to me."

My throat dried, and I swallowed to moisten it. "Yes. That's true."

"Can you describe what your home looked like?"

I lowered my gaze and shook my head.

Raiden grunted, a sound of disbelief.

The king said nothing, but I felt the weight of his stare chafing my flesh, just like his cloak had done on the carriage journey back to Coridon.

Finished with her needlework, the Sayeeda stood and bowed to the king, handing him the cloak. While staring at me, he flicked the garment around his shoulders, brought the material to his face, inhaling it as if it was a fragrant desert flower.

So, he had a thing for his Sayeeda. I wasn't surprised. Despite her cold, merciless manner, she was an exotic beauty. But really, there was no need for him to sniff the cloak she'd touched in front of everyone. It was off-putting in the extreme and curdled my empty stomach.

Flustered, I looked away and concentrated on stacking clean pots, crashing them together and making a mess of the job.

A heavy presence resonated behind me, and I gasped as calloused fingers gripped my chin and tugged my face around.

Silver eyes narrowed above me. "When you remember where you come from, human, I want to hear about it. Understand?"

I nodded, trying to ignore my frantic heartbeat, and the sweet, heady flavor of wine on his breath.

"If that is all, My King, we must get back to work," said the Sayeeda, dismissing him from her domain as if *he* was the servant. "As usual, I'll bring your infusion to your chamber at midnight."

The king stepped away from me, and at last, I could breathe again.

Any respect I'd had for the Sayeeda dissolved as I contemplated the fact that she had nightly midnight meetings with the king.

Gods knew what horrible things he made her do. Like me, she was nothing but a slave who lived according to the whims of her owner, and I wondered how such a magnificent, strong woman had fallen into his clutches.

The king nodded, the circlet of golden feathers glinting on his brow. Then he and Raiden stalked along the length of the kitchen toward the exit, like full-bellied, self-satisfied predators.

Little did they know that not everyone present held them in the same high regard as they held themselves.

In a daze, I watched the black cloak trail behind Arrow's calves, remembering how it had felt against the bruised skin of my breasts and thighs. The weight of it had been claustrophobic, yet oddly comforting.

What that said about me, I hated to think. Likely, I was a glutton for punishment. A masochist—attracted to the man who had enslaved me. To learn this about myself was a sickening disappointment, to say the least.

"*Green*," the Sayeeda shouted. "Are we keeping you awake?"

"Sorry." I covered a yawn with my palm, wondering how she would punish me for ogling her lover instead of tending to my duties.

On the other side of the kitchen, Grendal coughed to hide her laughter.

I angled a pot of stew on its side and scooped the leftovers into a large container. The contents would become the servants' dinner, which we ate in our rooms after our work was done. My belly rumbled loudly. I hadn't eaten anything since lunch.

Out of nowhere, golden fingers seized my wrist, and the Sayeeda snatched the spoon from my hand and placed it on the bench. Then she gripped my cheeks and tugged my face to meet hers, staring into my eyes from only an inch away.

My pulse raced. Was she trying to hypnotize me? Or kill me with her obscure gold reaver magic? Dust knew what kind of power she possessed, but according to rumors, she could disappear at will, which sounded quite useful to me. A skill I wished I could employ at this very moment.

I flicked my gaze to the bench, searching for something I could use as a weapon. I wriggled my hand toward a ladle. Not ideal, but better than nothing.

"Your eyes," she said, jolting my attention back to her glittering lips. "They aren't pure green. You have sparks of gold in there, too."

Wonderful news, I thought to myself; the bench digging into my hip as the Sayeeda's hands fell away from my face.

"Tomorrow, Green, I think you should serve dinner in the Grand Hall."

I swallowed a protest. She definitely wanted to get me killed.

"What do you say to that?" she asked.

"I... I don't know how to serve the court."

Nor did I want to learn. It was safer here, Underfloor with others like me, a place where servants traded secrets and knowledge and went unnoticed by the mysterious fae above us.

"You'll learn fast enough," she replied. "Now hurry and fill the dinner trays for the workers. Grendal, go with her."

"To think, we were visited by the Storm King himself," said my roommate as we pushed a trolley along the servants' hall. "Weren't we truly gold blessed?"

I couldn't tell if she was being serious or not. "Hardly," I grumbled as we began dishing stew and bread rolls into partitioned trays on the floor in front of each black doorway.

At the Sayeeda's instructions, the guards left the rooms of the more docile servants unlocked, so when we weren't working, we were free to exercise along the length of the hall and visit the auron kanara in their cages. The entry to the kitchen was always guarded, and any overlong gatherings between servants were broken up pretty fast.

One day soon, I hoped my obedience would be rewarded and I could join the small parties of servants who were allowed supervised outdoor exercise, then I would commit to memory the lay of the city and any landmarks or exits I was lucky enough to see.

Knowledge of my past was mostly gone, but any new information I learned seemed to stay in my head, neatly organized and easily accessible. I may have been struck dumb by the sight of Arrow in the kitchen tonight, but I wasn't entirely foolish.

After we'd emptied the trolley, we hurried toward the kitchen to wash out the containers, eager to return to our room and eat our dinner.

Before we reached the guard stationed on the kitchen threshold, I turned to Grendal. "The first time I saw the king, he was heavily armed. There were knives hidden all over him and at least two swords. Tonight, I didn't notice any weapons on his body. Do you think that's because the court is mostly peaceful?"

"Arrowyn has storm magic." She snickered. "And did you not see his breastplate? Each feather is a dart, filled with a lethal dose of gold serum. One pluck. Whoosh, thunk. And you'd be dead."

"Oh," I said, feeling the guard's eyes on us and pretending to check the trolley's wheels to stall for time. "I'd better behave in the Grand Hall tomorrow night, then."

A wicked smirk crinkled her gray eyes, then a dose of serum hit, and they glazed over. "Yes, Green, you had better."

Other than the three servants we found mopping the floors, the kitchen was empty. When our jobs were done, Grendal took my hand and tugged me along the center aisle toward the stairs that led to the Grand Hall.

"It's late. The Sayeeda must be busy with the king, which gives us the perfect opportunity to prepare you for tomorrow evening," Grendal said, the serum definitely impairing her decision making.

"Good thinking," I said, checking over my shoulder as we dashed up the stairs to be sure no guards had entered the kitchen behind us.

As I peered around a carved gold column at the top of the stairs, my breath hitched. Squeezing Grendal's hand, I released a slow breath. "It's incredible."

The Grand Hall was at least five times larger than the massive kitchen. The marble floor, visible between long dining tables, flowed like a dark river, with veins of gold flaring under the light of hundreds of candelabras.

Scores of silent servants slid wheeled ladders beneath them, slowly extinguishing the flames. I marveled at the hours it must take them to illuminate and darken the hall every night.

The Court of Storms and Feathers' Grand Hall was a glorious testament to wealth, power, and magic, manifested in jaw-dropping architecture.

I couldn't recall what my home looked like, but I was certain I'd never entered such a grand and lavish place before.

My hungry gaze devoured the view. Enormous arched doors that led to starlit terraces lined both sides of the room, their golden frames etched with feathers and bolts of lightning. Palm trees and other monstrous-leaved plants towered around the oval hall. The largest two framed a black dais, reached by nine clear-crystal steps, upon which sat a throne of feathers enveloped by a sculpture of golden wings.

Grendal's nails dug into my hand. "Look closely at the throne," she whispered.

My eyes adjusted to the dais's dark glow, revealing a figure slouching between the massive wings. The male released a loud sigh, then leaned forward, gold hair tumbling around hard, annoyingly beautiful features that sparked flames deep in my stomach.

Arrow.

The feathers around his neck chimed as he tossed a goblet onto the floor and stood up. "Enough," he boomed, and the servants scurried off their ladders and left the hall through doors situated behind the dais.

For several moments, the king stared into the distance, his powerful arms hanging loosely at his sides, but his fists balled. He looked restless and troubled.

We should have left, but it felt like the soles of my shoes were stuck to the floor, and I couldn't look away from the king.

As his arms spread wide, reaching for the ceiling, violent shudders shook his body. Thunder rumbled outside and lightning struck the windows. He groaned as power flowed into him, an aura of blinding white light outlining his tall frame.

Wind whipped along the hall, cloud-like whorls of tiny clear feathers sweeping around the candelabras and extinguishing every last flame.

Darkness fell over the room, and the king groaned like a dying man. Glowing like the sun and moon combined, he drew the storm into his chest with three quick movements of his hands, then collapsed over the dais stairs. Head in his hands, he laughed like a madman, the sound disturbing.

What could the ruler of the most powerful kingdom in the realms possibly be unhappy about?

Grendal tugged me down the stairs, and we ran through the kitchen and into the servants' hall. Breathless, we stopped, both laughing as she clasped my face between her palms.

"Gods. That was something else. It was..." Her words trailed off as serum spiked in her blood, a milky haze veiling her eyes.

"Terrifying is the word I think you're looking for," I said, pushing her hands from my face. "His power is incredibly destructive. I had no idea."

"He's the King of Storms and Feathers. What did you expect his magic could do? Water the kingdom's gardens and pluck the chickens with great speed? You'd better take care in the hall tomorrow. Don't do anything to gain his attention."

Gazing over her shoulder at the pitiful auron kanara in their cages, I scratched the side of my head, and let my focus soften as if a dose of serum had hit me too.

"Don't worry, Grendal. I'll be the best dinner server that the king will never see."

Chapter 6

ARROW

"It is time you visited the mines," said Raiden's father, Stormur, from his seat beside me at the high table.

Stormur had been my father's trusted High Counselor, and now he served as mine. The fae was wise, fair, and extremely measured in his opinions.

When he spoke, it was in my best interests to listen. If he gave advice, I knew I should heed it. But whenever he brought up the Auryinnia Mines, my ears suddenly became defective.

"There is no logical reason not to resume your duties at Auryinnia," he continued. "Enough time has passed since the incident, and now you must honor the agreements between the reavers and your kingdom."

I nodded absently and let my attention slide from his frowning brow as I inspected the chaos playing out in the hall. Burnished by candlelight, my courtiers ate, drank, sang, and groped and fought each other with joyous abandon, reveling in their good fortune to reside in the most prosperous kingdom in the realms.

Over thousands of years and an ocean of sweat and blood, my ancestors created order from mayhem. They established peace between the four fae realms and formed a system that not only benefited the indispensable reaver elves, but regulated the gold trade.

Of course, since Light Realm fae controlled the supply of auron kanara feathers to the elves, we also controlled the gold and all the wealth in the realms. An extremely fortuitous side benefit for my kingdom.

Watching my court enjoy themselves pleased me greatly. Let them dance and fight and hump each other senseless on the floor of my hall. Part of me longed to tell Stormur to shut his mouth so I could leap off the dais and join them. Instead, I sat in my gilded chair and let my counselor berate me for neglecting my diplomatic duties.

I took a slow sip of wine. "As king, I thought I wasn't required to do anything that didn't please me immensely."

"Your father certainly ruled according to that principle," said Stormur. "*I* was under the impression you wanted to be a different kind of king."

Stormur was right. I had loved King Darian, but didn't much *like* him or the way he ruled Coridon. He was a good father, occasionally a devoted husband, a frequent violator of courtesans, but much too self-indulgent to rule a great kingdom with the necessary discipline.

Discipline happened to be my specialty, a passion that had developed after my family died. Any form of control made me feel good. Made me stronger. And I particularly enjoyed wielding it over others.

"Arrow," Stormur leaned close, his dark curls sticking to the sweat beading his forehead. "Granted, your first visit since the accident will be uncomfortable—"

"Accident?" I slammed my goblet on the table, and Stormur's wife, Ildri, who sat beside him, dropped her spoon in her pheasant stew. "What happened to my family, Counselor, wasn't a slip of fate or an unfortunate alignment of circumstances. It was a calculated attack. I should have blown the mountain and all the gold inside it to dust on the day it happened."

The boom of their carriage exploding, the sight of what was left of their bodies, nothing but bone and gore, those sounds and images haunted my dreams and plagued my days.

Three years ago, in the time it took for my heart to beat thrice—my father, mother, older brother, and sister—everyone I'd cared about was killed, obliterated from my life, changing me forever. Transforming me into the man I was today—a king without a heart. A fae who would never be so weak and foolish as to love anything or anyone again.

For indeed, love was the worst, most insidious of weaknesses.

"Remember," said Stormur, gripping my arm, "your parents chose to ride in an unmarked carriage that day. The gold raiders assumed it carried valuable cargo. And the humans responsible have been punished. Quite *severely.*"

Yes, indeed they were. I remembered it well—the power of the storm moving through me and the smell of scorched flesh as it burned off their bones. Days later, the scent was still with me, in my nose, on my skin, as difficult to eradicate as the guilt that had infected me because I'd survived and my family had not.

"Your father went against my advice that day, and you, Arrow, to avoid a similar fate, vowed you never would. Wearing a crown of anger and guilt does not serve you."

I took a deep drink. "But being an irresponsible son, I chose not to join them and, instead, rode with Raiden at the back of the procession. Perhaps if I'd been with them I—"

"No," barked Stormur. "You couldn't have."

Ildri tucked long red hair behind her ears and concentrated on her meal, wisely not giving her opinion on the matter. She was terrified of rousing my temper since it had scorched her so often in the dark days following my family's death each time she had tried to console me.

Her son, Raiden, who sat on my left, leaned closer to reinforce his father's point, recounting stories about recent sightings of gold raiders moving along the border between our kingdom and the Sun Realm, recruiting humans for future attacks on the mines.

"Arrow," said Raiden, "if you show your face at the mines, even briefly, any reaver elves who had plans to help the humans steal your gold would rethink them."

Those close to me assumed I had withdrawn from the Auryinnia Mines because I was terrified to confront horrific memories. They were right about my fear, but for the wrong reason.

I worried that when I saw the enormous golden columns that flanked the mountain's opening, I'd do what the gold chasers had done to my family and turn the mine and every elf and slave within it to dust, singlehandedly destroying the source of our kingdom's wealth, power, and supremacy over the realms. A fucking stupid thing to do.

I shrugged a shoulder at Raiden.

"Do you not believe me?" he asked.

"No. You're right. My presence would deter the gold chasers. It is my duty, and I should return. I know I must, and I will... when

I'm certain I can control my fury. In the meantime, we'll send soldiers to patrol the border with orders to kill any raiders on sight. We'll even lead some parties ourselves. The hunt will be entertaining, don't you think?" I asked, trying to shift his focus.

Leaning back in his chair, he patted my shoulder, satisfied for now. "You look tired," he said, tipping his head toward the courtiers below. "You should have some fun for a change and follow Esen's lead."

"Last time I checked, I was the king, not you. Shouldn't I be issuing the orders?"

Scanning the hall, I found Esen's blue head amongst the revelers and laughed. A bearded fire demon drew her onto his lap, feeding her grapes and sucking her neck as she ate them.

I grinned at Raiden. "I think I'm too big to fit comfortably on that demon's lap."

Raiden laughed. He knew my tastes ran toward curvaceous, obedient female fae. At least, that was the case before my family died. Lately, I'd had little interest in bedding anyone—fire demon or not.

The Sayeeda appeared in the hall, and Raiden's attention shifted toward her. His longing to be near her was an intense energy that ignited the feather glyphs on my hand, turning them from dark red to glowing gold.

I should dismiss Raiden, let him join her. But I didn't. Those damn control issues again.

I surveyed the crowd, skimming over the servants in their plain gold tunics, my attention snapping back to dark hair escaping a girl's headband and framing the edges of a rosebud mouth.

The servant's body was lithe and compact, her movements confident and deliberate despite the fact that only days ago, she had been weak from starvation and abuse.

It was the slave I'd purchased from the Farron Gilt Market. The girl who claimed to possess no memories. The human I should have killed the moment I caught her trying to escape from the market.

My reflexes sharpened, muscles readying to pounce, like I was a desert panther sighting prey. It was likely I could single this girl out from a crowd of thousands by the unconstrained hate burning in her brilliant green eyes. I recognized that emotion all too well, for I saw it in my own gaze each time I caught my reflection in a mirror.

Last night, in the Grand Hall, I saw her and another servant spying on me from the kitchen. They had witnessed the might of my power and the high price I paid to wield it—exhaustion and a terrible weakness. My strength renewed eventually with rest, experiencing a surplus of positive emotions, or by taking a careful dose of gold serum.

Two of those things did not come easily to me, and the third could be lethal if I misjudged the dose.

The Sun Court envoy who was visiting my court set his fork down and smoothed his palm over the nameless girl's hip as she refilled his wine cup. My fingers clenched around my goblet. He had better get his fucking hands off my property.

"Ari," I barked out at the same time the girl snatched up the fork and drew it back, as if ready to strike the envoy's neck.

Standing nearby, my Sayeeda's head flicked up, and within moments, she appeared at my side. I directed my chin at the commotion below. The envoy had grabbed the servant's wrist and stopped the fork from lodging in his throat just in time.

I longed to kill him, but couldn't afford to break the peace treaty with the Sun Court and their powerful fire mages. So, instead of marching down the stairs to tear his head off, with great difficulty, I swallowed my violent urges and beckoned Ari closer.

"Give the envoy my apologies. Tell him that tomorrow, he will leave my kingdom with an extra crate of gold, free of charge, as thanks for his clemency toward my valued slave."

Her golden eyes flickered, a flash of confusion crossing her face. "And the human?" she asked.

"I haven't decided yet."

She nodded, and then hurried to follow my instructions.

The envoy's frowning fury dissolved as soon as Ari gave him my message. He resumed guzzling my finest wine and gorging on my food, content that he would return to his land with an extremely valuable boon.

At Ari's signal, a guard marched from the shadows, grabbed the human by the arm, and led her back to the kitchen. She went easily enough, her spine and shoulders rigid, her features a blank mask, and I wondered how she remained so calm.

After her reckless, violent action, surely she feared a painful death was imminent.

A mystery, with no name or known birthplace, this human was a tough one. It would not be a simple task to break her. I could kill her. I *should* kill her. But it was more entertaining, no *thrilling*, to keep her alive.

Why? I dared not ask myself.

As king, the Sayeeda served me first, and I was always one course ahead of the rest of the court. Soon, Ari would deliver a fragrant bowl of saffron and rose petal pudding to my table, the smile she reserved only for me shining brightly on her golden lips.

When she returned to my side, she brought no dessert tray, and a scowl marred her lovely face.

She leaned close and spoke in a low voice. "How should I punish the human, King Arrowyn? Is it to be the fires for her tonight?"

"No, not that. I want her to serve the dessert you neglected to bring."

"To serve *you?*" she asked incredulously.

"Yes, me. Who else does she belong to?"

"Now?"

"Yes, of course."

"But she has shown herself to be dangerous."

I rubbed my face, hiding a grin. "You doubt my ability to best her?"

"No, My King."

"Don't *my king* me. Just see it done. Bring the girl to me. And hurry, if you will."

"Yes, King Arrowyn." Ari bowed, then hurried away.

"You're not usually so merciful when your energy is low," said Raiden, absently scraping food around his plate.

"And you usually divert me over dinner with amusing stories of your father's knife juggling obsession."

Raiden glanced at Stormur and snorted. "Point taken. I'll watch the human closely in case she tries to plunge a spoon into your eye while serving your pudding."

"I'd prefer you were busy somewhere else. Go and ask Ari about her recent correspondence from the mines. I'm interested to hear the latest news from her people. But don't leave the hall in case you're needed."

At the mention of the Sayeeda's name, Raiden bolted onto his feet, dishes rattling on the table as he bowed before rushing toward the kitchen. I hid my grin behind my wine cup and took another sip.

My oldest friend didn't realize his infatuation with my bonded gold reaver elf was clear to every single being in the court but him—the very fae consumed by it.

Tapping my fingers on the table, I mulled over Ari's suggestion to throw the nameless girl into the fires. For the misfortune of being born human, this was the fate she deserved.

I hated her species with a passion. Most were gold chasers, serum-addicted fools, fated to be enslaved in my service or die in the great fires of the Gates of Amon.

If not for human greed and addiction, my family would be alive, and I would be *Prince* Arrowyn, not a bitter king of twenty-seven years of age, bound to a gilded throne of pain that should have belonged to my dead brother, Karln.

This human girl had dishonored her vow to my Sayeeda and threatened an envoy from another Star Realm Court. She should already be dead, but I couldn't give up the pleasure of seeing my own inner demons reflected in her luminous gaze. Not yet, anyway.

She deserved punishment—ample pain and torture to justify the hatred of fae kind, hatred of *me*, that blared from the depths of her rebellious eyes.

My glyphs tingled, and I looked up as the girl weaved along the edges of the hall, her steps unhurried, and her forest-green gaze fixed on the bowl she carried. Those eyes were a soothing color of respite—the very opposite of this slave's nature.

"What took you so long?" I asked as she placed the steaming bowl on the table, her hands steady.

"Sorry," she said, ignoring my question and stepping back to leave.

I seized her wrist, tugging her until her torso hovered over my lap, her weight balanced on one leg. "What do they call you Underfloor?"

"Green, my lord, as you heard the Sayeeda call me last night in the kitchen."

Even now, her words were a subtle reprimand, as if I should have paid more attention and remembered her name.

"I'm King Arrowyn to you."

"Yes, King Arrowyn," she repeated in a dull voice.

The serum affected her and doused the defiance in her eyes, which was unfortunate. It turned the servants into golem-like creatures. Lifeless lumps of clay fashioned into humanoid shapes and brought to life by dark magic to serve their masters' whims. I bit back a grin, realizing that in *her* case, that master would be me—and I would prefer her clear-headed and able to defy me.

"You still don't remember your birth name?"

"No, but if I did, I would hardly tell the man who'd enslaved me."

My brow rose, but I said nothing, inspecting her slowly while she stared at my breastplate of golden feathers. I grabbed her stubborn chin between my thumb and finger, parting her lips and revealing the gap in her front teeth that I'd first spotted in the slaver's cage. Back when spite and rage were the only things keeping her alive.

What a triumph it would be to tame such a rebellious creature.

"As punishment for this evening's crime, your ankles will be cuffed," I informed her. "The chain will make a pretty chime, don't you think?"

She met my gaze. Her eyes flashed, the color as clear and bright as new leaves.

I stroked her cheek. "You're small, and your flesh isn't soft and pliant, but your green eyes please me."

"Then hand me your knife," she said, "and I'll cut one out and add it to your pudding."

"Know this," I growled, squeezing her throat until her face flushed red. "If you harm yourself, I will spend my fortune, use the last traces of my power, hunt any living relatives of yours and cook them on a slow spit with lightning." I loosened my grip. "It's not a pleasant way to die. Do you understand?"

"Yes, *King Arrowyn*," she said, her voice trembling at last.

A chuckle rumbled in my throat. This girl amused me. My hand glided from her throat to her chest, pressing against the warm skin over her collarbone. "You're trembling like a blade of grass in a breeze. You are nothing, a leaf blown about by storms, used and abused for the wind's pleasure. From this moment on, you shall be known as Leaf. There... I've given you a better name than Green. Make sure you answer to it."

"Yes, King Arrowyn," she said again, and if looks could kill, I'd be a pile of charred bones and ash upon the gold-veined marble of my hall.

"Tell the Sayeeda I want you to return to your room while I consider your punishment."

I pushed her back onto her feet. She stumbled, then bowed and retreated, hurrying down the dais steps.

Beside me, Stormur laughed. "Am I dreaming? A human commits such an offense in your hall and simply walks away?

Since your return from the markets, Arrowyn, you haven't been yourself."

I couldn't argue. My High Counselor was correct. Shrugging a shoulder, I beckoned a guard over and instructed him to give Ari the same message I gave the girl in case she refused to relay it.

"I'm going to bed," I said, rising and leaving my favorite dessert untouched. "The council will meet in the morning to discuss a plan to deal with the gold raiders."

"My King," Stormur and Ildri said, standing and bowing as I left the dais.

As I strode through the hall, Raiden and Esen peeled away from their conversation with a group of guards and fell into step with me.

Instead of leaving by my usual exit, I took a detour through the kitchen, nodding at Ari as she descended the cellar steps.

I exited the kitchen into the servants' hall, a movement catching my eye at the far end. Three guards were tussling, partly hidden behind an auron kanara cage. My gut tightened, something telling me it was more than horseplay.

A few more strides down the hallway, revealed they were assaulting someone. It crossed my mind to let Raiden deal with it, and I stopped, about to turn away. Then a pair of green eyes flashed, staring unfocused over a guard's shoulder armor.

They were attacking my human, who, by the looks of her, had regressed into a state of shock. If they supposed her lapse of obedience in the hall made her a fair target for their games, they couldn't be more wrong.

"Arrow, wait," said Raiden, reaching for my arm.

I pushed him away. "Stay out of this."

The pungent scent of a storm infused the air as I marched forward and flung the guards off the human, their bodies hitting the opposite wall with three satisfying crunches.

"Leave," I growled out. "Wait for me Underfloor, and do not move."

The two that could walk scurried away like dung roaches. The girl slid down the wall, her body bruised and bleeding, the torn gold tunic exposing nail tracks on her breasts.

"Did they breach you?" I asked, whorls of blue lightning swirling my limbs.

She blinked. "What?"

"Inside you. Did they get inside your body?"

A slow head shake was her only answer.

"Esen, inform Ari that the girl, now known as Leaf, is in my service. She belongs to me and will remain in my chambers for as long as I desire. She will be chained and serve only me. Also, tell Ari the girl's wounds need attention and to bring her salves to my pavilion."

Esen shuffled her feet. "You can't be serious?"

"And *you* cannot mean to question me. Hold your tongue or lose it."

With a splutter of outrage, she turned on her heel and followed my directions.

"Raiden, take the girl to my quarters. I'll follow shortly."

Nodding at the guard on the ground, he said, "Shall I remove this one?

"No. I'll deal with him."

His mouth in a grim line, Raiden bowed, no doubt biting his tongue in half to stem the flow of questions that I could predict with certain accuracy.

Had I lost my mind?

Possibly.

What need did I have for a human chamber slave?

Absolutely none.

And finally... why?

I had no idea.

But never again would another male touch her. I would make certain of it.

"Thank you," the girl whispered as Raiden lifted her to her feet. "Thank you for... stopping them..." She shuddered, her words trailing away.

"Best you don't give your thanks too fast, little Leaf. You may find me a difficult master."

As Raiden guided her toward the elevator, she shot me a look over her shoulder, her eyes wide with shock. She looked vulnerable. Innocent. But it was only a matter of time before her bitter heart made her attempt another act of rebellion.

But the truth was, whatever she did next, I would gladly welcome the diversion.

Bending, I gripped the guard under his arms, tossed him over my shoulder, then took the stairs to the slave cells two at a time.

It would be a while before I got the rest I needed.

Chapter 7

LEAF

Raiden led me up two flights of stairs, then shoved me inside an elevator tucked in a corner of a hall on the palace's third floor, a place I'd never been before.

The doors slid open on the seventh floor. When we entered a well-guarded corridor, I wondered if it would take us to the tallest of the palace's seven golden domes. The ones I'd seen from the carriage the night I arrived at Coridon.

As we started up a staircase, a spiraling marvel of carved gold, I turned to the tight-lipped Raiden. "The king lives in the highest tower?"

Raiden nodded, his grip on my arm tightening.

"Of course he does," I said, keeping my voice level and hoping Raiden couldn't feel me trembling. "What does Arrow mean to do with me?"

Dark eyes frowned down at me. "On first name terms with the king, are you?"

I ignored his question and asked my own. "Will he kill me tonight?"

The thud of Raiden's boots on the steps was my only answer.

"Come on. Give me a clue. Should I prepare for torture? A slow death, where he'll slice a piece off my body every day until I'm nothing but a heart beating in a pile of gore?"

"And to think humans call us fae gruesome minded. Be quiet or I'll begin the king's work myself and cut your tongue out."

I supposed that answered my question. I clamped my lips together firmly.

As we climbed alternating stairs of solid gold and white marble, Raiden set a gentle pace. Perhaps in consideration of my bruises, or perhaps not. Then we arrived at a foyer on the bottom level of the king's apartment.

Arrow's home ranged over three circular levels of black-and-white marble, braced by soaring gold columns. Carvings and etchings of tiny palm leaves and the king's beloved feathers decorated most surfaces. I shook off Raiden's hand and spun on my heel, taking it all in.

The night breeze fluttered gauzy material in front of floor-to-ceiling windows. From this great height, I could see the lights of Coridon and the desert beyond sparkling in every direction I turned. There were barely any walls to speak of, and as a result, moonlight bathed the apartment in a wash of cool silver tones.

The bottom floor contained a river that flowed along a deep, winding channel in the marble. Palm trees, rocks, and groupings of low couches and tables surrounded it, creating the feeling of a luxurious retreat. Arrow's sanctuary, away from the chaos of the court.

The king's elevator, decorated in swirls of gold, stood opposite the stairs that swept up to the second level. And, of course, several auron kanara cages gleamed between archways in what looked like a sitting room above.

"Incredible," I said, walking along the river edge. I followed it to the end, where the water fell through a window before cascading into a large rectangular pool that ran along an external wall of the palace.

Leaning my palms on the sill, I stuck my head out of the window and let the water cool my skin as it rushed past me, sparkling like liquid stars.

"I wouldn't recommend jumping," said Raiden behind me. "You'd die before you splattered on the pavement."

"Most likely," I agreed, then pushed my weight off the column that braced the window and turned to face him. "This is beautiful."

"Enjoy it while you can. I doubt you'll spend much time in the river room." He seized my arm and led me up another flight of stairs.

Comfortable lounging furniture covered in jewel-toned cushions and rugs decorated the second-floor sitting room. Everything that could be gilded had been and flashed now in the moonlight, set in ideal places to enjoy the views through gigantic arched windows.

"These are the quarters that should interest you." Raiden gestured toward a narrow, wall-less stone bridge that connected an outdoor platform to the far side of the sitting room.

More soaring gold columns held up the platform's vaulted, domed ceiling. And all sides of the circular room dropped away to the gruesome death Raiden had taken pleasure in describing.

Perched high above the city, it appeared to be an elaborate gilded cage—a beautiful death trap from which there was only one way to escape. Through the Storm King's chambers and past his guards.

As Raiden walked me toward the pavilion, I noticed a long gold chain screwed to the center of its tiled floor. This pretty cage was about to become my new residence. But whether I should hope for a long or a short-term stay, I couldn't decide.

My limbs shook from both exhaustion and building terror as Raiden guided me along the narrow walkway onto the pavilion. With a palm on my shoulder, he pressed me to sit on the floor, wrapped thin, gold shackles around my ankles, and locked me in place.

I took slow breaths to settle my racing heart and stared up at him. "Does your friend do this often?"

"Do what?"

"Chain slaves in his chamber."

"Only the annoying ones." Crinkles appeared at the edges of his brown eyes, a flash of dry humor.

I shook the chain between my ankles. "I figured Arrow found everyone annoying. I'm surprised it's not more populated in here."

"You should see it on a Saturday night," he replied, stepping back and tucking dark hair behind his ears. Like all fae, his face was unnaturally handsome and his smirk etched with conceit. He chewed on the corner of his lip and seemed to consider his next words carefully.

"The old king had this pavilion built for unpleasant purposes and used it frequently. His son has more refined tastes and quite a different temperament. Behave yourself, Leaf, and you may survive."

"That's not my name."

"It is *now*. Better learn to answer to it."

A flash of light over Raiden's shoulders drew my eyes to the floor above, the top level of the king's apartment. I inhaled sharply.

The front section of the bedchamber floor cut away in the shape of a large crescent moon. A pair of white stairs swept from either side of the sitting room, the level my prison attached to, and wound gracefully up to the king's bedroom.

From where I sat, I had a perfect view of the Storm King's enormous black and gold bed, and from it, he would have a perfect view of me, chained and helpless below him. The only place he likely couldn't watch me from was the river room on the first level. But as Raiden had warned, I probably wouldn't spend much time there.

Nausea rushed over me as my new reality tightened like a band of gold around my chest, squeezing the breath from my lungs. I was just like the pathetic auron kanara, trapped in a pretty cage, my life reduced to making noise to gain attention and hoping that someone would remember to feed me.

The only way to escape the chains and get past the guards would be with help. If I survived long enough, perhaps Raiden or a servant who attended the king's chambers would eventually take pity on me. Unlikely, but it was probably my only option to get out of here and return home. Wherever home was.

Slippers whispered on the stairs, then the Sayeeda appeared on the landing carrying a tray that held tiny ceramic jars and a bowl of water. As she approached, Raiden's breathing visibly quickened. He stepped backward, away from me, and cleared his throat.

Interesting. The king's guard wished he had a Sayeeda of his own.

Without looking at Raiden, the Sayeeda gestured for me to stand. With a gentle touch, she inspected the damage from the asshole guards, then cleaned my scratches with pungent herbal water and dried my skin with a soft towel.

Her golden eyes stared into mine as she applied cream to my wounds. She tapped the crease of my elbow, where the pinprick mark had crusted over. "You inject serum?" she asked.

"Doubt it. I don't remember ever doing so."

"I believe you. Your eyes are too clear for you to be an addict. But you have been injected with something."

I squinted at the mark. "It could be an insect bite."

"No," she replied, pressing it with her thumb. "This was made by a needle." Gripping my cheeks between her palms, she turned my face left, then right. "Where are you from, Leaf?"

Her voice dipped low when she spoke my new name, as if it rankled her to say it out loud. Perhaps she was jealous that the king chose it.

"You speak the common language well enough, but your forest eyes don't hide your cunning quite as well as you think. I doubt you come from a tribe of gold chasers. If you'll trust me with whatever it is you're hiding about your origins, perhaps I can help you."

It took cunning to recognize it in another, and out of all the fae, elves were known to be the sliest. The Sayeeda was not only untrustworthy, but dangerous.

"As I've already told you, I don't remember my home. The lump on my head and needle mark on my arm indicate that someone has successfully stolen my memories."

She patted my cheek and released me. "What has been forgotten, will be remembered. We'll make sure of it." She placed the lids on her jars. "What do you think of the name the king gifted you?"

"It's hardly a gift," I replied.

A smirk flickered over the Sayeeda's shimmering lips as she wiped her hands on a cloth, then placed the jars on the tray. "That remains to be seen." She untied a gold shawl from her waist and held it out. "The night breeze is cool. You will need this."

I accepted the woolen shawl, hugging it to my chest. "Thank you for your mercy."

"What you did this evening was an offense punishable by death, if my master chooses. It isn't my mercy you need."

As I met her shrewd gaze, I let my focus soften, pretending to be affected by a dose of serum.

The Sayeeda collected her tray and murmured something to Raiden about the king having taken his medicine already. Then they walked across the stone bridge and left the king's apartment by the stairs on the right.

Unfurling my clenched fists, I wrapped the Sayeeda's shawl around my shoulders and strode forward until my chain pulled taut, discovering I could walk around the pavilion's perimeter with ease.

At least if I became desperate, I could fling myself over the edge and hang from my ankles until I died or wrap the chain around my neck and strangle the last breath from my lungs.

Rough stone grated my skin as I leaned against a column and slid to the floor. I curled my knees into my chest and studied the night view while the breeze sifted through my hair, soothing my nerves.

Stars sparkled in an indigo sky, shining brighter than the city lights below. The crescent moon illuminated a dark mountain range in the distance, storm clouds rumbling above them.

Those guards might have killed me tonight if the king and his party hadn't arrived when they did. Arrowyn saved my life, or at the very least, my virtue—if I still possessed it. The slavers from the gilt market could have done anything to me while I was unconscious.

Also, I was unaware of my people's traditions. Were we reserved or free with our bodies?

Despite how hard I tried, I recalled no memories of heated kisses or caresses. But in the servants' hall at night, people sneaked into their lovers' rooms, and I found the noises they made stimulating and entertaining.

And in the hall tonight, I'd seen fae tongues swiping across lips and delving inside painted mouths. Hands had caressed breasts, and bulges rose in the males' laps. Rather than feeling shocked, I'd been curious to see what raged beneath the material of their pants. So at the very least, I guessed that meant I wasn't a prude.

But later, in the hallway, when the guards' cruel fingers and hips moved against me, they'd laughed and joked, enjoying their game, their sour breath coiling tendrils of fear and disgust inside me.

I had felt no pleasure.

Only pain.

And if the king had more of the same in mind for tonight, then I wished he hadn't bothered to save me.

By the position of the moon in the sky, I estimated about an hour had passed when I finally heard the thud of boots against the stairs. They grew louder, then a crown of golden feathers appeared, followed by the king's tall form. Fear shivered down my spine.

Arrowyn had arrived.

He clicked his fingers and lightning globes like the ones in the servants' hall spread a warm glow throughout his living space. As he strode forward, removing his breastplate of deadly feathers, his gaze fell on me, and an unpleasant smile crossed his face.

"Ah, little Leaf. How do you like your new residence? A spectacular view, no?"

To stop myself from roaring at him, I dug my nails into the side of my thigh. To survive, I needed to be meek, obedient, but I hated him so much I wasn't sure I could manage it.

He stalked across the narrow footbridge, his chest bare, but with his stupid crown still glowing on his brow, then he stopped in the middle of the pavilion. Planting his feet wide, he crossed his arms and inspected me.

"Those chains suit you well," he rumbled, prowling forward until he stood within arm's reach.

"And you look good, too," I said. "I prefer you without your chest plate, weaponless."

Broad shoulders moved with each deep breath he took. "I'm hardly defenseless, human. What dangerous tricks do you hide beneath your tunic?"

"None," I whispered.

His hand shot out, and I flinched. Warm fingers rubbed the shawl over the notch between my collarbones. "Ari is too soft-hearted," he murmured.

The Sayeeda soft-hearted? That was debatable. His gilded slave was about as kind as a starving lioness protecting a prize kill. I smiled, realizing in that scenario, the slab of meat would be the very king who frowned above me.

He moved closer and sighed into my face, his right hand wrapping my throat, lightly choking me. The smell of sandalwood, cinnamon, and wine clouded my mind, a destabilizing combination that made me sway.

The intricate feather glyphs that twined his chest and heavily muscled arms burst to life, blazing gold, like flowing lava. If he noticed the phenomenon, he made no visible reaction. Glowing silver eyes traced my face, the thumb of his free hand parting my lips. He rubbed the gap in my front teeth, seemingly fascinated by it.

"Fae don't possess such curious imperfections," he mused.

My heart pounded as I pictured biting down and spitting the tip of his bloodied thumb onto the tiles.

A dark chuckle rumbled in his chest. "I see your thoughts as clearly as if you'd spoken them. Bite me and I'll toss you over the edge and leave you hanging all night from your ankles, the blood pooling in your brain as you asphyxiate. You will die before I wake."

I had no doubt the ruthless bastard would do it.

As we stared at each other, intense energy crackled in the space between our bodies. Self-disgust flushed through me when my skin prickled with a different awareness, heat burning low in my belly.

My cheeks flamed as he inhaled sharply, grinning at my reaction to his touch. It was base and instinctual, exactly like an animal's.

He dropped his hand to my hip and stroked lightly over my tunic. "I despise humans," he said.

"I wonder how you can bear to touch me, then?"

His perfectly curved mouth lifted in a sneer. "Your race is weak, greedy, and small-minded. You people are willing to destroy anyone and anything to obtain your desires... food, gold, control. You don't care as long as you achieve your ends."

"Are you any different?" I asked. "What would you do to retain your power, protect your kingdom and your family?"

Releasing a harsh breath, he recoiled from my words. "Don't speak about my family."

"Why not?" I remembered what Raiden had told me about Arrow's father. "Have they never been ruthless in pursuing their desires? As no two fae are alike, all humans shouldn't be tarnished by the actions of a few. I'm not the same as the ones who have hurt you."

A groan of anguish rumbled deep in his chest, then he shoved me backward and paced around the edges of the pavilion. I turned on my heel to keep him in sight.

Without warning, he lurched forward and gripped my chin, raising my face to his. "How do you imagine I'll punish you for tonight's transgression?" he asked in a husky whisper.

"First, you'll rape me." I forced frost into my glare, trapping my fear behind a sheet of ice.

"You're wrong, little Leaf." I tried to turn my head away, but he held it firmly in place. "Some fae require another's fear and pain to maintain their cock stands. But I do not. My pleasures run in the opposite direction."

"What does that mean?"

"It means I'd rather hear you beg for my touch."

I let out a shocked laugh. "Keep me here forever, and you'll never hear that."

"We shall see, my trembling Leaf."

I swallowed as his hand released my throat and trailed over my stomach. His fingertips came to rest over my pelvis, and heat exploded beneath his touch.

To stop his hand from roaming lower, I gripped his wrist. "What happened to the guards who assaulted me?"

His breath grew ragged against my skin, a disturbing sensation. "I burned the conscious pair alive and removed the other's favorite organ with my blade. When he woke, which was immediately, I stuffed it down his throat. That one took a while to die."

A shudder arched my spine. "Why commit such horror against another being? Inflict such suffering?"

"No one touches what is mine without permission."

I blinked in silence for a moment, astounded by his arrogance and capacity for casual cruelty.

"But I'm not yours. I would have to give my life to you in an act of love or deep friendship for that to be true. Know this, Storm King, I will never give myself willingly to you."

"Never is a long time. And I predict that in time, you will do just that."

I shook my head, and his palm shifted, his fingers dipping into the standard-issue tightly woven undergarment that court servants wore. A long finger glided through the mortifying moisture at my core, just the once, before he slid it out and swept it over his tongue, tasting me.

"Very nice. For a human. Sleep well in your cage, my defiant bird," he said, moving away. "I look forward to turning your bitter fury into something more palatable."

"What?" I spluttered. "You're leaving?"

"I've got better things to do than argue with a human—like sleep."

"I hope nightmares plague you all night long," I replied, immediately wishing I could bite my tongue off.

If I couldn't curb my temper, my lack of self-restraint would soon get me killed. Fear would make most sane people cower and behave cautiously. But not me, it seemed. What did that mean? Was I insane? Did I have a death wish?

With my reckless boldness, knowledge of weapons, and keenness to use them, I was beginning to think that, back home, I'd been some kind of soldier.

The king lurched forward and ripped the shawl from my shoulders. "You don't deserve this. I don't care if you freeze your bony ass off."

"No idea how I escaped a beating," I murmured softly to myself as he swaggered along the footbridge toward his sitting room.

"Me either. But since my guards have already damaged you, and I'm too tired to exert myself, that might have something to do with it," he mocked. "But tomorrow is another day. Anything is possible. Anything except you getting out of those chains."

As the king padded up the stairs to his bedroom, I sank to the floor while he stripped off items of clothing, dropping them as he went—two gold arm cuffs, a metal-studded belt, and then his black leather pants.

Curled on my side in the middle of the pavilion, I stared at Arrow's outline in the moonlight as he stood in front of the bed, his glyphs glowing a dull bronze color, illuminating his body.

Wiping tears from my face, I hugged my aching, hollow stomach. "I'm hungry," I told the star-studded sky beyond the arches.

"Whose fault is that?" said the dark lump beneath the king's bedcovers.

"Is there anything you can't hear?"

"Not really. And if you had any sense in that dull human brain of yours, you'd understand why no one fed you dinner tonight."

"Food is a basic right, even for prisoners," I shot back, thinking of the Sun envoy I'd tried to stab and the way his nostrils had flared as he squeezed my hip, his palm moving lower.

"Your existence in this realm, or in *any* realm, is entirely at my discretion," said the bed lump. "The moment you tried to kill the Sun envoy, your entitlement to any *rights* was destroyed."

"I wasn't trying to kill him, just mortally wound him."

Arrow laughed, and a cold shiver rolled over me. "Goodnight, King Arrowyn," I said, a sneer in my tone.

Only the flap of a single auron kanara bird answered me.

As I curled into a tighter ball, I pondered who might have given me the large bump on my head. Was it the same person who had injected me with an unknown drug? And why did they want to steal my memories?

I thought of the green-eyed boy in the forest, and warmth infused my shivering limbs. I sensed no evil, no bad emotions linked with the lush, green landscape from my flashbacks. The forest was home, a safe place, where friends and family awaited my return. I felt certain of it.

To find this beloved home, I needed to survive the pavilion. I had to earn food, grow strong, and make an ally who would help to break me out of these chains.

The seventh time my stomach growled, I resolved that no matter what the king did to me or *made* me do, I would bear it with detached silence.

Perhaps then he would feed me.

Chapter 8

LEAF

My feet were on fire as I trampled through the undergrowth, branches and twigs snapping beneath them. Sun blazed between tree trunks and vines. Tiny cuts bled between my toes, but I kept running until I reached the largest ruin in the forest—the crumbling walls of a once-grand palace.

My heart pounded and my legs ached, but I laughed gleefully as the boy chased me. Moss-covered walls soared into view, and I pumped my arms harder, making a leap for a low ledge that I planned to hide behind. A vine wrapped my ankle, and I went down with a thud, biting my lip to swallow a yelp of pain.

In three heartbeats, the green-eyed boy landed on me, tickling me as I rolled over. "Got you, Sapling," he said. "Knew I was still faster than you."

"You only caught me because I tripped. I'll always be faster than you, Ash. I plan to make sure of it."

"Oh, and don't I know it," he replied, his grin teasing. "But don't worry. What has been forgotten will be remembered."

Those words sent fear bolting through me. I shook it off and smiled at him.

The sun shone on his dark brown hair, and I tucked a thick lock behind his ear, which was rounded like mine. Not sharp like Arrow's.

"You're too heavy," I complained. "My back hurts. Get off!"

"I'm not on you," said the smooth voice of the Sayeeda, waking me from another vivid dream of home. I kept my eyes closed as she prattled. "Your back aches because you've slept on hard stone." She dug a finger into my heel. "And the midday sun has burned your feet."

"Is it midday already?" I sat up, gaping at the city below the pavilion's arches. Scores of fae roamed below, their clothes of burgundy, bronze, and gold fluttering behind them as they hurried about their business.

"I see you somehow lived through the night," she said, and I wondered if she wished I hadn't.

If any of the fae in the streets happened to look up, they would see me in my spectacular marble and gold prison. I'd look tiny, more like a carving of a woman than a real one, but when I moved about, they'd know the rumors were true. King Arrowyn's slave girl lived to see another day.

Rolling my shoulders, I made the mistake of looking up at the domed ceiling covered in mosaic-tile scenes of winged fae ripping each other apart on battlefields. Not a comforting sight.

My ankle chain rattled as I clutched the Sayeeda's shawl to my chest.

How did I still have her shawl when Arrow tore it off me last night?

I glanced up at the king's neatly made bed, then scanned the visible areas of the apartment. No Arrow in sight. The Sayeeda must have taken pity on me earlier when she came to perform her morning services for the king. Whatever distasteful acts they entailed, I hoped I never had to witness them.

My foot scraped over something rough—a drain about the size of my spread hand set into the middle of the tiles. My stomach dropped.

"Is that what I think it's for?" I asked, humiliated by the thought of squatting over the drain.

"Yes, among other things. It makes cleaning easier for the chamber servants, but you'll be given ample opportunities to use the first-floor bathroom when it is convenient for me to take you. At other times, feel free to use the drain."

My nose wrinkled, then I spied the breakfast tray on the ground, my mouth watering as the Sayeeda lifted the lid. "Is that for me?"

She gave a slow nod, her eyelashes glittering. "Before you eat, I want you to consider something. Living in this windy cage is a far better fate than dying in the fires. And if a slave serves their master well, their life improves a great deal. Remember that. You cannot change the past, but from now on, I suggest you choose your words and actions more carefully."

Long fingers tipped with gold pushed the tray closer, and saliva filled my mouth again as the rich smell made me swoon. I hugged my knees to my chest to stop myself from lowering my head and eating like a pig over a trough.

"When you call me the Sayeeda, my focus is drawn back to the slave cells, not a place I wish to think of often. If you survive the next few days, we will see quite a bit of each other. So you should call me Ari, as the king does."

To hide my shock, I dropped my chin and let dark hair fall over my face, focusing on a bright feather-shaped tile near my toe. The high and mighty Sayeeda had seen fit to share her private name with *me*—a disgraced human slave who might not even live through the night. My thoughts raced as I tried to understand why she would do such a thing.

Golden eyes studied me as I offered her a tentative smile, but her face remained an impassive mask.

My stomach gurgled, and I pointed at the toasted bread and boiled eggs arranged on a bright-blue ceramic plate. "May I begin?"

"Of course."

I bit into an egg, crunching through the shell while inspecting the beautiful Sayeeda. Even her eyeballs glimmered with a metallic hue, her lashes and brows studded with tiny nuggets of gold, as if she was more statue than living being.

Although she looked young, reaver elves were an eternal species, so she could have been hundreds or even thousands of years old.

Frowning, Ari peeled the other egg, then mashed it on the bread with the deft movements of a practiced cook. Perhaps that had been her occupation before she became the Storm Court's Mistress of Slaves and Spices.

Moaning as butter and dill melted over my tongue, I made short work of the toast, barely chewing between bites, the Sayeeda watching me far too closely as I ate.

"This is much nicer than the pile of rotten vegetables I was expecting," I said, licking the last crumbs from my lips.

"Yes, all things considered, you're very fortunate."

Still crouching on her haunches, she reached for a cup, filled it with water from an earthen jar, then passed it into my trembling hands.

"Thank you," I said, finally remembering my manners.

I gulped the cool liquid, then wiped water from my chin and placed the cup on the tray. "Were you born at the Court of Storms and Feathers?"

"No. Reaver elves don't live in the Storm Court by *choice*," she said, her tone hot but her expression cool.

Interesting.

Anyone who'd seen her fawning over Arrow would have a hard time believing that she lived in his kingdom under sufferance. She seemed to adore him, but perhaps her actions only modeled what she'd mentioned before, a slave's good behavior affording them a better life.

I longed to ask how she'd become the king's bonded servant who held a high rank in the court, but thought it best not to be too nosy for the time being.

Scratching a scab on my elbow, I searched for a more neutral line of questioning. "Are you originally from the gold mines?"

"That is none of your business." She rose to her slippered feet in a single movement, then bent and collected the tray, leaving the jug and cup on the tiles beside me.

I pointed at them. "Aren't you worried I'll smash those and use the pieces to slit my wrists?"

The smile that crossed her face wasn't pleasant. "You're welcome to try it. But your death would be slow and regrettable."

After helping me stand, she inspected my scrapes and bruises. "These require more ointment, but not until after you've washed."

I touched her wrist to get her attention. "Is Grendal all right?"

"Your friend has a new roommate, and since they are both obedient servants, all is well."

Ari unlocked the chain from the shackle on my ankle and fastened it to a plain gold collar around my neck. She explained the various ways she could use the chain to restrain me—by linking my two hands together, my hands to my feet, and so on.

She slid a bar through the end of the chain and used it to lead me along the death-trap stone walkway into the sitting room. "I'd prefer it if you walked beside me," she said as if she had entered my mind and heard me calculating the short, sharp actions required to wrap the chain around her slender neck and choke her.

Raising her eyebrow as I stepped beside her, she patted the knives that hung on both sides of her hips against her metallic dress. I wondered if Esen had told her about my weapon-pilfering skills.

I sighed. There was no point in killing the Sayeeda. If I wanted to escape this damned apartment and the city without being captured, and then somehow flee in the right direction, I would definitely need her help. And she might prove a useful source of information in time, if I could worm it out of her.

Transparent curtains fluttered in a light breeze as we strolled past the auron kanara cages, then down the stairs to the river room. We crossed the river and went up another set of white stairs to an antechamber on a raised platform of marble.

The small bathroom we entered was windowless and contained a toilet, a copper bathtub, and a long basin that curved in a semi-circle around the walls.

Ari turned the faucets over the bathtub and clean water gushed from them. She gestured for me to use the toilet while the bath filled, refusing to leave the room and give me privacy. I did as I was told, then stood and scowled at her.

"Don't look at me like that. Trust must be earned," she said as I climbed into the tub and sank up to my neck in sweet-smelling water. "At present, Leaf, you have much to atone for."

After I bathed and dressed in a clean gold tunic, she attached my chain to a link on the floor below the window that the river flowed through. While she tidied the room, she let me sit on the sill and watch the water cascade over the sloping marble into the city pool below.

"You have many duties," I told her. "The king's cleaner, food server, and his slave master. Why don't other servants perform some of the lesser tasks?"

Arranging cushions on a couch, she snorted. "Because he wishes me to do these things. Also, not everything is as it first seems."

I couldn't argue with that slightly cryptic statement, so I turned my attention to the pool below. It looked several feet wide and flowed through a quieter section of the market district. Opposite it was a city wall lined with a bank of thick bushes that were just the right height for a person to hide behind without being observed from the street.

The drop from the sill to the water was considerable, and I wondered how deep the pool was. Raiden was likely correct; the fall could be deadly.

A shiver ran down my spine, and my vision tunneled, images flickering at the edges of my mind, memories of me chasing the green-eyed boy through the forest.

This time, we followed a creek to its end. It spilled over a cliff overlooking an undulating landscape of trees and distant mountain ranges. Below us, a waterfall rumbled into a river.

With loud yelps, the boy and I leaped over the edge, our arms spreading out like wings to steady our descent. I felt the wind rushing past, freedom sizzling through my blood. I was alive and flying like a bird.

This wasn't a dream but a memory of a real event. Something I felt sure the boy and I had done regularly. A fun game. Something we had survived over and over.

Hope beat against my ribs as I studied the king's waterfall and the city pool it flowed into with a new purpose. What I needed to do was painfully clear.

No matter what, I had to gain the Sayeeda's trust, if not her friendship, so that one day, she would leave me alone and unchained as I sat in this exact position.

The sudden frantic fluttering of the auron kanara disturbed my thoughts. "Can't you feed them, Ari, and stop that horrible sound?"

"Gold reavers cannot summon the lightning they feed upon, hence why we elves need the Light Realm fae."

"For what exactly?" I asked.

"We cannot control the storms nor harness the lightning, and yet we must eat the auron kanaras' feathers to survive. Gold runs through our veins, which we feed back to the soil and rivers. Our elemental magic creates the gold that lies beneath the Auryinnia Mountain, always renewing. We mine it and sell it to the rulers of the fae realms."

"And also to the black marketeers," I added.

"That's true. Some reaver elves work with gold raiders and trade the information that allows the humans to intercept gold deliveries throughout the lands. But not many elves are willing to take such a risk. As you can imagine, the punishment if they're caught is severe."

Ari hummed as she ran her fingers along the cages, and the birds stilled, as if listening to her song. Water lilies drifted on the river's gentle currents at the far side of the room where the water entered Arrow's apartment, defying nature as it coursed uphill, growing stronger as it neared the waterfall window I sat upon.

"How does the river work?" I asked.

"A combination of machinery and magic. If you behave yourself, when I return to tidy the river room tomorrow, you can keep me company and enjoy the waterfall again. I can see it soothes you."

"Thank you. If I'm still alive, I'd love to," I said. "Ari, if what I did to the envoy was so bad, why hasn't the king killed me or at least beaten me senseless?"

"I'm sure he has more creative punishments in mind, Leaf."

Ari walked over, took a key from around her neck, and unlocked my chain from the floor. Fighting the breeze, she tucked a gold curl behind her ear and narrowed her eyes at me. "How are you coping with the serum?"

Shit. I'd forgotten to pretend I was drug-affected.

"It's fine," I said. "Since last night, it hasn't seemed as strong. Probably because it's providing pain relief from the bruises those guards gave me."

"Perhaps," she said, not looking convinced.

We mounted the curving stairs that led to the sitting room, but before she returned me to the pavilion, she stopped at a closet and rustled through clothes, pulling out sparkling lengths of material.

"I've had an idea," she said, holding them out. "Put this on."

"What idea?"

"Just do what you're told."

I took them, and she tucked the end of my chain underneath my tunic so it wouldn't get in the way while I changed. For a moment, I pictured strangling her with the chain, her gold eyes bulging as the life drained out of them.

Guilt heated my cheeks. The Sayeeda was as much a prisoner of the Storm Court as I was.

"What is this?" I asked, stretching the linked bits of material between my hands.

"New clothes. Something I hope will bring out King Arrowyn's merciful side. Despite what you think, he does have one. His father dressed all of his chamber slaves in such alluring outfits."

It was likely the Sayeeda had serviced Arrow's needs many times over, so she should know what excited him. By the dust, I'd rather work in the mines than spend even one night arousing the fae who owned me. But then again, if I wanted to buy time to plan an escape, what choice did I have? The king's whore I would have to become.

After I removed my tunic, she helped me tug on the material that only just covered my breasts before it crossed over my stomach and wound around my waist. More linked pieces formed tiny pants, the entire outfit little more than glamorous underwear.

Ari applied ointment to my cuts and bruises, then attached my chain to the ring bolted into the center of the pavilion. When I asked if the king would return to his chambers today, she said she didn't know and that he had instructed her to feed me and tend my wounds, nothing more.

After she left, I inspected the chain and the ring, tugging and twisting to test their strength. I walked the perimeter of the pavilion, studying the city and the landscape beyond, committing both to memory. A city roofed and paved in terracotta and gold and the Auryinnia Mountain range to the north. I only wished I knew where Coridon's exits lay in relation to them.

Once again, I considered wrapping the chain around my neck and leaping off the edge of my pretty prison, but I was too stubborn to end my misery and desperate to solve the mystery of my identity.

A fae merchant below dressed in desert yellow looked up, shading his eyes to better view me. I waved, but he glanced away and hurried along the street, as if he was too frightened to interact with me.

Sighing, I decided to use my chain and the pavilion's columns to exercise and build my strength. I ran on the spot, and then used my bodyweight to work my arms, legs, and stomach muscles, vowing that I would do this several times each day, so when the opportunity to flee arrived, I would be strong and prepared.

What else could a caged human do to pass the time?

I had no wings to flap like the fascinating and irritating auron kanara or pots and pans to scrub, like Grendal had.

All I could do was endure the punishments Arrow delivered, while hiding my determination to one day defeat him.

Chapter 9

LEAF

On a crumbling stone dais, a handsome older man sheathed his sword as a green-eyed woman at his side smiled up at him. A mass of trumpet-shaped flowers tumbled over the ruined building's walls. Sunlight speared through towering trees, illuminating the woman's auburn hair and the silver flecks in the man's dark beard.

The green-eyed boy and I stood below them in a forest clearing, dressed in worn fighting leathers. This time, I was aware I was only dreaming—asleep, while caged in the Storm Court and lost in memories of my past life.

In the dream, pride swelled in my chest as the woman clapped her hands, and the man shouted indistinct words of encouragement, laughter warming his voice.

I raised a heavy sword above my head, my muscles straining, then ran toward the boy who lifted his own blade and met my attack head on.

Using his panted breaths as a gage, I timed my lunges, twists, and strikes to the staccato rhythm of his breathing.

With my mouth sealed tight, I inhaled lightly through my nose, controlling my heartbeat.

We circled the clearing, lunging forward and back with speed. When he moved into the right position, I raised my sword and invited him to strike, blocked his blade high in the air, then gave a swift kick to his balls. With a pained grunt, he stumbled before recovering and lifting his weapon again.

In a few quick moves, my sword kissed the side of his neck, poised to remove his head from his shoulders. Above us, the man and woman cheered.

"Well done," she said, her green eyes flashing.

"And so, you won *again*," said the boy, squeezing me in a one-armed hug, his smile charming as he wiped sweat from his brow with an embroidered sleeve. "Congratulations. Your viciousness is admirable."

"I'm not vicious," I replied. "I'm determined. You're an accomplished fighter, but you're lazy and don't train as often as I do."

"Don't worry, sister. I aim to remedy that one day and surprise you."

I shoved his shoulder playfully. "I won't hold my breath."

Sister, the boy had called me.

He wasn't my lover or my friend.

But my *brother*.

The couple who stood smiling in the ruins were our parents. They had to be.

"Come," said the man, beckoning us forward with a strong arm. "Van will have returned by now. Let's go home."

Van? Who was Van?

My brother opened his mouth as if to speak, but before he could, a sharp pain stabbed my bare foot, and I bent to rub it. Then something hit my cheek.

"Wake up," said a familiar voice. "It's the middle of the day. Why are you sleeping again?"

"What?" I lurched up and saw the Sayeeda crouched beside me, a wooden fork lying near my foot. "Did you poke me with that?"

She smiled, flashing her golden teeth. "Several times."

I squinted in the blinding light of the pavilion. The tiles beneath my palms were hot, and I was as thirsty as a desert rat caught in a trap. Noises from the streets below drifted up, carriage wheels grinding over paving stones, snippets of conversation, laughter, and the mournful notes of someone singing a murder ballad.

"What day is it?" I asked.

"It is your second day in the king's apartment. Your eighth in Coridon. And for most of the fae in the city, it's lunchtime, but... if you prefer to sleep through it, well then, I'll happily take this tray of food back down to the kitchen."

"A rare joke from the Mistress of Slaves and Spices," I said, taking the cup of water she offered and draining it.

As cold as Ari had first seemed Underfloor, I'd since learned she possessed a dry humor, cutting in its directness, but a sense of humor, nonetheless.

"Only day two of my enslavement to your king, is it?" I stretched my arms and rolled the kinks from my neck, feigning a calm confidence, while mild terror simmered in my blood. "Feels like I've been up here forever."

"Yes. It certainly does." Ari inclined her head at the floor in front of me. Freshly baked rolls stuffed with greens and strips of juicy meat teased me from a lunch tray. My stomach groaned its approval.

Today, the Sayeeda looked relaxed, unperturbed by tending a dirty, disrespectful slave, but I supposed she was used to seeing people at their worst Underfloor. A bronze headband kept her long gold hair from her eyes, then it fell in loose curls around her shoulders like a glittering cloak.

"This king of yours seems to have disappeared," I said around a large mouthful of bread. "He didn't sleep in his bed last night."

"He's busy," Ari answered.

"Doing what?"

She sighed. "Shall I tell him that you're asking after him?"

"No. Please don't do that."

For the thousandth time, I wondered why the king wasn't in a hurry to punish me for attacking the Sun Realm envoy. I opened my mouth to ask Ari's opinion, then shut it, deciding to just be thankful instead.

Wiping my hands on a cloth, I took a moment to enjoy the blissful sensation of a full belly, fragments of my dream filtering through my mind as I watched an eagle soar above the distant mountains.

Three iridescent, gold-tipped black feathers fluttered on the edge of the pavilion, catching my attention. They were quite similar to the auron kanaras' feathers, but much larger.

I tipped my chin toward them. "Did one of the bird's escape this morning?"

"Not that I know of," Ari replied, rising to collect the feathers and tuck them into the pouch slung across her body on a woven strap.

"What kind of bird left them behind?"

She squinted at the mountains and ignored me, then canted her head in that peculiar elven way she had, studying me. "You were dreaming again."

"Yes, of my home."

"Will you tell me about it?"

My heart pounded as I considered her request. To gain her help, first I needed her friendship. Sharing part of my dream would build trust, the foundation of all good relationships. And another benefit—perhaps Ari knew of my people.

I took a big breath and nodded. "In my dreams, I'm usually in a forest with a green-eyed boy. Today, I learned he was my brother. My parents were there, too. Ari, these are people I must return to, people who'll be worried about me."

"What made you believe they were your family?" she asked.

"The boy called me sister."

She leaned closer. "If anyone spoke your name in this dream, I urge you to tell me. It will help me find out who you are."

"The boy sometimes calls me Sapling—to tease me."

"And his name?" she asked.

I shook my head. "I called him Ash," I said, not sharing that it felt more like a nickname than his real one.

"I'll make inquiries into Sapling and Ash from the Earth Realm. Is there anything else you can recall from your life before the Storm Court? Anything at all that might help me?"

"Only the forest—playing and training there."

"You trained in weapons?" Ari asked.

"Yes, with swords." Silently, I cursed my foolish mouth. I didn't want the Sayeeda to think of me as dangerous, someone who needed to be watched every moment of the day.

I needed her to think I was weak, so she'd leave me unchained and unattended, hopefully in the river room.

"Did you only have one brother in these dreams?"

"Yes." I didn't tell her how much the face I saw reflected back at me in her shiny food trays resembled Ash's and that I thought he might be my twin. I would keep that information to myself for now.

Without warning, her fingers seized my jaw, gripping it tightly as she brought my face close, inspecting my eyes. I softened my focus, kicking myself for forgetting to affect the daze of a serum-addicted servant yet again.

The auron kanaras screeched in their cages as the Sayeeda's eyes bored into mine. She released me, then slid three thin strips of gold leaf from her pouch.

"Eat these," she said, rolling the strips into a perfect mouthful.

"Why? Are you trying to poison me?"

"Eat it or I'll call him here to begin your punishment."

Him.

I knew exactly which *him* she meant.

I stuck my tongue out, and as the gold melted on it, she watched me closely. I counted my heartbeats, waiting to feel its effects, my palms damp with fear. For a moment, I considered acting drugged, but I wasn't sure what the symptoms of such a large dose were.

Ari's impassive mask flickered, but she made no comment, only leaned over to inspect my bracelet and make sure its tiny teeth were still embedded in my skin correctly.

Gold was a highly addictive substance for humans, and eating it had the strongest effect. Grendal said that, at first, it made users feel powerful and gave them insightful visions. But after a time, those visions became self-indulgent fantasies that the gold eater believed and, worse, acted upon.

In my mind, I ran through a list of questions I could ask to divert the Sayeeda from thinking too hard about the reason why ingesting three sheets of gold seemed to have no effect on me. In truth, it was something I spent a lot of time pondering myself.

"Shouldn't a lower-ranking servant serve my meals?"

Ignoring my question, she asked, "Do you feel well?"

There was no point lying to the Sayeeda. I was almost certain her sharp gaze penetrated through skin and bone to my soul, uncovering my every sneaky thought of escape. "Yes," I said. "Perfectly fine, all things considered."

"That is... unusual." Ari rose and glided toward the stone walkway that led to the sitting room.

I scratched the side of my head. "Ari, is there any chance you can shave my hair?"

Frowning, she turned to face me. "You want it shaved off?"

"Not all of it. Only the shorter side."

She froze, her expression unreadable. "I doubt I could get permission. Disobedient slaves cannot hope to indulge their vanity."

Thinking it wasn't a matter of vanity but comfort, I said nothing, disappointment heavy in my chest.

"Behave yourself until I return this evening," Ari said, then turned on her heel and left.

To pass the afternoon, I exercised until my muscles shook, then sat on the edge of the pavilion and watched the fae move through the streets below. I meditated, trying to manifest visions of the forest to learn more about my home, but grew frustrated, only summoning images I had already seen before.

When night finally fell, the smell of garlic and spices rose from the street vendors, and Ari returned with my dinner. After

I'd eaten, she accompanied me on a well-overdue visit to the bathroom.

Not long after she left, the city's gongs struck, and the storm wielders filed into the sitting room to feed the auron kanara. Thunder shuddered across the pavilion's roof and floor, the vibrations traveling up and down my spine and prickling over my skin.

I hugged my knees to my chest and watched the lightning zigzag across the sky then strike the three silhouetted fae. Smoke curled from their fingers as they willed the storm energy into the birds' gaping beaks.

Half an hour passed, then the weavers left, and I was alone with the contented birds as they preened their feathers and settled down to sleep for the night.

Stargazing in the dark, I pictured my forest home and re-lived every word spoken in my dreams and visions, recalling the laugh lines on my parents' faces, my brother's wide grin.

When I finally began to feel drowsy, heavy footsteps sounded on the stairs below, each thud causing my heart to skip a beat.

The king was on his way.

Relax, I told myself, forcing my fists and teeth to unclench.

No matter what he does, just breathe and survive, I chanted to myself. Should be simple enough.

A dark shadow moved through the sitting room that my pavilion connected to. Strips of moonlight flashing between the arched windows illuminated Arrow's fierce expression. Items of clothing made soft thuds and clangs as they hit the floor. And then he stalked along the walkway toward me, his feather breastplate shining darkly.

I scuttled to the far edge of the pavilion, wishing the night would swallow me whole and praying he'd turn around, retrace his steps, and stride all the way up to his bedchamber.

But suddenly he was in front of me, a great looming shadow, his hand swooping out to grab me. I flinched and bit my lip so I didn't scream.

"Little Leaf," he said as he picked me up by the throat and placed me on my feet. "Are you enjoying your pretty prison?"

Coughing, I tripped over my chain. He lifted me by my shoulders and propped me against a column, his hard body pressing against mine as golden feathers from his breastplate dug into my skin.

Grabbing my jaw, he raised my chin until I stared into sinister silver eyes. "Well? Answer me."

I hate my prison almost as much as I hate you, I thought, clamping my lips together to suppress the words.

Out loud, I said, "I'm grateful you've allowed the Sayeeda to care for me. I'm thankful for the food she serves and that you haven't harmed me."

"*Yet*," he growled.

I ducked my head to appear timid, but also to hide the anger that seethed inside me.

"You look well," he said, turning my face to each side for his inspection. "Even by starlight, your eyes glow with good health." His hand slid down my throat, along my chest and stomach, stopping at my hip. "As yet, you haven't been punished for your crime in my hall. How shall we remedy that?" he murmured.

My pulse raced, my breath coming out in ragged puffs of terror.

The stone column grated my shoulder as he shifted his weight and plucked a golden feather from his chest plate. I gasped, the sound echoing in the still night air.

He chuckled. "You know what these do?"

I nodded.

"Tell me, then."

"They're... poisonous."

"Yes. One prick and you'd be dead."

Since the serum had no effect on me, I wondered if that was true. And speaking of pricks, I was looking at the realm's most obnoxious one—at his face... that is.

The sharp end of the feather ran along my cheek, Arrow's fingers pressing it into my flesh firmly but not hard enough to draw blood.

His face dipped closer, warm breath ghosting over my lips, and as his weight shifted, his hips ground into me, his hardness a skin-tingling shock of heat against my stomach.

A groan rumbled in his throat, and fire rushed through me, melting my muscles.

Fear, or something like it—perhaps exerting control over a weaker being—seemed to excite the Storm King. And, worse, his excitement had a terrible effect, waking something dark inside me. Something sick that actually enjoyed and craved his touch.

Shaking, I gripped his forearms, and the glyph patterns on his skin came to life beneath my touch. "King Arrowyn." I breathed out roughly as the poisonous feather skimmed my cheek, my lips, then my throat.

His attention lifted from my mouth to my eyes, checking my response.

"Do it," I said. "Pierce my flesh. Kill me now. What have I to lose? The butter sauce dumplings your Sayeeda might serve for dinner tomorrow? More bruises from your fists on top of the ones I earned sleeping on the hard tiles? Death doesn't scare me. And pain? I can probably bear it."

"You speak rashly," he said, shifting back a little, the air cool in the space between our bodies.

"No, I speak the truth. It's the one gift I'm prepared to offer you. Can any of your courtiers do the same?"

His hand dropped to his side, the feather clutched in his fist. "Yes. Ari, Raiden, and Stormur always speak the truth to me. And now you," he said.

"So, including me, there are only four."

A sneer twisted his handsome face. "Perhaps you fancy yourself a story crafter? If you're hoping to barter tales for your life, let me tell you my court is full of talented story weavers. But there is something of value I want from you."

"What?" I whispered.

"I wish to know what makes your flesh crawl and your heart pound."

"I'm surprised you need to ask. *You* do," I said hoarsely. "You scare me."

His head tilted, and he inhaled slowly, running his nose along my neck. My breath hitched.

The king froze, his face pressed to my hair, his hand wrapping my throat again. Then he drew back and stared at me.

"What you said is true. You smell of fear. And you're not afraid of pain." His lips brushed mine as he bent his knees and ground his hips into me. "But you're afraid of how you react to this."

Long and hard, his length slid through the damp material of my pants.

"Please..." I begged. "I don't want that."

"And now the truth-teller becomes a liar. You reek of desire. You're afraid of yourself."

"No..." I denied it.

Grabbing my hand, he guided my palm down my stomach, pushing my fingers beneath the fabric across my hipbones, then lower. "Feel the evidence of your lie, Leaf. Feel how your body betrays you."

My skull rasped against rough marble as I looked to the stairs, a padding sound drawing my attention.

Then the soft voice of the Sayeeda floated across the room, breaking Arrowyn's dark spell. "My King," she said.

Muttering a curse, he stepped away from me, and I dragged my hand out of my pants, shame scalding my cheeks.

"Yes, Ari, what is it?" Arrow said calmly.

"I've brought your medicine."

He grunted. "Of course. Come in."

Her gaze averted, Ari climbed the stairs to the sitting room, carried her tray past my pavilion, then up to Arrow's bedchamber.

His breath tickling my ear, he leaned close. "Thank you for clarifying what frightens you the most." To emphasize his point, his heated gaze dropped to my core. "Don't get too comfortable sunbathing and eating butter dumplings. Your punishment starts tomorrow."

I slid to the floor and curled under the Sayeeda's shawl, praying she hadn't witnessed my shame. What a fool I was, turning soft-kneed, my body weeping for the very man who had locked me in a cage.

My legs shifted on the tiles, my hips aching. I groaned, wishing I could drown out the sounds of Ari and the king murmuring to each other.

The Sayeeda's silhouette lit a candle by Arrow's bed, then she lovingly spooned a tincture between his lips, as if he was an ill child or worse, her beloved.

Between doses, his voice rumbled. She soothed him with whispers, then hummed a soft song that also calmed my frayed nerves.

I wondered if she was running her palms over his body, and if his feather glyphs blazed like they had done for me earlier.

As night hawks called to each other in the distance, did Ari's golden lips press kisses on the king's chest, his stomach, and over the hard rod I'd felt pulse against me?

No matter how I strained my ears, I heard no noises of passion, only whispered words, and at one point, the rare sound of the Sayeeda's husky laugh. Just when I thought I'd never fall asleep, Ari's lullaby began again, but this time, she sang the lyrics, words in the reaver language I didn't understand.

It sounded so beautiful. I wanted to hear it all the way to the end, but my eyelids grew heavy, and before long, my surroundings changed from the chilly desert to the humid forest of my dreams.

After a surprisingly restful sleep, I woke to a sky streaked with pink and orange and lurched into a sitting position.

The king was already gone from his bed, and instead of lying on hard tiles, I was on a mattress made of large cushions, my body covered in a thick blanket of softest alnarah goat's wool.

As I stroked the blanket and marveled at my new comforts, I reminded myself to thank Ari for her kindness the next time I saw her. The Sayeeda may have been a fool for the king, an unlikeable trait, but she wasn't half as unkind as the frosty mask she wore suggested.

The self-satisfied Arrow was another matter, far more dangerous than a regular cruel master who taunted and abused his captives for fun.

The Storm King attacked with his heated touch, with the hardness of his body, making me desire him, and it pained me to know I was defenseless against such weapons.

I needed to stay vigilant against his strikes and do everything I could to resist him.

Chapter 10

ARROW

"**A**re you hungry?" I asked, looking up from my bowl of soup.

The human stood beside me while I sat at the dining table in my chambers, the air crackling between us as she fought her nature and tried not to lash out in anger.

Provoking her was fast becoming my favorite form of entertainment.

"You withheld my breakfast this morning," she said. "So, yes, of course I'm hungry."

"Yes, King Arrowyn would have been the appropriate reply."

"Yes, King Arrowyn," she said, repeating my words in a dull tone that failed to hide her longing to stab me with a spoon.

The delicious aroma of lentil soup curled up from my bowl in steamy wafts, likely torturing her. Good. It was about time the girl suffered for her impudence.

I leaned over the bowl and sniffed. "The mint is perfect, but the cumin is a little overpowering," I said, glancing at her downturned mouth. "And I did not withhold your breakfast. Ari was busy, and I forgot to arrange for someone else to deliver it."

She said nothing in response.

"Sit on the floor in front of me while I eat." I pointed to the cushion opposite the table.

She shifted her weight from one bare boot to the other. "Why?"

"Because I wish to look at you."

I picked up my spoon and said, "If you don't obey, I'll forgo the soup and have you for lunch instead."

Quick as lightning, she sat on the floor in front of the table, her legs crossed and eyes blazing like emerald flames as they trailed over the glyphs on my arms and stomach. The weather was humid, so I wore only a pair of loose silk trousers and my breastplate of feathers.

"Have you never seen a half-naked male before?" I asked, smirking as I ate.

I studied her, and she stared at the floor.

Roughly cut brown hair the color of cocoa beans fell to her shoulders. The right side was shorter, framing broad cheekbones, a petulant mouth, and feline green eyes. At first glance, they seemed too big for her heart-shaped face, but in truth, they enhanced her fragile human beauty tenfold.

Initially, the girl's appearance deceived observers into thinking she possessed a sweet nature. But when they looked closer and noticed the lean, compact muscles and fiery gaze, the smart ones realized she was trouble. A slave who needed discipline and a strong master. Someone like me to tame her.

Questions circled my mind.

I wanted to know what her last memories were before she woke in the cage at the gilt market. And if she'd remembered her birth name. But I said nothing, listening instead to her rapid heartbeats, which were louder than the noise of the auron kanara and the bubbling river on the floor below.

The burn of curiosity replaced hunger as I ate my lunch.

I beckoned her to rise with a flick of my hand. "Come here."

She shifted on the cushion, hesitating.

"I said come here. Now."

Slowly, she rose and padded to my side. I nodded at the flatbread next to my bowl. "Soak the bread in the soup and feed it to me."

"What?" Her mouth fell open, revealing the enticing gap in her front teeth. "Why?"

"Because it will amuse me. Wait too long to do as I bid, and you'll serve me tonight in the Grand Hall, where the whole court can watch you feed me."

Hand trembling, she swiped bread through the rich gravy, then held it in front of my mouth. Taking my time, I ate from her hand, then licked the juice from her fingers. At the first touch of my tongue, she drew backward. I narrowed my eyes in warning, wrapped my lips around her fingers and sucked again, laving her flesh.

Scraping my teeth lightly along her fingers, I eased them from my mouth and pointed to the cloth napkin on the table. "Clean the mess you made."

She wiped her hand on her clothes and stared at the soup splattered on my lap, digging her fingernails into the outside of her thigh, something I'd noticed she did when she was cornered, her gaze remaining blank and distant.

My pulse quickened as I crossed my arms and awaited her next move. Picking up the bowl, she tipped the rest of the soup into my lap.

With a snarl, I seized her wrist. "Now that wasn't very nice of you, was it?"

She stumbled backward, staring at me with wide eyes and the scent of fear emanating from her pores. A lick of heat burned in my gut. It took all of my resolve not to throw her over my shoulder and carry her to my bedchamber.

Slowly, I wiped the soup from my lap, then placed the napkin on the table. With my chin still angled down, I looked at her. "Run," I whispered.

Without a word, she fled down the stairs to the river room. The chain dragging between her feet barely hindered her progress. I should order it shortened, but the truth was I liked to see her limbs free and body mobile. All the more fun to catch.

My chair crashed across the floor as I leaped to my feet, my hunter's instincts roaring for me to give a quick and brutal chase. But I repressed the power firing in my veins and stalked slowly down the stairs instead.

Sunlight slanted over the rocks and plants surrounding the river. Other than the soft cooing of the auron kanara, traffic noises drifting up from the street below, and the gentle rush of the water, all was quiet.

I stopped near the water's edge, widened my stance, and scanned the room, listening for the girl's staccato heartbeats.

The air sizzled as clouds left the mountains and sped toward my dome-topped apartment, summoned by my heightened emotions.

"Not now," I mumbled, shifting my focus to keep the storm from breaking. The elements obeyed, clouds retreating, and I switched my attention back to the girl. "Where are you, little Leaf?"

Moving broad leaves aside, I prowled through the vegetation, hunting my prey, taunting and teasing her as I went, savoring the game. I inhaled deeply, seeking her scent. Yes. Found her. She was hiding behind a thick copse of ferns on the other side of the river. Triumph swelled in my chest.

"No matter where you hide, I will always find you," I reminded her.

Crossing the low footbridge, I made sure she heard me approach, not bothering to soften my steps. Leaves rustled, then she burst out of the garden and leaped into the river. She splashed to the other side, climbed out, then raced over the bridge toward the ledge that the bathroom perched on.

I broke into a run, catching her on the threshold. "There's nowhere to hide in there," I said, sweeping my arms around her waist, then swinging her over my shoulder.

With one hand, I gripped her ass firmly, snatching a bunch of grapes from a platter on a sideboard as I passed. I settled on a couch under a palm tree with a view through the open arches of the golden desert and let my shoulders sink back into a pile of cushions. Dragging Leaf forward until she straddled my waist, I grinned, then placed the grapes on my chest.

She stared at them with raw hunger, the way I aimed to make her look at me.

"Stay still," I said, gripping her hips when she struggled, the chain between her ankles cool across my legs. "There's no point fighting the inevitable. When will you learn?"

She huffed, wriggling once more, the warm center of her body an exquisite torture against my stomach. Breath ragged, anger blazed in her eyes.

"You must be weak with hunger. Does it pain you?" I asked, fighting a smile.

"As if you care. You're the king. I assume you've never gone without food or water for longer than an hour in your entire life. But I'm fine. Thanks for asking."

She didn't *sound* very grateful.

And she was wrong. As children, all Light Court fae trained as warriors, and none suffered deprivations more than the princes and princesses of our realm. To be assets to the crown and help our family rule, we needed to be strong, never weak, and able to survive the harshest of conditions.

I plucked two grapes from the bunch and ate them slowly.

Moistening her lips with her tongue, she stared at my mouth.

"Since you're fine, I suppose I'll eat them myself."

"I am hungry," she admitted.

I raised an eyebrow. "Really? Would you like one?"

"Only if you promise not to choke me with it."

This girl couldn't hold her tongue for anything. One day, it would be the death of her.

"It was a simple question," I replied.

"Yes, I would like as many grapes as you're willing to give me... please, King Arrowyn."

"Then you shall have them." I held two grapes in front of my lips. "You can try to take them from me."

Her nostrils flared as she lifted her fingers.

"No. You must use your mouth."

"My... *mouth?*"

"Yes, I can see you possess one." I placed the grapes on my tongue.

Her nails dug into her thigh, but she said nothing. I blinked, and her mouth pressed down on mine, her lips clumsily searching for a grape. Her tongue pushed too eagerly, and one slid down my throat. Choking on fruit and a laugh, fire sizzled through my veins. My glyphs burned and my hardness turned to marble.

I palmed her thudding heart. "Wait. You need to improve your technique. Take your time. Don't rush. I promise I won't bite."

Evidently, she couldn't promise me the same thing. Her eyes flashed with her desire to rip a chunk from me.

"Here... let gravity help." I shifted my torso up the cushions, changing the angle of my body. "Try again."

I placed another two grapes in my mouth. This time, she slanted her head for better access, her lips and tongue searching. It took a while for her to extract them.

"More," she demanded after swallowing them, her cheeks flushed and breath rough.

"Your technique is still lacking," I said. "At this rate, it will take all day to fill your stomach. But I am not without mercy. For a price, I'll put them in your mouth myself. One kiss for every two grapes seems more than fair."

Beneath my bravado, hot shame simmered in my blood. I didn't know why I wanted to kiss her so badly, but I did. Perhaps to punish myself for turning out to be like my father after all—a king who desired his slave. A fucking *human slave*.

It was a weakness, a terrible character flaw. But how could I eradicate it when every time defiance lit Leaf's eyes, it never failed to inflame me?

I squeezed her waist. "Do you agree?"

She bit her lip and nodded.

Seizing her cheeks with my palms, I dragged her mouth to mine, groaning as she surrendered and opened for me, my tongue seeking hers. Fire licked over my skin as I tasted the soft velvet of her mouth, my teeth grazing gently and lust spiking, addling my brain. When she leaned in for more, I pushed her back.

"Here... you may eat," I said, placing two plump grapes on her tongue.

She sighed, and as she swallowed the last mouthful, she launched herself at me, hungry for more. Surprisingly strong fingers dug into my shoulders, and it took all my willpower not to throw her on her back and enter her warm body in one savage thrust.

At first, her movements were clumsy, as if she'd never shared a kiss before or had forgotten how to do it. But she was a fast learner, and in no time, the glyphs on my skin burned as my elemental magic fought to be released. The feel, scent, and taste of the human were more drugging than gold serum to a human.

As we kissed, soft moans came from her throat, her need for food replaced by desire. At that moment, the last thing I cared about was punishing her.

My lips teased as my hand glided down her stomach until my fingers stroked the moisture at her core. I slid her damp pants to the side, exposing her velvety folds to my ministrations.

I considered raising my head to watch myself strum her body into a frenzy, but I refused to break our kiss and didn't want to destroy the spell that had bewitched her. Didn't want to stop her moaning. No. All I wanted was to be buried inside her, taking her higher. Taking everything.

Then her thighs began to shake. Her breath sawed out between desperate moans, and I couldn't resist watching my hands move over her skin. "That's right," I groaned. "Good girl. Let go. Come for me."

Roughly, I plunged two fingers inside her, and she gasped, her eyes flaring open and thighs shuddering harder. Her hips circled against me. She was close. So close.

As she rose onto her knees over me, I gentled my touch, coaxing the release from her. "Let go," I urged.

"I can't." She shook her head. "Stop," she commanded, as if *I* was the slave and she was in charge.

My hand froze, my body straining toward her heat. "Why?"

"Aren't you afraid..."—she caught her breath—"that your precious Sayeeda might appear like a golden wraith and catch you defiling a servant?"

"Why should I care? Ari has seen the worst of me countless times." I grinned, feeling her body clench around my fingers as I trailed a palm along her sternum between the ripe mounds of her breasts. "Also, I instructed her not to visit until later."

"Because you didn't want your lover to see you touch another?" she asked, her voice rough with unfulfilled need.

I slid my fingers from her heat and braced my hands on her hips, holding her in place.

Confusion danced over her features, and for a moment, it plagued me, too. She thought Ari was my lover?

"There's no need for jealousy," I said, a strange sensation, similar to pride but a thousand times stronger, swelling in my chest. "You're all I crave. If you kiss me as you did before, you can eat as many grapes as you wish and every piece of fruit on the platter over there." I hitched my thumb toward a low table near the windows.

"I'd rather starve."

"So be it," I said.

This would have been a good time to reveal that Ari would soon arrive with a meal for her, but I pressed my lips together.

"Tomorrow," I said, scratching the stubble on my chin, "I think I'll chain you to my dining chair."

"Is that the only way you can keep a girl's attention, King Arrowyn?"

I laughed. "There are many ways to keep your attention, Leaf."

"Resorting to brute force to get what you want is a character flaw, not something to brag about."

"Do you think so?" I said. "In my opinion, wielding lightning that can liquefy bones is a skill to be proud of. Is that not *brute* force?"

"I've never seen you use magic," she lied.

I hadn't forgotten the night she'd spied on me in the throne room.

"And you believe that means my power is insignificant? I am the King of Storms and Feathers. Do you really think I would be the weakest of my people?"

"It's possible," she said, pretending to contemplate the idea. "You don't look particularly strong, and I've seen many fae use storm magic in your court. What makes you so special?"

Laughter boomed out of me. "A courtier's magic can roast a nice duck; mine razes cities."

"And again, nothing to be proud of," she said.

I wrapped my hand around her throat, preparing to teach her a lesson in manners with my mouth, my fingers, and the organ currently trying to tear its way out of my pants.

"My King," called a silvery voice from the level below. "May I enter?"

Gold be damned. Trust the Sayeeda to arrive early and at such an inopportune time. *Again.*

Sighing, I pushed the girl off me and swung my feet onto the floor, bracing my elbows on my knees. "Your arrival is more than a little premature, Ari, but, yes, come in. Why not? Feed the feral human a delightful feast from my kitchen before she bites my nose off my face."

Ari appeared in the river room. "Bite you? From where I stood, it looked as if you were kissing each other with equal enthusiasm."

Leaf's face flushed scarlet.

"Indeed," I said, getting to my feet and stretching. "Be sure to lock her in her cage before you feed her."

"Yes, My King." Ari placed the lunch tray on the nearest table, then bowed, a smirk glimmering on her face as I passed by, then took the stairs to my bedchamber with speed.

The Sayeeda was right to mock me.

I should never allow myself to take pleasure in a human, neither in their company or in their bodies. Gold chasers had killed my family. Humans repulsed me. But did that make it right for me to use this one rebellious girl to atone for the grievous errors of her species? And if it was wrong, did I even care?

Pausing at the entrance to my bathroom, where I planned to stroke myself to completion on the memory of the dreaded human's soft sighs and ragged moans, I watched Ari help her stand. The gold chain rattled as Leaf followed her over the footbridge to the pavilion, her face still a fetching shade of pink.

Leaf despised her body's response to me, hated herself for melting under my touch, perhaps almost as much as I loathed myself for being fascinated with her.

Very well.

I had found a suitable punishment for my rebellious human.

By making her surrender to her desires, I'd conquer her defiance, and before long, she would beg me to claim her many times over. And each time she did, she would hate herself more and more.

Meanwhile, I could pretend the result in some way justified my own foolishly burgeoning obsession.

Stupid, yes, but at least I was self-aware.

Chapter 11

LEAF

Another night passed in the pavilion with only the luminous stars and the cool breeze for company.

After yesterday's mortifying grape-feeding incident, Arrow had mercifully disappeared. Ari said he and a group of soldiers were hunting gold raiders that were reportedly hiding in the Aureen Mountains. The ones we'd passed through on our journey from the gilt market.

I'd spent last night tossing and turning, terrified the king would return and make me betray myself again, horrified by my behavior.

When he'd touched me, I lost control of my senses, melted against him, making pitiful noises, like a cat in heat.

What was wrong with me? And how could I crave the touch of a man I despised?

After breakfast, despite trying to rid myself of thoughts of the Storm King by exercising until sweat soaked my skin, his heated kisses still plagued me. I gave up fighting it, then spent hours indulging the stomach-fluttering memories, reliving the torture. Pathetic, but it certainly made the time fly by.

At lunchtime, Ari arrived with a feast of still-warm bread, cheese, and salty strips of grilled vegetables. I devoured the lot as soon as she placed the tray in front of me.

"In case you haven't realized, Leaf," she said, watching me lick my fingers clean. "It is in your best interests to please him."

"Who, Raiden?" I asked purely to unsettle her, hiding a grin as her golden skin blanched white.

Did the great Sayeeda think I hadn't seen how hard she blushed in Raiden's presence? Or that I didn't notice how often he found excuses to visit the dome when she was tidying Arrow's apartment?

"You know exactly who I mean," she replied. "Arrowyn is not the monster you believe him to be. You continue to defy him, and he hasn't once beaten you, has he?"

No, I thought to myself. What he'd done was much worse—made me crave his touch and dream about his penetrating silver gaze.

"I suppose it depends on your definition of a monster," I said. "Has he ever hurt you, Ari?"

"No. And even if Arrowyn did enjoy harming others, he wouldn't dare touch me. I am too precious. A bonded gold reaver is a king's most valuable asset, and my good standing in the kingdom is essential to maintaining the accord between Coridon and my people, the elves of Auryinnia."

"That explains why you think him a better man than he is. He's not allowed to treat you badly."

"I assure you, he doesn't *want* to harm me."

I grunted, and her lips compressed with frustration.

"Where is Arrow's family?" I asked. "Is he related to Stormur and Raiden?"

"No, he is not. And his family is dead."

"Oh." That partially explained his bad attitude. "When and how did they die?"

"That's not my story to tell."

By the look on her face, she wouldn't be cajoled into telling me more.

"I keep forgetting to thank you for the cushions and the blanket," I said as a peace offering. It wasn't wise to argue with Ari. Other than Arrow, she was the only person I could talk to, and I liked her better than him a thousand times over.

Ari busied herself arranging dishes on a tray. "It wasn't me who put them in the pavilion."

I opened my mouth, then slammed my jaw shut as the truth hit me. It must have been the king himself who had given me those comforts.

"Oh, I see. I owe my thanks to King Arrowyn, the sweet benevolent angel, do I?" I said, tucking hair behind my ear. "What have you got there?" I pointed at a silk-wrapped parcel Ari lifted off the tray and smoothed her fingers over.

"I can't show you until the king arrives."

"What?" I lurched onto my feet in one quick movement. "He's coming here? Now?"

"Well, these *are* his living quarters," she said as the elevator opened in the river room below.

Then a moment later, Arrow strode toward me. He was dressed in full Light Realm armor, engraved and embroidered with lightning bolts and feathers, a dark cloak swaying against black boots.

I remembered how that cloak had felt against my skin, the weight and texture of the fabric, and the warmth, as if it had magically held onto his body heat.

Thunder shook over the pavilion's roof, the sky flashing from azure to silver as though in response to his presence. I clenched my fists to hide my trembling as he swaggered onto the pavilion and stopped beside the Sayeeda.

"Leaf." He inclined his head in greeting. "I have a present for you."

My stomach clenched, fear convulsing the muscles of my throat. What did he mean by a gift? Whatever it was, I was certain I'd despise it.

Ari lifted the cloth from her palm, revealing a neck cuff of overlapping layers of gold leaves encrusted with tiny green gemstones. Arrow picked it up, turning it over, and I noticed the back section was thin and curved, as if designed for comfort instead of security.

"Beautiful, don't you agree? I had it made for you. See? The leaves are lined with the finest emeralds."

"Why would you bother?" I whispered.

"Because you're mine and deserve the very best of everything."

He nodded at Ari, who passed him a key before she retreated to the bathroom.

Arrow's fingers were warm and gentle as he unlocked and removed my plain collar. Ari returned with a basin and folded cloths. The king washed my chafed neck with slow, deliberate strokes that made my skin prickle before he rubbed it with sweet-scented oil.

"This collar will be much more comfortable to wear," he said, locking it in place. "Tonight, you will serve me in the Grand Hall."

Terror iced my veins as my gaze met his. He couldn't be serious. I'd do anything to avoid the humiliation of standing like a placid fool at his side before the entire Storm Court. What would Grendal and the kitchen servants think of me? How could I convince him not to make me to do this?

For a mad moment, I considered bartering my body, then came to my senses. There was no power in that when he could already do what he wanted with me.

The Storm King and the Light Realm fae could all go to the fiery hell realms together. I would stand on his gilded dais with my head held high and stare down every single one of them.

"Aren't you worried I'll tip another bowl of soup in your lap?" I asked mildly.

"No." Silver eyes gleamed back at me as he shrugged a shoulder. "And if you did, I would punish you severely—now that I know what appalls you."

He stroked the base of my throat, then nodded for Ari to attach the chain to my new collar. "Don't worry, little Leaf. In the Court of Storms and Feathers, it is a great honor to serve a king."

Oh, I was sure *he* thought so. But we would have to agree to disagree on the matter until the day he killed me or I escaped. Eventually, one of us would get the upper hand, and I was determined it would be me.

"Prepare her well," he told Ari, turning with a flap of his cloak before thudding down the stairs and departing via the elevator.

I sighed. "Doesn't your king ever bother to rest or bathe?"

"He has urgent meetings," Ari said. "I assure you he'll do both later. I have a herb supplier to meet. You will accompany me."

I blinked at her.

"Don't look so shocked. This is an opportunity for you to earn my trust and therefore the king's. And the court will have a chance to view you in your new role. It is my hope it will ease your discomfort and allow you to serve the king with grace tonight. Always bear in mind, Leaf, that trusted servants are given greater freedoms than those who disobey. Instead of feeling sorry for yourself, I suggest you consider my advice."

"It almost sounds like you want to help me, Sayeeda, which strikes me as odd."

"It's not odd at all," she replied. "Once, I was very much like you, railing against my fate and lashing out in anger, making everything worse. But listen to me... everyone carries a story within them, and I'm interested in how yours unfolds. While you are chained in that pretty cage of air and gold, your tale is at a standstill and no one, including yourself, can know how it ends. Be grateful for each freedom you earn, no matter how small it seems at the time. This is the key that will open your cage."

The Sayeeda was right, and I thought about what she'd said as she led me into the elevator and along the palace's golden halls. We went through the kitchen and down an external staircase that ended in a busy courtyard, where servants carried baskets and parcels.

Ari settled in a chair at a long table set with ledgers and jars of ink cradling feather quills, then directed me to sit beside her. I obeyed, watching a bearded trader approach. He took a seat opposite and began discussing the deliveries that were occurring around the courtyard's mosaic-lined pool.

My chain hung loosely at my feet, as if I was a member of Ari's kitchen staff and a necessary part of the meeting. I listened carefully to the talk of orders, payment terms, and delivery dates with the man who was a fae trader from the Ice Realm, in case I could learn anything useful.

Courtiers stared at me, but I ignored them and kept studying the exit and entry points. I tried to make connections and draw a map in my mind from the king's dome to the courtyard, knowing it might prove useful at some point in the future.

Auron kanara birds chirped in their cages and bright sunlight beamed through palm leaves, the atmosphere busy but pleasant. I took a deep breath and smiled.

It felt good to be out of the pavilion, participating in a small part of court life. And even when Esen strutted past with another guard, both shooting me glares, it couldn't dampen my sense of satisfaction.

The trader completed his business, bowing to both of us, and Ari gave me one of her rare smiles, a reward for my compliant behavior, then guided me back to the king's dome.

In the afternoon, Ari presided over two fae servants who bathed and oiled me, then braided my hair to the point of pain before dressing me in an elegant but extremely revealing gown.

Made of fine links of gold and studded with rubies, the dress's long sleeves draped when I lifted my arms. The neckline swooped low, and the hem slashed across my thighs on the diagonal, trailing lightly behind me as I walked. Semi-transparent material glided across my body like snakeskin, alluring and sinuous.

It was a definite improvement over my outfit of glorified golden bandages that only just managed to cover the interesting bits. But even dressed in such finery, it was clear I was a plaything made for the Storm King's pleasure, an indignity I had no choice but to bear.

When dusk fell, Ari and the maids finally left me alone, and Arrow arrived soon after, ignoring me as he bathed, then dressed in black leather and gold metal. From the pavilion, I watched his muscles ripple and his brow crease as he scowled at his clothes as if they'd done him grievous harm.

Arrow seemed deeply troubled. But he ruled the most powerful kingdom in the realms, controlled the gold trade, and enjoyed absolute dominion over every courtier and slave in his city. What right did he have to be unhappy?

As he stalked toward my pavilion, his silver eyes devoured me from head to toe. When he reached me, he held my face between his palms and leaned close. "You look good enough to eat, little Leaf. Tell me, will you be an obedient servant in front of my court tonight?"

The scent of rosemary and mint on his damp hair teased my senses, but I did my best to ignore it, softening the set of my mouth and widening my eyes innocently.

I nodded in reply, concentrating on memories of my family in the forest, vowing to appear biddable and meek if it would help me find a way back to them.

Power vibrated around his body, and I clenched my teeth, determined not to show how his nearness affected me and turned my limbs to jelly.

"Come," he said, unfastening my chain from the bolt in the floor and attaching it to a cuff around his wrist. "Control your spite tonight and reap the rewards."

What rewards? I wondered. Did he think I was stupid enough to want him to feed me grapes from his mouth again? I had no desire to repeat that mortifying game. Just the memory sent heat blooming in my stomach—and lower still. I dug my nails into my leg to distract myself from the nauseating feeling.

In silence, we entered the elevator and dropped down, exiting into a gilded antechamber flanked by two guards. They led us to the Grand Hall, crowded tonight with gold-adorned fae. Lit by thousands of tiny candelabra flames, the courtiers glimmered like stars.

Feathers floated from the ceiling and drifted in the air currents. I reached up and caught one, folding my fingers around it.

The Sayeeda bowed to the king and gave me a nod of encouragement as a guard announced Arrow's arrival. "All rise for his Majesty, King Arrowyn of the Light Realm of Storms and Feathers."

Hundreds of chairs scraped across marble as the courtiers rose like a surging wave, conversations pausing until the king took his seat at the long dining table at the front of the dais.

Raiden appeared and attached my chain to the king's chair. With a flick of Arrow's hand, the feathers circulating through the room dissolved. I uncurled my fingers, the feather I'd caught no longer lying on my palm.

With my eyes downcast, I stood loose-limbed between Arrow and Raiden's chairs while servants served the soup course. I fixed a mask of bored disinterest over my face as Arrow engaged the burly, bearded man seated to his right—Raiden's father, Stormur—in heated debate.

The king wished to close an official trade route because black marketers used part of it to transport gold to camps in the Earth Realm, something he seemed passionate about preventing. But Stormur believed the financial gains justified keeping it open.

Stormur's wife, Ildri, sat beside him. She was an elegant redhead who wore ear cuffs resembling forked lightning and turned her mouth down each time she glanced at me.

After servants cleared the first course away, Ari served the king a plate of crumbed fish, liberally doused in white sauce. Arrow's arm wrapped around my waist, and he pulled me onto his lap. "You shall feed me, little Leaf."

Not this again. Why was he so obsessed with feeding me and being fed? Keeping fury from my expression, I held a piece of fish in front of his mouth.

His eyes fixed on my face as he took slow bites and sauce dripped over my fingers and down my wrist. When he had eaten the last piece, he sucked my fingers, licking them clean.

"You've made a mess," he said, pointing at splotches of sauce on my thigh. With his hands on my waist, he raised me to my feet, then knelt in front of me. "I despise waste," he murmured, as if that was an excuse for depravity.

To block out the sight of the court, I closed my eyes, which had the adverse effect of heightening the sensation of his tongue on my skin.

As the king opened his mouth and sucked gently, my legs quivered, my heart fluttering like the weak wings of the auron kanara against my ribcage.

I fought the need to knock his crown of feathers off his head and weave my fingers through his dark gold hair. I locked my knees together and imagined plucking a poison feather from his chest plate and stabbing him in the eye with it.

I promised myself that one day, I would do just that.

He took his time, drawing out the ridiculous display just to spite me. Soothing images of the forest flowed through my mind. The comforting smell of decay, the humidity and feel of sweat on my skin as I ran through the trees until my muscles ached. And when I finally opened my eyes, I found my fingers curled in the king's silky hair, gripping hard.

Dust save me, I was an idiot.

I gasped, and silver eyes met mine, a wicked smile on the king's lips.

"Well done," he purred. "It's your turn to eat. You must be famished."

He took his seat and drew me onto his lap, waving a hand at the Sayeeda. She stood against a carved wall of massive golden wings at the rear of the dais that reminded me of the ones on the king's throne. But at his signal, immediately started toward the kitchen stairs.

A few minutes passed while Arrow conversed with Raiden and Stormur. They both ignored me, perched there on the king's lap as if I was an auron kanara he'd let out of its cage for entertainment.

Surrounded by the chaos of the court's revelry, I forced my mind to linger in the forest, where everything was calm and safe. The opposite of how I felt.

Ari returned, placing another plate of fish on the table. Arrow ran a piece through the white sauce before holding it to my lips. "Blow first, or you'll burn that stubborn mouth of yours."

Starving, I obeyed without delay, unable to drop my gaze from his as I groaned in pleasure. It was delicious. The Sayeeda was most definitely an excellent kitchen mistress who planned the tastiest menus, but she was very wrong about the king. He *clearly* enjoyed tormenting me. The evidence was outlined in his leather pants, pressed against my thigh, too sizable to ignore.

Unashamed, he gave me a smug smile. There was no denying Arrow was the most attractive man I would ever lay eyes on, but he wasn't right in the head.

Swallowing self-disgust along with the fish, I ate quickly and licked his fingers like a good little slave when he gave the order. I'd had many sips of wine from his cup, and before long, my head spun with the effects. I stared brazenly at the courtiers on the floor of the Grand Hall, daring them to mock and laugh at me.

"Will you dance for me?" Arrow whispered, stroking my gold collar.

Not understanding what he wanted, I shook my head. With a dark chuckle, he lifted me by the waist and arranged my legs, spreading them on either side of his lap so I faced him. "Show my court what an obedient slave you are."

Silent, I held his gaze and raised a brow.

A smirk curved his mouth. "Go ahead, dance for me."

Instead of smacking him, I held the image of the family I longed to return to in my mind, pressed my palms against his chest, preparing to stand.

"No. Stay where you are. Haven't you seen a lap dance before?"

Of course the asshole wanted a lap dance. I'd seen many of them performed in the hall—designed to humiliate the giver and tease the receiver into a frenzy of lust. Could I do it in front of the fae of the Storm Court? If it would keep me alive and give me time to learn the city's weaknesses, then yes, I'd do almost anything.

Gritting my teeth and staring at the king, I rested my palms against his shoulders and raised my hips, my thinly covered ass on display for the entire hall to view. Slowly, I undulated my hips over the leather-covered bulge in his pants and pretended Stormur, Raiden, and Ildri weren't beside us.

Arrow's head fell back against the gilded chair as he watched me through a hooded gaze, waves of heat shimmering from his muscled body that made my stomach tighten.

Every indignity leads me to revenge, I reminded myself as a feeling not unlike power snaked through my blood, bolstering my confidence. Desire seemed to weaken him, and *that* could be exploited.

Bringing my face close to his, I made a breathy sound, teasing my hips over his erection and watching his pupils dilate. Feather glyphs glowed as he made a guttural sound and dug his fingernails into the chair's armrests.

"Fuck," he breathed in a low voice. A large hand caught my hip, stilling my movements. "Are you *trying* to kill me?"

I gave the only answer I could—the truth. "Yes."

"Congratulations, it's working." He turned me so I sat sideways on his lap, right over his hard length. "By the gold," he muttered, shifting beneath me. "Stay still or suffer the consequences."

Unsure what he meant by consequences, I obeyed. My heart pounding as I stared blank-faced at the courtiers, their glowing eyes assessing me in the golden light of the hall.

The few fae who possessed wings flicked them in my direction with lustful interest. Let them look. I doubted Arrow was the sort of man who liked to share his things with them. I was safe enough up here on the dais. For now.

As a line of dancers wearing tall golden crowns and not much else snaked through the hall, the king grunted his dismay at the entertainment and bid his friends goodnight.

Pressing his lips against my ear, he said, "I have a better form of recreation in mind back in my chambers. Come, Leaf. It's time for us to retire."

Time for us to retire. As if I had any choice in the matter.

As he led me through the crowd encircling the dance floor, the gold chain hanging loose between us, courtiers' sharp features blurred before me.

I stared back, refusing to give the Light Realm fae the satisfaction of cowering before them. I imagined the groping touches on the backs of my arms and legs were only the soft brushes of giant fern leaves as I hunted through the forest.

A green hand shot in front of me, swiped between my legs, and squeezed hard. I yelped, suppressing the reflex to elbow the Sun elf's nose deep into his skull. Arrow whirled around, his eyes shooting toward the male who walked beside me, still assaulting me.

With a roar, the king knocked the elf to the ground. Thunder groaned nearby, lightning flashing, and all at once, the auron kanara screeched as if they were under attack.

Arrow's hands wrapped the elf's throat, and he thumped his dark head against the floor. "You're fucking finished," he yelled.

The elf begged and pleaded, tears streaming down his pinched face as he whispered the words *please King Arrowyn* over and over in a strangled voice.

"Arrowyn," said Raiden, coming up beside me. "He's a Sun Realm fae. Remember the treaty."

"I don't give a fuck about treaties. Do not touch what is mine. *Ever.*"

Lightning bolts forked through the windows, seven striking Arrow as he leaned over my assaulter, the force buckling his body. A blue current sizzled over the king's skin, down his arms, burning out his fingertips. Dark, acrid smoke fouled the air.

My attacker's face turned deep scarlet, spittle forming on his lips as he muttered nonsensical words. Pity opened my heart. No matter how much I resented the Storm Court fae, I didn't want this. I didn't want anyone to lose their life because of me if I could help it.

"King Arrowyn," I murmured. "I'm so tired I can barely stand up anymore. And you forget our entertainment..."

The lightning rewound up his arms as he looked over his shoulder at me and blinked. "Yes. Of course. We should leave."

Esen stepped forward and pulled the bloodied elf to his feet, glaring at me as if I'd forced the stupid male to put his hands on my flesh and make the king lose his already unhinged mind.

Arrow straightened to his full height and faced the court, tiny bolts of lightning still curling from his hands and circling his limbs. He looked dangerous, feral enough to destroy everything and turn his hall into a smoking pile of rubble.

He seized my hand in a bone-bruising grip and skimmed a smoking-hot gaze over the crowd.

"Court of Storms and Feathers, I command each of you to heed my words... I will fry the brains of any fae who touches the girl known as Leaf. This human who stands before you is mine. Do not make me prove it to you with a more explicit demonstration than the one you witnessed tonight."

All around us, fae bowed, whispering words of deference.

Arrow shuddered as he drew the last remaining storm magic inside his body. Then, leaving my chain dangling like a gaudy ornament, he picked me up and carried me in his arms from the hall, past slack-jawed guards and into the elevator.

As the door slid shut, he said, "Leaf, I find myself torn. Should I reward you for tonight's good behavior or punish you for your past transgressions?"

I offered him a weak smile in reply, unsure of how best to advise him.

After all, I was only biding my time, pretending to be a biddable servant, while he was the king, whose idea of a reward was probably my definition of a punishment.

He would have to decide for himself.

I just hoped I survived the night.

Chapter 12

LEAF

When we crossed the moonlit floor of his sitting room, he veered away from the pavilion. He put me on my feet before settling his large frame on a divan, then drew me down beside him.

In the darkness, his eyes glowed like almond-shaped moons. He stroked my cheek, then rubbed his thumb over my lip. "Ideally, I would spend the night making you scream, little Leaf," he said. "But using my power in the hall has left me depleted."

"Using storm magic leaves you weak?" I asked, excited to learn about a deficiency I could exploit.

"Yes. I must rest." He turned his palms up and lightning sizzled over them. The auron kanara birds screeched in response from their cages, the noise making me grimace.

"You dislike the auron kanaras?" he asked.

"Only when they make that terrible racket. The storm wielders fed them this afternoon. They shouldn't be hungry."

"Some storm makers yield better lightning than others, so the kanaras' food quality can vary. The birds are reacting to the scent of my magic. Come, I'll feed them."

His power licked against my skin as he helped me to my feet, then prowled toward the nearest cage. The birds descended into a delirious frenzy as their king, their lightning god, approached.

"I thought you said you needed to rest."

"Why rest when I can show off first?" he said, flashing a grin.

He whispered to the birds, and they settled, ruffling their feathers and emitting soft, expectant chirps. Then without warning, lightning exploded in the sky, forking through the tall windows and burning the veil curtains to ash.

Thunder boomed as storm energy entered Arrow's body, his back arching. Shuddering, he strode to the center of the room, threw his head back and stretched his arms wide, his fingers straining with the effort of controlling the force. Blue lightning coiled like serpents seeking prey, the ribbons of light winding into the birds' open beaks.

Arrow moaned as the power moved through him. It was a sound somewhere between extreme pain and pleasure that made warmth bloom in my core and shame redden my cheeks.

"Follow me," he said, moving along the seven cages.

I gave him a curious look, wondering how much energy he would have left to attend to me after he'd fed the birds. Hopefully, not much.

The dome roof shuddered above us, the marble floor below, and the whole apartment lit up with the blue fire of lightning. Fear snaked through my stomach.

Over the last few days, I had watched many storm wielders feed the auron kanara, but this... this was something else. The power Arrow wielded was of far greater magnitude, so immense it appeared difficult to control.

In no time at all, the king had visited every cage, and the birds within were satiated and silent. A blue aura sizzled around his body, the residue of storm energy. Leaning over his knees, he blew out a hard breath, then straightened, cracking his spine as he beckoned me to follow him up to his bedchamber.

Without ceremony or warning, he took off his clothes, placing his feather chest plate on a short pillar beside the crescent-shaped bed. Unable to turn away, I took in every inch of his hard body, fascinated by the feather markings glowing blue and orange over his chest and arms.

Lowering his large frame onto the bed, he turned onto his stomach and pulled the silky black sheet to his hips. "Rub my shoulders and work the kinks out of my muscles."

I swallowed my fear, perched beside him, and began massaging his tight muscles as instructed. Deep groans reverberated through the room.

"There's oil in the nightstand," he said.

Twisting my torso, I opened the top drawer and withdrew a glass vial. I pushed his wavy hair over his right shoulder, poured a generous dollop of heavily scented oil on my palms, and then rubbed his back briskly.

"Slower. And harder," he commanded, his voice gruff.

I adjusted my position and put more of my weight into the work.

If the price to wield storm magic was energy depletion, I wondered how Arrow's particular species of fae recharged their powers. Many humans ate gold for the initial benefits it gave them—as a painkiller and to receive prophetic visions, but it also boosted energy. Perhaps the Storm Court fae did the same.

"Do you ingest large amounts of gold serum to replenish your magic?" I asked, curious to see if he would answer my nosy question.

"Not often. Too much is poisonous. Rest is the safest method, and of course there is..." He let his words trail off, unwilling to disclose a third method.

"A high dose of serum is poisonous to all fae?"

"Yes. Straddle me." With his head turned and resting on his folded arms, the bulge of his flexed biceps muffled his voice.

"I... I don't understand," I said.

"Straddle the back of my legs and press your knuckles on either side of my spine. Then work down slowly and put all your weight into it."

With my gown's long sleeves getting in the way, I tried to obey. I did my best to ignore the animal groans Arrow made each time I leaned forward and dug into the heavy cords of muscle that ran down the middle of his back. My thighs grew damp from his hot skin, the cool air a shock each time I settled back on my heels, the sensation making me dizzy.

"What gods rule over the Light Realm?" I asked.

He made a scoffing sound. "The people pray to many, but there is only one official god. The king."

I choked out a laugh. "You're a god?"

"So they tell me," he replied, wry amusement in his voice.

"Do you really believe that?"

Instead of answering, the king rolled over, his hooded gaze searing me as his thumbs stroked my hipbones. "I need to sleep." He flipped onto his side, knocking me off balance. "Keep stroking my back," he ordered.

As he lifted the sheet, I slid in behind him, and he tugged a light woven blanket over us. I couldn't believe how soft and warm it was and even more luxurious than the Sayeeda's shawl.

For a moment, I stayed still, just watching the movement of his shoulder blades as he breathed in and out.

Why hadn't he chained me to a bed post? He probably believed I wouldn't dream of running. And he was right. At least for now. If I tried, I wouldn't make it past the guards that secured the apartment. There was only one other way out, through the waterfall window, and I wasn't foolish enough to leap out of *that* in the dead of night. It would be difficult enough sleeping in this ridiculous dress, let alone trying to flee a kingdom.

"Why have you stopped stroking my back?" he growled, jolting me out of my thoughts.

I ran my fingers lightly over his skin, drawing patterns and tracing his pulsing glyphs, their color silvery under the moonlight. I stroked his neck, played with his hair, running my nails over his skull, then around the glittering feather glyph that curled over his cheekbone.

"Don't think you've gotten away with your offenses," he murmured, half asleep. "You have much to atone for, Leaf. Not tonight, but soon. I promise."

After those ominous words, he fell asleep, and I spent far too long marveling at his bone structure, the sculpted shape of his mouth. And I wondered how someone so physically perfect could be so rotten on the inside.

Perhaps with fae, the greater the beauty, the bigger the asshole. Maybe that rule applied to every species.

Finally, his solid warmth lulled me into a drowsy state, and I drifted into the lush, green dreamworld of my forest home.

What felt like moments later, but was more likely a few hours, a sound of agony woke me. My heart in my mouth, I jolted upright, shocked to find myself still sprawled in the luxurious bed.

Beside me, the king thrashed his bare limbs, the covers now twisted around his ankles. "Fucking gold chasers," he moaned on repeat, his mind caught in the tight grip of a nightmare.

"Arrow," I whispered, gently palming his shoulder.

His eyes flew open, and even by starlight, I saw horror blazing inside them. Fisting the sheet, his big body shook like he was having a seizure.

"It's all right. It's only a dream," I said, stroking his cheek. "It's not real."

Why did I soothe my enemy? Not because I was falling for him. I hadn't fooled myself into believing that, deep down, he was a man who deserved pity. No.

Instead, I was the type of fool who couldn't just stand by and watch another creature suffer. Even monsters deserved compassion. I hated Arrow, but I couldn't stand to see him in pain.

Awareness sharpened Arrow's gaze. "Leaf," he said, blinking twice to clear his dream.

"Go back to sleep," I mumbled, turning my back to him.

Arrow's arm wrapped around my waist, and he dragged me against him, tucking my head under his chin. "Stay close. Your nearness chases the demons away."

"What demons would dare to torment a king?" I asked.

"Demons of fire and blood."

"Is that... is it anything to do with how your family died?"

He sighed, his breath rustling my hair. "Gold chasers blew up their carriage. I should have been with them. But I was selfish, thought only of enjoying myself, and rode behind with Raiden."

Humans killed the Storm King's family. That explained why he hated me but also wanted to keep me alive. I was an easy target, and whenever the mood struck, he could avenge their deaths slowly... bit by bit... and day by day, using me as a scapegoat.

Shivering, I dug my fingers into the back of his hand that braced my stomach, sickly sympathy swelling in my chest. "And if you'd been in the carriage with them," I said, "how do you imagine your kingdom would be faring now?"

A hard shudder wracked his body, but he didn't answer.

Arrow's pain shouldn't bother me. In truth, I should relish it. But something about the way he clung to me cracked my heart wide open. I didn't want to feel compassion for my captor, but I understood the pain of loss. The urge to ease his anguish overwhelmed me.

"It wasn't your fault, Arrow. You couldn't have prevented what happened. If they had time for any final thoughts, your parents would've been so relieved you weren't with them."

My breath caught in my throat as he squeezed me tighter and slung a heavy leg over mine. In that moment, I realized Ari hadn't delivered the sleeping medicine that kept his nightmares at bay.

"Shall I ask the guards to call for your medicine?"

"No. If the dreams return, you can catch them for me."

"I'll do my best," I said, squeezing his hand tightly.

In his current vulnerable state, the king seemed almost human, far removed from the cruel-eyed fae who had bought me as if I was chattel for the slaughterhouse.

But he had caged and humiliated me. And I hated him for that. Someday he would pay for his cruelty, but not tonight.

I would work to earn his trust, and before long, he would turn his attention away from me just long enough for me to steal his blade and slit his golden throat.

Chapter 13

LEAF

"**W**atch where you're walking," the Sayeeda warned, tugging me out of the path of another servant.

We descended a staircase that scaled an outside wall of the palace. It led down to a palm-tree-filled courtyard with a fountain glittering in the midday sun in the center of a rectangular pool.

"Sorry, the light distracted me," I said, squinting at the yellow ball in the sky as my palms grazed the wall for balance. "Doesn't the sun look wonderful from the ground? I'm used to seeing it from the pavilion."

"Not wonderful enough to fall to your death over."

"You could unchain me," I suggested, flashing a smile as I glanced back over my shoulder at her. "Then I'd be safer."

The gold chain attached to my ankles made an escape attempt today, not only foolish, but impossible. But at least it couldn't stop me from studying the angle of the sun and how it aligned with the city's landmarks.

"What lies north of Coridon?" I asked.

"Thinking about an escape attempt? I wouldn't bother if I was you."

"Oh? Why's that?"

"Outside the gates, you would find desert, the Auryinnia Mountains, and not much else. If you traveled in a northwesterly direction, you'd eventually come to the coast and the Port of Tears. On horseback, it's about a two-hour ride. On foot, well, you'd likely fall into the hands of gold raiders before you reached the port."

"Maybe I'd be better off with humans than remaining a prisoner of the Storm Court," I replied.

"You, in the possession of raiders? No, I don't believe that would be an improvement in your circumstances."

Ari was entitled to her opinion, but the prospect of reuniting with my own kind sounded pretty good to me. Worth the risk of being caught by raiders or Storm Court soldiers. All I had to do was work out how to get rid of my chains and steal a horse. Should be simple. Or maybe not.

Either way—that was my goal.

"I don't know, Ari, I think I might be an optimistic risk taker so..." I let my words trail off with a laugh, and she scoffed loudly.

In the courtyard, we wove through a line of servants carrying supplies to the kitchen, baskets balanced gracefully on their heads. As if I was invisible, no one returned my curious glances. Clearing my throat, I smoothed the gold tunic over my legs.

"Why are they ignoring me?" I asked as we stepped through a doorway at the end of the courtyard. "I'm dressed exactly the same as the other slaves today."

"We prefer to call them servants."

The fae could call us anything they liked, but it still didn't change the truth.

"Why do you think they might be afraid to look at you?"

My cheeks warmed. "Because the king told them not to?" I guessed.

"You are not so stupid after all, Leaf." She grinned, her gold teeth sparkling.

Damned Arrow. Why did he need to control not only my body and emotions, but everything around me? I couldn't wait to be free of him.

A week had passed since I'd first slept in his bed, and no matter how late he returned to his moonlit bedchamber, every night, he would unchain me from the pavilion so I could perform my duties.

For what seemed like hours, I worked kinks from his back, my breath catching in my throat when he turned over and stared up at me. His big chest rose and fell as I straddled him, massaging his neck and arm muscles.

My heart would pound in suspense as I waited for his hands to move, wondering if this would be the night he'd finally do more than touch me, but he never did. Because the Storm King took sick pleasure in delayed gratification.

Most nights, I barely slept as I lay in Arrow's arms, unchained and alert. I waited for his grip to loosen so I could leap through the waterfall window—possibly to my death. But each time I shifted a muscle, his arm would tighten like a band of steel, and I'd curse him silently until sleep finally took me.

"Hurry, Leaf. Don't fall behind," Ari said as we walked along a series of covered outdoor corridors.

I made a game out of the shafts of sunlight that divided the red ground into strips of shadow and light, only walking on the bright patches and avoiding the dark.

"Does the king have many lovers?" I asked. "Since I've been in the dome, no one's visited his bed."

She arched a golden brow. "Well if someone did, you'd have a spectacular view from your pavilion."

My skin flushed hot. I'd rather strangle myself than watch Arrow engage in bed sport.

"Do the dreams still plague him at night?" Ari asked.

I nodded, wondering how much Arrow had told her about the duties I performed in his bed.

"Then it is good he asks you to soothe him. Much better than ingesting the sleeping medicine every night. It clouded his mind and affected his moods. Now he is happier."

"And his lovers?" I said. "What do they think of a human sla... servant soothing their king's troubles?"

"Should I come across any of these mysterious lovers, I'll be sure to ask their opinions. But my spies tell me he visits no brothels or courtesans' quarters."

I stopped walking and gripped her wrist. "Ari, is the king perhaps not... *interested* in such pursuits? Doesn't he like to..." I couldn't think how to say it without causing offense.

"Fuck? Yes, I assure you he does."

I dropped her arm, shocked to hear such a word come out of the Sayeeda's elegant mouth.

She smiled and urged me into motion. "I make it my business to know who Arrowyn spends time with. Lately, he sees only his inner circle—friends and counselors. There is much on his mind and, of course, now he has you to entertain him."

Ari had given me a lot to think about as I followed her along a web of pathways in the city's industrial area, always looking around for places I recognized. We turned a corner into an open area of low buildings, and I spotted the golden dome of the king's chambers and the columns of my pavilion soaring in the distance.

The waterfall pool was probably my best chance of escape. I needed to find it and take mental notes of the landmarks surrounding it, then locate the nearest city exits. Because the day I jumped out of the river room window, I had to know which direction to run in.

Though where my home was, I still had no clue.

What is forgotten will be remembered, I reminded myself. I would get home eventually.

I just had to make my way to the Earth Realm, get back to the forest, where, hopefully, someone would recognize me and sweep me away to be reunited with my family.

Laughing green eyes flashed through my mind, and I smiled at the vision. *Brother*, I thought. *Wherever you are, please wait for me. I'm coming to find you soon.*

The scent of cinnamon and cardamom wafted on the breeze, and even though I'd not long ago eaten lunch in the king's apartment, my stomach rumbled.

Arrow. I pictured the grotesquely pleasing form of the King of Storms and Feathers for the hundredth time today. All that smooth golden skin wrapping around an unnecessarily tall, muscular package. In isolation, his features were too chiseled, too strong. But together they formed a jaw-dropping masterpiece of lethal, masculine beauty.

Taking a deep breath, I gritted my teeth. It was fortunate I wasn't attracted to him. His lips were dangerous. His touch was worse. And thankfully, I wasn't the least bit impressed with his brooding temperament.

Chanting variations of Arrow-denouncing sentiments under my breath, I stomped along gold-paved paths, wiping sweat from my brow under the heat of the midday sun.

I really wished I could stop thinking about him.

Dust knew why the king wanted a slave to keep his nightmares at bay. But if it stopped him from sending me to the mines or those terrifying fires the fae often spoke about, then I was more than glad to do it. Kind of.

We arrived at a covered cargo bay where servants were unloading wooden pallets from three mine carriages, the process overseen by Raiden and Esen, the king's ever-present guards.

Raiden eyed me with suspicion while Ari advised him of the king's wishes. Arrow wanted me to spend part of my days in useful occupation, and today, I would assist with the unloading of the latest gold delivery.

"I'll return for you in a couple of hours," the Sayeeda said, then marched away before I could protest.

Raiden indicated the third carriage rowed up against the loading dock. "Take as many bags from the pallets as you can carry without dropping them, follow the other servants into the palace foyer, and leave the gold on the trolleys in front of the service elevator."

A sour taste filled my mouth when I saw Esen presiding over the carriage Raiden had assigned me to. Taking a brief break from striking the slower servants with lightning magic to get them moving faster, she glanced up and shot me a glare.

I rolled my eyes and turned away as a slave with curly gray hair passed by. The older woman grinned over the bags of gold in her arms, and I did a double take at my ex-roommate, Grendal.

"Stop staring at the others like an imbecile and get to work, king's harlot," Esen growled, flicking her head toward sacks piled on pallets near the carriage.

King's harlot, she'd called me. That was unfair and, so far, untrue.

Would Esen be kinder if she realized that instead of sweating over her king as I rode him from dusk till dawn like she imagined, I was only rubbing his back and soothing him to sleep with low whispers?

Likely not.

She was a cold bitch who probably only smiled when she scratched her ass and accidentally inserted a finger into the tightly puckered hole.

I grabbed a heavy sack and hurried to catch up with Grendal who was mounting the stairs that led inside the ground floor of the palace.

"Leaf, it's good to see you," she said when I pulled alongside her. "I was beginning to believe the stories about you being thrown to the fires. Where have you been hiding?"

"In the king's chambers," I replied. "And as you can see, I'm alive and well. And if I do die of anything soon, it'll likely be from terminal boredom."

"Have your memories returned?" she asked.

"No, unfortunately."

Grendal's gray eyes twinkled. "Perhaps you can't remember anything because you spent your days in the human forests serving others, and it's too depressingly similar to your current fate. So you're repressing it."

"That's possible." I laughed and ducked through a doorway into a palace foyer, a large service elevator visible on the other side of it. "How are things in the kitchen?" I asked.

"The same as always. Rumor and delight ran rampant the night you served the king in the hall and he got down on his knees before you. I truly wish I'd seen it. Shame he hasn't dined in the hall this past week." She nudged my ribs. "The entire court would appreciate a repeat performance."

I groaned. "How humiliating. And thankfully, you won't see the king in the hall anytime soon. The Sayeeda says he's been busy murdering raiders during the day. He often doesn't return until the early hours of the morning."

"That's a pity," said Grendal.

Under the watchful eyes of the elevator guards, we dumped our bags of gold on the floor and followed the line of servants back to the loading bay.

"So the king goes on raiding missions without his faithful guard dogs, Raiden and the blue-haired shrew?" asked Grendal.

"Ari said they're the only two he trusts enough to oversee the gold deliveries. Apparently they're very *special*," I said, grimacing.

"They certainly think so. But it sounds as though you're gaining the Sayeeda's trust. That's a good thing. Maybe one day, she'll even help you get out of here."

"She's very loyal to Arrow. But at this point, she's definitely my best option," I agreed.

"If a plan eventuates, be sure to let me know. Perhaps I can help." Wearing a wide grin, she bumped her hip into mine. "And maybe even come with you."

"Thank you. It's nice to know that someone in Coridon is on my side. And I've got your back, too."

As we went back and forth moving the gold, I asked Grendal if she knew anything about the king's waterfall pool. She didn't but suggested I take a peek around the passage at the bottom of the stairs that we traipsed up and down to see what lay around the corner.

It was a risky move, but the dock was crowded, and if I ran as fast as my chained ankles would allow, I'd only be gone for a few minutes and no one would notice me missing.

We waited until Esen entered the carriage. Then, when we reached the base of the stairs that led into the palace, Grendal dropped her bags with a yelp and collapsed on the ground. Servants crowded around to assist her, and with my heart pounding like a drum, I scrambled through their legs.

As fast as I could, I ran along the corridor, the chain scraping the ground between my feet.

The path hooked left, then right, and then left again before it opened onto a beautiful garden arranged in four quadrants that stretched as far as the eye could see. I clenched my fists, spying the moat-like waterfall pool against the palace wall in the distance.

I couldn't see the water that poured through Arrow's river room, but I heard it—a great gushing noise that sounded to me like freedom. My heart thudded while I scanned the area, committing landmarks to memory.

"Leaf!" a deep voice boomed behind me, and my heart stopped beating entirely.

I whipped around and gasped. *Arrow*. Shit. I was in so much trouble.

"What do you think you're doing?" said the king as he stepped around a column painted with black and gold feathers.

He was dressed in full Storm Court armor, his favorite gold-feather ear cuffs, and the black cloak he'd wrapped me in that day at the river. He looked as if he'd just leaped off his horse and hurried over to the loading dock, hoping to catch me doing something wrong.

Well, he'd caught me. So now what? If I had to bet on it, I'd say nothing very good.

Just in case I never got to see it again, I stared briefly up at the cobalt sky, then down at my gold-painted toenails—anywhere but at the king. I already knew what I would see if I looked at him—storm-lit eyes blaring his strong desire to grab my neck and snap it.

"Leaf? Answer me," he said, stalking forward.

Damn. This looked like an escape attempt, and nothing I could say would change that. Surely now he would throw me into the fires without ceremony.

I swallowed hard and took a deep breath. "Admiring Coridon's exotic architecture?" I said, more of a question than a statement.

The air crackled, and blue light circled Arrow's arms as he sighed, one hip hitched forward and boot tapping the paving.

"I'm helping unload the gold, like Raiden directed me to."

"Not now you aren't. And according to Esen, you weren't doing a very good job of it before anyway."

My blood boiled in my veins.

"Did she also happen to call me the king's harlot?"

His lips compressed, and he stared at me grimly.

"No? Of course she didn't. I wonder what else Esen says behind your back."

A wry half-smile lifted his lips. "She reads poems in my honor, no doubt."

Arranging my face in a mask of innocence, I took a step toward him, my palms raised in supplication. "I was curious, that's all. I spend most days alone, and I'm bored. I only wanted a glimpse of the city. I'll head straight back to the bay now and return to work."

Staring past his bulky shoulders, I marched forward.

"Stop," he said. "Did that bag of gold help you better admire the streets?"

I looked down at the gold in my arms. "Damn. Sorry." I held the bag out. "I know how this looks. I meant to drop it, but somehow... I forgot."

He ripped it from my hands, and with a straight face, dropped it on the ground between us, like it was an insignificant bag of potatoes.

I made a quick bow and tried to step around him.

"Not so fast, Leaf." His fingers seized my wrist. "The only place you're going is where *I* say."

"But I have work to do. Ari said..."

Silver eyes blazed down at me, and his brow twisted in a hard frown. "*Ari* answers to me. And *I'm* telling you that you're coming with me. Did you really think you could escape so easily?"

"No! I told you. I was just curious. I'm sorry, King Arrowyn," I said, keeping my chin dipped but my eyes foolishly fixed on his.

Whatever he saw in my gaze—probably anger as hot as the desert sun—made him laugh. Then he grabbed my arm and tugged me in the direction of the palace.

"You're a liar, little human," he growled, glaring at the workers who stared slack-jawed at us as we weaved our way through the crowd.

Struggling to keep up with his long strides, frustration loosened my tongue. "You're hurting me. Why do you have to be such a dust-damned giant with tree trunks for legs?"

"Really? You're going with that *now*?" He stopped dead, jolting me backward by my arm. "It's not my fault you're so tiny, is it?" Then he tossed me over his shoulder, his fingers digging into my flesh in an uncompromising grip. "Despite what you say, you're definitely not sorry now, Leaf. But I promise that you soon will be."

Shit. I was pretty sure my luck had run out and I was about to see a side of Arrow that he kept reasonably well-leashed. The dark side.

The question I asked myself, as I bounced against his back, my head spinning with fear and something even worse, was so far from sensible I wondered about my sanity.

I should have asked myself... would I die tonight? And if so, how badly would it hurt?

But no.

I didn't.

Whatever Arrow had planned, my foolish, blood-pooled brain was wondering if I might *like* it.

Chapter 14

ARROW

Fury burned inside me as I strode through the sitting room. The human dug her fingernails into the backs of my thighs but, wisely, made no sound of protest, not even a squeak.

How dare she leave her assigned work and then pretend she wasn't sneaking around looking for escape routes? No matter how innocent her gap-toothed smile made her look, the girl was a liar and would flee the city the first chance she got. But she was mine, and I would never allow her to leave me.

The sooner she understood that, the better her life would be.

I chained her to the center of the pavilion, then stomped up the stairs to my bedchamber and removed my travel armor. My bones cracked as I rolled my shoulders and then tugged on pants that hung loosely on my hips.

I breathed a sigh of relief and pushed the memories of human screams and hacked limbs and gore from my mind.

Murdering raiders was far from my favorite pastime. But someone had to instill fear in those who thought they could steal gold from my people without consequences. I hoped the gruesome remains of today's hunt would serve as a warning that the risks were not worth the gains, no matter how considerable.

A warm breeze blew through the apartment, whipping my hair around my face as I went downstairs and crouched to unchain the girl. She shivered at my touch but stayed silent. Gathering her into my arms, I carried her down to the river room and threw her in the water without warning. I tossed a cake of soap in after her.

"Bathe," I commanded as she surfaced, the water level at her hips and her poisonous green glare murdering me over and over.

With a laugh at her impudence, I dropped heavily into a chair near the edge of the water and lounged backward, my knees spread wide as I watched her through hooded eyes.

Even suffering profound exhaustion, my body reacted to hers, a response I relished as much as I despised it.

Glistening wet, the girl shivered in her thin tunic, but not from the temperature of the water, which I knew was always mild. I was willing to bet every kanara in Coridon City that suppressed anger caused her shaking. My little Leaf dreamed of killing me. The urge shone darkly in her eyes. But even that wasn't enough to stop me from wanting to touch her.

Ravish her.

Consume her.

Take her over and over again until she had nothing left to give, until every muscle in her body was weak and all she could see, hear, and think about was me.

But she was determined to never obey me. Never be malleable and meek. So what stopped me from giving this ungovernable human to the Fires of Amon? The challenge she posed as being the first female who openly defied me was one possibility. The novelty of the situation.

And also, because her warm body and hushed voice somehow subdued my nightmares, I wouldn't be casting her aside anytime soon. That was as good an excuse as any to keep her chained to the pavilion forever.

"Do you plan on obeying my command anytime soon?" I asked, my voice deceptively calm.

Leaf stared at me, her chest rising and falling. The sneer on her lips told me that she too was thinking of the time I'd thrown her in the Auric River on the day I purchased her—a wretch of a girl, half dead and stinking of the gutter.

Crossing my arms, I raised my brow, and she finally obeyed my instructions and dipped down into the water, making a show of finding the soap and washing her hair.

After a while, I stripped off my pants and entered the water. Her gaze skimmed over my chest, then lowered, sliding away to avoid viewing the indisputable evidence of how much I'd enjoyed watching the water flow over her supple limbs.

Throwing the soap at me, she pointed at my face and neck. "You're streaked with the blood of the humans you murdered."

I scraped my fingers over my cheek, then rubbed them together, inspecting the rusty brown dirt under my nails, the color of death.

The human raiders had been terrible fighters, and we hacked them to pieces without need of magic. The memory of the ragged scream of an older man with eyes the same shade as Leaf's shivered down my spine. I shook off the horror and refocused on the problem in front of me.

"I was thinking that instead of wandering where you shouldn't, you could use that pent-up energy to prove yourself trustworthy." I waded closer to her as I scrubbed my hands and nails with the soap. "Then I would allow you more freedom. You could accompany me throughout the palace at certain times and satisfy that gold-damned curiosity of yours."

The water cascaded over her breasts, turning the tunic transparent as she surged onto her feet again and walked toward me, her breathing uneven.

Those emerald eyes lifted, settling on my mouth as her palms came to rest on my chest before gliding to my stomach. My muscles leaped under her touch, and I stifled a groan.

"What must I do to prove myself trustworthy, King Arrowyn?" she asked in a voice she evidently hoped would pass as docile.

I knew how my title must have tasted on her tongue, but if she would let me, I'd happily lick the bitter flavor away. At least now, her words and actions proved her willing to pretend compliance, which was *something*.

A mix of triumph, heat, and disappointment roiled through my veins, but in truth, it killed me to see her yield even this negligible amount. Eventually, I would bend her to my will, then I'd hate myself for breaking her fierce, reckless spirit.

Yes, one day soon, she would beg for my attentions—her body craving only me—and on that day, I would both win and lose simultaneously. Never before had I experienced such conflicting desires, craving another's destruction as equally as I longed for them to prevail against me.

Though she fought the urge admirably, her gaze kept skimming my body, catching on the glyphs pulsating around my length. Had she never seen a naked male before?

Curving my lips slightly, I stayed silent. Let her sweat and guess what would please me best. Throughout the short period she'd lived in my apartment, I had given her many clues.

It wasn't her pain and fear that would delight me, but her tears of frustrated longing.

Her palms trembled against my skin as she stood on her toes and tilted her face toward mine. "Would a kiss be a good first step in building this trust?"

"Why don't you find out?"

With a shaky breath, her rosebud lips parted, the gap in her teeth flashing, and then her mouth pressed against mine. My gut contracted, and I groaned as she answered with an animal whimper. I cupped her breast, ran my thumb over the hard nipple, then bent and suckled it through the wet material of her tunic. She cried out, her knees buckling.

Kissing her, I lifted her legs, wrapping them around my waist, reveling in the feel of her against my stomach, the scent of her desire a heady fragrance.

"You like this?" I asked, needing her to say it.

She nodded, her head falling back as I laved the long muscle of her neck down to her collarbone.

"Tell me," I demanded.

"Yes... I do. It feels..." Her words trailed off on a moan.

"Feels what?" I urged, closing my teeth around her ear lobe and biting to the point of pain.

She hissed in a breath. "Wonderful."

With clumsy, lust-fueled movements, I carried her to the curved steps that wound out of the river. I laid her down, ready to thrust inside her before I came from the sight of the wet tunic bunched around her waist, revealing her glistening slit.

"But don't feel too pleased with yourself," she said, looking up at me through a feline gaze. "It's only a natural response to physical stimulation, not the result of any particular skill of yours."

With those words, the lust fog cleared from my mind, and I laughed. This girl was unbelievable. Even when her life depended on it, she couldn't control her vicious tongue.

Fine. I would teach her a lesson.

I draped her over a flat boulder on the edge of the stairs, then got to work, my lips and tongue torturing her as they traversed the peaks and valleys of her body. I licked down her center and kissed her inner thighs, torturing her sensitive folds with my warm breath. I licked deeper, her creamy, earthy flavor bursting over my tongue, driving me wild.

"Arrow," she said in a broken moan, spurring me to suck harder and slide two fingers inside her heat.

"Fuck, Leaf," I groaned as she writhed against me.

When her nails clawed my back, I shuddered on the precipice of my own climax. I lifted my head and let a smirk form on my lips, the effort to appear in control nearly breaking me. "Shall I continue?" I asked.

Her fingers wound into my hair, tugging me back to where she most ached for relief. "Yes. Oh, gods yes."

"Your pitiful Earth gods can't help you now. Beg to *me*. From now on, I am the only god you shall pray to."

"Please, King Arrowyn. Continue," she rasped.

I pushed onto all fours above her, staring into her desire-filled eyes, now a heated jade color. "If you're going to beg, do it properly."

She shook her head.

"*Beg.*"

"I asked nicely," she said, her chest rising and falling rapidly. "Isn't that enough to satisfy your ego?"

"Obviously not." My thumb caressed her lips. "Now use that pretty mouth to beg."

Her head thrashed. She cursed and moaned. "Never."

My hand froze on her cheek. "What did you say?"

"I'll never beg you. Not for anything."

"Very well." I pushed onto my feet, my restraint near to snapping as I drank in the picture of her spread across the rock. Water lapped where my tongue had been, and her eyes burned with anger and unfulfilled passion.

I offered my hand, and she turned her head away, ignoring me. I scooped her up by the waist, tossed her over my shoulder, and returned to the pavilion.

After I locked her chain in place, I went into the bathroom. I leaned against the marble wall and gripped myself, stroking and stopping on the edge over and over, my whole body shuddering.

I drew the agony out, needing it to last as long as possible, but then the three words she'd uttered—*please, King Arrowyn*—whispered through my mind, and in four firm strokes, I exploded with a groan, thick ropes of seed coating my chest. As my breath sawed out of me, I pictured my climax decorating the human's petulant mouth.

When my self-control was restored, I bathed and dressed for dinner, and on the way to the hall, stopped by the kitchen and advised Ari to deliver a tray of food to Leaf. Then, barely listening to Stormur and Raiden discuss the day's gold delivery, I hurried through my meal, pleaded exhaustion, and then returned to my chambers.

In the moonlight, twin bolts of green glared at me as I unchained the human—the catcher and keeper of my nightmares. I silently cursed my way through her torturous massage, my hardness rubbing the sheet with her movements and her moist heat searing my skin.

To keep my wits, I recalled today's hunt, counting each strike of my blade on the raiders' flesh. I only just stopped myself from turning over and slaking my need with Leaf's hot little body. I kept reminding myself that a more powerful release awaited us both on the day she eventually submitted to me, and that was worth waiting for.

As I settled down for sleep and drew Leaf against my chest, she wriggled several times, pressing her perfect ass into my hardness, the musk of her arousal an agonizing temptation. But I refused to give in to her body's unconscious demands. I was her master, and she would bow to my will, not the other way around.

"Your guard dog was right about me," Leaf said in a sleepy, barely audible voice.

"My guard dog?"

"Esen."

"Tell me what she said."

"Why should I?" Leaf asked. "You'll only believe her word over mine."

"Likely true. Tell me anyway."

"I already did tell you at the docks, and you pretended not to hear it." She sighed. "Esen called me the king's harlot."

My jaw tightened. "Jealousy has long been Esen's curse to bear."

"Because she's your lover?"

"No. I've rejected her advances more than once. I don't sleep with my soldiers."

"Just with girls you can chain up."

"So it seems."

"Will you tell her that I told you?"

I smiled against Leaf's neck, wishing I could see her face. "It seems only fair that I should. Esen informed on you when you disappeared at the loading bay today. Now you've returned the favor. I'd say the scales are balanced."

"Great. Now she'll want to throw me in your famous fire pits more than ever."

"Then don't go near them."

"Or... if you'll tell me where they're located, I could throw Esen in instead."

I laughed. "Go to sleep, ruthless one, and wreak revenge inside your dreams."

Within minutes, she was asleep in my arms, leaving me to wonder where such a fierce little human had come from. Then worse, if there was a human male out there searching the realms night and day to get her back.

If so, let him search.

I would never let him find her.

Chapter 15

LEAF

"Swallow it," Ari said as I turned my head toward the sun's glare, away from the vial of gold serum she held in front of me.

"Why? I'm beginning to think you know it has no effect on me. I've stopped pretending that it does. So what's the point?"

"Swallow, and I will explain."

Rolling my eyes at the bright azure sky visible through the pavilion's columns, I tipped my head back and drank the vial's contents.

Each morning, the Sayeeda and I repeated this exact scene. I refused the serum, and she insisted I take it, but this was the first time she'd offered to explain the reason behind the routine.

Smiling, she sat back on her haunches. "I needed you to ingest the gold for a long enough period to be certain."

"Of what?"

"I will tell you everything when it is safe to do so. Plans must be made first. At least now, we can dispense with the farce of topping up the serum in your bracelet. You are right; it has no effect on you."

"Ari! When *what* will be safe? And what plans are you talking about? Please don't leave me in suspense."

"For your safety, I must." She fastened the chain between my ankle cuffs and stood, handing me a gold tunic. "Put this on. Esen will be here any moment."

"Esen?" My heart thudded against my ribs. "Why? I certainly didn't invite her. Can't you get rid of her?"

"King Arrowyn wants you to visit the gold foundry with her, and also Raiden and Ildri. It will be a chance for you to satisfy your troublesome curiosity. Those are the king's words, not mine."

Speechless, I blinked at her. It was an incredible opportunity to scout for exit routes from the city. I only wished the sour-faced, blue-haired demon wasn't coming. And Raiden's mother—that was odd. Why would the elegant Ildri be joining such an unusual excursion?

As I slid the tunic over my head, Ari said, "Be nice to Ildri, won't you? She is a particular friend of mine and may one day prove helpful to you."

I took a breath to ask what she meant, but swallowed my words as Esen strode through the sitting room, scowling as she greeted Ari with a brisk good morning. Clearly, she wasn't happy about spending the day with me either, and there was some satisfaction in that, at least.

We took the elevator down to the ground floor of the palace, Esen silent, staring straight ahead with her hand on the hilt of one of her many swords, ready to thrust it through my heart at the slightest provocation.

Outside the large stable complex, a coach waited, the doors emblazoned with Coridon's royal insignia—a coat of arms with two lightning bolts on a background of floating feathers. Raiden, dressed in his usual soldier's garb, and Ildri, wearing a green and gold gown more suited to a feast than a foundry visit, were already seated inside it.

Ildri smiled as I settled into the plush cushions opposite her, and her son, sitting beside her, skimmed a dark gaze over me.

Forcing a grim smile, he said, "Leaf, are you looking forward to viewing our city's famous foundry?"

"I am. The view from the king's dome has grown boring. I'm curious to see more of Coridon from the ground."

Both Ildri and Raiden looked away, as if embarrassed by the reminder of my status as the king's personal slave.

"What was your home like?" Ildri asked in a gentle voice, fixing me with her violet gaze.

I shrugged. "I don't really remember. But I often dream about a forest that I believe is located in the Earth Realm. I have a family waiting for me there. I'm sure of it."

Ildri's bejeweled fingers patted my hand. "I hope you can return to them one day, Leaf."

Raiden glared at her, as if in shock. Well, that made two of us who were surprised by his mother's words. I'd never expected to hear expressions of sympathy from a high fae of the Storm Court.

Esen pulled a parcel from her satchel, unwrapping it to reveal a pile of small cakes glistening with honey. As the carriage jolted into motion, the fae began munching on them, moaning and raising their brows in delight at the apparently delicious flavors.

"Aren't you going to offer one to Leaf, Esen?" Ildri asked.

"When I've had my fill, I might consider it," she replied.

I wouldn't be holding my breath waiting for *that* to happen.

Ignoring the mouth-watering smells of cinnamon and cardamom, I drank in the sights outside the window, my breath hitching when we passed Arrow's waterfall pool and I realized I had a perfect view of the streets surrounding it. I committed to memory as many landmarks and possible hiding places as I could.

A flash of yellow cloth caught my eye, and I craned my neck to get a better look. "That man disappeared through a hedge," I said, pointing at a wall that was possibly only a ten minute walk from the waterfall pool.

Laughing, Ildri gave my knee a maternal squeeze. "That was a gold reaver elf, like our Sayeeda. What you saw was a doorway, an exit from the city that only opens for the reavers."

Rubbing my clammy palms on my tunic, I gritted my teeth to stop myself from asking questions. Even the most innocent of them would raise my companions' suspicions.

My mind raced as I wondered if there was a way to force the mysterious door open without reaver magic. Perhaps I could coax some details about it from Ari tomorrow.

As she worked in Arrow's apartment, she often answered my questions distractedly and revealed more about the court and city than she probably intended. Especially if I peppered vague comments about Raiden into the conversation.

"Human, you can have the last cake," Esen said, offering the sweet to me on the cloth, her lips twisted in the approximate shape of a smile. "The king asked me to be nice to you today. It's a peace offering."

"Thank you," I said, taking the cake before she changed her mind. I was too hungry to refuse a delicious treat just to annoy her. I scoffed it down, then licked the honey from my fingers.

"Got any more of those in your satchel?" I asked. "I'm sure the king would approve if you gave me another."

Esen laughed, a harsh unpleasant sound.

Last night I'd stayed awake too long, waiting hours for Arrow's grip to loosen, and now tiredness overwhelmed me. I yawned and let the fae's conversation wash over me, angled my body toward the window, and studied the view.

Coridon was a large, bustling city, and I stared wide-eyed as the carriage rattled along gold-paved pathways past shops and dwellings. Gold glinted from arched doorways and high turrets, flashing brightly in the sun and making me squint.

After a while, the faces of the fae traveling on carts and carriages blurred, my thoughts floating in a haze, and growing duller, as my error slowly dawned on me.

The cake... Esen had poisoned me.

Feeling sick to my stomach, I studied Ildri. Her eyes seemed clear. Her smile and words were sharp as she chatted, sharing her hopes that before long, the court would visit the Auryinnia Mine again.

Beyond my control, my eyes closed and didn't open until Esen shoved my shoulder, hissing in my ear, "We're here. Wake up."

Raiden and Ildri stood out front of an enormous black-stone building, which I assumed must be the city's famous gold foundry. Instead of slapping Esen's smirking face, I shot her a glare and climbed out of the carriage, trying not to trip over the chain between my legs.

Raiden steadied me as I swayed on the pavement. "You all right?"

I nodded and shook him off.

Concentrating on every step so I didn't fall flat on my face, I caught up to Ildri, who threaded her arm through mine and guided me gently forward. I couldn't tell by her inscrutable expression if she knew that Esen had drugged me. Perhaps she didn't care.

The foundry manager, a tall elf with long gold hair and bronze-colored wings folded against the back of his uniform, met us at the entrance. With a proud smile, he swept us into the building, eager to begin the tour.

Inside, a hellish nightmare of heat and flame enveloped me, the air reeking of coal smoke and magic that made my already reeling head spin faster. The manager's pale eyes flicked down to my chain, then quickly away, and I wondered if the king had warned him to pretend not to notice it.

Hoping I didn't pass out, I stared over a railing at the floor below, where enormous clay crucibles hung above large furnaces. Fixed on bars, the crucibles tipped, pouring gold into ornamental casts. The manager told us that when they cooled, they formed the sheets of gold, filigree feathers, and lightning bolts that the builders used to decorate the city.

Rows of fae sat in front of the fires, dressed in loincloths and blowing air into the bottom of the flames with leather pipes they held to their mouths. The heat was so intense that they probably only remained conscious by using magic. I didn't envy them their jobs.

I longed to pester our guide with questions, but in my fuzzy, drugged state, all I could do was nod and pretend I understood his lecture. I focused my energy on staying upright, the crash and bang of irregularly beaten metal in the distance shuddering through my teeth and bones.

"What's wrong?" Raiden asked. "You look pale."

"I'm fine," I lied, focusing on his face with great difficulty.

He gave me an odd look, then headed toward the guide, who beckoned him over to watch a demonstration of new gold beading equipment.

A wave of nausea swamped me, and I fell behind as the party moved into the next room. Clutching my stomach, I ducked between some inactive machinery and vomited on the floor.

"Poor little human," Esen said from behind me. "Feeling unwell, are you?"

Wiping my mouth, I turned and faced her. "Thanks to you."

Holding a short knife by the hilt, she strode forward with hostile intent, and I bolted sideways, tripping on the chain between my ankles. Her hand shot out, dragging me backward, and with the knife at my throat, she bent me over a railing positioned directly above a simmering vat of gold.

"Bit slow today, aren't you, king's whore?" She laughed. "This is too easy. One little push and over you'd go. Never to be seen again. And with the way you've been blundering about today, no one would doubt me if I told them I saw you stumble and fall into a vat."

Rage shuddered through me, and I spat in her face. "If you hadn't poisoned me, you'd have no hope of cornering me. I'm not the helpless human you'd like to think I am."

A sneer twisted her lips. "Oh, I didn't poison you. It's only a large dose of hashish oil dulling your senses." Keeping the blade at my throat, she shifted her other hand to my shoulder. "Just a tiny little push and—"

Using all my strength, I kneed her thigh, sadly missing her groin. She made a satisfying grunt of pain as footsteps sounded behind us. "Bad luck. Too slow," I whispered over her lips. "Spent too long gloating."

"Esen!" On the other side of the room, Raiden's voice boomed from the shadows. "Drop the knife and let her go. Now!"

With a growl, Esen stepped backward, sheathing her blade.

"I thought your king ordered you to be *nice* to me today," I said, rubbing the sting from my throat. "I'm not sure murder fits that definition. What do you think he'll say when he hears about this?"

Esen's face paled. A common failing of the overconfident schemer, she likely hadn't considered that her precious Arrowyn might learn of her wicked deed.

Raiden grabbed her arm and tugged her toward the exit. It was pleasant to see someone else being hauled about for a change, especially the obnoxious Esen.

"*Arrow* won't be hearing of it," he said, flicking his head toward the door and directing me to follow. "And if you tell him, Leaf, we'll just say you're a liar who attempted to escape. Who do you think he'll believe?"

On the silent journey back to the stables, my mind ran wild with far-fetched schemes of escaping from the king's apartment. Now that I knew how serious Esen was about getting rid of me, the need to leave Coridon was more urgent than ever.

I had to sweeten up Ari, who thankfully grew more trusting every day, and please Arrow to the best of my ability, no matter how much I hated bending to his will.

The next day, after breakfast, I accompanied Ari to the river room. I sat in the waterfall window as usual, and we chatted as she arranged platters of fruit for the king's pleasure. Not bothering to bolt my chain to the floor, she'd attached it to a single cuff on my wrist and left the end lying loosely over my thighs.

Over the past couple of weeks, her frosty demeanor had slowly thawed. And right now, I'd never been so grateful that the king's Sayeeda and I had become friends. Or at least, something quite similar.

"Was yesterday's foundry visit interesting?" Ari asked as she swept a broom around groups of chairs and low tables along the edge of the river.

"Extremely," I replied, recalling my sweat-soaked skin as Esen had held my torso in the air above the vat of molten gold.

"You should ask Arrowyn to take you to Auryinnia. He's long overdue a diplomatic visit to the mines, and I think you could convince him to make the journey."

"Me? I doubt that. Wasn't his family killed near there?"

"Yes. But three years have passed, and it's time he upheld the contract his ancestors made with my people, the reaver elves. We have allowed him time to recover, but the Zareen's patience is running out."

"The Zareen?" I asked. "Who is that?"

Ari's skin paled, and she waved a dismissive hand before marching off to the other end of the river room to throw a bucket of sweepings out a window. She collected her broom and called out to me. "I must clean the bathroom. Remain there if you wish. I won't be long."

With dread and excitement churning in my stomach, I nodded and returned her smile. A few moments later, I heard her broom thudding against walls as she swept the bathroom briskly. The Sayeeda had just given me what might be the only chance I'd get to escape from the king's chambers.

With a pounding heart, I scanned the river room for what I hoped would be the very last time.

Translucent veils danced over the floor-to-ceiling windows, framed by gold and black columns. Dappled light cast intricate patterns over the marble floors and the dark green leaves of tropical plants. The atmosphere was uplifting and tranquil, like a refuge. A haven.

I turned my face away from the beauty and fixed my attention on the waterfall that rushed past my legs and over the windowsill I sat on.

Stupid idea or not, if I was going to do it, I needed to act fast.

Water sprayed my body as it gushed past, the urgent sound spurring me into motion. I got to my feet and studied the ground around the pool. The street appeared quiet, with only a lone cat wandering by.

The drop was high, but the rectangular pool below was deep and wide. I might survive the jump. Or I might not. Either way, one thing was certain: I'd had enough of living at the whim of the fae of the Storm Court, waiting for Esen or Arrow to kill me whenever the mood struck them.

If I died today, so be it.

And if I lived, only sheer luck would get me beyond the city walls.

And if I somehow got out of Coridon, then what?

Where could a person with no memories go?

That wasn't entirely true, I told myself. There were things I remembered. The forest and the boy whom I believed was my brother. My smiling parents. And on the day that Arrow bought me, I had known immediately that he was fae. I was aware of the fae courts and cities and knew that the realms were five lands and that gold was the most valuable commodity in all of them.

I also remembered things I liked. People whose laughter and kindness comforted others—be they human or fae. Blue skies, never stormy ones. The deep green of trees and vines, the familiar brown of dirt and stone. Weapons. Training hard until my muscles ached. The sensation of honey melting on my tongue. And freedom. I needed freedom to be happy, like I needed air to survive. Of that, I was certain.

I hated hunger. Chains, neck cuffs, and cages of all kinds, no matter how pretty they were. Glittering gold. Cruel people. Esen. And most of all, the arrogant fae who shuddered through his dreams each night, squeezing me so hard that sometimes I almost lost consciousness. And lastly... heights.

I remembered heights scared me.

Fortunately, in the forest, I'd trained myself to deal with that.

Images flickered through my mind—me and the boy running through the forest and skidding to a halt at the edge of a cliff. Then laughing as we leaped over into the water far below, my brother flipping his body backwards, like an acrobat, as he descended.

I let the feeling of flying fill my lungs and my blood.

I wasn't a nobody, like Esen wanted me to believe. I was real and as worthy as someone like Raiden or Stormur—or even the Sayeeda herself. And I was ready... prepared to take a leap of faith, life or death be damned. But I had to do it now. Before Ari, who I could hear humming in the bathroom, returned.

I could do this.

I crouched on the marble windowsill, wound the chain around my arm, then gripped the end tightly in my fist so it wouldn't knock me out as I fell. I straightened, counted out three heartbeats, then bent my knees and jumped off, falling feet first—down, down, down.

As the wind rushed past, I stretched my arms out wide to maintain balance, and swallowed a shout of joy.

As the pool got closer, I took a big breath and clasped my hands tightly in front of my body, shielding the place Arrow had recently tortured with his tongue.

For dust's sake, I couldn't believe my last thought in this life might be of the fae king and his stupid tongue.

With a gasp, I broke the surface of the water, sinking into darkness before my feet pushed off the pool's slimy bottom, then I swam as quietly as I could to the wall. Disorientated, I peeked over the tiled edge at the street.

Several city dwellers walked in the distance, and not one of them looked in my direction. The noise of the waterfall and street musicians drumming nearby must have masked the sounds as I plunged into the pool.

I slipped out of the water and bolted for the tall shrubs flashing bright green as they crawled up the city walls. I pushed my way through them until the wall's rough render scraped my back, the greenery hiding me from the street.

Pushing wet hair off my face, I sat on the ground, and tried to catch my breath and recall the direction of the gold reaver door I'd seen yesterday from the carriage. I needed to go left at the crossroads at the end of this street, then keep going, heading south toward the gold foundry.

Scrambling along the wall, I fought my way through prickly branches and foliage until I came to a section I couldn't squeeze through. I ducked onto the street, my heart beating wildly, and picked up a cracked ceramic jar lying on the pavement. Hoisting it over my right shoulder, I hid my face from foot and cart traffic until I turned left on the gold foundry street. Within a few minutes, I found a place to push back through the hedge, safely hidden once more.

As I hurried along, I dragged my fingers along the wall's surface until I felt a different texture—wood at last! I stopped and ran my palms over the outline of a frame, a dark green door becoming visible against the tangle of leaves.

This was definitely the reaver door. Hope made me dizzy as I searched for a handle, not surprised to find that there wasn't one. Perhaps I could hide there until night fell, then sneak through the town's shadows and hunt for a tool to break the door open.

It was a high-risk venture, destined to fail, but I'd rather die trying than spend one more day trapped like an auron kanara in Arrow's gilded palace.

With a frustrated grunt, I shoved my palms hard against the wood and stifled a triumphant yell when the door opened with a soft click. I stepped through into an expanse of blue sky and breathtaking, glorious freedom. Of course, it was probably the worse kind of freedom—sadly, incredibly short-lived.

As I whipped my head around, my vision blurred. I swallowed bile, fear and thirst making me dizzy.

In the rush of adrenaline, I'd lost track of time and didn't know whether it was minutes or hours since I'd jumped out of the window.

The Sayeeda would have reported me missing by now, so the palace guards must be searching for me. Raiden closing in with orders to cuff me and return me to my cage. Or Esen leading the pack with her sword raised, determined to take my head off. I took slow breaths, willing calm into my lungs and bloodstream.

If they caught me, so be it.

If I failed, at least I'd tried to make my way home. The face of the bearded man from the forest—my father—swirled in my mind. With his arms open wide, he beckoned me forward, encouraging me, calling me his little Z. What Z stood for, I had no clue.

"I'm coming, Father," I whispered as I crouched in the shadow of Coridon's massive wall. I squeezed my eyes shut and prayed the kind-eyed man and the loving family were as real as the gold-flecked dirt beneath my bare feet.

Shit. I really needed to find myself a pair of boots.

Wiping the sweat from my face, I surveyed the environment. The line of the city walls snaked to my right, and to my left, a wide road split the golden-red desert in half. I quickly calculated which direction to take.

Straight ahead, a collection of tiny buildings dotted the horizon. It was most likely the outpost town I'd heard Arrow and Raiden discuss called Bonerust. It provided services to travelers, such as transport and storage for hire, and had a small tavern that offered basic accommodation.

Maybe once I got there, I could steal a cloak, some food, and, if I was lucky, a horse that would carry me all the way to the Port of Tears. And I'd better not forget about those damned boots. I wouldn't get far without them.

Ari said the coast lay in a northwesterly direction, which made Bonerust the perfect first stop on my journey.

All I had to do was not die of thirst before I arrived. And pray the Storm Court guards were having a bad day.

Chapter 16

ARROW

"**R**umors of a gold chaser resistance building in the forests of the human realm grow more frequent by the day," said Raiden, his armor creaking as he walked by my side. "We can't ignore them much longer."

As we stepped into my sitting room where the Sayeeda would soon serve food and wine while we recovered from the tedium of this morning's council meeting, the auron kanara gongs rang out.

The birds shrieked, beating their wings against their cages and increasing the painful throb in my temples. Praise the gold that the lightning wielders would soon arrive and shut them the hell up.

I unstrapped my arm bracers and threw them on a couch. "As you said, Raid, they're only rumors. Every time we send a party to search the forests, they only return with tales of ruin and decay. I've gone myself, and all I've found are insects, birds, and animals."

"But it's more than just hearsay," Raiden insisted. "Humans do still live around the old city. Fae in other realms are detecting their energy and some have found signs of people moving through the forest."

"If it is true, then those that remain are part of a dying race. Their city is long gone. The survivors deserve our pity, not our fear. Stop worrying about it."

The noise of the birds reached a feverish pitch, which was odd. Hearing the gong usually soothed them because they knew food was coming. The skin on the back of my neck prickled. Something felt off. I whirled on my heel to face Leaf's pavilion.

It was empty.

Heat burned through my veins, then I willed myself to calm down in order to think straight. Perhaps she was with my Sayeeda in the kitchen, gossiping as she ground cloves with the servants.

No, Ari would have told me of her plans.

"Ari," I bellowed, unease churning in my gut.

The gold reaver appeared from behind a palm tree in the river room below me, her expression as tranquil as always.

"I've been waiting for you," she said as I descended the steps three at a time.

When I stopped in front of her, I noticed her skin was so pale it looked silver.

"Leaf jumped out of the window into the pool below. She's gone, Arrowyn."

"*What?*" I growled as Raiden arrived at my side. Lightning struck the dome, storm magic circling my limbs. "When?"

"A few hours ago," Ari said, her voice calm.

Raiden reached out and took Ari's hand, as if he wanted to touch her one last time before I turned her into a pile of smoking ash. "You've sent guards to check if she survived?" he asked.

"I didn't want to create a fuss, so I sent cleaners to the fountain," she replied. "They didn't mention a body in the pool, so I assumed she made it out of the water."

What the fuck? She didn't want to create a *fuss*?

I took a deep breath, loosening my clenched fists. The reckless human was alive. She couldn't have got out of Coridon. And I would burn the entire city down, if that's what it would take to find her.

My hands wrapped around Ari's slender throat.

"Arrow," Raiden said.

"Be quiet," I warned him, focusing on Ari. "Next time you can't find Leaf, alert me immediately or I'll send you packing to Auryinnia, the first bonded gold reaver to be dismissed by a Light Realm king. Where have the guards searched?"

Ari swallowed, her golden gaze not meeting mine. "As I said, I wanted to speak to you before I raised the alarm."

"Ari, she could be *dead*. Crushed by a cart. Stolen by any number of fae leaving the city."

Raiden marched toward the elevator. "If she's still alive, I'll find her, Arrow."

"Not without me, you won't." I used magic to draw my armor and cloak through the air toward me, tugging them on as I walked. "But first, I need you to tell the guards that if they find Leaf, no one has permission to touch her. No one but me will lay a hand on her. Understand?"

"As you command." Raiden dipped his head, his mouth grim.

As the elevator's barred door closed, I stared at the Sayeeda, my glare promising she would pay for her unforgivable inaction today. By doing nothing after Leaf jumped, Ari may as well have pushed the girl out of the window herself. And now, my human was alone, vulnerable prey in a city of hunters.

With Esen, Raiden, and a small party of soldiers, we searched Coridon from top to bottom, no bale or stone left unturned.

Where the fuck was Leaf hiding?

As night fell, our horses stamped the dust near the city gates, and I wheeled Yanar around, a flash of light on the horizon catching my eye. Dark energy tore through my gut, and I knew without a doubt where Leaf was.

Fucking Bonerust.

Somehow, she had escaped the city, a near impossible feat for a human. Perhaps she'd hidden in a cart or begged a ride with a traveler who was foolish enough to think they could use her, then discard her broken body in a ditch. If I found her in the possession of such a man, fae or human, I would fill his veins with lightning, boil his brains, and crush his bones to a pulp.

A storm gathered in the sky, thunder rumbling, and my horse reared, his front legs lashing the air. "Raiden, you and three others come with me. Esen, remain here and continue searching with the others. Scour every surface of the foundry again. Earlier, I felt an energy disturbance on the balcony that overlooks the vats. It held remnants of the human."

Esen recoiled as if I'd shot an arrow through her breastplate, her cheeks flushing. Then she turned without a word, and her horse galloped toward the center of town, several armored riders following in her dust trail.

I spurred Yanar through the gates and rode as fast as the wind allowed, not stopping until we arrived at the corroded spiked gates at Bonerust's entrance, smoke and the stench of roasting meat thick in the air.

Two guards bolted forward as Yanar stamped the dirt and blew hard through his nose.

"My King," said the brawniest guard, his heavily bristled face partly visible beneath his helmet. He was human, which surprised me. They weren't considered strong enough to guard the entrance to a fae town, and I wondered briefly how he got the job. "Welcome to Bonerust. It is an honor to—"

I urged Yanar forward until he loomed over the guard, tendrils of storm magic curling from his nostrils. "A slave girl escaped from Coridon. Has she passed through your gates?"

"A whore was found sneaking through the gin gates on the eastern wall, Your Majesty."

A muscle twitched in my jaw. "A whore, you say?"

"She wore a fine neck cuff but had a mouth on her like a Port of Tears sailor. Guards who found her said she didn't sound like a court servant."

Sheet lightning flashed across the sky as I leaped off Yanar and wrapped my hands around the guard's throat. "Who has the girl?" I snarled.

Magic seeped from my pores, blue ripples circling my limbs, and the man squirmed in pain as the contact burned his skin.

"Who found her? How long ago?" I asked. "Lie to me, human, and I'll snap your neck."

Words garbled through his spit-flecked lips. "The blacksmith. About three hours ago."

The fucking blacksmith scum, who called himself the Rust King, was about to learn that my dominion over all things in the Light Realm included him, the slobbering son of a goat lover.

"You better hurry," wheezed the guard, his neck muscles straining beneath my grip. "He finishes smithing about now and will be turning his attention to his new acquisition."

His acquisition. Leaf was my property. And the blacksmith would pay the price of presuming otherwise.

I shoved the guard, and he flailed to the ground. My fae companions watched somber-faced from their horses, not uttering a single word between them.

"Let's go," I told them, leaping onto Yanar's back.

Within minutes, we had bashed through the blacksmith's door, finding Leaf in a cell at the rear of the shop, naked on the filthy floor, and the smithy kneeling above her with his cock in his hand and pants around his ankles.

"Gorbinvar," I ground out, keeping my tone neutral as Raiden and I marched through the barred door of the makeshift cage he'd foolishly left open. I didn't want him to crush her skull in panic, and considering who he was, I had to play this carefully.

"What?" His bear-like head whipped around, the drool hanging from his tusks threatening to land on Leaf's split lip.

While he was distracted, she released a banshee's cry and punched his snout.

"You bitch! I'll gouge your witch's eyes out, then fuck the empty sockets until there's nothin' left of your skull."

"Do that, and my spirit will rub cayenne pepper on your prick for all eternity," she snarled, ever the foolish provoker, who as yet, hadn't even glanced in my direction.

The self-proclaimed Rust King was from the Sun Realm and skilled with flame and metal. But from our past exchanges, I knew his mind was dull with dreams of power and riches... and looking at the state of his body right now, lust for my human. If he possessed any other talents, thinking wasn't one of them.

The smithy grabbed a fistful of Leaf's hair and thumped her head against the stone floor.

"Gorbinvar. Look at me," I growled.

The bristles around his tusks vibrated as orange eyes met mine. I held my finger to my lips, bidding the human to be silent, shocked when she actually obeyed.

"King," he said, unflinching.

"What right do you have to imprison this girl? To hurt her?"

"The same right I have to do anything in this city. Like a ship rat, this one scurried past my warehouse. My men brought her straight to me."

"A mistake. Because now you have your puny cock on my property."

"She's yours?" Fear twitched over his face. "How so?"

"The stamp of my house is on the bottom left of her collar. See for yourself. She is mine, no one else's, and you, blacksmith, have made a grievous error."

Beneath a sweaty kerchief, his throat bobbed as he ran a dirty fingernail over my mark on Leaf's collar.

"Enough," I snarled. "Get your hands off her before I break them."

He pushed his weight off her, stumbling backward, his arms raised to protect his ugly face.

The room shook. Thunder crashed over the roof, storm power gathering in my chest as it sizzled silver, then blue, circling my neck, arms, and wrists, the strength of the current wild, almost ungovernable.

Like her. Like Leaf.

"King Arrowyn. Wait... How was I to know she was yours? You cannot blame me for..." His words trailed away, the smell of piss assaulting my nose.

I smiled.

No one moved. Not Leaf or a guard. Not even Raiden. And especially not the terror-stricken smithy.

At chest level, I pressed my hands forward, and lightning forked from my palms, burning the fingers off Gorbinvar's right hand. Another strike hit the top of his barrel chest, just far enough away from his heart and lungs to keep him alive.

He was a fire fae, and I couldn't afford to kill him. As much as I longed to char the flesh from his bones, then spear his troll head on the city gates, Coridon's treaty with the Fire King prevented me from satisfying my rage.

First, Gorbinvar's knees hit the ground, then his face, his whole body shuddering like a partially squashed bug. Finally, he rolled over, vomited blood, then pointed one of his remaining thick fingers at me. "Arrowyn Ramiel, on my father's tusks, you will burn in the Hell Realms for all eternity."

I laughed. "Curse me a thousand times if it pleases you, smith, but you know well I'm immune to your hexes. So, go ahead and do your worst."

"Fuck your storm magic," he said, spitting out a broken a tooth.

"Tie him up," I told Raiden, then noticed him shaking his head in what looked like disgust at Leaf. "Hey! Don't even look at her. I fucking told you before not to look at her."

Raiden's brow arched. "Actually, you said no one could *touch* her. And you've never given a damn *who* looked at your servants before, naked or not. Why start now?"

Good question.

Lightning magic flared over my skin, and Raiden cleared his throat and quickly got to work on Gorbinvar, my soldiers helping him truss the blacksmith up like a boar ready for the spit. For a fire troll, his men finding him with his pants around his ankles would be a fate worse than death. Their most prized possessions were their inflated pride and vanity.

Crouching beside Leaf, I tucked my cloak around her trembling body. "Looks like I got here just in time," I murmured.

"Of course," she said hoarsely. "You wouldn't want anyone else to ruin me."

I had a lot to say on the matter but only grunted in reply as I stood and swung her into my arms. Holding her tightly, I strode outside to where Yanar waited.

As I began to lift Leaf into the saddle, she said, "Wait. Please, Arrow. Set me down for a moment. I need to adjust the cloak."

Gripping her hand, I scanned the rusted-metal buildings and the encampments of fae gathered around fire pits. They drank and talked in quiet voices, hoping to avoid my notice. My mind wandered, and I pictured Gorbinvar crouched over the human, anger heating my blood again.

"I'm ready," she said as Raiden and the other soldiers exited the smithy and marched toward their horses.

"I'm not," I growled. "There's something I need to do before we leave."

Still holding her with one hand, I clenched my other fist. My back buckled as I unleashed my rage, channeling white-hot energy through my palm until it became a spinning orb of blue light. With a roar, I threw it, and the forge exploded, the Rust King disintegrating inside a chaos of rubble and smoke.

One day soon, there would be hell to pay from the Sun Realm for killing Gorbinvar, but not tonight. Tonight, I had only two things to worry about. Leaf. And deciding how I would punish her for escaping.

Residual magic swam like angry wasps in my head, nausea churning my gut, but then a feeling of absolute satisfaction eclipsed the pain. I closed my eyes, willing my heartbeat to slow, the magic to settle. And when I opened them, Leaf was gone.

When the power had me in its thrall, I must have loosened my grip on her hand.

Fuck.

In the alley to my left, I caught a glimpse of golden feathers flashing on black material before it whipped around the corner. There she was! I bolted after her, not bothering to alert Raiden or the others.

It had to be me who caught her.

It could never be another.

Drunks crowded the narrow street, their fumbling limbs slowing my progress. I relished bowling them over as I passed, gaining upon my human with every breath.

The after-affects of the lightning blast still clouded my vision, but I didn't need sight to find her. Fragments of her sweat infused the air, a heady scent that caused hunger to pulse through my blood, demanding to be fed.

Fury honed my focus on the human.

Not *the* human—*my* human.

Mine.

She was mine and always would be.

In the distance, I saw her duck between a scorpion male's outstretched arm and a low-swinging lantern, his pincer snapping at her brown hair. She scrambled out of his way, ducking under a long bench piled with hawker food.

When she burst out on the other side, I was waiting. I grabbed her hair, tugging her against my chest.

"Caught you, little Leaf," I whispered against her ear. "No matter how far the wind blows you, I will find you. *Always.*"

"But for the love of dust, you bull-headed brute of a Storm King, *why?*" She turned in my arms, her fists pummeling my chest armor. Once. Twice. Three times. "I don't belong here, Arrow. Why don't you just let me go?"

"Because I... I can't. I'll never release you."

"As king, you can command crowds of courtiers to cater to your every whim. The last thing you need is a slave who comes from the very species you claim to despise."

I thought of her soft fingers moving through the shadows of my bedchamber, her whispered words that warded off my nightmares. I needed her all right. More than I could bear to admit.

The crowd buffeted her sideways. My arm jerked tighter around her waist as I shuffled backward until I hit the wall, moving her out of the fray.

"What if instead of these crowds of courtiers you mention, *you're* the only one I want to command?" I rocked my hardness into her body to illicit a reaction. Any number of responses would do fine—a quick writhe of her hips, a lusty moan, tears of frustration.

"Deriving pleasure from someone else's fear is a sickness," she said, disgust twisting her features. "You don't need a slave. You need help."

"You? Afraid of *me*?" I laughed. "You fear me in roughly the same way the moon cowers from the sun, which is to say not at all."

"That's different. The sun doesn't threaten the moon, does it?"

Frustration made me tighten my grip on her. Why couldn't she see me as I wanted her to? Why did she misinterpret... *everything*? "But think, Leaf. You constantly defy me, and still I haven't hurt you. Does that mean nothing? I would never take more than you're willing to give."

"Keep telling yourself that if it makes you feel better. But look at us—king and slave. We are not equal," she snapped. "Anything I give you is only the price I pay for comfort. Think about *that*, Arrow. Then decide what kind of man you are."

A heavy weight settled on my chest, winding sinuously like a serpent bearing the regrettable name of Guilt. I tore its phantom head off, tossed it to the ground, and loosened my grip around Leaf's neck ever so slightly.

Night noises of Bonerust floated through the air—snatches of drinking songs, laughter, an argument nearby—and I let my thumb stroke softly over her throat. A musky scent rose from her skin as her breath grew ragged from so little stimulation.

My pulse raced, heart pounding in my chest.

She was a liar. My nearness affected her. The evidence permeated the air.

"Leaf..." I groaned as pleasure spiked through my blood, and I snaked my hand lower, seeking her warm, wet center.

Sharp pain struck as she slapped my face so hard my skull thudded against the wall. Her hands formed fists at her sides as she drew a shuddering breath, realizing what she had done.

Attacking a king of the realms was an act of treason. On top of her escape attempt today, rules and common sense demanded I kill her without delay.

I could have—no *should have*—finished her off right there, freeing myself from this strange obsession. But instead, I pressed my palm against my cheek, its heat calming my rage.

Turning swiftly, I shoved her against the wall, my hand around her throat again. Like a demon caught in a trap, she spat a curse as her spine crunched against the stone.

"Listen to me." I pressed closer, caging her between my forearms braced on the wall. "Since you were nearly raped—"

"Oh, let me guess," she interrupted. "You think you're the right man to finish the job."

I sighed through my nose. "And this is how she thanks me for saving her life!"

"*She?* Is there another girl you're harassing around here?"

I let out a low laugh as she broke eye contact and stared at the ground between us. I watched the pulse beat at her throat.

She smelled so delicious, so tempting, and I longed to drink her down in one long, balls-tightening, mind-blowing draft. But I reminded myself that self-restraint was my specialty. Or at least it *had* been until the day I stared into fury-filled green eyes through the bars of a gilt market cage.

At the side of my vision, fae stirred with interest, and I was glad of the hood covering my head, hopefully concealing my identity. Anyone who recognized me likely knew the consequences of drawing attention to my presence, so kept their mouths shut and gazes fixed elsewhere.

"Let me begin again," I said. "You've had a bad day. But every misfortune was of your own making, and it seems you don't learn from your mistakes. When we return, know this: you will feel the sting of my anger in equal measure to the force of your slap."

Her eyes widened, then she shook her head with resignation and collapsed like an exhausted stray kitten, soft and pliant in my arms as I picked her up and returned quickly to my horse.

"Wrap your arms around my neck," I said.

She obeyed, and power licked over me where her cool fingers touched my skin.

To secure her in the saddle, I took a rope from Yanar's saddlebag and bound her waist to mine with care.

On the journey back to Coridon, I would allow her the sleep she needed.

But when we reached my chambers, well, that would be another matter entirely.

Chapter 17

LEAF

"You fool," the Sayeeda said, her nails digging into my scalp as she washed my hair with rough movements. "What were you thinking, destroying the king's trust like that?"

Water splashed in the copper tub as I hugged my legs to my chest, my kneecaps sticking out like pale mountains rising from a sea of lavender and rose petals.

I willed tears away, refusing to let them spill onto my cheeks. I wasn't afraid of what might happen to me, only burning mad at myself for getting caught. Just my luck that the hole at the bottom of Bonerust's so-called Gin Gates led into a tavern courtyard frequented by unsavory types. They'd been raucously pleased to pluck me off the ground and deliver me into the meaty paws of their boss, the vile smithy.

"But I had to try, Ari. Please don't be mad at me. I bet you'd have done the same thing if you were in my position, shackled like a criminal in a gilded prison. I know you would have."

"Stupid girl, we *are* in the same position, only *my* bonds are invisible, forged by traditions, linked by tenets and rules, and hammered in place by the weight of my love for my people."

I swiveled to face her. "But unlike you, I've made no such bargain. I was stolen from my life. *He* purchased me like I was nothing but cheap livestock for the slaughter."

Water poured over my face as she rinsed my hair. "Smart folk learn to judge when to fight their circumstances and when they should shut up and make the best of them. Jumping out that window today was an ill-timed decision. Arrowyn was beginning to trust you."

"Is he very angry?" I whispered, not really wanting to know the answer.

"Did you think he'd be happy he had to rescue you from another man's clutches? Of course he's mad! I've never seen him so enraged." She pinched the edge of my jaw and shook my head in frustration. "Arrowyn may be ruthless, but fortunately for you, violence does not bring him the same pleasure as it did his father."

I supposed the Sayeeda would know.

"Why didn't you set the guards on me as soon as you realized I'd jumped? Surely you must hate me for taking away your reason to visit the king each night with his medicine."

"By the gold, why would I?" She snorted. "I have enough duties to fill my days and nights. I'm glad you soothe Arrowyn's nightmares. And contrary to what you think, I don't want you to perish." She dipped her chin, lowering her voice. "When you escape, you must have a solid plan, one made with allies who will ensure you won't get caught."

A strange emotion swam in her eyes. Perhaps I only saw what I longed to, but that look could be interpreted as a promise. Was the Sayeeda hinting she was the ally I badly needed?

"Come, get out of the bath before your skin wrinkles like an old man's ball sack and Arrow has another reason to be angry with me."

A towel wrapped around my body as I stepped from the tub, water pooling on the floor at my feet. Ari helped me dry off, then applied a pungent ointment to my scrapes and bruises.

I swallowed hard, then took a breath for courage. "How did he punish you for not calling the guards straight away?"

Ari sighed. "In three days' time, my dearest friend was to make her yearly visit to Coridon, but... no longer."

Guilt filled the hollow ache in my chest. "I'm so sorry, Ari."

She spun me around and handed me the outfit of golden bandages that I despised, which, of course, was Arrow's favorite.

"If there was even the slightest possibility that you would find your freedom, I would do it all over again. Get dressed. And hurry. The king will be here soon."

Before she left, she locked my chain to the center of the pavilion, giving me a final piece of advice. "Pretend to be who he wants, Leaf. That is your first step forward on the path home."

The warm night air brushed my skin and bright stars winked down from the black sky as I sat on the tiles and awaited my fate.

On the edge of the pavilion, one of the mysterious black and gold feathers that often appeared from nowhere danced in the breeze. I picked it up and trailed the soft tip along my cheek and mouth, inhaling the rich, musky scent, wondering what desert bird smelled so good.

Without warning, the elevator doors clanged open, and Arrow stepped into the sitting room. Silently, he glided like a forest panther toward my lofty prison. As he moved, he stripped off his molded leather armor, revealing the plate of gold feathers that rested against the muscles of his chest.

Feather glyphs floated over his skin as he tugged off his belt, then tossed it to the floor. Thankfully, he kept on the tight leathers that hugged his thighs and other interesting parts of the male anatomy.

For now.

As he walked over the footbridge, I scrambled to my feet, studying his movements. His limbs seemed too loose, his gait far too relaxed for a fury-filled fae, hell bent on revenge.

Wearing a smirk, he stopped about a foot in front of me. He swayed slightly as his hand whipped out and snatched the feather from my grasp, tucking it into his back pocket next to the smallest of his obsidian blades.

"Don't look so worried, little Leaf," he drawled. "I'm not going to murder you. Not tonight, anyway."

"You're drunk," I said as realization hit me. His lazy smirk, the unsteady swagger and slightly unfocused, mocking silver gaze were evidence that the Storm King was smashed on fae wine.

"Still tempting fate?" he asked.

Damn. He was right. Tonight of all nights, I was in no position to criticize him.

He stepped closer, looming over me as he ran a fingertip down my cheek, neck, shoulder, all the way to my wrist. "Look what you've done to yourself, marred your lovely skin."

"A small price to pay if it meant I might not be a prisoner anymore."

Shut up, I told my unruly tongue. *Please, just shut up.*

A sigh parted his lips. "Why are you so determined to leave? I don't beat you or make you scrub my floors and wash my walls until your back breaks."

"Sometimes I think I'd prefer it if you did."

Resting his hands on his hips, he chuckled. "No, you wouldn't, foolish human," he said. "What am I going to do with you?"

"You could let me go."

"Where?"

"Home."

He slid the gold strap off my shoulder. "You don't even know where this mythical *home* is. Could be anywhere."

"I would find it."

"Yes, you probably would, if you didn't get fucked and mutilated by half the fae in the land before one of them decided to shut your belligerent mouth up for good."

"Are you any different from these men who plague me?"

"Of course," he said huskily, silver eyes flashing in the darkness. Then he stilled. "Are you saying someone's taken you against your will before?"

I nodded. "He didn't rape me, but he would have if he hadn't been stopped."

"A man from your old life?"

"No. In the Underfloor cell. Another slave."

Before I could blink, he jerked me close, cruel fingers biting into the flesh under my chin, forcing me to meet his steely gaze. What I saw burning in those silver orbs terrified me. Why did I open my big mouth?

"*Who?*" His fingers dug deeper. "Tell me who did this."

A shudder rolled down my spine, the urge to flee following in its wake. "You saw your guards attack me that night."

"Liar. That didn't happen Underfloor. Give me a name or by the gold, I'll find every male slave still alive that was in that cell with you and rend their bodies apart piece by piece, guilty or not."

My mind raced. I couldn't bear the thought of Arrow stealing my revenge from me, but worse was the thought of blameless souls paying for one man's despicable act.

"His name was Davy," I grudgingly admitted.

"Last name?"

"I don't know it."

"But he was sent to the mines?"

"Yes."

"Then he is likely already dead. Cast him from your thoughts," Arrow said, his voice silky, but an unnerving shadow flickering over his hooded gaze.

A shiver skated down my spine as he tugged my top below my breasts, exposing me to the cooling breeze. My nipples pebbled instantly, and Arrow's eyes fluttered closed, then cracked open as he tugged me forward, closer to his heat.

"Try to be good, and this may not go so badly for you," he said against my lips, his hand cradling my skull as his mouth forced mine to open with a perfect, mind-spinning kiss.

"You have a strange idea of punishment," I whispered when he broke away and cupped my breasts, his thumbs grazing the hardened peaks.

He grunted in reply, and despite my best efforts to remain unaffected, the rough sound made heat pool low in my stomach. Why did he have to be so magnetic, his arrogant face so breathtaking?

His beauty was excessive. Almost sickening. And only made me hate him more. At least that's what I told myself as my knees weakened and I fell farther into his embrace.

I kissed him back with clumsy enthusiasm because the terrifying, wonderful things he made me feel transported me away from this prison. Made me forget I was a human with no name in a city full of supernatural predators.

I hated Arrow. *Hated him* with a passion. And yet, right now, I felt like I would die if he didn't touch me and fill the ache inside me.

Obviously, my mind was a mess. Awash with relief that the Storm King wanted to torture me with his kisses instead of a variety of sharp instruments.

I moaned as his tongue brushed mine, first soft and then demanding.

"Yes, that's it," he said, smiling against my lips. "Let go."

His hand palmed my breast, then traveled slowly down my stomach, coming to rest over my molten center. His smug smile skated over the side of my neck as he discovered the evidence of my body's betrayal, no doubt delighting in my blatant need for *more*... more pressure... more of *him*.

No matter what I did, I couldn't seem to get enough of his touch.

"Arrow..." I moaned, lifting my hips.

"Leaf," he whispered, a hint of amusement in his voice as his thumb stroked over the damp material of my pants. The bastard was enjoying my undoing. "Off with these," he commanded, tugging the edge of them.

Wriggling my hips, I slid the material down to the tiles, my eyes locked on his. Although it would cost me my pride, my self-respect—my only possessions of worth—I wished he would

hurry up and make me forget everything. Everything except...
him.

He bent and ripped my pants away from the chain still attached to my ankle, then when I was naked, turned me carefully, inspecting my body. His finger traced my lower spine, and he made a tsking sound. "This bruise on your back is especially bad. If I knew who did this, I would—"

"What would you do? Kill them like you did the blacksmith?"

The wildness in his gaze told me that was exactly what would happen.

"Prepare to punish yourself then, King Arrowyn."

A frown creased his brow. "I... I didn't do this."

"You did. When you slammed me against the wall in Bonerust."

His breath hitched. "I was angry... afraid for you. I shouldn't have been so careless... All I want is for you to stop disobeying me."

Ari's words swam through my mind. *Pretend to be who he wants. That is your first step forward on the path home.* As much as I disliked it, deep in my heart, I knew she was right.

"Instruct me, and I promise I will do your bidding without complaint. I'll give you my complete obedience tonight as penance for—"

"For what? Your betrayal of my trust today?" Flames from a sconce lit up his eyes, and they darkened from mirror-bright to slate gray as he released a rough sigh. "Fine. Come here."

I closed the small distance between us, and he wrapped a hand behind my neck, taking control of my movements while his other hand snaked up my body to knead my breast. Slowly, he teased his hardness against me, squeezing my sensitive nipple until I moaned his name with shameless abandon.

A chuckle grazed my ear. "You enjoy that—pleasure laced with pain." A statement, not a question.

Fever gripped me as he pressed hot kisses over my chest, then suckled my nipple deep, his tongue teasing, making me writhe and burn. With a curse, I surrendered completely, bucking against his fingers as they danced over my drenched folds.

"Oh, God," I moaned, and the asshole had the nerve to laugh.

"Nice of you to remember."

That he was a god? No, Arrow was most definitely not a god, despite what his deluded courtiers believed. But... if it stroked his ego, I'd be willing to call him anything to further my cause. Which I reminded myself was to gain his trust again, not satisfy my own reckless and disturbing urges.

"Would it please you to be called a god, King Arrowyn?"

"No... not a god. Say my name... just... Arrow."

I smiled and trailed my finger down his chest, skirting around the poisoned feathers. "Then let me feel you, Arrow," I said in a husky whisper as I pressed my palm against the bulge in his leathers.

With quick, rough movements, he tugged at the laces on his pants, then his erection sprang free. Dust be damned, it was thick and long, with veins pulsing beneath a glyph that snaked around the length, reminding me of forked lightning. I wondered if it would be painful to touch.

"I won't hurt you," he rumbled, noticing my fear.

I had no clue if I'd ever touched a man in this way before. When I took him in my hand, would he feel my inexperience? And if so, would he throw me to the fire pits if I couldn't satisfy him?

Carefully, I encircled his girth, the velvety feel of his skin a shock as I shifted closer to his heat. A bolt of energy slammed into my chest, the warm buzz of Arrow's power spreading through my limbs.

My thumb rubbed the bead glistening on Arrow's tip, and he gritted his teeth.

"Wait a moment." He collected cushions and piled them on top of each other in front of me, then hard fingers gripped my shoulders and pushed me down. "On your knees, my trembling Leaf."

I stared up at the king, his feather breastplate gleaming on his bare chest in the moonlight. Thunderclaps echoed across the sky as his rod bobbed above my face, storm energy sizzling around his hips.

I swallowed nervously, lifted my hand, then let it fall to my thighs.

His eyes narrowed. "Didn't you just promise to obey me?"

I nodded.

"Then take me in your mouth," he said, his voice strained and body vibrating with unslaked lust.

Thunder crashed again, shaking the roof of the pavilion.

"I don't know how to please you this way." My voice was low and husky, and I sounded disgustingly eager to learn. I couldn't remember if I'd done this with a man before, but right now, all I wanted was to taste him.

He grasped my wrists, placing one of my hands on his hip, securing the other at his thick base. "Lick, suck, kiss. I promise you can't go wrong."

My heart pounded against my ribs, my mind spinning at the thought of what I was about to do. I closed my eyes and angled his pulsing length toward my lips, then pressed a kiss against the tip, tasting his salty essence.

"Gold's sake," he cursed, his hips bucking once.

Emboldened, I licked along his veined shaft before wrapping my lips around the broad head. I moaned as moisture pooled between my thighs and magic buzzed on my tongue, a strange but wonderful sensation.

As his fingers weaved through my hair, his stomach muscles twitched, and he muttered curses that I suspected made no sense in any of the realm's languages.

Guided by each sound and movement he made, I got to work, swallowing as much as I could, then slowly drawing back. When I bobbed on his length, his fingers seized my throat in a tight grip, holding me in place, rocking into me, using my mouth for his pleasure.

"Reavers. You're too good at this," he said. "You're fucking ruining me. When I explode, you'll take my seed and swallow every drop. All of it, understand?"

I tried to answer, to tell him I'd do anything he wanted, but all I could manage was a muffled, "Yes, Arrow," making him huff out a desperate-sounding laugh.

Then he thrust into my mouth, while I clung to his hips and tried to relax my throat. Thunder crashed against the golden pillars as blue light buzzed around our bodies, wrapping our limbs with such fiery heat I thought I might pass out.

He jerked and shook, cursing and muttering my name, his breath sawing out of him. Then with a full-throated moan that shook me to my core, the king came apart, his essence pouring down my throat. I swallowed as fast as I could, but some escaped my mouth, dripping down my chin and my breasts.

I watched him shudder, thrilled by the power I had over his body, and I finally understood what Ari had been trying to tell me. A man might grant many favors to the person who helped him lose himself so thoroughly. Slave or not.

I trembled at his feet, waiting for Arrow to touch me. For him to take me apart, just as I had done to him.

Slowly, his breathing settled. He smiled down at me, an unnamed emotion glittering in his eyes.

He ran his thumb over my lips, and I opened my mouth, panting for more. He slid it in, and I sucked hard before he dragged it out with a popping sound.

"Time for your punishment," he said, running his wet thumb over my chin, his gaze filled with wicked promise.

Good. The sooner he freed me of this ache the better.

"What will you do to me?" I asked, waiting to hear the lewd act described in his deep, rumbling voice.

He gave me a crooked grin as he tucked himself back into his pants, then prowled along the bridge toward the living room.

When he returned, a towel hit my chest. I said nothing as I took it and cleaned the mess from my body. Metal clinked as Arrow threw another chain on the ground, thumping down a flagon of wine beside it.

"I'll fix these chains to your wrists and your other ankle, splay your limbs wide so you can't press your thighs together and soothe away the ache."

My heart leaped. "What? No. That's not fair..." I let my words trail away as he moved my limbs like I was a rag doll. He quickly pinned cuffs in place, chaining me to them, then spreading me out like a five-pointed star... like the fucking fool I was.

Every teasing brush of his fingers caused shock waves to ripple through me, my core clenching. The urge to have his body pressed against me, pushing *into* me, was an agonizing, visceral need.

"Arrow," I said when he stood up and stretched his powerful frame above me. "Don't leave me like this. Don't let your

Sayeeda see me this way in the morning. I know how much you care for her. I once saw you breathe her scent from a piece of clothing like it was the last drops of a life-saving elixir."

The wine flagon stilled halfway to his mouth. "Ari's clothing? When did I do such a thing?"

"After she fixed your cloak in the kitchen that night you and Raiden visited."

His deep laugh echoed through the night, the sound rippling over my body like a breeze across the surface of a river. "You're mistaken. It was your scent I wanted from the cloak, Leaf. You had been wearing it. Remember? I specifically asked her not to wash it."

I stared up at him in astonishment.

"You've a dirty mind." He smirked. "I've never touched Ari in the way that you imagine."

Another gulp of wine, then he straddled my bare body and bent and sucked my nipples, giving both equal, fervid attention, the tickle of his long hair lighting flames along my skin. Bumps prickled over me, and heat surged through my blood like poison, my stomach twisting in knots of frustration.

"Are you doing this because you're too drunk to continue?"

By the bulge in his pants, I knew this wasn't the case. But I'd never seen him so intoxicated before, and I was curious to know what sorrow he was intent on drowning.

"Shhh, stop talking. You'll only make things worse for yourself. I must check my work." He plunged two fingers inside me, and I ached for three or four. "So wet for me," he rasped.

Feverish, I writhed against them. Once. Twice. Squeezing my muscles around him, desperate for relief. Then ever so slowly he withdrew his fingers and stood up, grinning.

He made a noise of disapproval, stepping away from me. "You've been a very bad girl. And tonight, you're finally being punished for your transgressions."

"Arrow!" I thrashed against my restraints. "Fuck you!"

He breathed a laugh through his nose. "You wish."

"If you let me go," I said, all my pride dissolving, "I'll do anything, kiss every inch of your body all night long if you want."

A winged brow lifted. "A tempting offer." He took another long drink from the flagon, then raised it in the air as if making a toast. "Which is why I need to drink a whole flagon of this cock-numbing rubbish—in order to say *no* to you. Because tonight, Leaf, you must suffer." His gaze raked my body. "Don't worry. You will take your pleasure another day, when I allow it. And after you've begged hard enough and long enough."

"I hate you."

"I know," he replied.

"I'll *always* hate you," I insisted, thwarted lust making me reckless. I wanted to inflame him, make him change his mind and ruin me completely.

"So be it," he said, dousing the spark.

He tossed a blanket over me, arranging it quickly so it covered all but my neck and head. It was so *nice* of him to keep me warm. The prick.

"Sleep well," he said, walking backward toward the footbridge, leaving me spreadeagled like some virgin tribute.

"I doubt I will."

He laughed, his body a hulking silhouette in the moonlight. "Don't attempt to escape again. If you keep pushing me, eventually, I'll have no choice but to throw you to the fires."

"I had good reason to want to leave. Esen tried to kill me at the gold foundry."

A hard breath rushed out of him.

"That's right," I said. "Your blue-haired guard dog went against your orders. If Raiden hadn't arrived when he did, I'd be dead, melted into sheets of gold, and not your problem anymore."

"And you're sure Raiden saw this?" he asked, a muscle twitching in his jaw. "He never mentioned it."

"Yes. Definitely."

The king raked a hand through his messy hair. "So, the three people I trust the most have betrayed me. Fantastic."

"Well, at least you know what to expect from me," I said, the downturned corners of his mouth causing pity to surge in my chest. "I'll betray you every chance I get."

"One day, Leaf, that might change," he grumbled.

"I wouldn't hold your breath."

He made a scoffing sound. Then stalked toward the elevator, leaving me alone with my damp thighs, the taste of him on my tongue, and one idea tumbling through my mind on repeat...

Arrowyn Ramiel was far from a god.

He was an asshole, through and through.

Chapter 18

ARROW

Storm energy circled my limbs as I stomped along the passage toward Raiden's chambers. My rage manifested in fiery showers of blue sparks that swirled around me unbidden, the heat in my blood almost unbearable.

Try as I might, I couldn't expel the sight of Leaf on her knees from my mind, couldn't stop remembering how she'd looked and felt with her lips wrapped around me. Those memories, coupled with the fact that one of my oldest friends had almost killed her, were fucking torturing me.

It took all my willpower not to return to the pavilion, bury myself inside her, and fuck her until every last scrap of hate had left our hearts—even if it took a week and nearly destroyed us.

Everything would be simpler if I just threw the little human into the fires. I knew my inner peace would improve tenfold. But I couldn't do it. I just fucking couldn't.

"Move," I barked at the guards flanking Raiden's doorway. They scuttled sideways, flinching when I slammed past them into his chamber.

"Raiden! Get out of bed."

He jolted upright, the bedcovers pooling around his bare waist. "What's happening? You're lit up like a bonfire. Is the city under attack?"

I inhaled and sucked the storm energy inside me, the air crackling as magic moved through it. "Not Coridon. Only you and Esen."

"Fuck." Swinging his legs over the edge, he sat on the bed and rubbed sleep from his eyes. "Let me get dressed."

"Don't bother. Why didn't you tell me Esen tried to kill Leaf at the foundry?"

"*Why?* Because I didn't want you to turn her into a pile of fucking ash. I was protecting her."

I couldn't fault him for that. He'd always had a soft spot for Esen. I did, too. Someone had dumped her at the city gates when she was a child, and Raiden's parents, who'd had no luck conceiving more children, jumped at the chance to foster her.

But even as a seven-year-old, Esen had been ruthless, biting chunks off her foster parents and attendants as she'd struggled to adapt to her new home. She was ruthless, yet rarely suffered consequences. And lack of suitable punishment had turned her into a scowling, self-righteous tyrant. A living warning against over-indulgent parenting.

Tonight, that would all change.

I couldn't kill Esen, but I could certainly scare the hell out of her.

"I've felt like shit hiding this from you, Arrow," said Raiden, his dark eyes pleading. "My magic has dried up. I can't sleep."

Letting him sweat, I paced across the room before stopping at a wall of bookshelves. I selected a volume with a gold-embossed spine, then turned it over and studied the cover.

"Mayrian's Golden History of Reaver Elves." I smirked as I read the title. "Is this entertaining? If it contains a chapter on reaver elf courting practices, be sure to read it carefully."

A grin spread over his face. "You're mocking me about Ari. Have you forgiven me, then?"

"Not in the slightest. But I do understand why you kept it from me. In your place, I'd have done the same. Esen's crime is another matter."

Raiden shot to his feet, stumbling as he shoved his arms into an embroidered robe. "Arrow, think of all she has done for you—"

I pushed my palm out, halting his advance, then opened the door and called a guard inside. "Take three other guards with you and go to Esen's room. If you don't want your eyes knifed out, you must restrain her, then bring her to the Gates of Amon without delay."

"Arrow..." Tears brimming in his gaze, he squeezed my arm. "Please, not the fires."

I patted his back. "Come, we'll meet them at the Gates."

"Will you at least let me get dressed first?" he asked, sweat beading his brow.

"Yes. If you hurry. I'll be waiting in the stables." In the doorway, I turned back to him and drew the night clouds closer, reigniting the storm magic in my chest so it sizzled around my body again. "Raid, if you ever keep anything important from me again, especially if it concerns Leaf, I'll burn you to a cinder."

Face grim, he nodded. "Understood."

During the brief journey to the crater in the desert, which was known by all in my kingdom as the Gates of Amon, I drove my horse, Yanar, at a punishing speed. Mainly to stop Raiden from begging for Esen's life the entire way, something I was in no mood to endure.

Burning for as long as Light Realm fae could remember—thousands upon thousands of years—the pit of flames was visible glowing in the desert from some distance.

When we arrived, we dismounted downwind, the heat of the fires unbearable as we stared transfixed at the flames that licked the edge of the deep crater. The two largest pyres burned in the middle, embers flowing around them, a sea of brilliant lava.

Raiden appeared at my side. "You're not going to throw me down there, are you? It's too fucking hot."

I grunted. "No. Unfortunately, I still need you."

"Because I'm the only one who laughs at your jokes," he stated dryly.

"I wasn't aware that I made any. Listen, when Esen arrives, just follow my lead. All will be well. I promise."

He huffed out a hard breath and nodded. "I know you don't want to hear this, so I'll only say it once. Please try and remember her past. Forgive her mistakes. She'll learn from them, I'm certain of it."

I nudged his shoulder with mine and pointed. "They're here."

In the distance, five horses moved toward us, the rider up front holding a torch on a long pole. Before long, the guards pulled their horses to a halt and dismounted. Then they helped a trembling Esen slide from a steed that glowed like liquid silver in the moonlight.

With her wrists tied together, she was barefoot and dressed only in a robe. Esen's magic connected to the thunderhead cloud above, and weak forks of lightning curled from her fingertips.

All Light Realm fae possessed storm magic of varying degrees and strengths, and we all paid the same price for using it. Extreme depletion of energy that could only be recharged with sleep, careful dosing of serum, or by experiencing strong, pleasant emotions.

With each use of the immense and destructive power, storm fae risked being consumed by it. Fire and ice roared through the wielder's veins, shuddering painfully over their sinews and bones. And if not well-stabilized, the force could kill them within seconds.

Over generations, great power had been honed in my bloodline, making powerful kings of my ancestors and me the strongest magic wielder in the realm.

As a child, Esen's power was so strong she could have trained to become one of the city's lightning wielders who fed the auron kanara. But no amount of storm magic would save her from my wrath tonight.

"Come forward, Esen," I said coldly.

A gentle smile of reassurance on Raiden's lips, he squared his shoulders and nodded at her.

Esen stared at my boots, her face pale with fear. "Please, Arrow," she said, dropping to her knees. "I only wanted to protect you. To free you from the hold the human has over you. How can I make amends? I'll do anything. Anything you say."

"Enough," I boomed as lightning flashed, a bolt forking into the middle of my chest. Thunder crashed a heartbeat later.

I glared down at Esen, my face impassive. "You dared to raise your hand against my property. You knew I counted on your loyalty, your friendship, and yet you still betrayed and hurt me." I let silence hang between us while the scorching wind howled, whipping the desert sand into glittering, star-lit vortexes that eddied around us. "Stand up."

Esen's teeth chattered as I turned toward the pit of fire. "You wouldn't," she whispered. "Please, Arrow."

Terror contorted her features as I dragged her to the edge of the pit. She had betrayed me and needed to face the reality of the harshest consequences.

Hair blew over my face as I thought about what it would feel like to shove my traitorous guard into the flames. It was only what she deserved. And with Esen gone, it would be much safer for Leaf at my court.

Raiden called out, "Arrow, remember the persimmons."

"What?" I snapped.

"When we were children, remember how you hated them with a passion? Your mother made you eat them with every meal to strengthen your magic. And for years—even though Esen despised them too—she ate yours and never told a soul."

Images of our shared childhood flashed before my eyes. The sad girl Esen had been. Unloved, until Ildri took her in. Esen gagging on those fucking persimmons.

My mind was already made up. I didn't want to hurt her. I couldn't *kill* her. But I needed her to understand the gravity of her actions. And that my authority was law.

Esen had to be punished.

I clapped my hands together, a wave of magic exploding from my palms, and I directed it between her shoulder blades. "It pains me to hurt you, but your betrayal cannot go unpunished."

Her spine buckled as she cried out, her fingers clawing the air before she collapsed on the dirt, unconscious with her limbs jerking.

Drawing the energy inside me, I stepped back, and gestured to Raiden. "Return Esen to her chambers. The healers may attend her, and you can stay with her until she wakes. When she does, tell her that the next time she so much as looks at the human with ill-intent, I won't hesitate to send her through the Gates of Amon."

Raiden let out a long shuddering breath, then gathered Esen into his arms. "Thank you, my friend. I won't forget your mercy. Esen loves you. As do I. You must know that everything we do is to protect you."

Without responding, I turned away, my heart heavy with the knowledge that those who professed to care about me could be disloyal when it suited them. Perhaps this was a hard truth all beings faced—kings or not.

When Esen hurt Leaf, she may have convinced herself she was only protecting me, but jealousy was her unconscious motivation. She saw the human as a threat. And in truth, so did I. But for very different reasons.

There was nothing special about Leaf. She had no magic, hidden or manifest. No power. She was an unremarkable human, a member of the species who had killed my family. When I found her in Bonerust, I should have killed her without a second thought. But I didn't. Couldn't.

Why did she have such a terrible hold on me? Why did I care about someone I should despise? These were mysteries that needed solving.

First thing in the morning, I would send spies to scout the Earth Realm. If anyone was missing a gap-toothed troublemaker, my men would soon hear about it.

Then my curiosity would be appeased, and gold be willing, the girl's insidious grip on me would loosen. At least enough for me to breathe properly again.

Chapter 19

LEAF

"**H**as Arrow lost his mind?" I asked Ari as I rode beside her on a rather flatulent dappled gray mare. "Yesterday, I escaped, you hid it from him, and today he's letting us ride off together into the sunset, and I'm not even wearing chains. He's unhinged."

"This is a test. And I must point out that the sun is still high in the sky, so there's no sunset to ride into."

I huffed a laugh. Ari often took my words literally, context and nuance evading her. But what she said about Arrow rang true. This was a game. And the games he liked best were the ones where only he understood the rules.

"A test of what?" I asked. "How far I can flee on horseback as opposed to on foot?"

"Of our loyalties." Ari tucked a metallic wave of hair behind her pointed ear. "He's giving us a chance to prove we can be trusted."

"But can we?" I asked with a grin.

"Of course. Our most important task is to earn the king's trust back. The very last thing you should do today is ride away on that horse."

"I wouldn't get very far on her, anyway. She prioritizes flatulence over moving fast."

Smiling, she raised an eyebrow and steered her fawn-colored horse away from mine. "The king proves he is no fool by giving us the laziest mounts in his stables. But we will get you home one day, Leaf. Do not doubt it."

My heart slammed into my ribs, and I bounced clumsily in the saddle, out of sync with my horse's trotting motion. "*We?*" I asked, bracing myself for crushing disappointment.

"Yes, *we*. You have allies in this court. The time to utilize them draws near."

"Allies?" Shock prickled the tiny hairs on my forearms. "Who? The Storm Court fae don't care about me. They hate humans."

"There are very good reasons for some of them to want to assist you. When you are safer, I shall explain in more detail."

"*More* detail, Ari? So far, you've given me none."

She laughed and nudged her horse a little faster up a sand dune. Mine slowed to a walk and begrudgingly followed.

"Just be grateful these allies exist and learn to behave yourself around Arrowyn. I know it isn't in your nature to be compliant, but for all our sakes, please, Leaf, at least try."

"I will try. I *am* trying."

"Befriend the king, if you can. Out of all the Light Realm fae, it is he who despises humans the most because of what the gold chasers did to his family. Make yourself indispensable. That is all that matters for now."

"How was Esen punished?" I asked. "Did she at least lose her position as Arrow's personal guard?"

"No, but she's lucky to be alive."

That meant all Arrow likely did was threaten Esen, which didn't make it any safer for me to spend time alone with the blue-haired fae.

"What are we supposed to be doing today?" I asked, brushing a green-tailed insect off my nose and raising my brows at the Sayeeda's bulging saddlebags.

"Delivering spices and kanara feathers to a small village that functions as a leisure town for reaver elves who are between shifts at Auryinnia."

I wiped sweat from my brow. "You once said reavers eat the kanara feathers?"

"That is true. They enable our blood to absorb nutrients from other food. We couldn't survive without them."

That was... *interesting* information. "So, are auron kanaras kept in reaver cities?" I asked.

"No, the birds need to eat lightning, which only the Storm fae can wield. Because of this, thousands of years ago, it was easy for Arrowyn's ancestors to take control of them and make it an offense punishable by death to keep them outside of Coridon. We can't even trade in their feathers without special licenses. We reavers must live in accord with the Light Realm fae because without the feathers, we would die. There are, as you can imagine, complicated arrangements, laws and rules in place to maintain balance between our people. A certain number of reavers must reside in the mines at all times, feeding our blood to the underground rivers and burying the bones of our dead in the earth around them."

"And that helps form the large quantities of gold that the Light Realm own?"

"Correct. Without reavers, the King of Storms and Feathers and his land of dust and gold would be nothing."

My heart thudded slowly as that sank in.

"Why don't you get rostered for shifts in the mines?" I asked.

"The Gold Accords stipulate that a reaver elf must reside at Coridon at all times, a bonded servant to the king, who is highly valued by him and the court, venerated and protected."

"And that's you."

"Yes. Until my death, that shall be my fate. If any harm befalls the royal Sayeeda, the Gold Accord is broken, and that would bring... kidnappings of lightning weavers, war, famine, endless bloodshed for all of the five realms."

"Now it makes sense why Arrow hasn't punished you more harshly for not calling the guards when I jumped out of the window."

"Unless he wants his people to suffer upheaval, he will always show me great leniency. And we can use this to our advantage."

With this information spinning through my mind, we rode for another hour in a southwesterly direction from Coridon. We passed three small reaver settlements before stopping at a fourth that morphed from the desert like a shimmering mirage. It was nestled in a shallow valley full of tropical trees, and a bright blue river wound through it that reminded me of a serpent asleep under the blistering sun.

We passed through gates not unlike those at Coridon's entrance, but on a humbler scale. The rich colors of the town were striking and very different from what I remembered of my origins—a life lived in a subtle palette of green, brown, and gray.

"What's this place called?" I asked as we dismounted at a large rammed-earth building capped with a golden dome and circled by a series of similar smaller structures.

"Auron K," Ari replied.

"After the birds?" I gaped at the green palms and elegant metallic-skinned elves who greeted the Sayeeda with friendly smiles as they strolled past in the dappled shade. "That seems a little gruesome."

"Why?" she said. "Just because we eat their feathers? Don't be foolish. We revere the auron kanaras and treat them extremely well."

"I'm sure you do, while you're plucking all of their feathers out."

Ari's cheeks reddened. "They molt frequently, and we do *not* pluck them bald."

"I believe you. I'm only teasing." I looked around, searching for a more neutral topic. "How is everything kept so lush out here in the desert?"

"The same way Coridon does it, with underground streams and magic feeding the city. And we have our beloved river."

We unloaded our saddlebags and passed the packages to reaver elves who wore long golden robes and swords on their backs that were nearly as tall as them. They bowed to Ari and narrowed their eyes at me.

As we made our way toward the main domed building, I asked, "Why would the king let his valued Sayeeda travel without guards?"

"Reavers possess efficient methods of protection."

I grinned and raised an eyebrow, prompting her to explain.

Ari sighed. "We place cloaking spells around ourselves, energy fields that make us invisible. Targets are difficult to strike if assailants cannot see them." She smiled and opened the thin ceremonial cloak she wore over her usual gold dress. "And I have these."

A necklace of the same golden feathers that Arrow wore adorned her upper chest.

"Is that the king's breastplate?" I asked.

"No. This is mine. Arrowyn had it made for occasions such as this."

"Would you let me practice throwing one on the way back to Coridon?"

"Absolutely not." She tapped a golden feather. "I can't have you knowing the secret to plucking one from Arrowyn's plate and trying to murder him in his sleep, can I?"

Dust knew I'd tried many times, but the damn things never budged.

Inside the building that rivaled Coridon's Grand Hall in its abundant use of gold, scores of elves greeted us with great enthusiasm. I watched Ari's face light up when the reavers held her close, making me wonder if living with the Storm King was more difficult for her than she let on.

No doubt she felt lonely without her people.

The pain of longing contracted my ribs, and I closed my eyes and let my dream forest envelop me, the dark scent of decomposing pine needles teasing my nose. Distant laughter carried on the crisp Earth Realm air, the green-eyed boy's voice echoing as he called me to follow—to what place and for what purpose, I didn't know.

I shook my head to clear the vision and smiled as Ari introduced me to the reaver elves.

Surprisingly, during an elegantly raucous dinner, the elves treated me as an honored guest, not a disgraced king's slave. Their curious stares and constant questions were clues that they rarely, if ever, entertained human visitors at Auron K.

After our meal, Ari attended meetings with three solemn reavers, leaving me with a group of card players who taught me the complicated rules of their game and laughed at my many mistakes.

As the moon rose in a violet sky, we bid the reavers goodbye and departed Auron K, using Ari's magic to cloak us as we traveled. Along the journey, I pondered my conversations with the elves. Some of what I'd learned surprised me.

Arrow had earned the respect of his people, but his father, King Darian, and his heir, Karln, were more feared. According to rumors, before their deaths, they'd regularly treated slaves and courtiers cruelly.

On the outskirts of Coridon, we passed a rowdy group of drunken trolls and orcs who were heading toward Bonerust. Dread shuddered down my spine as one of them frowned and sniffed the air, unwelcome memories of the blacksmith's cell assaulting me. Fortunately, Ari's invisibility cloak held, and we passed by them without incident.

When we were alone again, I pushed the memories aside and concentrated on the sound of the ballad Ari sang in the lilting reaver language, her melancholic voice rising above the jingle of our horses' tack.

Just inside the golden gates of the storm city, Esen herself waited on horseback. Dressed in the royal guards' black and gold armor, her face bore the smile of a malevolent forest sprite who hoped to lead an unsuspecting wanderer off a cliff edge to their gory death.

"Welcome home," she said as Ari greeted her with a slow nod. "I was beginning to think you weren't coming back."

"What business is it of yours?" I asked.

Ari's horse led the way as Esen pulled her mount alongside my gray mare, whose stomach was rumbling ominously.

"Arrow instructed me to advise him of your return."

"Well, then," I said, giving her a bright smile. "You'd better hurry off and advise him, like the obedient servant you're pretending to be."

"That's a role we both must play. But let me warn you, the royal chamber slaves have expiration dates, after which time they become unpalatable to our kings, dispensable. A month maximum before they get fed to the fires. The really unlucky ones go to the gold mines, become gold eaters, addicts if they weren't already, and labor until their flesh rots from their bones. This is your future, human."

Surely she was speaking about the old kings of Coridon. Arrow was far from sweet and benevolent, but as yet, he hadn't beaten me, even after he recaptured me from Bonerust.

What he'd done was possibly worse—tortured me with his body, then left me to burn with unresolved desire, staked out like a virgin sacrifice all night long.

At some point, I'd make the asshole pay for that.

Esen nudged her knee into my mare's flank. "Your days are numbered, human."

"As may yours be, Esen, if you disobey your king again."

She snarled. "Arrowyn will always take my word over a human bed-warmer's. *Always.*"

"I guess we'll see about that," I said, smiling.

My thighs tightened around my horse's belly, and she released an overlong belch. Actually, the sound may not have originated from her mouth. Then off she trotted toward the stables, moving faster than she had all day.

For some time after I'd disappeared from Esen's sight, her outrage burned like hot daggers between my shoulder blades. An extremely satisfying sensation that was almost as gratifying as picturing her bitter scowl floating in a cloud of stench.

Chapter 20

LEAF

As I stared up at Arrow's empty winged throne three nights after my visit to Auron K, my resolve not to ask about his recent absence finally broke.

"Where has your king been hiding lately?" I said, turning to Ari, who sat at a table beside me on the floor of Coridon's Grand Hall.

Arrow hadn't returned to his chambers since the night he'd found me in Bonerust, and I was tired of waiting for someone to tell me whether he'd fallen off the edge of the kingdom or not.

"Thanks to you, Arrowyn is currently in the Sun Realm. The envoy whose eye you nearly took out was King Azarn's cousin, and let's just say he was more than a little upset by the assault."

"*Near* assault," I corrected, gnawing on a spicy chicken wing. I tossed the bone onto my plate. "Why does Arrow care what the Fire King thinks?" I asked. "I can't imagine him bowing before anyone."

Seated on my left, Ildri coughed to cover a laugh and muttered, "Except you."

Smiling, I raised a brow and waited for her to continue.

She cleared her throat. "We rely on the Fire Court's transformational magic to keep the portals open between our realms. And on top of your misdemeanor, Arrowyn killed Gorbinvar, who was a Sun Realm fae, so there was much to be atoned for." Ildri leaned closer. "The debt was paid in large quantities of gold and a night or two spent drinking King Azarn's wine to soothe his fragile ego."

Tonight, Ildri looked like a queen in a gown made of silver and gold scales and with a circlet of feathers weaving through her tumbling waves of red hair. Since the night I'd first seen her seated at the king's table, her frosty demeanor had thawed significantly. And I couldn't help wondering if she was one of my secret allies.

"The portals certainly explain how Arrow travels great distances and yet returns so quickly, often on the same day," I said, taking a sip of wine.

The Sayeeda made a strangled noise, and Ildri only nodded at me before turning her attention to the line of fae dancers weaving between the tables. Musicians tapped out a hypnotic rhythm on small goatskin drums they held high above their heads as they followed close behind them.

Ignoring the dancers, I drank more wine and crossed my legs carefully, so the chain attached to my ankle didn't rattle. I contemplated the sky through the arched windows, the night so black the throne room appeared to float in a sea of shimmering stars.

I didn't know what to make of the fact that Arrow had instructed Ari to chain me to my chair in the hall. Perhaps he worried that, in his absence, I would attempt to stab another courtier, which was a ridiculous concern. The Light Realm fae had storm magic, and all I had to protect myself with was my mildly ruthless nature.

I stared at the surrounding fae, their beautiful features morphing in the flickering candlelight. Framed by the gilded feathers and lightning decorating the circular walls, from one moment to the next, they looked like angels, then monsters. And I couldn't decide whether to be impressed or terrified.

Like Arrow, some courtiers' forms were more human-like, well-built and muscular. But many of them had twisted horns, metallic wings, and odd-shaped limbs and fingers. The orcs, trolls, and shape-shifting jinn had tangled mops of hair on their heads, but other fae wore elaborate styles that shone like spun gold. The latter were the high lords and ladies of the court, who looked down their regal noses at me at every opportunity.

All beings that inhabited the four realms were considered fae, including the reaver elves. Humans from the fifth realm, the Kingdom of Dust and Stones, well, we were just *human*, without magic or power, and viewed by most fae as little better than vermin.

Each fae realm had their magical specialty, unique powers expressed in the courtiers' physical attributes. But centuries of inter-species breeding and migration across courts had led to a varied and happy mix of inhabitants. It was the kings and queens and counselors of the realms who were obsessed with controlling borders, wealth, and power, their machinations creating untold anguish and misery for their people.

A few kohl-rimmed eyes flicked my way, but most fae, no doubt in fear of their king's wrath, ignored me, gossiping, singing, or dancing around me, as if I was invisible. Three fan-tailed ravens unaware of Arrow's rules, zipped between tables, then flitted around my shoulders, tangling strands of my unbound hair together.

"Away with you, wretched beasts," I said, smiling as I swatted at them. With high-pitched croaks, they flew through an archway and winged away over the city, toward the mountains. I patted Ari's arm, drawing her attention. "How many of these portals you mentioned are in Coridon?"

She laughed. "Oh, Leaf, your thoughts may as well be written across your face in cursive script. You're wondering where they're located and how easy it would be to cross through them, yes?"

My cheeks flushed. "Is it hot in here tonight?" I said, sucking in a big breath of frankincense-and-jasmine-scented air.

"Except for the Realm of Dust and Stones, one portal exists between each of the realms, linking them together," Ari said, then quickly added, "Mundane methods must be used to travel to the human lands, and other than sailors and traders, most fae have no wish to go there."

"Which means there's no easy way out of Coridon for me."

Ildri smiled. "Where there is need, cunning plans fall into place. As you know, gold chasers killed Arrowyn's family three years ago, when he was a young warrior of twenty-four. Now he wears a crown that he never wanted and spends his days with counselors instead of soldiers. He despises humans, but somehow, you are an exception. *This* weakness of the king's—his desire for you—will be your way out of his city."

I lifted my ankle, rattling my chain. "You're wrong. Arrow despises me the same way he does all humans."

Ildri squeezed my shoulder gently. "No. I think what he feels for you is similar to an obsession... and obsessions are exploitable. His trust is the key that will open your shackles. Do what you must to earn it. And do it quickly."

Arrow obsessed with me? Not possible. But then out of nowhere, a memory—something Ash, the boy in the forest, had once told me—echoed through my mind.

The difference between hate and love can rise and fall on a breath, a single heartbeat in time, the slightest shift of light and shade. People will do anything to control what they most fear. There is no point in hating them for it.

There was no point in hating them for it... I mouthed his words softly. I had no idea what my brother had meant, but the general idea seemed to align with Ildri's advice. If I could cast the right amount of lingering touches and admiring glances the king's way, he might eventually grow careless and leave me an opening to escape through.

Courtiers' rumblings rose throughout the hall, then as if my reeling thoughts had conjured them, the king and Raiden appeared on the dais above us. Arrow stood in front of the throne, its majestic golden wings sweeping on either side of his broad shoulders as though they were a living part of him.

Before he noticed me gawking, I swiveled around and faced the other direction.

"Ah, there she is—the troublemaker herself," Arrow boomed. "Feasting and drinking while I've been atoning for her crimes."

I swallowed thickly but kept my gaze on my empty plate.

"Raiden, bring the girl to me. I wish to look upon her and decide if she was worth the price that I paid to keep the peace between two kingdoms."

The courtiers laughed, and a moment later, Raiden appeared at my side. With a quick smile, he dropped to his knees and unlocked my chain.

"Don't worry," he said under his breath as he helped me rise. "Arrow loved every moment he pretended contrition and told the tale of *his Leaf,* who almost murdered their envoy. The Fire King is a fool. Arrow would have paid ten times the price for the chance to smear the insult of your deed over Azarn's smug face for three whole days and nights."

"Did you just try to comfort me, Raiden?" I murmured as we walked up the dais steps.

His dark hair swung over his face, almost hiding his smile. "Apparently, you're not quite as diabolical as you first seemed."

"Now you've really shocked me." I glanced back to the table where his mother sat staring at us with a blank, all-too-innocent face.

"What?" Raiden laughed. "With your violent attitude and prickly demeanor, you can't blame me for initially thinking the worst of you. And as much as I hate to admit it, he's been less agitated since you've been... how shall I put this, *diverting* him?"

The king slouched on his throne, tousled hair of copper and gold framing cut-glass cheekbones, his black leather-clad knees spread wide, and the golden feathers on his chest plate glinting in the subdued light of the hall.

It was almost a shame that before long, I'd have to stick a blade somewhere deep and painful in that startlingly attractive body. But all good things came to those who waited, and for now, I needed to try to make him *like* me.

As the intensity of his stare radiated over my skin, both my knees and my resolve to despise my captor weakened ever so slightly, which I supposed would make my job to re-frame myself as indispensable a little bit easier. It would be no real hardship to let this magnetic creature touch me all over.

To achieve this elevated status, I needed to bed the king with such authentic abandon he could think of nothing else but repeating the act over and over. I had to gain his trust and make him depend upon me for more than just soothing his nightmares.

I curled my damp palms into fists and reminded myself that fooling him was a type of vengeance in itself, albeit a rather cruel one.

As I stepped in front of Arrow, the kanara gong rang through the city, and a swirl of feathers burst from out of nowhere and eddied around the king's body like a halo, a jarring but mesmerizing sight that made me smile. The storm king was far from an angel.

Arrow selected a feather that had landed on his bare stomach and held it out to me. "A feather for my wandering Leaf."

Unsure whether he was accusing me of trying to flee again or reproaching me for my past attempts, I took the feather and tucked it behind my ear as Raiden bent and detached the chain from my ankle cuff. He handed it to the king before bowing and bolting down the stairs toward Ari's table.

Wearing a disarming crooked grin, Arrow patted his thigh, and I perched between his spread legs. He draped the chain around my neck as if it was a fine piece of jewelry, then ran his finger around the admittedly beautiful neck cuff.

"Yes, I believe I would pay the price many times over." He flicked the band of sparkling material that made a pretense of covering my breasts. "Although this outfit pleases me, I think I will order a dozen enchanting gowns for you to wear at court. Would you like that?"

"Thank you," I said, pretending gratitude as I inserted a feather that had floated onto my lap into the side of his crown.

His smile grew, then he kissed me. My head spun as his mouth gently opened mine. The entire court might have been watching us, but I pushed that thought away and gripped his biceps, shifting so that my weight pressed over his hardness.

Drawing a ragged breath, his silver eyes shot open. "Time for bed," he whispered against my lips.

I steeled my jaw and forced the protective shields from my eyes, allowing real desire to shine through.

"I've tried to punish you as I should, defiant human, spent countless hours picturing all the ways to hurt you. But cannot and will not. Not ever. Do you believe me?"

"Yes," I lied, watching his hand tremble with lust as he gestured for me to rise.

Fear clenched the muscles between my ribs, my heart pounding erratically because I was about to surrender to the Storm King. I prayed I could allow myself to do the one thing that pleased him the most... the thing I'd sworn I would never do.

Beg for what I wanted.

And what I wanted was to feel his heavy weight crush me as he moved inside me in long, punishing thrusts, while I dissolved in reckless abandon in his arms. Not too much to ask for, surely.

But if he kept me writhing on the precipice again, unless I begged... well, I didn't know what would happen.

And as the king led me from the hall, I wondered for the thousandth time if I had ever allowed a man to do such things to me before.

And if I hadn't, would Arrow be able to tell?

Chapter 21

LEAF

"There is more than one way to punish someone," said the king as he exited the elevator into his bedchamber with me draped over his shoulder like a living, trembling cloak.

Without ceremony, he dumped me on the bed. I flailed on my back, wriggling until I perched on the edge, and stared up at him with what I hoped passed for a sultry gaze.

As he loomed above me, his powerful muscles flexed, a storm brewing in his eyes, and for a moment, terror seized me. I was at this fae beast's mercy. If he lost control, he could kill me with a single click of his fingers, melt the flesh from my bones without raising a bead of sweat. It wasn't an overreaction to think that this might end quite badly.

Trying to look docile, I smiled sweetly, and he grunted a laugh in response.

I was in so much trouble.

He stepped closer, his fingers threading through the shorter hair on the right side of my head, tugging on it. "Why do you keep asking Ari to shave this side?"

I licked my dry lips. "I... don't know for sure. But I assume I used to wear it like that back home. The way it is now feels... wrong."

One side of his mouth curled up as he sifted through longer strands of my hair. His expression could be mistaken for the fondness a rich lord shows for their favorite pet, but I knew better. Thrilled by finally seeing fear shine in my gaze, Arrow delighted in watching me tremble.

As if in response to his mood, a storm gathered outside. Lightning flashed through the arched windows, veils blowing in a gust of wind, followed by the bone-shaking crash of thunder.

"Are you causing that fuss?" I asked, nodding toward the windows circling the half-moon of his bedchamber.

"Not intentionally. I know you won't believe this, but my purpose isn't to scare you. I want you to admit you're at my mercy. Say you're mine and no other's."

"That makes no sense. I'm human. You hate me."

A muscle in his jaw twitched. "Do I?"

I sucked in short, fast breaths, yet I couldn't seem to get enough air in my lungs. "Why would you want that from me?"

A king who looked like... *that* could demand obedience from countless others who'd act the part with greater conviction than I ever could.

"Not your business." He pushed my legs apart, knelt between them, and all sensible thought evaporated.

His thumbs stroked the edges of my gold pants, dipping under the material, teasing me. "Leaf?" his deep voice rumbled.

"What?"

"Tell me who you are."

As his torso pressed my thighs apart, I moaned—whether out of fear or pleasure, I wasn't sure. "I don't know."

"Stop lying." Warm breath caressed the shell of my ear, bumps prickling over my skin. "Confess, and I'll reward your honesty."

Confess? If I suddenly realized my identity, in a moment of madness, I'd probably shout it from my pavilion, and the whole Light Realm would know it, too.

"How will you reward me exactly? Set me free? Or help me find my home and my people?"

"No. The person you were is your past. This is your present, here, with me." His lips pressed against my throat, hot kisses moving downward. "You're mine to torment, Leaf. Mine to pleasure. *Only* mine. Understand?"

"If that's true, then why should you care who I was before you found me?"

His chuckle vibrated over the notch between my collarbones. "Someone wanted you to disappear. They took your life away, your memories. Hurt you. Sold you. And that person must pay. Tell me who they are. Tell me everything you remember, and I will ensure they can never hurt you again."

"I barely remember anything," I said, sighing. "A forest, a family that may already be dead. That is all. I promise you, Arrow."

"Liar," he breathed, his hand wrapping my throat as the other one traveled lower.

Calloused fingers slid through my mortifying wetness, and he groaned at the discovery.

I hadn't lied. But I'd omitted the information about Ash, my green-eyed twin. Whether he was dead or alive, nothing good would come of giving Arrow *his* name.

I couldn't satisfy the Storm King with information about my identity, but I could say other things that might please him.

"The only name I have is the one that you gave me. You named me, and as you've said—now I'm yours."

Squeezing my throat, he kissed me hard, his fingers stroking and teasing below to build a tumultuous storm inside me. Oh, gods it was horrible. My head spun as my stomach muscles coiled tighter. Shaking with need, I gripped his wrist, not sure if I wanted to remove his hand or keep it there all night long.

Chuckling, he slid his fingers from my pants and held my face between burning-hot palms, slanting his mouth over mine, demanding I succumb to his control. With a needy sound, I surrendered, giving in to the desire that snaked through my veins, giving in to *him*—to the Storm King.

This time, I tugged his wrist with a manic focus, certain of where I needed his attention. Where his touch would relieve me from the pulsing ache that wound through my core.

"Tell me what you want," he said.

"This feeling to end. Please, I can't stand it. Arrow, I need—"

"You need to come."

I wasn't sure what that word meant in this context, but I had a rough idea and a strange feeling that no matter what he did to me, it wouldn't be enough. I'd want more, more, more.

"How do you get the things you want, Leaf?"

"I ask nicely and say please, like you taught me." I hissed in a breath and forced the words he wanted to hear through my gritted teeth. "Please, Arrow, I need more."

"That wasn't so hard, was it?" He lowered onto his haunches, his laugh huffing against the drenched material of my pants, then with one quick movement, he tore them off.

With a hand on my chest, he pushed me backward and slung my legs over his shoulders, exposing me to the night breeze and his carnal view. I wriggled and tried to cover myself, but he growled and made a tsking sound.

"Let me look. Let me taste you."

Good gods. What was happening?

And then he bent his head and went to work.

First, he pressed soft kisses on my inner thighs, his breath tickling my most sensitive skin. When his tongue gently laved along my seam, I cried out, shocked at the sensations wracking through me.

His thumbs parted me, opening me to his ministrations. I bucked and writhed and moaned, a terrible, wanton heat rushing through my blood and pumping my heart faster. This felt wrong. Shameful. But I wouldn't let him stop for anything.

While he nibbled and sucked my flesh, his fingers fumbled at the fastenings of his chest plate, the golden feathers chiming as they hit the marble floor. The sound barely audible over my loud, ragged breaths and his low, animal moans.

I squirmed, levering my weight onto my elbows so I could see what he was doing. The sight of his head between my thighs, those beautiful lips moving over me, savoring my slickness, nearly undid me.

"So good," he whispered, curling two fingers inside me, another sweet torture.

I dropped my head back, my hips bucking as my thighs shook. I was so close to something that was both amazing and terrifying. So ready to come apart. "Gods, Arrow. Please don't stop."

A snarl vibrated against my skin, and he muttered curses as I ground against his face.

"Fuck, Leaf," he growled and shoved away from me, standing up.

"No! Arrow, come back," I said, squeezing my thighs together in an attempt to end the agony.

"Do not move or I'll lock you in the pavilion and stand over you, stroking myself to the sight of you lying there helpless and aching for me."

"You wouldn't."

"I most definitely would. Have you learned nothing about my nature?"

I let out a frustrated sigh. Of course the prick would do it and probably enjoy every moment.

The black leather pants were peeled off and thrown aside. Then he stood naked except for the gold bands and blue magic circling his arms, glyphs moving like dark blood over the muscled canvass of his moonlit skin.

Drinking me in, he laughed at my expression. My gaze fixed on the thickly veined length jutting proudly from his body, and as he gripped it in his fist as if to taunt me, I reached out to touch it. He swatted my hand away. "Did I say you could do that?"

I shook my head.

"Do you know what I'm going to do next?" he asked.

"I hope so. It better be what I think."

"First, I'm getting rid of this." He tore the stretchy bands of gold from my chest, then buried his face against my breasts, worshiping them with his lips, tongue, and teeth.

When he finally came up for air, his eyes were black and his breathing a mess. "You've done this with a male before?"

"I... I think so," I said, even though I wasn't certain.

"Good. Because from the moment you beg for it, I won't be gentle, little Leaf."

At his words, heat blazed down my spine, bursting in my belly, then pulsing lower.

"So, if I refused to beg, would you stop?" I asked.

He nodded. "And punish you in the way I described."

I couldn't bear to watch him slake his desire and not touch me. The raw sight and sound of him would be agony to witness. For the sake of my plan, I knew I had to beg. There was no other choice, and what was even more disturbing—I wanted what he offered. I wanted Arrow's power, his body to fill mine and make me forget for a night that I was a prisoner.

I could pretend to be a queen instead. The queen who ruled over him—Arrowyn Ramiel, my devoted king.

Self-disgust wormed through me. I was stupid to indulge in such pathetic, implausible fantasies. But before I could berate myself any further, his hands hooked under my arms, and he pushed me to the center of the bed.

Then he knelt between my thighs. "Beg me to claim you without mercy. Beg for what you need, Leaf."

As the broad head of him teased through my wetness, the barely there pressure maddening, making my hips lift, my self-control broke. "Please, Arrow, I need you now."

"Need what?" He slipped between my folds, and I gasped, then panted, clawing at his forearms.

"I need you to... I don't know what fae call it."

A chuckle rumbled in his chest. "The same thing it's called everywhere. Fucking. What you want, Leaf, is for me to fuck you."

"Yes." I ran a hand down his stomach, the cut muscles leaping under my touch. "Yes, I do. Please."

"Say it."

My head thrashed against the silky covers, the words hovering on my lips.

"Say. It." His tip edged inside me, then withdrew.

"Arrow! I can't."

With a growl and a hissed curse, he thrust hard, seating himself deep inside me. Pain knifed through my center as something tore inside me, the agony blinding. Lightning flashed outside, visible behind my tightly closed eyelids. He had split me apart. Broken me in two.

My breath hitched, and I bit down on my tongue, blood pooling in my mouth as I trembled in his arms.

Above me, Arrow stilled, his thickness like a column of marble inside me, and his grip around my waist excruciating as his muscles tightened.

A curse parted his lips, then a groan. "And once again, you lie. You *haven't* done this before."

"I couldn't be sure. You know I'm not afraid of much, so it seemed reasonable to assume that I would have."

He kissed my temples, the tip of my nose, then my lips with surprising tenderness. "This is as it should be. No other man has had you, and no other ever shall. You are mine. Only mine. To take. To use. To revere and worship. Hear my words, Leaf, for they are a spell that binds us. King to slave. Fae to human. Lightning to blood."

As his hips began to move slowly, he kissed the sighs from my lips, and praised me with each breath he took.

He told me I was beautiful. Willful. Powerful. Sweet and diabolical. And I was his. Only his.

A kind of joyous delirium built in my mind and muscles as I wrapped my arms around his neck and clung to him, undulating my hips to increase the pleasure, to reach the end, to keep experiencing it forever.

His bowed head lifted, his gaze boring into me, and I earned a grin for my efforts. "Fucking hell, Leaf. Yes, that's it. You take your punishment so well."

My hips bucked erratically, but he continued to thrust slowly. The pleasure of his body grinding against me, then the agony as he dragged back, leaving me empty, spun me into madness.

"More," I breathed. "More, Arrow. More."

He grunted, then laughed. "As you desire."

I more than *desired* it. I needed it in the same way I craved freedom. I would die if he didn't finish this and bring me down from the cliff edge as soon as possible. My heart would give out. My mind would crack apart.

His body shifted higher, seating himself more deeply, rubbing a spot inside me that wrung the breath from my lungs with a ragged moan.

He wrapped his hand over my neck cuff, then made a sound of frustration before moving two fingers in a quick pattern over it. The lock sprung open, and he tossed the shackle aside, cuffing my throat with his hand and holding me pinned as he pounded into me.

My thighs burned as I dug my heels into his back, the increased pressure exquisite.

"Are you trying to kill me?" he asked.

"Not right now. You've a job to finish."

Capturing my lips, he breathed a laugh into my lungs and began to move in earnest. He pulsed inside me, and I raked my nails along his shoulder blades, urging him on.

He pinned my wrists above my head and raised his upper body, the angle forcing him deeper. I bit my lip but couldn't hold back a scream. It was too much. Too wonderful.

His mouth seized mine, and he whispered against my lips, coaxing. "Relax, angel. Let go. Come for me."

He slipped a hand between our bodies, thrusting deeper and deeper, losing his rhythm and moaning and cursing. "I knew you'd feel so fucking good impaled by me. So hot and tight. Oh, little Leaf, your mouth tells lies, but your body always speaks the truth. It tells me everything. Everything. You love this. You love me."

"No," I said, shame fighting ecstasy inside me. "Because of you, I have no freedom."

"Yes. Tell me how much you despise me."

"I do. I—" I bit my lip, humming as his fingers went to the place I throbbed the most, his thumb circling, and the pressure sending shock waves along my spine.

He gripped my wrist and dragged my fingers to circle his base. "Feel me. Feel what I'm doing to you. Only I can bring you this pleasure. Only me."

He moaned—a low, filthy sound—then hissed a breath, his gaze intent where our bodies joined. "You are a small, fragile human, but feel how well your body takes me, bending to my will. Tell me this is the most blissful thing in all the realms." Another long moan. A husky curse. "It's all that is good and right. Tell me you agree."

The power of his thrusts shook my jaw. "Not like this," I said. "Not when I'm nothing more than your possession. It's wrong, and you know it."

His laugh vibrated in my core, pushing me closer to the edge. "Liar," he said. "You're a fucking liar."

His mouth slanted over mine, his fingers winding in my hair as I bit his lip, an iron tang coating my tongue. He swore, and I laughed. His blood was the same as mine. The King of Storms and Feathers tasted like a human. He wasn't invulnerable. If he bled too much, he would surely die.

I tensed, expecting him to retaliate, but he only groaned harder, pistoned faster. "So tight. By the gold, you make me burn."

Gods, the things he said. So raw and base, they made me blush as I writhed beneath him.

With his free hand, he squeezed my breast, his lips searing as they took the aching point into his mouth. An inferno raged inside me, lava flowing, needing to erupt before it destroyed me.

"Arrow," I moaned.

As I tugged on the silky mess of his hair, his thrusts turned vicious. Soon he would break me into pieces. Ruin me. I couldn't take much more. But why did it have to feel so damned good?

"Beg," he demanded. "Beg for mercy. Do it now."

"Please," was all I said.

"Let go for me," he commanded. "Come."

My lips parted on a broken cry as my muscles spasmed, coiling so tight the tendons felt like they would tear from my bones. White light, purple, then blue flashed around me as pleasure peaked in my core, my whole body pulsing with an intense sensation that felt like... death.

I was dying.

This was death and life and everything in between. And he, *Arrow*, was the god who controlled me.

The king threw his head back, and a low growl rumbled in his chest, turning into a roar as he froze, then he came in hard shudders that wracked his body. With every jerk of his hips, a warm wave crested inside me. Lightning streaked throughout the room, tiny bolts of blue forking over our skin.

As our convulsions eased, the king stared, his gaze flitting between my throat and my breasts. Deep, ragged breaths moved his chest like bellows.

I gasped as I felt him harden inside me again. Vicious silver eyes glittering down at me, he drew his head back, then his lips parted, revealing long, gleaming-white fangs.

A warm hand slapped over my mouth, muffling my scream.

Gods, was he a vampire? If so, how had he hidden it from me? This must be the punishment he'd spoken of. He planned to drain every last drop of blood from my body. I tried to bite the soft webbing of his hand and to butt him with my head. But I could barely shift a muscle. Arrow was too big, too strong for me to rise against him without a weapon. Or magic.

Whatever this was, I had no choice but to lie still and endure it.

In a rush, sounds, smells, and images of the forest washed over me, transporting me from the horror of bearing witness to my own death. I closed my eyes, my heartbeat slowing, and I let the humidity of the woods, the tang of pine needles, calm my panic.

An animal snarl vibrated against my throat, then two sharp fangs pierced my skin, sliding into my flesh. "Relax," the king whispered as his hips moved rhythmically and he drew on my vein. Soft feathers floated through the air, drifting over my skin, then landing on the bed.

"Don't move." A crude slurping sounded as he spoke, his voice muffled and hoarse. "Just feel me inside you. Remember what I said... I will never hurt you."

The pain subsided, and I was shocked to feel my core heat, a wave of desire cresting through my stomach and all the way to my fingers and toes as Arrow drank.

Another feral snarl vibrated over my skin, his focus on one thing only—the fulfillment of his need, his pleasure.

He might not have planned to kill me, but it would be so easy for him to take too much. To drain me dry.

And despite the dawning possibility of my death, my inner muscles pulsed in sync with the draw of my blood, another climax building, its intensity making me cry. Tears streaked my face, and Arrow's thumb wiped them away with the gentlest touch.

He swelled inside me, our bodies shivering then shuddering as my back arched off the bed, and his weight pressed me down again. Moaning, we came at the same time, warm wetness filling me as our breaths sawed from our lungs.

With my muscles still pulsing, I stared at the gilded-dome ceiling in shock as he licked my throat wound, then looked at me and grinned shamelessly. Stunned, I lifted my head, finding black and gold feathers scattered over my body.

"You bit me with no warning! You're an asshole," I said, forgetting the need to be nice and compliant so I could escape him forever as I slapped his smug face.

He laughed. "Am I? I didn't hear any complaints when I drank from you."

"So you're... what? A *vampire*?"

"I am fae, and the most powerful fae at my court bear fangs. All the better to increase your pleasure, don't you agree?"

"I'm not so sure." I eyed the red welt on his cheek with a sliver of regret, wishing my default response when threatened wasn't always instant violence. "Show them to me again."

"Kiss me, and I might." He flung onto his back and slid me a sheepish glance. "The fangs are connected to..." he waved his hand between our bodies. "... to fucking. I can suppress them, but in this case, I didn't want to. When I drank, I marked you. Now no other fae of power would dare touch you."

"You did what? And what about the fae with lesser powers? Could they touch me?"

"If they were foolish or somehow didn't recognize my mark, then they wouldn't live long enough to regret it."

"To do that... to mark me—whatever that is—without warning... it was wrong."

"I am king. I can do what I like, and it was worth your anger to ensure no other fae could claim you. I would pay the price a thousand times over."

I rolled my eyes. "Since you're so obsessed with *paying over and above the price* for things, if I never spoke to you again, would it still be worth it?"

Raising his upper body, he leaned on an elbow and laughed, trailing his fingers along the side of my face. "Yes. Now that I know what makes you sigh and moan, I could simply force you to talk to me."

I made a scoffing sound.

"Deny it all you like, Leaf, but the next time I touch you... the proof will be in your tears of ecstasy, your words of praise. May lightning strike me dead if I lie."

His confidence was astonishing, and I hated to admit, likely justified.

Lips curved in a smug shape, he tucked golden hair behind his ear, and I ran my fingers along its outer ridge to the tip. He seized my wrist in a bruising grip. "Don't do that."

"Why not?" I rubbed his ear firmly. "Does it hurt?"

Instantly, he hardened, drawing a ragged breath as his length pulsed against my belly. "If you're ready to have me drink from you again, then by all means, rub my ears, my reckless Leaf. Pinch and bite them, but don't say I didn't warn you."

I snatched my hand back and curled my body into him, flinging an arm over his waist. His throat bobbed in surprise, but he gripped my wrist that was tucked against his chest, his thumb stroking my skin.

"Where do the feathers come from?" I asked. "The ones floating around you in the hall tonight and while we were... you know... just now?"

"Fucking?" he said with an evil smile. "It's a side effect of my elemental magic. Certain emotional states draw the room's loose kanara feathers toward my body."

I thought of the scattered feathers in the streets and halls under the cages throughout Coridon. "I see." I considered my next question, then decided to risk it. "Arrow, are you going to put the collar back on me?"

Silence thrummed through the air for several moments. "When I'm not with you, yes, and perhaps sometimes even when I am present, for example, in my bedchamber. The cuff symbolizes who you belong to, and at times during our bed play, I will enjoy the sight of it around your pretty neck." His fingers strummed the large vein in my throat, but his gaze fell to my breasts. "Of course, there are other types of decorations I wish to see on your skin. White pearls would suit you in particular."

Unsure what he meant, I smiled at the gleam in his eyes that promised it was likely something shocking, and after the way I'd responded tonight, I imagined I might enjoy it.

"You're the king of the Light Realm, so why do you continue to show mercy to a slave?"

"Because tonight, when we were joined, I didn't care whether I was a king, a jinn, or even a gold-damned fucking human. All that mattered was how it felt to be inside you, hearing you cry out, feeling you shatter beneath me. I will always protect you, Leaf, from the discomfort of golden collars, from every fae in the realm, and even from yourself, if necessary."

But I didn't want his protection. I wanted to go home, with or without his help.

I wondered if he knew how frequently the thought of leaving consumed me, if he realized that if it came down to a choice between his life or my escape, I would slit his throat in a heartbeat.

I swallowed hard and pressed my palm over his cheek, gently, where I had hurt him. "Marked or not, collared or bare, you must know I still hate you." I spoke the words softly, like a caress.

I shouldn't have uttered them at all, and, yet, I still couldn't lie to him.

"Yes," he said calmly. "I know."

My fingernails pressed tiny crescents into his skin. "Nothing you do will change that, Arrow."

He scraped a length of hair away from my lips, stroking it behind my shoulder. "We'll see about that, my vengeful Leaf. We shall see."

Chapter 22

LEAF

Sheets of warm rain fell from the sky as I sweated through my morning exercises, the sound drowning out the restless chirping of the auron kanara. Whorls of steam rose from Coridon's streets, carrying the mouth-watering aroma of spices frying in the hawkers' pans up to the pavilion.

A haze of moisture muted the town's bold terracotta and jewel tones, and even settled the gold dust that often shimmered like fireflies over the undulating hills of the desert.

Light Realm fae, who rarely hurried, dashed between covered walkways and buildings, clutching their intricate hairstyles and gossamer silks, holding them in place. A wave of wicked satisfaction warmed my chest. It was nice to see them scurry around like roaches for a change.

When my muscles shook, I took a break from exercising and sat on the edge of the pavilion, kicking my heels as I watched chaos play out in the city below.

After a while, soft footsteps sounded on the stairs, and Ari approached, carrying a tray.

"He left you unchained again?" she said, raising a golden brow.

"Yes, as you can see." I grinned, shaking my ankle and proudly displaying the chain-free cuff, proof I'd been working hard to gain Arrow's trust.

"I thought you might like an early lunch today." Ari's lips formed a sly smirk. "When I delivered breakfast, you were still fast asleep beneath the king's bedcovers."

Heat flooded my cheeks, pooling low in my stomach. Ten mornings had passed since I'd surrendered to the king, and each one had begun the same way. For breakfast, we ate fruit with spiced yogurt, then for dessert, we had each other, gorging on fiery lovemaking until we couldn't take another mouthful.

Arrow had warned he'd wear me down, that I would beg for his touch, and beg I *had*, many times over, disgusted with myself because my longing for him was genuine. But debasing myself had the desired effect, and I was officially his favorite pastime.

Each day, as soon as he'd finished his kingly duties, he would return to his chambers and indulge my wildest desires. There was hardly a place in his chambers we hadn't made use of—his bed, the river, the divans, the floors. And I'd be lying if I said I wasn't living for the moments when his voice rumbled against my flesh, raising chills.

The times that I'd accompanied Arrow to court were the hardest. Playing the placid concubine, smiling when he stroked my hair or clamped an arm around my waist, wasn't a role I enjoyed or one that came naturally. My rebellious nature screamed for me to lash out and scratch his cheek. But a darker, immensely stupider internal voice urged me to lead him back to his apartment, where I could kiss him senseless in private.

Every night, I dreamed about his kisses, his rasped commands, and begged in my sleep for his bite. I craved the feel of him drawing my life essence through my veins in hot pulses.

Yes, I still hated him. But whether I was asleep or awake, only two things consumed my thoughts: the Storm King and my family in the forest. My twin obsessions—one of which I needed to kill to escape and the other I'd kill to return to.

"Leaf, snap out of it," said Ari, clicking her fingers in front of my face. "I have a surprise for you."

"In recent experience, surprises are more like shocks. Will this be another one of them?"

"Take a look."

I glanced down. Two knives glittered on Ari's tray, one with a blade of the sharpest obsidian. Smiling, she placed a bowl of water and a cake of soap on the floor between us.

"What are they for?"

"First, I'm going to cut your hair, and then I'll shave it. But only the right side, yes?"

I nodded, still wondering why I wanted to wear my hair in a style I saw no humans or fae at court wearing. "Why now?"

"Because the king asked me to."

As she swept my hair aside, the Sayeeda gasped, her fingers trailing over the area where Arrow had bitten me that first night. "Arrowyn did this?" she asked, her voice weak.

"Yes. I had no idea that he had a vampiric nature."

"He doesn't, strictly speaking. As reaver elves need the kanara feathers to survive, true vampire fae require blood as sustenance. He bit you, leaving this mark, for a different reason."

I pushed her fingers away and massaged the side of my neck. "I thought it had healed."

"The wound is fine, but in its place, there is a feather glyph, indicating he has marked you as his Aldara."

"His what?" I asked, blood rushing through my ears.

"His Aldara. His chosen. The word translates from old Coridonian as 'winged gift'. It is a bond stronger than the most tightly contracted of political marriages, breakable only by death."

"That makes no sense." Tears stung my eyes as panic swirled in my chest. "Why would he do that?"

She laughed. "There is only one reason, Leaf. So no other fae can have you." Taking up the serrated knife, she cut one side of my hair close to my scalp. "This development is good. He has come to rely on you, desire only you, which means it's now safe for us to plan your escape."

Ari swept a soft-bristled brush through a dish of water, soaping my scalp before scraping the short hair off with the obsidian blade. "Both Ildri and I will put the idea in Arrowyn's head that he should visit Auryinnia Mines and take you along. It would be a perfect opportunity to impress you with his power and skills of diplomacy."

"I wasn't aware he possessed any such skills."

Ari snorted. "Fortunately, most males cannot resist showing off in front of their women. I am confident he'll agree to take you."

"You'd better organize the trip before he gets bored and tosses me through the Gates of Amon."

"All you must do," she said, drying the right side of my head with a towel with rough strokes, "is keep smiling at him, enjoy the bed sport, and leave the rest to me."

I swiveled and frowned at her. She smacked my bare shoulder, turning me away again, then braided what was left of my hair down my back in a thick rope.

When she finished, Ari raised a mirror, and I leaned forward to inspect her work. A strange feeling swelled in my chest, equal parts sadness and happiness. "This... this is how I used to wear it."

"Yes." She smiled. "I know."

"Thank you." I jumped up and kissed her cheek, then gave her a quick wave as I sauntered toward the stairs.

"Where do you think you're going?" she asked, her palm pressing her face where I'd kissed her.

"I've arranged to meet Grendal at the Tarneeq Courtyard for a cup of apple tea and some kitchen gossip. Please don't object to her having a break from work. We won't stay long, and she'll be back before it's time to prepare lunch."

"Of course. Leaf, wait a moment." Ari beckoned me over and unstrapped one of the ornate daggers that hung around her hips. "You must wear this if you're going to traipse about on your own."

"But if someone sees me with it—" I started to object.

"It will be fine." She wrapped the knife belt around my waist over my thigh-length gold dress, securing it tightly. "After what happened with Esen, not even Raiden would challenge your right to protect yourself in the court, and Arrowyn would send me back to my people in disgrace if I didn't keep you safe. Take care and stay out of trouble."

"Thank you. I will."

As I darted down the stairs, my hand sliding along the carved marble balustrade, guilt gnawed in my stomach. A few days ago, Arrow had given me permission to leave his chambers occasionally, as long as I was in the company of Ari or a member of his personal guard, with the obvious exception of Esen, who he'd forbidden me to be alone with.

It was wrong of me not to share the king's conditions with Ari, but she knew Arrow better than me, and she should have realized he'd want his prized slave guarded.

No doubt she'd been distracted, too eager to rush off and plant the idea of a tour of Auryinnia in Raiden's mind. And probably whisper the suggestion in her low, sensual voice, directly in his ear.

Watching their interactions these past few days, I was now certain Ari's favorite occupation was giving Raiden a hard-on he couldn't do anything about. One day soon, the tension would break, Raiden would retaliate, and the serene Sayeeda's world would never be the same again.

That idea amused me, but as I exited an elevator and stepped into the Underfloor servants' hallway, the smile slid off my face. I had arranged to meet Grendal here to remind myself that no matter how much I despised being the king's pet, my living conditions had improved immeasurably.

As long as I behaved, I lived in unchained luxury in Arrow's apartment, enjoying the view from the pavilion and swimming in the indoor river. All the while dreaming of following the waterfall right out of that damned window again.

After Grendal greeted me with a hug, I studied her serum-dull eyes, noting the lack of flesh on her bones, the sallow complexion, and her vacant expression. She was a mirror of how bad things could have gotten for me if I wasn't immune to the gold.

"Are you all right?" I asked as we walked along the corridor. "Have they stopped feeding you?"

"Of course not. I don't feel hungry, that's all. I'm fine."

We stopped at a cage of dozing auron kanaras. "If you don't take care of yourself, you'll end up like these poor sad fucks."

Grendal snickered. "Why do you despise them? It's not the birds' fault they're imprisoned."

"I don't hate them. I pity them. They're reflections of our fates. We're trapped in the Storm Court just like them, our survival dependent on the whims of a stronger species."

"For me, it's not so bad here." She stroked my arm, and I flinched at her cloying touch.

Grendal was much changed from the roommate I remembered. All the fire and fight had gone out of her. She sounded as if the fae had brainwashed her, and I regretted that I'd committed to spend time with her today.

"Look, someone forgot to lock this cage," I said, running my finger over a latch that hung open. "I should let a kanara out."

"You can't be serious," she hissed. "It'll be the fires for you if you get caught interfering with those birds."

"Probably." I turned and whispered to the closest kanara. Its beady red eyes fixed on me, then it pecked my finger. "I can't set you all free, but how about you, precious? You look adventurous," I said, patting the bird's golden head before lifting it out, holding it between my palms.

It began to flutter in panic.

"Quick! Let's go before a guard comes." Grendal took off toward the elevator, and the kanara flapped out of my grasp and flew back toward its cage. The foolish bird.

I leaped into the elevator after Grendal just as a guard strode along the corridor. The kanara landed at his feet. And as the golden doors closed, the frightened bird flew in his face, and he yelped, then ran in the opposite direction.

Grendal and I stifled laughter, and the solemn-faced elevator guard asked, "Which floor?"

"The ground," I replied, emulating the haughty voices of the high fae of the court.

"You have permission?" he asked, looking down his nose at us.

"Of course. We're only having tea in the gardens, not planning a servant uprising."

He grimaced and angled his spear at the center of my chest. "Don't think I won't check with the Sayeeda."

"Go ahead," I replied, giving him a bright smile as we stepped from the elevator.

We moved swiftly through the city's outdoor alleys and linked terraces until we arrived at the Tarneeq Tea Garden. In the small courtyard, golden lanterns swung above bright-colored mosaic tables dotted around giant palm trees. The coffee and tea bar, usually populated with high-ranking servants on their breaks, was strangely empty at noon on a sunny weekday.

"Where is everyone?" I asked as Grendal guided me to a table in the far corner, hidden behind the huge leaves of a balor palm.

"My friend, Sernius, manages this place," she said, slurring her words as I took a seat. "She agreed to give us privacy."

"Privacy? What for? Sit down. My neck's hurting from craning to look up at you. Do you think the guards will suspect that it was me who let the bird out of the cage?"

Still looming over me, her fists twisted into the material of her tunic, and her gaze shifted sideways. "I want you to meet someone."

"What? Are you telling me I won't get any apple tea today?" I asked.

255

Grendal ignored my joke and knocked on the surface of a narrow door concealed in the terracotta wall. A cloaked man, a human I'd never seen before, stepped through it.

"Took your sweet time," he growled, a puckered scar flashing white across the weathered skin of his cheek. Devoid of the tiniest spark of kindness, his pale blue eyes narrowed. Unease slithered through my gut, the cruel set of his features reminding me of the gilt market slaver.

"Sorry," said Grendal, her sour tone raising my hackles. "This one felt it necessary to release an auron kanara on the way here."

This one? Did she mean me?

As Grendal collapsed into the seat on my left, and the man sat directly opposite me, I glanced down, making sure Ari's knife was still attached to my hips.

Grendal pointed at the haggard male. "This is Marlewyn. He's my brother's friend. He can get you out of the city and onto a ship heading back to the Earth Realm."

I was sure that he could, and I'd also bet my life he'd throw me straight into the first slave cage he came across.

All my instincts screamed out not to trust this Marlewyn, but the real mystery was why Grendal did. The serum had destroyed her judgment if she couldn't tell he was at the very least a charlatan, and more likely an outright villain.

"That won't be necessary," I said, inching my chair away from the table. "Like you said before, Grendal, it's not so bad here, especially for me, being the king's favorite."

I studied the man's reaction. Did he know I was the Storm King's pet? Would the thought of Arrow chasing him down put him off whatever nefarious plan he'd hatched?

He grinned, revealing blunt yellow teeth and incisors of solid gold. "Time's running out. The guards at the south gate will change in fifteen minutes," he muttered. "I have a cart waiting through this door. Let's go."

My hand snaked to the hilt of my blade. "I'm not interested in going anywhere with you."

"Marlewyn, please give us a moment," said Grendal. "I'll talk sense into her."

The big man left through the door, and I turned to Grendal. "Are your eyes and ears no longer working properly? He's a fucking slaver."

"This could be your only chance to escape, Leaf." Her face flushed red. "And he said... well, he said he'd kill me if you don't go with him."

"What?" I whispered. "What the fuck have you done, Grendal?"

Behind me, the door scraped open, and a thick forearm wrapped around my throat. Marlewyn choked me as he dragged me off the chair, the paving stones scraping my heels in my sandals.

Stars swam at the sides of my darkening vision as I gasped, flailing and writhing against his hold. I would not lose consciousness. I would not lose...

Bucking wildly, I stopped tugging on his arm, snatched Ari's knife from its scabbard, and stuck it in his thigh. He grunted, dropped me, then raced straight for the door.

"Bitch ain't worth the trouble. If she wants a ride out of here, I'll wait in the cart for three minutes, no more."

"Come on, Grendal," I said as the door closed. "We'd better get out of here."

She stared back at me with vacant gray eyes. My head spun, and I took a seat at the table, shock slowing my movements. With shaking hands, I wiped the blade on my tunic, and beside me, Grendal sobbed like she was the one who had just been attacked by a slaver.

Her hands balled into fists, then she shrieked like a mad woman and snatched my knife from the tabletop, slashing it wildly, only just missing my face as I lurched backward.

"What is *wrong* with you?" I grabbed her wrist, and she struggled to lift the knife toward my neck. "You've lost your fucking mind!"

"Please, Leaf. I don't want to hurt you. But I promised that you'd go with him."

"That man is nothing but a fast trip to a slave market in a different gods-forsaken realm. Why would you want that for me?" Sighing, I gentled my voice and let her wrist drop. The knife clattered onto the table. "Forget him, and let's get out of here before someone finds us and wonders what we're doing in an empty tea garden."

"Please, Leaf. I'm begging you." Grendal leaped up. As I reached for the knife to sheathe it, she grabbed it, forcing me onto my feet and into another ridiculous scuffle.

Without causing harm, I tried to disarm her, blocking three clumsy strikes with my forearm. Losing patience, I pushed her against the stone wall and twisted her wrist, the blade she still clung to pressing against her throat. She thrashed her head and slammed her knee into my stomach, but my grip didn't weaken.

"Grendal! Just stop. You'll get hurt."

"You might as well finish me off." Her muscles loosening, the fight went out of her eyes. "He'll send someone to kill me."

"Who will? Marlewyn?"

Determination drew her features into a grimace. She screamed, gripping the back of my head with her free hand, pushing herself forward and thrusting the Sayeeda's pretty blade into her throat.

I cried out, adrenaline pounding through my system and nausea rising.

Blood bubbling from her mouth, she slid down the wall. On the ground, I cradled her in my arms. "Grendal, no, no."

The blade stuck out from her throat at a fatal angle, bright blood frothing from the wound. She didn't have long to live.

"I'm sorry," she whispered. "He promised to get serum to my son, Zaret... an addict in an encamp... encampment. He promised he would... take care of you, too. I told him you were valuable cargo, but... but not who you really are. I'm sorry, Leaf." She coughed, blood splattering my tunic. "Sorry I disappointed you."

Stroking blood off her cheek with a trembling hand, I attempted a smile, and then a poorly timed joke to distract her. "In truth, I'm disappointed. First no apple tea? And now this?"

She laughed, blood glimmering on her lips, like gruesome gemstones.

"I understand why you did it. I..." My words trailed off as her words sank in. "Wait. You said you didn't tell him who I was. What did you mean? The king's pet? Someone else? Tell me, Grendal. Please."

"No... not the king's slave, silly girl... you... your parents..." A final breath rattled from her lungs, the veils of impending death darkening her eyes. Her lips moved, but no sound came out. Jaw lax, her head slumped against the wall.

"Grendal!" I knew she was dead but shook her anyway. Tears streamed down my cheeks as I clung to her. I didn't care so much that she'd used me because the son she'd never mentioned needed help. That I could understand. But if she knew my real identity and didn't tell me—well, that was a betrayal I couldn't forgive so easily.

Soft hands drew me off Grendal, and Ildri lifted me onto my feet and into her arms. "Leaf, what have you done?"

"I didn't hurt her. I promise."

Raiden appeared beside me and bent to check Grendal's pulse. He looked over his shoulder and shook his head, confirming Grendal was dead.

Footsteps sounded, then Ari arrived at my side. "What happened?" she asked.

"I didn't kill her. She was trying to send me away with a trader, attacked me when I wouldn't go, and then pushed herself into my blade. I swear it."

Ari wiped my face with her sleeve. "I believe you. Come. Ildri will return with you to the king's dome."

"Where did this trader go?" Ildri asked.

I pointed at the door that was partially hidden in the wall. "Through there. He said he had a cart waiting that would take me to a ship. Grendal called him Marlewyn. And for a moment, I thought she might tell me who I was."

Ari's golden brow rose but she said nothing.

Raiden pushed on the door. "Doesn't open."

"It's a reaver door," Ari said, sticking her head through the wooden panel and holding it open. "The trader was part elf."

Raiden stepped over the threshold. "I'll catch him. Tell Arrow where I've gone."

"Must you go alone?" Ildri said, a mother's worry etched on her brow.

"I'll collect some guards to accompany me on my way through town."

Ildri blew him a kiss. "Be careful."

As Raiden disappeared, I turned toward the Sayeeda. "Why did you come here? To check on me?"

"We had good news to share and couldn't wait to bring you back to the king's dome to tell you." Ari looked up from removing the serum bracelet from Grendal's thin arm. "The king has agreed to visit Auryinnia Mines and plans to take you with him."

"When?" I asked.

"In seven days. The gold reavers need time to arrange a celebration. This is a long overdue and very significant visit."

"I'm sorry about your gown," I told Ildri, my hands shaking as I pointed at the blood-smeared fabric.

"It's fine, dear one. I have plenty of others. Let's return to the palace. Ari will arrange for the courtyard to be cleaned."

Cleaned... What would they do with Grendal's body? And who would help her son, Zaret, and tell him that she was gone?

As Ildri led me away, I glanced back at my friend crumpled against the wall, the front of her body bathed in blood, and her gaze fixed on the perfect, clear sky above.

The sky she would never see again.

Chapter 23

ARROW

I tipped my chin at Leaf, who sat opposite me in the carriage. "Come here." She rose, then settled in the curve of my arm, her palm on my thigh and her body warm and pliant. "Apparently, someone released an auron kanara from its cage last week," I murmured, watching her face closely.

Staring past me and out the carriage window, she toyed with the silky material of her gown. "Really? Did it escape the palace?"

"No. And, unfortunately, a guard injured the bird when he caught it."

She stiffened in my arms, confirming my suspicions. It was Leaf who set the bird free. That much was certain.

"I was sorry to hear of the death of your friend, Bronwal."

"Her name was Grendal actually, and as it turned out, she wasn't such a great friend—just another victim of the Light Realm's illegal gold trade. I'm glad Raiden caught the trader who was blackmailing her."

"Raiden caught him, but I delivered the punishment myself." Images of flesh peeling from bones flickered through my mind. The punishment had been harsh, but very just, in my opinion. Anyone who touched my Leaf without consent would suffer the same consequences, as dire as they were.

I stroked the shaved side of her head, then walked my fingers along her braid until they reached the gold-bound tip lying against her breast. "I like your hair this way. It matches the two sides of your personality—harsh and prickly versus sweet and soft."

She graced me with a sensual smile. "I don't have a soft side."

"Not true. Think of the tender way you soothe me through nightmares. How sweetly you beg to feel the sting of my fangs. And when I kiss you, you're softer, more delicious than butter. A delicacy to be savored."

She blew out a breath. "If you despise humans as much as you claim to, I don't see how you can find one *delicious*."

I traced the Aldara mark on her throat, my length thickening as our elemental bond heated and vibrated, like a woven cord of gold strung between our hearts. "I hate humans with an irrational passion."

A dark eyebrow arched. "Then it's not so bad to be your enemy."

"You know you are different, Leaf. You're mine. I knew I wanted you from the first moment your vicious gaze met mine through the bars of the gilt market cage."

"Liar. At the time, you didn't care what happened to me. When we arrived in Coridon, you tossed me to the Underfloor guards and let the Sayeeda decide my fate. She could have easily sent me to the cell that feeds the fires of Amon."

"Do you really believe I'm that stupid? It was no accident that I left my cloak around your shoulders. I knew Ari would see it and know that I had chosen you."

Green eyes narrowed as she studied me with suspicion. "And when you take a queen, will I become fuel for the fires, then?"

"I will never marry a fae of the realms."

"Then how do you propose to get heirs?"

My mouth curved. "*You* will give them to me."

She froze. "Me? A human? You're insane, Arrow. You just admitted you despise my entire race. Your entire kingdom would rise up to replace you on the throne if you had half-human children. And you believe that you could actually tolerate them? Be a father to them? I think not."

"Whatever you and my court think about my plans, it is irrelevant. You've seen the strength of my powers. I'm impossible to kill. They couldn't dethrone me."

Leaf laughed. "Oh, there is always a way to kill someone. Not even you are invulnerable. Everybody has a weakness. Think about how drained you are after you release a large amount of storm magic. An enemy only needs to wait until you're in this weakened state, then strike before you're able to rest and recharge."

Sighing into her sun-warm hair, I pulled her closer. "Then I am fortunate to have you by my side. You bring me contentment, and positive feelings recharge Light Realm magic far better than any other method."

A calculating expression crossed her face. "I don't imagine your emotions would be very positive when you're under attack."

"You'd be surprised," I replied. "Regardless, you are mine, and when the time is right, my people will accept you as my consort, the mother of my children, the creator of Coridon's golden princes and princesses. At that time, I will stop using the ore magic that has prevented impregnation, and you will conceive promptly."

"That's the first I've heard of this *ore* magic. But if it prevents pregnancy, then I'm grateful you've been using it."

A sensation similar to strong displeasure bristled over me, then she pressed a kiss against my chin, and gazed up at me, her expression a mix of pity and sadness.

"You're quite mad, Arrow, and I'm not sure if I like you better or worse because of it."

"Better, of course," I said, tucking stray hair behind the round shell of her ear.

"I'd like you a lot more if you abolished the Light Realm's slave trade. Evolved societies have no need or desire to trade in lives. Why should Coridon continue with such brutality?"

"Humans are notorious for their terrible treatment of slaves," I replied. "Our world is brutal, and we do what we must to create and maintain order. If you know of less savage ways to survive in the Star Realms, then please share them with me."

She frowned, her eyes glazing over as if she had entered a trance, a memory of the forest taking her away from me.

"Leaf, what's wrong?"

"Nothing. I was remembering a disagreement with someone from before. This person argued the merits of the Earth Realm's trade in servants, while I spoke against it."

"There, you proved my point. Humans are slavers, too."

"But Coridon sends humans to the mines, or if they're too weak, incinerates them. That's horrific."

"I disagree. Most who find themselves traded are gold addicts, lost souls. For hundreds of years, if not longer, my court has salvaged lives from the wreckage of their own dissipation. Gold eaters. Those who could not be saved, we ended their suffering, granted mercy. We punished those who had repeatedly harmed others and made miners of the ones who still might, using their strength constructively. And we gave low doses of serum to those who were addicted, keeping them healthy while they served my court in the kitchen or palace. Rulers of the Storm Court have displayed compassion to those who fall into the trade."

"That may be true, but under your rule, Arrow, you sometimes create addicts from humans who'd never touched gold before they came to your court. That is unforgivable. Every decision you make, big or small, adds to or subtracts from your worth, the final tally equaling the king you will forever be known as. Think about the kind of legacy you want to leave when one day in the distant future, the ash of your bones is mixed with the gold dust of your desert."

"I never said I was perfect, Leaf."

"No. Just hinted at it many times."

A haze of gold veiled the hills in the distance, and I gazed out the carriage window, stroking Leaf's arm bracelet, wondering again why the serum didn't seem to affect her. Who was this lost girl? And why did I care what kind of man she thought I was?

"I will consider what you've said. I don't wish to be remembered as my father is—a tyrant who gained respect through fear. Although, perhaps in that regard, I am a lost cause. If Raiden had suggested what you did, I would probably have punched him in the face."

"Arrow!"

I flashed my teeth. "What can I say? My upbringing was barbaric. But I am trying to progress beyond it."

She shook her head and smiled, revealing the gap between her teeth. I stroked her lips, my thumb dipping between the moist flesh. That gap always made me want to protect her and also fuck her to the edge of violence. Two opposing urges battling inside me that felt good thrumming through my veins, like the sweetest, most addictive of poisons.

Leaf. Her contradictions fascinated me. Soft but strong. Naive and sensual. Caring but ruthless. If I displeased her by either deed or word, she would transform from a playful sprite to an unhinged Valkyrie, intent on disemboweling me, and all in the space of a breath. I would never grow bored of her company.

If it weren't for her presence—a guilty comfort snuggled beside me—I wouldn't be in this carriage, about to confront my past.

Ahead, I spied the fork in the road that featured in my nightmares and sent tremors shuddering through my bones. One branch led to the old Aurum Road, which was once the primary route to the mines. And the other traveled toward the obelisk erected three years ago to memorialize the exact location where my family was ripped apart.

Fury spiked in my blood, wrenching my mind from this carriage and dropping me into a different one. Inside it, an arrogant boy prince reclined, self-satisfied and foolishly confident that his life would always be one of ease and indulgence. My youthful assumptions couldn't have been further from the truth.

The triple boom of explosions jerked my spine into a rod of steel. Then the screams started, mine and those of the spectators who'd lined the road. The courtiers had hoped to catch a glimpse of the royal family passing on their way to the Auryinnia ranges. Instead, their guts and bone fragments were sprayed across the landscape as storm clouds raced across the sky. The growl of thunder echoing in my chest was the only thing that kept my heart pulsing in slow, wet thumps.

Thunder crashed overhead three more times, and I opened my mouth to roar, but then... but then a small hand gripped mine, settling the tremors that wracked my body.

"Arrow?" Leaf asked. "Does the winged tower mark the place where your family died?"

A sound of pain brought me back to the present, and I relaxed my crushing grip on the fragile bones of her hand. "Yes," I muttered. "That's the place."

"I'm so sorry. It must have been horrific to see it happen."

Closing my eyes, I let my head fall against the leather headrest. "Because I was a privileged prick and had overslept, I was in a carriage at the rear of the procession, some distance away from theirs. But I was still close enough to see everything. It was a living nightmare, and no matter how hard I try, I will never be free of the memory."

"We're quite a pair, then, aren't we? A king with too many memories and a slave with almost none." Pulling my head down, she kissed my cheek, my lips, then cradled my face in the crook of her neck.

Apples and the scent of midnight-flowering auron roses filled my senses as I breathed her in deep, my fingers bruising her flesh. *Don't let go. No matter what, don't let go.*

"Poor little prince you were," she said, her tone not without sympathy. "And now you are a king, the strongest and most powerful in all of the realms. You could do anything you want. Hurt anyone, hurt *everyone*, and make countless, blameless people pay for every single tear you shed for your family. And yet you haven't. I admire you for that."

Like a cool dawn that breaks after a sweltering night, relief and gratitude infused my chest. These feelings were mostly foreign to me, yet they were comforting. Addictive. And they were the very reasons that wouldn't allow me to kill Leaf or ever let her return to the Earth Realm without me, no matter what crimes she committed.

She was precious. And I would burn all five realms to ash if it would keep her by my side for eternity.

"You're still shaking," she whispered.

"I'm fine."

"Tell me about this mine visit. What will happen today?" She crawled into my lap, straddled my thighs, then ran a finger down my chest plate, the feathers tinkling softly. "Explain in detail, and I'll distract you from your memories for a while."

Gripping her hips, I adjusted her weight over the bulge in my pants, grunting when a bolt of pleasure shot through me. "Once a year, the King of Storms and Feathers is meant to—"

"That would be you." She grinned, leaving moist kisses on my neck.

"Yes. That fact is often regrettable, but always undeniable." I sighed and refocused my thoughts. "According to ancient laws and traditions, once a year, the king should make a ceremonial trip to Auryinnia to deliver feathers. The mountain is deceiving; it contains not only the mines below ground, but the reaver elves' palace above. We will make camp around the mountain, and there will be politicking, feasting, and tonight, a revel. You will dance in my arms as gold specks rain from the ceiling and golden creatures play flutes, contorting their bodies into bewildering shapes as they hang from bars fixed into the walls at spectacular heights."

She hummed a sound of interest against my skin.

"Is that enough description for now?"

"Yes. It will do. Prepare to be rewarded and distracted." Her warm palms framed my cheeks, her tongue parting my lips.

My glyphs came to life, buzzing over my skin, and I groaned and pushed forward, preparing to flip her onto the seat and take her savagely.

"Oh, no, you don't. I'm distracting *you*, remember."

Distracting me? More like driving me to the edge of insanity. I ignored the reaver guards visible outside the window. They lined the road at regular intervals, their golden bows slung over their shoulders and quivers packed with arrows.

Instead, I watched my human lick her way down my body, her braid torturing my stomach muscles. She pressed open-mouthed kisses over my leathers, and then slowly unlaced them, her green eyes fixed on mine.

"Fuck," I breathed, my fingers digging into her shoulders. She gasped, and I had to force my muscles to loosen.

"Feeling distracted yet?" she asked as my weeping shaft sprang free, and she wrapped her hand around its base.

I grunted a vague affirmative noise as my hips jerked toward her smiling mouth.

"Shall I stop, then?" She blew a slow breath up my length, repeating the motion twice more. "Perhaps you'd prefer to gather your wits for your arrival."

My thighs shook, and my head spun with lust. "Not for all the gold in the realms," I choked out.

With the tip of her tongue, she traced my pulsing veins, teasing until I cursed again. Finally, her lips closed around the head, and she sucked, warm and wet. Just the once.

"Would you beg for more if I wanted you to?" she challenged.

"I would hand you my crown, if you promised to do that forever."

Fisting my root, her tongue circled, lapping the pearl-colored strands of lust, her teeth grazing sensitive flesh. I growled like an animal, then followed her suggestion and begged.

"Please... suck me. Now... I'm begging... can't wait."

Slowly, she took me deep inside her sweet mouth, her cheeks hollow with the effort. She dragged the blissful pressure up, then bobbed hard and fast on my tip before repeating the pattern thrice more.

I thrashed against the seat, thunder crashing outside in response. I was a wild creature, not a king, not a storm god. I was her slave, and this human was my queen.

"Good girl. So good. You're perfect." The sweet, musky scent of her arousal driving me wilder, I bucked into her mouth. "Tell me you're mine. Say it."

The suction and pressure was too good, almost unbearable. She wanted to send me out of my mind so I would forget what I had told her. Forget I'd asked her to say she was mine and always would be. I wanted to hear her say it so badly that I didn't even care if it was true.

My thumbs caressed her cheeks and lips where they stretched around my shaft, I shuddered and groaned, and... the carriage ground to a halt. Pleasure-drugged and moaning, I couldn't have cared if we'd arrived at the gates to the hell realms. I just needed her to finish what she'd started.

"Don't stop," I said, my voice harsh. The sight of her mouth enveloping me, her soft moans vibrating over my skin, brought me to the edge of madness again. "Fuck." My fingernails tore into the leather seat. I was so close, shuddering and about to erupt. Then two sharp knocks sounded on the side of the carriage.

Leaf's head jerked off me, her lips making a wet sound. She grinned as Raiden's armored back appeared in the far window, his face directed away from us as his voice rumbled near the door. "We've arrived, King Arrowyn."

"Give us a moment," I rasped.

Leaf parted her mouth, and Raiden cleared his throat. She dipped her head, but I motioned for her to wait.

"Arrow, the Zareen is standing not ten steps away, waiting to welcome you."

The lust fizzled from my blood, replaced by annoyance. "Gods damn the Zareen. Why must she always be punctual? It's a very vexing habit," I said, stifling a laugh as Leaf tucked me back into my leathers, then quickly fastened them.

"I'll finish distracting you in our tent," she whispered, her grass-green irises brimming with mischief.

"I shall look forward to it," I said, leaping from the carriage, then helping her step out.

I placed Leaf's hand on my forearm, and we walked along a carpet of wildflowers woven into a ceremonial pathway. It led us through the golden desert and past four carriages from Coridon containing Ari, Ildri, Stormur, Esen, and other members of my court.

Leaf's eyes widened as she surveyed Auryinnia. The mountain loomed before us, paved in gold all the way to the high summit. At the base, enormous gilded arches flanked a gaping entrance into its interior. And finally, the formidable Zareen herself, who stood statue-still before us, swathed in a gown of embroidered gold.

Like all fae creatures, the Zareen looked ageless. She resembled her sister, my magnificent Sayeeda, but as matriarch of the reavers, her elven features were even more enhanced.

Long elvish ears swept back from her head like scythes, framing her towering cone-shaped headdress.

She was the tallest reaver elf I'd ever seen, matching even my height, and every part of her body shimmered in hues of darkest gold. In looks and demeanor, she surpassed that of any god or king of any realm in existence, including me. Her serene presence was humbling, soothing, and today, I greeted her with a genuine smile of pleasure. I had missed her.

As was the customary reaver greeting, we bowed to each other, our hands pressed together and steepled under our chins. Leaf stood beside me and watched us silently, her fingers digging into the side of her thigh, the gesture that told me of her unease.

She was right to be nervous. The Zareen did not suffer disrespect with patience. If Leaf's tongue hadn't been so delightfully occupied during the journey, I might have thought to warn her to mind it when we arrived.

"So, warrior king," said the Zareen, "your first visit in three years, and you bring your human slave to meet me."

Leaf's breath hitched, and I stepped back and to the side so that my arm touched hers, a gesture of reassurance.

A smile on her face, the Zareen walked forward, her hands outstretched toward Leaf. "It is an honor to meet you," she said, grasping my human by the shoulders and pressing kisses on both her cheeks.

A wrinkle formed between Leaf's brows. "The honor is all mine. Auron tadar maleeka."

The Zareen laughed, delighted to hear the human greet her with the traditional reaver words that translated as *may the gold always flow to you.*

"And same to you, lost one. Ari has told me a lot about you. Did she instruct you to greet me in this fashion?"

"No. It just came to me then. I must have learned the phrase in my old life, back in the Earth Realm."

"Yes, you must have." The Zareen's eyes sparkled as she wove Leaf's arm through hers and strode forward without a word, forcing me to jolt into motion and take long steps to catch up with them.

We walked toward the entrance of the mountain, and the Zareen turned to the assembled crowd, reaver elves to the right and human miners and servants to the left. Several hundred beings stood motionless, waiting for her to speak.

"Citizens of Auryinnia, we welcome Arrowyn Ramiel, the King of Storms and Feathers, and his consort, Leaf of the Earth Realm of Dust and Stones. As it is written in the Book of Auron Ways, may the feathers always float the way of the fae and the gold flow between us, forever replenished by our friendship and alliance. Auron tadar!"

"Auron tadar," shouted the crowd in unison, before erupting in loud applause.

Raiden marched behind us as the Zareen beckoned us along the carpet of wildflowers. Ari joined her, and Leaf fell back beside me as we moved closer to the mountain's entrance.

Linking Leaf's arm through mine, I bent and whispered in her ear. "One day soon, you will admit the truth that you managed to evade in the carriage."

"What truth?" she asked.

"The truth of who you belong to."

"Not that again." She smiled and, in a cheerful voice, said, "Tell me, do you love me, Arrowyn, *warrior king* of the Light Realm of Storms and Feathers?"

"Love?" I spat the word out like it was bitter poison. "That emotion is for children who've never woken from nightmares with no one to wipe their tears. I am a man grown, raised in the shadow of violence and death, who has brought more of the same to the realm that I rule. Love shrinks from my being and will never exist within the bounds of my soul. I love nothing and no one, my little Leaf, least of all the *things* that belong to me."

After that declaration, I expected she'd scratch my eyes out, but she only shook her head and smiled sadly. "And you wonder why I don't rejoice in my position at your court. Anyone who was close to you would wish to deny it. For what could they gain by admitting the truth of it?"

Gold be damned, this human was a bold one. The truth hurt, everyone said. And as fire roared through my veins, burning that wretched organ in my chest until it felt like a charred husk, I agreed with the ridiculous platitude.

I swallowed a curse, forced my muscles to loosen, and slid Leaf's arm off mine. Then, gritting my teeth hard enough to break them, I strode with purpose toward Ari.

If Leaf believed I was unworthy, I would be happy to provide her with good reasons to want to belong to me. The main one being: no one had the strength and will to protect her the way *I* could. And if she required proof, then fine, I would give it to her.

Chapter 24

LEAF

C learly angry, Arrow stalked off. Like a typical king, he preferred to hear lies from his courtiers and servants, who were happy to withhold their honest opinions as long as it kept them in favor.

When would he realize I could never be content with lying to him?

As he reached Ari and the breathtaking gold reaver matriarch, he bowed his head and spoke rapidly, both elves listening intently. The Zareen gave a solemn nod, and a moment later, Ari shouted commands in the reavers' musical language before coming to stand beside me.

"What's going on?" I asked, my fingers catching the draping sleeve of her gown.

"Quiet. You will see. No matter what happens, you must say nothing. *Do* nothing. Do you understand, Leaf?"

With my stomach twisting in knots, I nodded.

Arrow, Raiden, and Esen stood in front of the mountain's entrance, their arms folded across their chest armor and boots planted wide in the golden-red sand. By their thunderous expressions alone, I knew that whatever was about to happen next, it wouldn't be good.

Sighing, I shuffled my feet, wishing Arrow would allow us to wait out of the sun's scorching heat. But that wasn't his way—to consider the comfort of others. I mentally swatted away memories of the times he'd given me warm blankets in the pavilion. Or delicious food that satisfied more than my hunger. And how he had ordered Ari to shave my head because he knew it was important to me.

If I was honest with myself, I had to admit the king had performed many kindnesses toward me. All because he wanted me to beg and plead and tell him I loved him, when I could never feel that way about a man who wouldn't give me my freedom.

But why did he need this from me?

I wasn't stupid and had an inkling of what motivated him—something dark and twisted to do with the death of his family. Something lacking in his upbringing.

I knew that once I'd surrendered and told him I was his, he would discard me as easily as if I was an ill gold eater in his service, unable to work, and throw me to the fires. Then he could proudly add another notch to the tally of human suffering that he'd caused in the name of vengeance.

Before long, two reaver guards dragged a chained male through the golden doors of the mountain. He wore the wide felt hat, brown tunic, and trousers of a miner. Although grime covered his skin and his once scrawny body had filled out, I immediately recognized the mean, dark eyes of my Underfloor cellmate who'd tried to assault me.

Davy.

Blinking in the daylight, he scanned the crowd, eyes widening to an almost-comical size when they landed on the king. But when he saw me standing on the carpet of wildflowers, my hair braided with gold strands and tiny nuggets, my shining, corseted gown split to each thigh, his mouth twisted, shaping soundless words, and underneath all the dirt, his skin blanched ivory white.

He forced a grimace-like smile. "My friend," he croaked out. "I knew you would come to my aid one day, just as I helped you Underfloor."

"Helped yourself to what didn't belong to you," said Arrow, stalking toward Davy, his voice like rolling thunder and faithful guards following in his wake.

"No. Wait—" I shouted as Ari dragged me backward.

"You cannot stop this, even if you're the cause of it. Accept it. Those who cross Arrowyn live to regret it. But they never regret it for long. Close your eyes if you must, but let it happen."

"Do you know that girl?" Arrow asked Davy in a mild voice, pointing at me.

Davy swallowed several times, likely aware that any answer he gave would be wrong.

"Leaf, come here," the king demanded.

Ari nudged me into motion, then we trudged forward together, stopping beside Arrow. I gasped as his fingers wove through mine, his grip crushing.

Davy's gaze dropped to our entwined hands, then violent shudders wracked his body. "Yes. I recognize her. We spent a night in a Coridon cell together."

Arrow released my hand and grasped the miner's face between his palms, dropping his voice to a deadly whisper. "And what did you do to her?"

"I... I gave her information. Tried to help her."

"And what else?"

"I touched her. I know I shouldn't have."

"You tried to use my property for your own disgusting gratification."

"I'm sorry... I didn't know that she..." A stream of urine darkened the front of his trousers as his words trailed off. "I didn't know. Please..."

Thunder rumbled, inky clouds traveling at light speed toward the mountain and darkening the sky to slate. Lightning flashed directly above us, forking down and striking Arrow between the shoulder blades, his body buckling with the force.

With a single twist of the king's wrist, Davy's body rose three feet off the ground, a scream straining the bulging cords of his throat.

I took a breath to speak, to stop the horror, but Ari touched my arm and shook her head. By rights, this revenge belonged to me. If I could, I would press a blade against the miner's throat and terrify him so he'd never think of abusing a girl again, but then, eventually, I'd let him go. Today, the Storm King would grant no such mercy. That much was clear.

The assembled crowd stood in silence. No one moved as Arrow growled, storm magic spinning the man's body like a child's toy, first sideways, then backwards.

"*Never*. Touch. What is mine," the king roared.

Tendrils of smoke curled from Davy's ears, and the king dropped him onto his feet, lifted him by the throat, and plunged a black dagger into his gut, slicing through his sternum all the way up to his chin. Steaming entrails spilled at my feet, and I gagged, swallowing bile.

The king shuddered as the storm dissipated, turning toward the mine guards. "Get rid of this filth." They bowed and hurried to do his bidding.

A heavy silence buzzed through the air, then a smattering of applause sounded, growing louder as the courtiers one-by-one decided that congratulating the Storm King for his savagery was the safest option.

Sighing, Arrow linked our arms, guiding us around the remains of what once was a desperate gold runner called Davy. "Have you no comment now that you've witnessed what happens to those who cross me, little Leaf?"

"Why? Is that a threat?" I asked, my chin raised and attention focused straight ahead. "Is that what you plan to do to me if I keep refusing to say what you want? To *do* what you want?"

He halted mid-step and stared at me. "Of course not. It pains me that you think I'm capable of it."

We began walking again, following the Zareen and Ari into the mountain's interior, and I took three steps to every two of Arrow's. "What you did was horrific and... unnecessary. If you'd shown the man mercy, he might have learned a lesson, changed for the better, and continued to work hard in your mines."

He gave me a quizzical look. "Mercy? But I did grant it because he told the truth and admitted his crime. Most fae present today could describe what an unmerciful death by my hand looks like, and it is a considerably more drawn-out process."

My steps faltered, dizziness sweeping over me, no doubt from the shock of beholding another example of the true nature of the man I belonged to. Taking a slow breath, I wiped sweat from my brow with the back of my hand.

Arrow beckoned a trembling Auryinnia guard over. "Send soldiers and at least two high reaver elves to ride to the nearest human encampment and inquire about a boy called Zaret. If you find him, return him to me safely. And be sure to treat him well."

My jaw dropped as I stared at Arrow, hope for Grendal's child blooming inside me.

"Yes, My King." The guard bowed and scurried away.

We entered a large gold-lined chamber, the walls carved with the familiar lightning forks and feathers of the Storm Court and long-lashed feminine eyes, symbols of the reavers' matriarchal society.

On either side of the room, open elevators plummeted into the depths of the mines, filled with miners returning to their days' work. Our small party entered a larger, ornate elevator set into the rear wall, which I assumed would carry us up to the reaver palace.

The filigree door clicked shut, and a shudder passed over me. To distract myself from my rising fear of confined spaces, I concentrated on the sounds of Arrow's courtiers setting up our camp outside, thankful that we would sleep under the open sky tonight.

As a child of the forest, I couldn't bear the idea of the weight of the mountain pressing down on me all night long. Although, if Ari's plan succeeded, I wouldn't spend much time in my bed tonight.

The elevator zipped upward, and I stole glances at Arrow's chiseled profile, my gaze tracing the hard set of his mouth that relaxed into its full, sensual shape when we were alone, the points of his ears cutting through tousled hair, and his crown of twisted feathers.

I wondered if he had been volatile before his family died, a man who could transform in the blink of an eye from an empathetic and reasonable person to one capable of monstrous deeds. Had he always been erratic and inconstant? If I could give him anything, instead of my absolute surrender, it would be the gift of peace inside his violent, bitter heart.

"Thank you, Arrow," I said, squeezing his hand as the Zareen addressed the king's entourage. "It means a lot to me that you're helping Grendal's child."

Silver eyes glowered down at me. Then he beamed, his broad smile twisting my heartstrings into knots that could not easily be untangled. I thought of Ari and Ildri's plan, and for a passing moment, I regretted that I was leaving him. Saddened that after tonight, I would likely never see him again. Never shiver under his touch. His kiss. Or his sweet, savage bite.

I shook my head and forced myself to recall every indignity he had made me suffer, remembering what he had called me earlier: his possession. There was no point in hoping to ever mean more to him. It was a futile dream. A dream I didn't even realize I'd been nurturing.

The reaver palace's gilded apartments and reception rooms spanned seven floors, each level growing narrower as we rose higher toward the pointed summit of the mountain, the interior lit with the same floating balls of lightning that illuminated the city of Coridon.

The air was thick with incense, and the atmosphere was cloistered but inviting. Every surface glowed in rich burnished hues, including the reaver elves themselves, who shone like golden stars.

On the top floor, we stepped into a grand hall of sorts. Located high in the mountain, its floor space was the smallest in the palace. The ceiling soared upward, growing narrower and narrower. And hundreds of shafts, built into the angled walls, cast bright beams of sunlight over the elves gathered around tables laden with large woven baskets.

The Zareen took a seat on a throne that was shaped like a bird in flight and set on a small dais only three steps higher than the floor. The outstretched wings of gold wrapped her shoulders, reminding me of Arrow's throne back in Coridon.

"Let the ceremony begin," she said, waving her hand toward a band of musicians who commenced playing a dramatic tune on their reed pipes.

A storm courtier appeared beside Arrow, handing him a brocade cushion with seven auron kanara feathers neatly arranged in its center. The king whipped off his cloak and passed it to Ari, his chest covered only in his plate of golden feathers.

Holding the cushion with great care, the king walked forward, dropped to one knee in front of the throne, and solemnly presented his offering to the Zareen.

She stepped down from the dais and knelt before Arrow, placing her hands on the cushion. After reciting a verse in reaver language, she said, "On behalf of the gold reaver elves of Auryinnia, I accept the Court of Storm and Feathers' gift with immense gratitude for our continuing friendship and alliance. As a symbol of my sincerity, the king and I will reveal our true natures to each other. By the will of the gold that flows through my veins, all glamours will now dissolve."

Standing on the left side of the gathering, I watched Arrow's lips curve into a smirk as a shudder undulated down his spine. His body wavered in and out of focus, and an enormous pair of wings appeared at his shoulder blades.

"What the fuck?" I whispered, nausea swirling in my stomach. I grabbed Ari's hand, crushing it. "Can he fly?"

She clicked her tongue. "Shush. I knew I should have prepared you for this moment, but Arrow swore me to secrecy."

The absolute prick. Why hadn't he warned me? I knew he relished every opportunity to unsettle me, but this was pushing the concept too far. By the dust, Arrow had wings? I could barely believe my eyes, but those baffling stray feathers that appeared in the pavilion suddenly made a lot more sense.

The Zareen's wings were made of iridescent purple-black feathers with tips of bright gold, a perfect match for the king's.

I bit my tongue and watched them leisurely flap their massive feathered appendages at each other as a constant procession of fae filed past and filled the baskets on the tables with ceremonial kanara feathers.

When the ritual was finally over, Arrow swaggered toward me, his smile transmitting a ridiculous degree of self-satisfaction. With a flick of his wings, strands of hair blew over my face, and the glorious feathered attachments disappeared as if they'd never existed.

I would have paid many gold feathers to learn about his wings, but I quashed my curiosity, took his offered arm with a smile, and pretended I hadn't noticed them.

A deep frown appeared between his brows, and I swallowed a laugh, pressing my lips together tightly.

Two could play the Storm King's childish games. When he woke tomorrow morning and found me gone, he would have no choice but to declare me the winner.

As the sun set in fiery shades of magenta and plum, Ari led me into the elevator, then back to the tent to prepare for the evening feast. Arrow and his inner circle remained in the palace, occupied with the affairs of state and kingdoms, and I was very glad not to be a part of it.

It baffled me that over a millennium, countless fae had murdered members of their own families, started wars, all for the chance to sit on a throne. Good luck to them, I thought, spending the rest of their days mired in politics, when instead, they could go fishing for river trout.

The Storm Court's domed tents dotted the landscape around the base of the mountain, and Ari escorted me to the grandest of all. The reavers had furnished the space with low couches, a bed of stacked feather mattresses set in a pillared frame, and far too many cushions and candles.

After I bathed in a narrow tub carved from a single trunk of the white sapoula tree, I dressed in swathes of gossamer silk, then Ari braided my hair in a style that covered as much of the shaved side of my head as possible.

"When you leave Auryinnia tonight, it is crucial no one sees your shaved hair," she warned.

"Why is that important?"

"Well... we don't want anyone to recognize you and report back to the king, do we?"

In the mirror, her eyes dropped from mine as she spoke, and a chill prickled my skin. She was keeping something from me, but I was nervous, my mind occupied with the escape plan, so I let it go.

"Tonight, when you retire to the tent, I will bring wine. As we've discussed, the king's goblet will be drugged, but only lightly. He will believe he is drunk, likely talk some nonsense, over share, and then fall into a slumber that I pray to the gold will last many hours. Wait until you're certain he's fast asleep, then slip out under the rear of the tent, behind the bed. I will be waiting directly outside with travel clothes and essentials, cloaked by reaver magic and invisible, but I will see you."

"And if he wakes while I'm casually ducking out underneath a flap of canvas?"

"Pretend you're sleepwalking. Ildri will occupy Raiden and Esen. The wine she gives them will also be drugged."

Guilt gnawed at my insides. Poor Ildri. It wouldn't be easy for her to drug her beloved son.

Ari gripped my chin between her fingers, studying my face. "I won't use kohl on your eyes tonight. It's too hard to rub off for the purpose of discreet travel." She grabbed a jar of gold paint and dusted some over my eyelids, my lips, and cheeks. "We'll speak more later. Go now before you're missed, and be sure to play your part well."

"I'll do my best. Wish me luck," I said and kissed her cheek before she could draw away.

Ildri entered, her red waves poppy-bright as they tumbled to her waist against a gown of shiny emerald and gold. Holding her arm out for me to grasp, she smiled. "Ready?"

"As I'll ever be. Thank you Ildri. For everything."

"One day soon, you will understand the balance Ari and I hope to maintain by returning you to your people. Tonight, you must trust us. That is all. Thank the gold you're a brave soul."

Although the night was warm, I shivered as we strolled through the campfire smoke toward the mountain. Soldiers cooked meat and drank ale, their raucous laughter only increasing my anxiety. But a sickle moon shone a calm light upon me, and I interpreted its presence as a soothing message, hearing it whisper in my mind: *all is well, human—do not be afraid.*

I wasn't afraid. Not much, anyway. I refused to think about what might happen once I left Auryinnia, and I concentrated on the memory of the forest and the bright-green gaze of my brother, Ash.

Because, tonight, what I'd dreamed of since the day Arrow took me from the gilt market was finally coming true. I had allies, people who cared about me, and they were helping me return to my home. To my family.

So what if a small part of me would miss the Storm King? After I learned of my birth name, I would scour that feeling off with dirt and stones, then bury it in the forest's dark earth. Along with the name Leaf and all memories of Arrow's sweet kisses.

"I was beginning to think you'd escaped again, little Leaf," said the king as he cut through the crowd celebrating in the reaver hall.

"I wouldn't be so foolish."

"Yes, because you know that no matter where you flee, I will follow. I will never let you go. You are my marked one, my Aldara, bound to me forever."

I rolled my eyes. "Forever is a long time."

"Indeed," he agreed, his gaze traveling over the panels of gold and bronze fabric that wrapped my body as soft as spiderwebs and almost as sheer.

When I finally looked away from his golden beauty, I scanned the room. The luminous bodies moving to the slow tune of the pipes and a singer's lilting voice came into focus.

The regal Zareen sat smiling on the dais, and most of the gold reavers were on the floor surrounding us, dancing in loose-limbed movements.

"Have you eaten?" Arrow waved his scarred warrior's hand, unburdened by rings or artifice, toward the far wall at a bank of tables laden with food platters.

"Yes, I shared a plate of meat and cheese with Ari earlier. I'm not hungry."

"Good. Will you dance with me?"

Interesting how he posed it as a question when we both knew I had no choice in the matter. Of course I would dance with him.

Gold dust fell like rain as I stepped into his arms, and he spun us in time with the hypnotic pulse of the music. Above us, golden bodies shimmered from high bars, swinging through the glittering air, just as Arrow had promised they would.

Compared to Arrow's Court, Auryinnia was intimate and serene, and I felt at home on the dance floor among the elves. In my five-plus weeks at Coridon, Arrow and I had never danced like this, our bodies close, hearts beating as one, as we stared into each other's eyes.

The Storm Court's musical revels had been much too raucous for romance—riotous reels and jigs, with drunken fae constantly tumbling over each other. Most nights I'd watched the dancers from Arrow's dais, distracting myself from the delicious torture of his fingers stroking my skin under the table.

And now, as we spun past Raiden and Ari, I tried to imagine how Arrow had held his invisible wings while he ate his meals in Coridon's Grand Hall or ravished me in his bed. Had they always been present or did he only manifest them at certain times?

I studied his strong features that never failed to stir an intense combination of disgust and longing inside me. Yes, I lusted after the king. And I also hated him. But was that all I really felt, or did something more worrying dwell in the depths of my heart?

Tonight, the skin around his eyes looked too tight for an immortal, even for a warrior king, who traveled his realm in a dusty cloak and bought slave girls from markets on a whim. He looked tense. Tired. And before I could suppress the emotion, sympathy swirled in my chest and burst right out of my mouth.

"Are you all right?" I asked.

"Of course. Why wouldn't I be?"

"Well, you've returned to the scene of a traumatic event, and—"

"Yes, I see what you mean." His lips quirked. "But I'm fine. Each time a memory threatens my composure, I turn my thoughts toward retiring to our tent. That distraction you promised me in the carriage helps me even now."

I smiled as he drew me closer, worry and that damned futile pity stirring again in the pit of my belly. How would Arrow cope tomorrow when he had to deal with his memories, magnified by my betrayal? And the nightmares... When I was gone, who would hold him close and soothe him back to sleep?

Between dances, we spoke with the Zareen and her consort, a good-humored male with a deep, booming laugh, called Jarveeya. With keen anticipation, they described tomorrow's events—in the morning, a tour of the mines followed by an afternoon hunt, where we would ride the reavers' famous eponars, the tall, sightless, bronze-furred creatures that were part jinn, part horse, and used magic to navigate their way through the desert.

Smiling brightly, I told the Zareen that I looked forward to the festivities. I felt genuinely sad that I would miss the hunt for the wild hares of the plains that would be spit-roasted for a feast every elf, storm fae, and mine worker would attend. Except for me.

Hours later, as the king bid the reavers goodnight and led me from the hall, I noticed Esen scowling over her dance partner's shoulders. I gave her a cheery wave before the elevator doors closed, hopeful it would be the last time I had to look upon her bitter face.

Dropping his glamour with a laugh, Arrow picked me up, spread his wings, and launched into the sky. I let out a single screech as my stomach lurched. Then I clung to him, enjoying the thrill of the wind in my hair and the sight of the tiny campfires burning below.

When he turned and swooped toward our tent, I dug my fingers into his shoulders, and yelled, "Can we not go farther? This is amazing!"

"No," was his clipped and only reply as he landed in a graceful crouch, then marched us through the canvas door.

Chapter 25

LEAF

Flames writhed in seven braziers, casting sensual shadows over the walls of the tent and Arrow's strong features. With an exaggerated grunt, he threw me on the bed, and I wriggled to the edge.

As he loomed over me, his gaze hungry, I reached for the laces on his leathers, eager to continue where we had left off in the carriage.

After all, it would be our last time.

"Not yet," he said, pushing my hand away, then stripping his armor and chest plate off while his eyes devoured me.

"Don't you want me to finish what I started earlier today?"

"I have no patience for that. I want you on your stomach, moaning my name. Quickly, do as I command. And leave your dress on."

With my limbs quivering, I scrambled onto my stomach, placing my arms at my sides.

He laughed. "Not quite like that." With a feral growl, he dragged my hips high and shoved my dress up to my waist.

"Gods, Arrow," I breathed as he stroked the edge of my underwear.

His fingers teased briefly, finding me ready, then plunged inside me. His other hand slid to my breast, tugging material and exposing my nipple to his brutal attentions. "Say my name again."

He ground his hardness against me, moaning like a dying man. My breath hitched as he fumbled to release his pants with one hand, then I nearly choked on a surprised laugh as he thrust deep inside me. I held on for dear life as he took me savagely, mercilessly, as if he'd somehow intuited that this was our last time together.

Through a haze of pleasure, I tried to picture what those dark wings would be doing if he had left them on display. Would they be spread high and wide above his shoulders as he thrust inside me? Or would they be curled protectively around my body?

I tried to turn and ask him to reveal them, but he rode my body too hard, controlling me, and I couldn't move.

I bit my lip as his incisors pierced my neck, sliding deep into my flesh, sharp pain, then the most intense pleasure I'd ever felt undulating through me. It was too much. Too perfect. And with a long moan, my core spasmed around his plunging shaft, the muscles gripping and releasing as I came loudly.

"No, Leaf," he moaned against my neck, his words slurred as he drew slowly on my blood. His big body froze, shaking, every muscle clenched, as he panted and tried to hold his climax at bay.

Outside, low murmurs and the hiss and crunch of fires being banked for the night traveled through the air, sounding muffled, as if they came from a distant realm. My head spun, and I panted, unable to catch my breath as I felt my entire body dissolve into the mattress.

Gods, how could I leave something so transcendent, so blissful, behind?

Arrow licked my wound, sealing it, then wrapped his hand around my neck, moving his hips excruciatingly slowly as he thrust in and out of my body, the wet sound mixed with his short, hard grunts and muttered curses.

"Tell me you're mine, Leaf. Say it," he demanded, thrusting harder, grinding against me.

Even now—our last time—I couldn't bring myself to fully surrender. My cheek against the bedcovers, I shook my head and stretched my arm, cupping the swaying weight of his sack between his legs to distract him.

"Gold damn you," he hissed out. Gripping my hips, he took control and slammed them back against his body again and again.

The pleasure was intense, too perfect, and sobs wracked my chest, tears leaking from my eyes. Arrow's movements grew rougher, and he pulled out and flipped me over, shuddering and groaning like a wild beast. Blue lightning sizzled over his skin.

One hand gripping his shaft, the fingers of his other hand still worked inside me as pearl-white ropes painted my chest and he came with a final intense groan. My muscles coiled tight, and I released a strangled cry, following him over the edge and climaxing again, violent spasms wracking my body.

With a rough sigh, he collapsed over me and framed my face with his hands. He kissed me slowly, as if we had all the time in the realms, then nipped my bottom lip and rubbed his nose against mine. "You were made for me, little Leaf. Only you bring me such pleasure. Only you."

Raking his gaze down my body, he pushed onto his feet and snatched a towel that hung over a basin of water. After wiping himself with rough strokes, he returned to the bed with a freshly dampened towel and cleaned my chest.

"So perfect," he said as he pressed a kiss on my sternum, his tongue teasing a response from my depleted body.

Three scratches sounded on the canvas door. "May I enter, My King?"

Ari. With the wine that would change my fate.

Arrow raised his eyebrows at me, and I nodded, drawing the sheet over my body.

"Come in, Sayeeda," he said, his voice a warm, contented rumble.

Ari glided across the rugs, her face serene as she carried a tray that held a carafe of wine and two full goblets—the king's cup engraved with feathers and lightning and mine encrusted with emeralds.

"Your wine as you requested, Arrowyn," she said.

"Requested?" He sat up against the bed frame and raised a questioning brow at me.

I shook my head.

The Sayeeda's steps faltered. "Oh, I thought... Ildri had said... It doesn't matter. I'll leave you in peace."

"Ari, wait. I am parched. I'll gladly take some wine. And you, Leaf, are you thirsty?"

My smile trembling at the edges, I nodded and took my goblet from the tray. Ari's eyes flicked to the full carafe, then briefly met mine. I understood her meaning perfectly. Do not drink the wine from the carafe. My goblet was fine, of course, and Arrow's was already drugged.

"Sleep well," Ari said before she turned and left us alone.

"To memories," I said, clinking my goblet with Arrow's. "When they return, may we conquer them with joyful hearts."

He grinned back at me as I sipped the spiced wine. "And may you always be mine, Leaf, and before long, declare it with unbridled joy. Many times over." Raising his cup, he drank deeply.

"I'm not sure I want to drink to that," I teased.

"But I do."

"Well then..." I refilled his goblet, and I lifted mine in another toast. "It would be discourteous of me to refuse."

Laughter rumbled in his chest. "Good manners have never made you do anything you didn't want before, but indeed, drink to our delightful future." He tossed his head back and drained the cup, slamming it on the tray and smacking his lips together. "Delicious... but I am still parched."

Waggling his eyebrows comically as if it was me he thirsted for, he shifted his weight on the bed, preparing to pounce on me. Before he did, I flung my leg over his thighs and straddled his lap.

"Arrow," I whispered as I held his face and kissed him slowly. "Is it possible you're not half the brute you pretend to be?"

A slow smile spread over his face. "What if I said I was thrice the brute and I'm willing to provide the evidence?"

"Before you do that..." I ran my palms over his muscled shoulders. "I want to ask you about something."

The bed frame creaked as his head flopped back against it. "Storms save me from my woman's endless questions. Tell me, will they be brief, so we can move on to more pleasurable pursuits?"

Of all the times for him to call me *his woman.*

Although I felt far from amused, I forced a laugh. The slur of his words and the loose movements of his powerful limbs told me the drug was beginning to work.

"Perhaps they'll be the most fascinating questions you've ever been asked," I said.

Wearing a dazed grin, he yawned and shuffled down the bed, wriggling against the mass of pillows to find a comfortable position. He tugged me close and wrapped me in his arms, his thumb stroking the edge of my collar, the collar I would soon be free of. "Can't promise I'll answer each one, but I am willing to hear them."

"What's the story with your wings? Are they an illusion or are they real?" Now that we were alone, I couldn't resist satisfying my curiosity about them.

He laughed, his breath ruffling my hair. "Yes, they're an illusion. The illusion is that they *don't* exist."

"So they've always been there?" I asked, gazing up at him.

Amusement sparkled in his slightly unfocused eyes. "Most nights, Leaf, you are kept warm in the feathered embrace of my wings."

"That can't be true! I would've had some inkling of their existence."

"Some fae are born with wings, inherited from either parent, but mine are connected to gold reaver magic. When a Light Realm king dies, a ceremony takes place to grant the new king his wings. Of course, after my parents' deaths, I didn't want the damned things. The Zareen had to come to my chambers and convince me herself to accept them. Fortunately, for the health of both our kingdoms, the Zareen can be very persuasive."

Silent, I tried to picture how those beautiful wings might have looked on past occasions. Slashing the air above his shoulders as we'd argued, or perhaps spread wide, ready for flight, as I slept soundly on the floor of the pavilion. What I wouldn't give to go back in time and witness him soaring around it.

"Why haven't I seen you flapping about the kingdom?"

"Excuse me? Storm kings do not *flap* about. *Ever.*"

"Oh, forgive me. I didn't know," I said, fighting laughter.

"There aren't very many winged fae in Coridon and none whose company I enjoy. So who should I flap about the kingdom with, as you so elegantly put it? Sometimes, if I cannot sleep, I fly alone at night. Your pavilion is a wonderful place to take off from."

"If your wings are always there, then why didn't you fly instead of ride when you chased me to Bonerust?"

"Until I had completed the Zareen's ceremony, renewing our alliance, I had no right to use my wings outside of Coridon. If I'd flown then, I would've risked losing the gift of my wings forever, and I do believe I will need them to keep you safe in the future. But if I hadn't found you in Bonerust that night, I would have flown to the moon if required, risked everything, to have you returned to me."

"Can I see them again?" I whispered, stroking his cheek.

"Tomorrow." He yawned again, stretching his arms above his head. "I promise to take you around the mountain in the morning. Right now, I'm so tired I might drop you."

"Gold forbid." I pressed my cheek against his chest, breathing in the scent of his warm skin.

I needed to stay silent and let him drift off, but the drug had put him in a gentle, generous mood, and before I walked away from him forever, I wanted to hear a little more of his voice.

"Arrow? Have you traveled over all the realms?"

"Most places, yes. But only briefly to the forests of the Earth Realm, which is the realm I'm sure you wish to hear about."

"The Earth Realm of Dust and Stones," I said. "It sounds like a bleak and desolate place, quite different from my dreams. And if that's true, I wonder why I long to return to it."

"It's understandable. You miss your family. But you must know they may not even be alive. Regardless, one day, I will take you to visit the forest you dream about so often."

My breath hitched in my throat, a feeling similar to regret sliding through my blood. There couldn't be a worse time to begin to *like* the Storm King or to feel real empathy for him, but at present, I came dangerously close to both.

Toying with a lock of his dark gold hair, I asked, "What have you seen in your travels that amazed you?"

"In each realm, insurmountable beauty exists, but I think my favorite place to visit is the Kingdom of Night and Stars. There's a magical glacier in the far north of their realm where one can stand on the summit and view the stars that fly around us with great clarity. Tiny newborn planets whoosh past, so close I could have reached out and changed their orbits with my fingers."

"Would you take me there one day?" I whispered.

He kissed my brow. "Indeed. One day, I most definitely will."

Little fantasies, alluring dream-like scenes of what my life might be like if I stayed with Arrow and toured the realms as his prized slave, consumed me. These visions appealed to a weak, undisciplined part of me that I quickly gagged and bound, because that cozy future with the Storm King could never be mine. I wouldn't let it be. Not ever.

Arrow's weary gaze dropped from my face, alighting on my fingers that were digging into my thigh.

"What's bothering you, my little Leaf?"

I forced a smile. "Nothing. I was wondering about my family again. That's all."

He sighed deeply. "When you first came to live in my chambers, many times during night flights, I glided around your pavilion, watching you sleep."

"Did you? Why?"

"Because I never felt lonely when you were nearby. I hope that one day, you will find the same comfort in my company."

Gods be damned. Why did Arrow choose the night I was leaving to speak to me in such a way? Ari warned that the drug might cause him to talk nonsense, so I did my best to harden my heart against this more open, vulnerable version of him.

As his eyes closed, I whispered one last question. "Do you promise you'll take care of Grendal's son, Zaret, no matter what?"

His hand sliding off my back, he grunted as he fell farther under the drug's spell.

"Arrow!"

He jerked half awake. "Of course... promise."

"Thank you," I said, and pressed a lingering, barely there kiss to his mouth. A goodbye kiss, thanking him for being a better king, a better owner than I'd imagined he would be when I first laid eyes on him through the bars at the gilt market.

I had vowed to stick a blade into his heart for imprisoning me, and worse, for making me desire him. I wanted to hate him so badly—but I didn't. Far from it. Even when I conjured the anger I'd felt that day he stripped me naked and threw me in the river, I still couldn't bring myself to hurt him.

Releasing a rough sigh, I relinquished the perfect opportunity to kill my captor.

Then to confirm he was fast asleep, I stroked his ear and waited, watching his chest move in and out, as regular as waves lapping at the shore. If anything would wake him, it would be this, since playing with his sensitive ears never failed to produce an immediate and impressive reaction.

But tonight, nothing.

After I'd committed each angle and precious curve of his face to memory, I slipped off the bed as quietly as I could and stole into the star-filled night. Toward the alarming promise of freedom.

Chapter 26

LEAF

"This is treason," I muttered, staring at the patch of night-dark grass between the travel boots Ari had given me and her delicate woven sandals.

I could barely meet her gaze as she slipped a key from her pocket and removed the collar Arrow's goldsmiths had made especially for me.

Not only was I finding it difficult to say goodbye to the Sayeeda, I was worried sick about what would happen to her when Arrow discovered her role in my escape. As he inevitably would.

"You and Ildri are risking your lives for me."

Bathed in moonlight, we huddled together in the eponar paddock on the western side of the mountain, away from the Storm Court's tents. Thanks to Ari's cloaking magic, we were invisible to all. But that didn't stop the sightless creature, who used magic to navigate, from rasping its sizable tongue along my neck in long, moist strokes.

"Would you stop that, Enyd? We won't get very far tonight if you plan to lick me the entire journey." I stepped sideways out of the creature's reach, and Ari checked my satchel for the third time since we'd slunk into the paddock.

"Enyd will carry the cloaking spell for as long as you ride her. Remember the gold nugget in your coin pouch. Don't lose it. Repeat the chant I taught you, and it will help you disappear if you're in danger. Mount quickly, head northwest toward the Port of Tears, and do not stop for anything. The eponar is fast. It should take you two hours at the most."

"Remind me about when I arrive?"

"As we discussed, an orc called Orion will meet you in the tavern in the hiding place we arranged and sneak you onto a ship, which will dock at the gold trader port in the Earth Realm. Head northwest, and when you reach the Sunken Forest, keep going in the same direction through the trees, and your people will find you."

I stuck my foot in the stirrup and swung into the saddle with a grunt. The eponar let out a deep honk, a sound I would probably find amusing if there wasn't a good chance a certain winged fae would be hunting me from the sky in the next few hours. Truthfully, the odds of me surviving the escape attempt were low, and at present, I was scared witless.

Sitting on this creature, with its long neck and narrow lumpy body, felt similar to riding one of Coridon's cantankerous camels—a blind one. I patted Enyd's bronze fur and prayed that everything Ari had told me about her was true—she was calm, obedient, intelligent, and, most importantly, faster than lightning.

"Ari, what will happen to you and Ildri when Arrow finds out what you did? Why risk your lives for me?"

With her golden eyes fixed on her clasped fingers, she said, "The risk is now greater, of course, since the king marked you as his Aldara."

"You're deflecting."

She sighed. "Ildri helps you because of her soft heart. And I help you because I know that you're needed in your realm. You really haven't uncovered a single memory of your true identity?"

My heart thudded harder. "If I had, I would have told you. Ari, if you have any knowledge about who I might be, even a hint, please, tell me."

She took a slow breath, her irises shimmering in the moonlight as she gazed at me. "I believe you come from the lost city of Mydorian, a city that, even now, stands strong in the Earth Realm."

"That's impossible. The city is nothing but vines and rubble."

What Ari suggested couldn't be true. My memories were of a family who lived rough in the ruins, surrounded by forest. There was no lost city of Mydorian. And if there was, and I'd lived there, surely I would have seen it in my visions.

"You're wrong." Gazing up at me, Ari gripped my knee and huffed. "The city is cloaked, hidden by a resident reaver elf. There is so much more I wish to tell you. The reasons the gold serum has no effect on you... why you were able to exit the city using the reaver door unaided... But there is no time. You must leave now, while you still can. Find the hidden city. If you still don't know who you are by the time you arrive, when your people see you, they most definitely will. Trust me. What has been forgotten will be remembered. I promise you."

I twisted in the saddle, leaned down, and kissed Ari's cheek. "Thank you for everything. I want you to know it was worth becoming a slave in the Storm Court to gain your friendship. I'll never forget you, Ari."

"Nor I you. Do your best to pass for a male if you can, and don't take that knitted cap off for anything," she whispered. "Now go! Travel swiftly, Daughter of Dust and Stone."

At her words, something twisted in my chest and coaxed the shadow of a memory from a dark corner of my mind. Not an image or a vision, just a feeling—of visceral fear.

"If you haven't enjoyed the full benefits of Raiden's... *friendship* yet," I said as I wheeled Enyd around, "for everyone's sakes, you should try to do it soon."

My heart squeezed at the sound of her soft laughter. The eponar lurched forward, leaping smoothly over a paddock fence instead of exiting via the gate I'd tried to direct her toward. Panic shivered down my spine as my mind careened from one disastrous scenario to the next.

If I made it to the Sunken Forest alive, which was reasonably unlikely, how would I find my way inside a city that was hidden by reaver magic? It seemed an impossible task, and I was insane to even attempt it. But I couldn't remain Arrow's slave forever, no matter how hard he made my heart pound. I had no option but to try to make it home—dead or alive.

Enyd sped through the desert under the light of a mauve sickle moon, bright stars illuminating the gold dust as it sprayed beneath her hooves. In the distance, glittering vortexes of sand spun as if by magic, and I looked over my shoulder, shivering at the storm clouds that gathered above Auryinnia Mountain.

I clung tightly to the eponar's neck and wrapped the reins of plaited gold around my left wrist, using my other hand to pat my body and check my coin pouch and knives were still secured beneath my cloak.

Before long, I tasted brine on the breeze, heard the squabbling cries of gulls, and saw white caps racing over a pitch-black sea, visible between low-lying buildings that hugged the ragged slope of the coastline.

On the outskirts of the small port town, I dismounted clumsily and fell into a scraggly salt bush, bruising both my backside and my pride. I leaped up and stroked Enyd's nose, kissing her unseeing eyes as I whispered my thanks for carrying me swiftly to my destination.

She nuzzled my neck, gave a too-loud honk, then took off in the direction of Auryinnia, where the Storm King hopefully still slept like a babe in our tent.

Holding the satchel strapped tightly across my body, I crept through shadows at the rear of the town until I found the rune-engraved wooden fence at the back of the reaver tavern that Ari had described in great detail.

I entered the yard via a narrow door in the wooden fence and hunkered down in a storage hut that smelled of rat shit to await sunrise and the arrival of Orion, the orc who was to help me stowaway on the ship bound for the Earth Realm.

The tavern was closed, but unfortunately, not all of the port's inhabitants were in bed. Groups of what I assumed to be drunken sailors and port workers stumbled past at frequent intervals. They sang tunelessly and laughed at vulgar jokes as they knocked into walls and clanged over containers and gods knew what else. No one ventured near my little hideaway, and I passed the hours nibbling strips of dried meat in uneasy peace.

Eventually, the drunks passed less frequently, their rumblings replaced by sounds of the port workers beginning their day. I listened to their shouts and piercing whistles as I pictured their carts rumbling over cobblestones and loading planks.

Through the hut's wooden slats, dawn burst in vivid strips of bright orange and purple, the light hurting my itchy, sleep-deprived eyes.

Not long after sunrise, the door cracked open, and a tall, gray-skinned orc entered the hut. He peered at me through a single, red-rimmed amber eye that took up nearly the whole of his rugged brow. I pulled the gold nugget from my pocket and squeezed it between my palms, whispering the three words Ari had taught me.

Auron khaban ana.

"Leaf?" he growled in a husky whisper, his bushy beard fluttering around bone-white tusks. "Is that you in the corner?"

Dust be damned. Of course Ari's disappearing spell didn't work. But hey, it was worth a try.

"I'll give you a hint, Orion," I called out. "I'm not your mother."

A dry chuckle rasped through the air, the sound not unfriendly. "Given she's been buried underground these past ten years, I'd be surprised to find the old orc crouching behind a woodpile."

"I'm sorry," I said, instantly regretting my joke. "That was cruel of me."

He grabbed my wrist and pulled me onto my feet.

"No need to apologize. She likes it down there, beneath the mountains with her bone collection."

Slinging my satchel over my shoulder, I puzzled over his words. Was his mother dead or not? In different circumstances, I'd be very keen to hear the story.

"Do you know what to do when I drop you off in the cargo hold?"

"Don't move until the ship docks, which will be when again?"

"Midnight. The captain has meetings tonight, so they won't be unloading any cargo until they dock again tomorrow, just heading to the taverns to pickle their brains. As soon as the ship docks, leave through the trap door in the far-left corner of the hold. It's under the flour bags. Then walk northwest toward the forest. Don't stop or even close your eyes. If you do, you're dead."

"What will—"

"You don't want to know. Men on horseback. Hungry wolves in desperate packs. Naiads in the rivers, spriggans in the trees. Demons. Many more things than dust and stones exist in that land, girl. And most of them have sharp teeth and claws."

"I thought you said you weren't going to tell me about them," I grumbled as I shuddered, watching him pull out a dusty blanket from a bag and unfold it. He lifted it toward me and grinned.

"Come closer. I'm going to wrap you in this, like a moth-girl in her silky cocoon, but not quite as tightly. Then I'll button you in this bag." Before I could protest, he started winding the blanket around me. On closer inspection, it looked more like a rug. "I'll leave the top buttons of the bag undone. You'll have plenty of time in the hold to work out how to get out of it."

"That's comforting," I said, my voice muffled by the folds of musty wool pressing against my mouth.

My pulse raced as my lungs filled with stale air, but I forced myself to breathe slowly and pictured my parents standing on the crumbling, sun-lit dais, surrounded by trailing vines and towering tree trunks.

"Thank you," I whispered even though I doubted Orion could hear me.

He laid me on the ground, and I felt him fumble over my body, fastening buttons on the bag I was now cocooned in, just as he'd warned.

I was silent as he hoisted me gently over his shoulder. The creak of the door opening and shutting covered my squeak as he wrapped a heavy arm around my butt and lumbered into motion.

With my muscles loose, I concentrated on sounds. Orion and the other sailors greeting each other, boots stomping on stones, then wood. Then even more blood pooled in my head as the angle changed, and we went downward into what was likely the hold of the ship.

As he placed me on the ground, the voice of another sailor boomed in the dark, and I did my best to stay calm. "What have you got there, Orion?"

"Bag of silk carpets from Coridon for the Sun Realm. They're the king's. So you'd best not get your grubby hands on them, Sindar, or the captain will twist your nuts off."

"Right. Reckon I need my balls, don't I?" The newcomer's laugh rumbled through the hold, sending chills over my skin. "Mighty tempted to take a peek at them, but it's probably not worth it. You sailing tonight?"

"Not on this run. Tomorrow," answered Orion.

A door thudded closed, and their voices dissolved in the darkness, leaving me alone with my raging fears. The cargo hold must have been packed earlier because after Orion left, only three other fae entered and left quickly before the ship set sail in a din of shouts and clanging sounds.

The hull creaked and rolled over the sea. And for far too long, I fought not only waves of terror, but swelling nausea that threatened to make me cast up my measly breakfast. Vomiting in the blanket might be worse than actually being discovered cowering inside it.

Eventually, I dozed off and dreamed of climbing slimy-rocked ruins and sword fighting in the forest until footsteps entered the hold and woke me. They stopped right next to my bag, and I recognized Sindar's deep mutters as he lifted me into the air, then thudded me down in a new position on the floor. I gave thanks to Orion for wrapping me in such a thick blanket.

"Bastard Fire King thinks he can keep all the nice things from Coridon, does he? Well fuck him and his orange-eyed sisters. Sindar here deserves some treats, too. Pretty rugs earn a nice sum of feathers at the markets. We'll see if they don't."

With a grunt, he tossed me out of the bag, and I rolled across the floor, still wrapped in the blanket, until I hit a solid lump, likely a bag of flour or grain. Glad that my hands were down by my sides, close to the knife strapped to my thigh, I focused, channeling fear into anger, weakness into battle readiness.

A chant whispered through my lips as I waited, blind in the dark and alert to the sound of the male's every breath and oafish move.

By branch and root, soil and stone, lend strength to muscle, heart, and bone. Crush all to live. Conquer and prevail. Mydor blood will never fail.

I had no idea how I knew this particular war song, but it drove all of my fear away. Violence hummed through my veins as every muscle strained to burst free from the rug and attack. Kill to survive. Because there was no way it would be me who died in this shithole of a hold tonight. It would be him. Sindar.

Come on asshole, I thought. *Hurry up. Let's get it done.*

Silence resonated, drowned out by the hard thud of my heart. Then, finally, something prodded my side.

"Heavy fucking rugs. Best Sindar takes a look at them."

Good, Sindar. Have a fucking look. I was ready.

And then, he unraveled me.

As a pair of blood-shot troll eyes widened in shock, I made myself wait, freezing my muscles solid for three seconds.

Friend or foe? Friend or foe? Come on, hurry up and reveal yourself, you bearded prick.

A lecherous, dark chuckle vibrated his thick, hairy lips, then he licked them with a wet, black tongue. "Looks like I found myself a little diversion. Last hour of a trip's always fucking boring. But not tonight, it seems."

A meaty hand reached for my cheek.

I ripped my knife out and plunged it into his leathery neck, grabbing the collar of his shirt and using his weight as he fell backward to flip myself out of the blanket. Then, before his dark blood could stain the wooden floor, I rolled him up and dragged him into the corner.

I wiped my blade on the bag Orion had hidden me in, then threw it over the troll, stood, and stretched my spine. "Sorry, Sindar," I said, sheathing the knife in my thigh belt. "You picked the wrong girl to abuse tonight."

Warm light from the hanging lanterns revealed hundreds of bags and barrels of various sizes stuffed into the large hold. A wide aisle of free space ran down the center.

Behind the dead troll's body, I moved aside bags of grain, searching for the trapdoor exit. I found it in the corner wall of the hull, along with a flat length of wood. I figured the plank attached to the outside of the ship and was used to access the dock that we'd soon arrive at.

I had found my escape route. My heart rate slowed, but I couldn't relax just yet. I wondered how much time I had before someone came looking for Sindar. Or came down here for any thousands of other reasons. I didn't have to wait long to find out.

Only minutes later, boots thudded down the stairs outside the hold. I drew my blade and hid behind the door, ready to strike, the battle chant racing through my mind again.

Mydor blood will never fail.

A latch clicked, then the door swung toward me. I shoved it as hard as I could, but it met with heavy resistance as a man cursed and kicked it open. I stumbled backward, my head cracking against the wall. When I opened my eyes, three human sailors stood in front of me. The one brandishing a long sword reached out to slam the door shut with a grunt.

The tallest one with narrowed mean eyes and a curling mustache whistled long and low. "By the gold, what have we here?"

I slowed my breathing and forced my arms to hang loose. Let them think me harmless. Let the assholes try to touch me.

"A very dirty, very fetching little bird, by the looks of it," said the second, his violent, black eyes clashing with his handsome face. "One we can mess up some more, me thinks."

The third, short and round, flicked his thumb toward my knife. "She's got a sharp beak this one. Want to bite us with that tiny thing, sweetheart?"

"I think if anyone's gonna do any biting," said mustache man, a bulge growing at the front of his tight leathers. "It'll be us taking pieces out of you." He took a step closer. "What's your name, green eyes?"

"Pain," I said, and attacked.

Moving fast, I slashed mustache's thigh, head-butted the short one, and kicked the handsome one in the balls. I lunged forward again, but unfortunately, they'd recovered from their surprise.

"You bitch," mustache yelped as handsome kicked my feet out from under me.

The moment I hit the ground, ignoring waves of blinding pain, I tried to sit up, but handsome's sword pinched the flesh under my chin, holding me in place. "We're gonna take our time ruining you, nasty little firebrand."

Snarling, I thrashed as the rotund one hooked his arm around me from behind and raised me off the floor, giving the handsome one access to my knives. As he removed them, my cap fell off. Mustache swooped and picked it up, then wiped it across his bleeding thigh.

"No sense in wasting energy fighting us, sweetheart. You fucked up. And now you're gonna pay the price." Oblivious to the pain of his knife wound, mustache laughed and grabbed me by the throat.

"Fuck, Darius, wait," said the beefy bald one. "Look at her hair."

While their wide eyes bounced between me and each other, I tried to drag my mind from my growing terror and focus on staying alive.

"Well, well, well." Handsome shoved his blade against my neck. "The gold has certainly blessed us this evening." He lifted me to my feet by the crook of my arm. "I have no idea how you got in here, Mydorian, but the captain would love to meet you, that's for sure. Am I right, lads?"

He called me a Mydorian. Were they aware the city was in ruins? Or like Ari, did they believe it still stood in the Sunken Forest, hidden by gold reaver magic?

As they dragged me out of the hold, I hoped the captain would at least give me some answers before he killed me.

Chapter 27

LEAF

A s it turned out, Captain Loligos wasn't in the mood to answer questions, which was a shame. He likely knew more about where I came from than I did.

I stumbled into his tidy, polished-mahogany cabin with my hands tied in front of me, and he looked up from his whiskey tumbler and smiled, his gold teeth flashing in the candlelight.

Yellow eyes trailed over Mustache, stopping at the blood seeping from his thigh. "*Darius*," the captain growled. "Get that seen to before you ruin my favorite alnarah rug."

Mustache nodded and left without a word.

On first glance, Captain Loligos looked human, but his unusual U-shaped pupils indicated he was fae. He wore a sea-green velvet jacket buttoned halfway up his brawny chest, revealing a billowy purple shirt underneath. Around his tanned throat, a necklace of polished crab shells and sharks' teeth gleamed. Ink-black hair curled past his broad shoulders, framing a handsome, rugged face, with a sly rather than kind set to his features.

"Well, what have we here, lads?" he asked as he leaned back in his chair and lit a cigar. "This one's an improvement on our usual quality of stowaways. Any idea how she got aboard?"

"Orion," said Shorty. "Rolled her up in a blanket, said it was a rug bound for the Fire King."

"Is that right?" The captain's strange yellow eyes raked my body. "You were in the hold?"

"They didn't discover me doing a circle dance on the deck," I muttered. As soon as the words were out, I regretted them severely.

With a horrible, moist crackling sound, the captain slid out from behind the desk, his eight tentacles slithering across the wooden floor. "I don't think you're in a position to backtalk me," he hissed.

"Sorry," I said, trying not to goggle at his writhing appendages. "That was stupid of me. My mouth often engages before my brain does."

A tentacle shot out and wrapped around my waist, dragging me close. The rest of them moved about wildly, some on the floor and others lashing the air like angry serpents, while his torso rose until he loomed over me.

Throwing myself backward, I swallowed a scream, but the tentacle around my waist only tightened.

Cold terror slid through my veins as I realized what Captain Loligos was—a cephalaean—a human octopus hybrid, that until this moment, I had believed only existed in stories. I truly wished that was still the case.

The water-filled tank that lined a wall of the cabin where a bed would normally stand made a lot more sense now that I'd laid my shocked, bulging eyes on him.

For one insane moment, I wondered why, instead of my name and entire identity, I remembered useless things, such as the times I'd spent running wild around ruins, and the names of fantastical creatures.

"Please pardon my rudeness, Captain," I wheezed, grabbing hold of the tentacle that circled my waist.

"Give me one good reason not to squeeze the life out of you," he said. A second slimy limb slithered around my neck, its grip looser than the first. "Will you promise not to scream too loudly while I spend the night removing your organs through your nostrils? I despise a noisy female."

The tip of his tentacle waved in front of my nose, and I retched and shook my head frantically.

"Wait, Cap'n," said Shorty, sidling up.

Loligos's lower arm shot out and knocked him across the room. Shorty collapsed beside the tank, then sat up, rubbing his head. "Just take a look at her hair."

The captain loosened his grip a little and studied me, his strange pupils dilating with interest. "What's your name?"

"Leaf."

The captain chuckled. "Leaf? I doubt that very much. Where are you from, little Leaf?"

Little Leaf.

A wave of sorrow swept over me at the sound of Arrow's nickname coming from the captain's foul mouth.

"I don't remember."

"Very mysterious." His smirk turned into a sneer. "Where have you been then? Before you bought your way onto this ship?"

"I don't remember that, either."

"Liar."

"I'm not. I swear it. A forest somewhere in the Earth Realm, that's all I know."

He sighed. "Listen, I've been at sea nigh on five centuries. I've witnessed almost everything there is to see in the realms, and I know when someone is feeding me a barrel of turned cod. Tell me the truth, or I'll throw you overboard."

"Someone drugged me. I have no idea who I am. Somehow, I ended up in a cage at the Farron Gilt Market. The Storm Court bought me from there and put me to work in their kitchen."

He grunted. "Now that tale has the ring of truth to it." He paused a moment, considering me. "Lads, I believe we'll lock this precious cargo in the cell until we dock. If anyone touches her, I'll stick a tentacle so far up their ass it'll look like their tongue wriggling out of their mouth. Understand?"

"But, Cap'n," said Handsome, his fists clenching at his sides. "As a reward, can't we have a little taste? Just a scrap of fun before we put her in the cell?"

"She'll be of no value maimed. But you did the right thing, boys, bringing the—this *daughter* of the Earth Realm straight to me when your *instincts* were screaming for you to do otherwise. There are only a couple of hours left until we dock, and I'll see that you get paid in gold for your restraint."

The captain's tentacle unraveled from my waist, then he slithered back to his desk, sat down, and began scribbling on a tiny piece of parchment.

From behind me, Handsome gripped my tied wrists and pushed his weight into my back. Praying silently that they wouldn't find Sindar's body anytime soon, I grunted as his knife pricked my neck. "Steady on. I can't do much to hurt you at the moment, can I?"

Loligos frowned in concentration, the tip of his cigar flaring red. He pressed his finger on an ink pad, then onto the note, stamping it with his print. He repeated the process on a second parchment. "Send these via gull—this one to the Regent and the second to his soldiers stationed at the closest port. Lads, he'll give us a tidy sum for this little thorn in his side, boil me alive if he don't."

"Cap'n, we'd never chuck you in a pot," said Shorty, taking the messages and pocketing them. "What should we do about Orion?"

"If he's smart, he'll already be in the Sun Realm. But if he ever shows his face around the port, you know what to do."

"Feed him to the sharks."

"Precisely." With a smirk, the captain waved me out of his cabin.

Handsome and Shorty pushed me along a lamp-lit hallway, down narrow stairs, and then shoved me into a tiny cell. Minutes later, Shorty reappeared and threw me a hunk of stale bread.

"Dinnertime," he announced, pointing at the barrel in the corner, from which the smell of foul water wafted.

When he left, I crouched against the far wall with my muscles strung taut, poised to respond to an attack from an unwelcome visitor. Though eating was the last thing I felt like doing, I forced myself to nibble on the bread and sip a little of the unpleasant water. Doing my best not to retch, I told myself I'd need energy, since an opportunity to flee might magically present itself.

For now, I had no choice but to hunker down like a rat in a trap and await my fate. I replayed everything that had happened in the captain's cabin, in case I'd missed any clues about this regent person who Loligos was so eager to sell me to.

I wondered why the captain seemed certain this man would want me and what I'd done to become a thorn in his side. Who did Loligos think I was? Perhaps a rebel fighter or a spy from Coridon? Whatever the truth, I wasn't looking forward to meeting him.

I grimaced as I took another sip of sour water, unsure if I wanted time to speed up or grind to a halt. My eyes burned with exhaustion. So I closed them for just a moment, my head dropping back against the cell wall.

Don't go to sleep. Not here. Not safe...

I jerked my head up and rubbed my eyes, determined to stay awake. A few moments later, my vision darkened as I fought sleep. Suckered vines wrapped my ankles, tripping me over as I chased a pair of vivid green eyes through the crumbling ruins.

Dreaming. Fuck. I was dreaming.

After I jerked awake for the fourth time, I stopped fighting it, telling myself a short nap would do me good, then I let the forest swallow me.

Sometime after, rough voices penetrated my dreams, trying to drag me back to unwelcome consciousness.

"Where the fuck is she?" said Shorty's voice.

"How should I know?" grumbled another. "You're the one standing in front of me. Move out of the way."

In the dream, I stood in the center of my pavilion in the king's apartment, naked except for my gold collar. "Do it again," Arrow said, stroking my throat. I relaxed, focusing on the piece of auron kanara feather in my mouth, chewing it slowly. Golden light burst from my chest, radiating out from my body, and Arrow laughed. "That's fucking brilliant. I can't see you anymore. But quick, Leaf, I can't bear it. Come back to me. Show yourself."

The rough voices sounded again, drowning out the words of my dream Arrow.

"Look. She's over there... in the shadows. Asleep. You must be blind not to see her. Better stop drinking so much rum, Jarl."

I jolted awake, keeping my muscles loose as I gripped the gold nugget Ari had given me and gazed at the men through cracked eyelids.

Shorty, or Jarl as the second man had called him, had his meaty fingers on the cell door, unlocking it with fumbling movements.

"Hurry up," said Handsome, standing behind Jarl, his arms folded and a filthy leer spoiling his pretty face. "Cap'n wanted her on deck twenty minutes ago. The Earth Realm soldiers are getting prickly. If he thinks we've been fiddling with her, he'll throw us in his tank and have us for his dinner."

My rope-linked hands flew to my side before I remembered they'd taken my blades. The sailors laughed.

"Touch me and I'll scream. I promise I'll poke your eyes out and bite your pricks off before you can kill me. Then what will Captain Loligos do to you? Sew them back on tenderly? I don't think so."

Muttering about how they would use me if only there was no captain to be feared, they led me up onto the deck. Under a star-flecked indigo sky, Loligos himself and five human soldiers stood chatting, all glancing up at my arrival.

As I walked past the crowd of sailors gathered to witness my handover to the Earth Realm soldiers, I held my uncovered head high. Not one of them spoke, and an eerie silence hung heavy in the air. I looked left and right, scanning the faces of the motley collection of humans and fae, disappointed that none were familiar.

A few of them dropped their gazes as I strode by, their hands twisting dirty caps in front of their chests, which struck me as curious. They looked frightened or embarrassed, and I couldn't understand why.

Finally, the truth struck me. They weren't used to seeing a woman on board. I was bad luck. But fortunately for them, they wouldn't have to suffer my presence for long. I was about to be whisked away. I only wished I knew to where.

"Ah, here she is," boomed the captain, his tentacles writhing with glee as he watched me approach flanked by Jarl and Handsome, their blades digging into my sides.

Loligos stretched his arm toward me. "Your Regent's precious cargo cometh. What do you think of her, Earth soldiers? Pretty little viper, no?"

"Indeed," answered a man who was dressed in a navy uniform trimmed with gold piping that matched the armor covering his chest and shoulders. "She is exactly as you described. The Regent will be pleased."

Ten bags that contained either coin or gold feathers were unloaded from a covered cart on the dock and dropped at Loligos's feet. A sailor opened the sacks and verified the contents with a sharp nod. The captain grinned like he'd just been served a juicy baby whale for his dinner.

"She's all yours," said Loligos as Jarl pushed me into the human soldier's arms.

As two of the men stepped forward and replaced the rope around my wrists with shackles and chain, Loligos drew on his cigar, then blew smoke in my face. "She claims to have no memories, but has all the pluck you'd expect for her type, so watch her closely or she'll cut your kidneys out and eat them while you sleep. Good luck, human. Give the Regent my regards, won't you?"

In a fond gesture of goodbye, I spat on the captain's boot. The Earth Realm soldier's slap sent my head reeling to the side. While I rubbed the sting from my cheek with the back of my hand, he dragged me across the plank and onto dry land, where I swayed on the dock next to a cart and five tethered horses.

"I'm Sonail, by the way."

"Impressive backhand," I said.

He grunted and dumped me on the cart bench seat. After he got comfortable next to me, he checked the handcuffs and chain lying in my lap, then picked up the horse's reins.

The four other men mounted heavily muscled steeds, moving them into position. One at the front of the cart, two on either side, and one at the rear.

Even restrained and unarmed, the Earth soldiers correctly viewed me as a flight risk.

I turned to Sonail and took his measure. Middle-aged, with reddish-brown hair tied neatly behind his head, he looked fit, strong, and despite the straggly beard growing in below his scarred cheeks, neat and orderly. Dark narrowed eyes stared back at me.

"And I'm Leaf," I said in a mocking tone. "Pleased to meet you."

"Leaf, is it? I don't think so." He shouted at the horse, lashing it into motion with a long whip.

"With only one horse to draw your cart, you might want to treat it better," I suggested.

He laughed. "Varlys is strong and the cart light. If I was you, I wouldn't waste my energy worrying about a horse. You've got bigger problems ahead, *Leaf*."

We set off at a brisk pace, soon clearing moonlit coastal dunes, then traveling along rough roads that cut through a hilly landscape marred by strange shadows. The air was cooler here than in the Light Realm, and the sounds were different, too. Instead of the haunting calls of night hawks and owls, wolves bayed from different directions, coordinating their night's hunt.

Without warning, two of these hungry creatures shot out of the darkness, snarling as they attacked one of the horse's legs. A wolf yelped, kicked away by beating hooves, and Sonail whipped out a pistol and dealt with the other, the shot echoing through the wasteland and bouncing off nearby hills.

"So, this is the Earth Realm," I muttered to myself. "What a hospitable place."

"I'm glad you like it," my companion replied. "It is your home, after all. The wolves are hungry. And like them, you'd probably bite my fingers off the first chance you got, wouldn't you?"

"No doubt. But then I'd spit them out and crush them under my boot. I'd rather starve than task my gut with digesting your rotting flesh."

"Charming," Sonail replied.

"As are you."

He sighed so hard he nearly choked on his saliva, and I had to swallow my laughter or risk angering him further.

"Speaking of food, what are my chances of getting something to eat and drink soon? Or are you hoping I'll perish along the way to wherever you're taking me?"

"If you'll be quiet, I'll make sure you're fed and watered when we make camp. If not, then perhaps I will let you perish. It's not a bad idea."

"You know, Sonail, it really bothers me that you don't care whether I make it to our destination alive or dead."

He shrugged. "I might be bluffing. You really have no idea where we're going?" he asked.

Light from the rising sun revealed a lightly treed, softly undulating landscape that I was sad to find completely foreign to me.

At some point soon, I hoped the environment would begin to look familiar.

"That's right. I have no idea."

"And no memory of who you are?"

"I don't remember anything before I woke up in a slave cage roughly six weeks ago."

He grunted. "That's probably for the best," he said, his words sending a cold shiver down my spine.

Lost in our own thoughts, we fell into an uneasy silence, traveling all day and barely speaking until sunset when our small party made camp in a cool forest.

The fresh scent of damp earth and pine needles made my chest ache. Finally, something I recognized. It smelled like home, and I knew that at last, we were getting closer.

After Sonail watched me pee, as promised, he fed me a portion of the juicy rabbit his men had roasted on a spit, and then tied me to a tree trunk in sight of their campfire.

For an hour or two, the soldiers drank, their revelry culminating in a tedious song that listed their heroic deeds and all the lands they planned to conquer before their deaths. Then, finally, they fell asleep, leaving me to stare into the darkness, every muscle aching as I listened to them snore, sounding like a family of wild boars.

In the dead of night, something sharp poked my chest, and with a gasp, I jerked out of a light doze, expecting to find one of Sonail's men leering at me. Instead, I found one of Loligos's human sailors crouched over my legs.

His hand slapped over my mouth as he ducked behind me and whispered in my ear. "Don't scream. I'm here to help."

I nodded, and his hand fell away. "Who sent you? And why?"

"We'll talk about that later... when we're three hundred miles away from here," he said, cutting through the rope that bound me to the tree.

"I'm handcuffed, too."

"Not a priority now. I just need to get you out of here. I'm Aallon."

"Leaf."

My blood rushed in my ears. *Hurry up, hurry up*, I chanted under my breath, my teeth chattering.

I kept my eyes fixed on the sleeping bodies of the soldiers visible on this side of the dying campfire—only three—and prayed the other two were fast asleep.

Aallon sheathed his knife, threw me over his shoulder, and pulled an ax from his belt, running deeper into the forest. He was fast, his body strong, and all I could do as I bounced against his back was hope he was a good man and, also, very skilled with that ax.

Could Arrow have sent Aallon to retrieve me?

My skin crawled. Fear and something else, something deeply worrying, slithered through my belly. With shock, I realized it was excitement. I was excited at the prospect of seeing the Storm King again, if only briefly, before he fried me with his lightning magic as punishment for escaping.

It pained me that even now, my thoughts were twisted in my head and I very likely fancied myself in love with my ex-captor.

What a spectacularly bad time to realize it.

We hadn't gotten far when a voice boomed behind us. "Put her down."

Fuck. Sonail.

As Aallon turned, throwing his ax, a shot rang out, and he grunted, dropping to the ground with a thud. I rolled off him, stumbled up, and ran like the desert wind, the crunch of footfalls chasing me through the trees.

Blinded by terror, I smashed into a tree trunk, recoiled, and took off again. Two breaths later, Sonail threw himself on me, taking me down to the ground. We rolled, and when we came to a stop, his knife was at my throat, his nose dripping blood on my face as we panted at each other.

"Good try," he said, leaping to his feet and pulling me up. "But not good enough. The men are breaking camp. Take a piss. We'll be on the road until early afternoon."

As he tugged me toward the campsite, I looked over my shoulder at the body on the ground. "Do you know who that human is? Are you just going to leave him there?"

"The wolves will deal with him. Relax. Soon you will be home sweet home."

Yes, I was beginning to worry about that. Perhaps home wasn't the blissful, happy place my visions had led me to believe.

Sonail didn't punish me for my attempted escape, and I wondered why. Could he not be bothered? Or did he figure that when we arrived at our destination, my punishment would be severe enough?

As the cart rolled through a valley that wound between a lush mountain range, I couldn't stop thinking about Aallon. I wondered why he'd risked his life to free me, and even though it was true, I tried hard to bury the thought that I had caused his death.

Of course, there was a chance he'd planned to take me somewhere worse than wherever Sonail and his men were delivering me. He might have handed me over to an even bigger monster than Arrow or the mysterious regent who had paid for me with bags of gold. But somehow, I doubted that. My gut told me he was genuine. And thought I was worth saving. Gods knew why.

Once we cleared the mountains, we followed a river through long grasslands dotted with scraggly gray scrub, not stopping for lunch and eating dried fruit and meat as we traveled. Then a few hours later, we dropped over a hill and descended into a thick forest where the energy changed so swiftly it felt like we were approaching an invisible forcefield or barrier.

Every hair on my body prickled, my heart battering my ribcage as my eyes darted over the trees and vines that suddenly looked so similar to my visions.

This was home. But where in the realms was it?

I stopped breathing and strained my ears, hearing nothing but the scrape of our horses' hooves over dried twigs, the gentle creak of saddles and cartwheels. No birds. No water tinkling nearby. No leaves rustling in the breeze.

This place felt like a void in time, a dead space that repelled every living being from getting too close. Standing in front of the barrier reminded me of how I felt in my dreams as I waited on a cliff edge with Ash, ready to leap into the writhing river below. Afraid, but intensely excited.

"Do you see it?" Sonail asked me.

"Are there ruins here?" I said, certain I was close to where I remembered training with Ash.

"On the eastern side, yes," said Sonail. "But not here."

The soldier on the white horse to my left studied me curiously, then turned quickly and stared ahead.

Relaxing my focus, I gasped as a convex veil of light bent over the foreground and soared as high and wide as my eyes could see. It was translucent, and yet it reflected the trees and foliage beside and behind us, like a magical mirror. A trick that made you see what wasn't there and not see what was right in front of you.

I strained my eyes and mind trying to make sense of it.

"I see something. We're going to go through that?" I said.

"Yes. The barrier isn't visible to everyone, which suggests you've seen it before. That you know what to look for."

"But if we can simply go through it, then surely anyone can."

"No. Its magic works to repel folk. Most simply find a way around it without even realizing what they're doing."

"And what's on the other side?" I asked.

The soldiers laughed, a heartless sound.

Sonail glared at them, then touched my arm, startling me. He unlocked my handcuffs, and I made a sound of pain and relief as I rubbed my wrists.

"Brace yourself. This might hurt a little."

Frowning, I looked up at him. "What do you mean?"

Ignoring me, he whipped the poor horse, and we lurched forward through the strange barrier that undulated like a wave of heat shimmering off the desert sand. Tiny teeth tore at my skin, and I cried out, thrashing to escape the pain, then with a wet popping sound, we broke through the barrier and everything changed.

I made a noise of confusion and blinked at the scene before me.

People. Everywhere.

A massive crowd of humans gathered around wide iron gates as if they had been waiting for our arrival. Through the gate, a sprawling palace of black stone loomed. Its round turrets were lined with silver and countless sparkling arched windows filled with clear glass. In a semi-circular pattern, smaller dark buildings ranged around it.

Deep-green ivy and a flowering vine with black petals crawled over the buildings as if it was trying to consume the entire city. Perhaps it was. But it would fail. The city looked strong, as if it could endure anything, even its own rumored demise.

"Behold the Lost City of Mydorian," said Sonail at my side, his voice full of pride as he lifted me from the cart. "To allow you some dignity, you can walk beside me unchained. Please note, I'll be holding onto you very tightly, my soldiers watching your every move. Don't make me regret my moment of compassion."

A wave of humans surged forward. Young, old, and every age in-between. Many were gold addicts, their eyes a dull golden color and rough patches of glittering skin marring their faces, but the majority of Mydorians seemed healthy enough.

Excitement and fear clenched my heart. These were my people, and I was home, exactly where I had longed to be since the moment I woke in the gilt market slaver's cage.

"Move!" Sonail shouted, pushing people so hard they fell to the ground as we passed. "The outlaw princess, Zali Omala, has been captured. Make way so she can be returned to the capitol and face trial."

Zali Omala?

Zali was my name? And I was *what?* A princess? Crazed laughter bubbled up my throat. Heat and ice filling my veins simultaneously. No. That was ridiculous. *Impossible*. Sonail had it wrong.

None of this made sense. I didn't feel the slightest flicker of recognition, not a single revelatory twinge of ownership of the rebel princess's name. It couldn't be me. How could I forget, not only my whole identity, but also the entire city my family supposedly ruled?

No... No way. I wasn't this Zali person. It wasn't even remotely possible.

"Shit," I muttered, my legs beginning to shake as I realized something that was indeed true.

I had been a fool, wanting to return to this place. I should have stayed with Arrow and remained his little Leaf forever, instead of this... Zali, the outlaw.

He would have kept me safe, made me laugh and cry with his powerful hands and body. And I would have fought his rule with every breath, every nip of my teeth.

Arrow would have loved it.

Perhaps I would have, too.

As my breath sawed in and out of my aching lungs, Sonail tugged me through the gate. While bodies buffeted us, pushing and shoving, I relieved him of a small blade that fit neatly inside the pocket Ari had stitched in my shirt.

At least now I'd be armed when I met the regent. And all going well, my visit to Mydorian would be a short one.

Chapter 28

ARROW

A storm rumbled in the distance, the sound invading my sweat-soaked, alcohol-induced dream. I moved slowly inside my human, moaning blissfully, somehow aware I was still asleep.

Thunder cracked, and I woke with a start to find cool air on my chest instead of Leaf's warm body. My eyes still closed, I flung my hand out, patting over empty silken sheets. I inhaled deeply, seeking her scent in the air, not finding it in the camp. Not finding it *anywhere*.

Gone. My human was gone.

"Ari," I bellowed, sitting up, rubbing my temples and wondering how much wine I'd drunk last night. My head throbbed, and my eyes burned when I tried to focus on... fucking anything.

I leaped from the bed, stumbling as I threw on a shirt, then my chest plate and leathers. "Ari! Where the fuck are you?"

I strapped on a sword and ducked out of the tent. The Sayeeda and Ildri strode through the mist-filled camp, their faces grim like they were marching toward their executioner.

If the news they bore was as bad as I predicted and it explained why Leaf wasn't in my tent, then the storm of the century was about to break.

Energy sparked from my knuckles as I cracked them and flicked my wings out. Then I tore across the field to meet Ildri and my Sayeeda. "Where is she?"

Ari stared at my wings that whipped the air above my shoulders. It was rare for me to display them in front of my courtiers, but my blood rushed like wildfire through my veins, and I longed to shoot into the air and find my human. My Aldara.

She was more necessary to me than my crown of feathers, than my whole fucking kingdom. Why? I didn't know, and I didn't care. All that mattered was that it was true.

Thunder rumbled closer, black clouds gathering above. "For fuck's sake, Ari, where's Leaf?" Without thinking, I wrapped my hands around her throat and lifted her off the ground.

Ildri stepped forward, touching a burning glyph on my arm. "Be calm, Arrowyn," she said, her eyes gentle. "You'll need to be calm to listen. And to then take the right action."

Action? What the fuck was she talking about? What was going on?

Ari's sandals hit the grass as I lowered her. "She's gone, My King."

"*Gone?* Where?" Lightning forked above me, the golden morning turning into darkest night.

"Home."

"With your help I take it?"

The Sayeeda nodded, her eyes downcast.

"You drugged me last night."

"Yes, she did," said Ildri. "And I helped her."

Fury exploded inside me, an aura of blue and orange energy crackling over my body.

Panic flared in Ildri's violet eyes. "Arrow. Please, you must listen—"

"*I* must listen? I must listen to those who have betrayed me? Are you fucking serious?"

Lightning bolts struck the campsite, setting fire to a cart and two nearby tents, thunder shaking the ground beneath my feet.

"Arrow," said Ari, her voice level and face as serene as a lake on a windless day. "If you don't gain control of yourself, you'll burn everyone in the camp to cinders. I know you don't want to hurt your people."

"Don't I? I'll raze the whole fucking realm, turn it into a wasteland to get her back, Ari. The sooner you realize that the better."

"If you want to know where she is," she said, "if you want our help, you will need to play nice. When your father died, my life was bonded to your will, but know this, I'll only help Arrowyn, my friend, not the king currently ruled by rage. Tear me to pieces if you must, but acting rashly today may be as good as signing Leaf's death warrant."

I shut my eyes and forced a fake sensation of peace through my blood, into my lungs, then sent it to the storm clouds above. Rain poured down, drenching everything in the camp within seconds.

"Fine. Tell me," I commanded. My body shook with the effort of not roaring at Ari as I stared at her through my wet hair.

"I will, Arrow. I promise. But first, let us return to your tent, where we can have a civil and private conversation."

For several heartbeats, I glared at her, then stomped toward the tent, streaks of silver shooting across the sky and thunder rumbling in my wake. I focused my anger, my fear, and chased the darkness and the rain away, restoring a gloomy gray light to the sky.

In the tent, I slumped in an armchair, grinding my teeth. The canvas flap opened, and Raiden marched in, followed by Ari and then Ildri.

"Arrow," he said, rubbing his temples, no doubt suffering the aftereffects of being drugged, too. "My mother... please, I beg you—"

Silencing Raiden with my outstretched palm, I turned to Ari. "Talk."

Taking her time, Ari poured water into a cup, then handed it to me. "We had good reason to think it was necessary to help Leaf return home."

"To what?" I shouted. "Ruins in a forest roamed by raiders and gold addicts? What you've done is send her to her death. A very unpleasant one. That is something I will *never* forgive you for."

"No. I am certain that at least some of her family remain there. She deserves to be reunited with them."

A low table flew across the tent as I pushed it away, lurching upright and grabbing Ari's face between my hands. "What Leaf *deserves* is to be protected by *me*." Of their own accord, my wings raised themselves above my shoulders, trembling hard and ready to lift me into the air. "Tell me where she is. I'll retrieve her now and deal with you when I return."

"I can't. Not yet, and you'll never find her on your own. Reaver magic hides her location."

My brow knitted as I searched her face, fury flowing through my veins.

"Threats won't work, Arrow," she whispered, reading my intentions correctly. "Return to Coridon. By the time we arrive, Leaf will be safe at her destination. Then I'll tell you everything and help you find her if you still want her back."

"Fuck," I breathed, releasing Ari and pacing across the floor of the tent. *If* I still wanted her? Hadn't she been paying attention? "I could take you with me now in my arms. We'll fly back to Coridon. It'll be faster."

"No, I need more time, not less, before I am prepared to tell you everything."

Stifling a growl, I kicked the water goblet across the floor, my head pounding. "Raiden, activate our spy network. Any whispers or rumors about *any* travelers, even if the descriptions don't match Leaf, I want to know about them. Send the information to me without delay. By any means. Understand?"

Mouth a grim line, he nodded, his dark eyes flicking to Ildri. "And should we decamp, My King?"

My king? Raiden had never called me that before except in jest, and the title coming from his lips now was an insult. To stoop to using it, he must rightly fear for his mother's life.

Ari stilled my hand from raking through my hair, her expression shockingly devoid of guilt. "It is your best move, Arrow. Go home. Rest and restore your power. You'll need to be strong if you intend to travel to the human realm."

"I fucking hate that I have to wait, but you're right. I need to recharge my power. Dismantle the camp immediately."

Raiden bowed and hurried away.

"Ari, go quickly and give my apologies to the Zareen. We'll leave as soon as my carriage is ready."

"As you wish." She turned and glided out of the tent, seemingly in no particular hurry.

Ildri's gaze dropped to my clenched fists, and she risked a gentle smile. "All will be well if you trust us, Arrow. I promise you."

I doubted that very much.

And on the journey home, try as I might, I couldn't control the storms that besieged our procession of carriages and carts, depleting my power further. My gut screamed that Leaf wasn't safe. Every instinct inside me writhed and raged, insisting that I take to the sky without delay and search until I found her. Search until every feather was ragged or broken, if that's what it took to get Leaf back.

But I wasn't a fool. I could search forever without success, while Leaf lay buried in a shallow grave as I flew in vain above the Earth Realm forests.

With Ari's information, we would waste no time. I would find my Aldara dead or alive.

If the former, Ari would pay. Ildri would pay. And Raiden would suffer the loss of both females he loved.

Of course, if it was the latter... if Leaf was alive, I would bring her home, no matter what circumstances I found her in. I would take her. I would carry her back to Coridon.

Because she was mine.

And always would be.

Chapter 29

LEAF

The hidden city of Mydorian was nothing like the decaying ruins from my dreams and visions. As Sonail led me up sweeping steps toward the palace's entrance, two things astonished me: the building's grandeur and how unfamiliar it was.

I recognized nothing. Not the guards' bearded faces or their black and gold uniforms. Nor the dark stone beneath my feet or the sulphuric scent of gold smelt in the air. If this was indeed the place I grew up, it seemed odd that I remembered none of it.

But when silver double doors glided open and revealed a long rectangular throne room, something stirred inside me. Ghost-white trees grew up through the edges of the hall's pale wooden floor, their branches soaring upward to cradle the ceiling, open to the sky in the center.

An image of the bearded man from my dreams—my father—flashed through my mind. He was standing on the low dais, his hands braced on his hips. On a solid throne of white marble, my mother sat beside him, regal in a shimmering gown and wearing a crown of rubies and golden thorns on her brow.

I shook the vision from my mind, my heart stuttering as I dragged cold air into my lungs. My eyes widened at the green-eyed boy from my dreams, who was currently sprawled over my mother's white throne.

Sonail's grip on my arm tightened, and he pulled me toward my only real memory of home.

"Ash," I whispered, my heart a painful lump in my throat.

Lifting his gaze from his lap and casting it about the room, Ash tapped long fingers against the throne's armrest as memories rushed over me. Ash and I swimming, laughing, racing through the forest, sword fighting, fist fighting, more laughter. Love. Light. Happiness.

Home.

It was really him—my brother there in front of me.

I hardly dared to believe it, but I was finally home.

And I was safe.

While I waited for him to look at me, the word *brother* sounded on repeat in my head, growing louder and louder until it took on a nightmare quality.

Finally, my brother's eyes met mine, a cold smile spreading over his face, his features a creepy mirror image of my own. Nausea churned my gut. That face of malicious glee didn't make sense. Ash's expression was all wrong. Out of place.

Unless...

As I walked closer, my flesh crawled as if maggots wriggled beneath my skin, eating me alive.

Unless this man... this regent who had bought me... was my twin.

I stopped three feet from the dais, and he leaned over his knees, moving slowly like a reptile in the sun. He looked me up and down with eyes that were no longer bright green, like in my dreams. Translucent gold, they matched the scaly splotches of shimmering skin that marred his handsome features.

An obvious gold addict, his face was a beautiful ruin, like fruit left out too long in the sun that was still juicy and bright enough to tempt you into taking a bite. So changed was he from the boy who had appeared in my dreams, that just looking at him soured my stomach.

Bitterness bled from his pores. Did he no longer love me? Perhaps every memory I possessed of him was a lie. A trick. Some sort of glamour or spell.

Laughter rasped from his gold-touched lips. "Do you know who I am?"

Clenching my fists, I raised my chin. "Of course, you're my brother, Ash."

A slow blink, then one of his dark brows rose. "The name's Quin, actually. Ash was only a nickname."

Quin. Yes, I remembered that name. "Tall as an ash tree," I whispered.

"Precisely. Welcome home, sister. I must say you look a little worse for wear. Rather filthy and bedraggled. You must be hungry. Exhausted." He coughed and shook his head. "Are you pleased to see me?"

I forced an expression of calm. The only way to play this was to pretend I thought this alarming man on the throne wasn't my enemy and be ready to attack.

"Ash, I can't believe it's really you. Somehow, I got lost and woke up in the Light Realm with nearly all of my memories gone."

"Nearly all?" The ruby crown our mother had worn tipped on Quin's brow as he slouched back against the throne. "So, you retained some memories? Interesting. Tell me about them."

The icy teeth of fear nibbled down my spine, and I swallowed hard. "I dreamed of when we were children, roaming the forest together. I remembered the fun we used to have, how much we loved each other. And our parents—"

He waved a hand, cutting me off. "They're dead. Thanks to the fire fae who found them in the forest outside the barrier six months ago."

The knot of twisted muscle in my stomach turned to stone. I had suspected my parents were dead. But to have it so flippantly confirmed by the boy I'd assumed was searching for me the whole time I was in Coridon was a brutal kick to the gut.

I glanced over my shoulder, noting the positions of the four guards—two flanking the entrance and the others facing each other halfway down the sides of the hall.

"You may leave us, Sonail," said my brother, not bothering to thank his soldier for returning me in one piece. Maybe Quin would have preferred it if Sonail had presented me in a bag of dripping gore instead.

Sonail hesitated, then dropped my arm and bowed. "Yes, Regent."

I waited until the sound of his heavy footsteps disappeared, then took a deep breath. "Regent? Who exactly are you standing in for?"

"Why, for you, of course, sister dearest. Upon our mother's death, you should have been crowned Queen Zali Omala, the three hundred and thirty-third Empress of the Realm of Dust and Stones. It has quite a ring to it, doesn't it?"

Yes, I thought as I gritted my teeth, the weight of the title making my head spin. The brother of my dreams was a traitor, no better than the power-hungry fae of the realms. And if he was capable of stealing a crown, what else had he done?

Fury wiped sense from my thoughts, and I gave up pretending that we were on the same side. "So you disposed of me just because you wanted the crown for yourself?"

"No, because I knew I'd make a better ruler than you."

"We could have ruled together. My memories indicate our bond was strong. Every recollection of you was fond and loving. Why turn against me?"

"Perhaps I grew tired of watching you win all the time. And was bored stupid by everyone talking about how special you were. The golden child that was blessed with everything—natural fighting skills, the apple of our parents' eyes, beloved daughter of our people. And perhaps because of this..." He ran stained fingers over the gold marks streaming from his eyes and down his cheeks.

"Because of the serum?"

"Yes. You'd taken Mother's side in the argument about the slave trade and could go on about nothing else. The very trade that all five of the realms rely on. Under your rule, our family's power would have diminished until we were nothing."

"But, Quin, we *are* nothing in the other realms. The fae kingdoms believe our city is long gone and only ruins and decay stand in its place."

He smirked. "Not all of the kingdoms. The Sun Realm is still aware of our glory and of our remarkable connection to the gold reavers."

Ice slid through my veins as the truth of what my brother had done hit me like a bolt of lightning. "It was you! Fuck, Quin. You had our parents murdered. You're a fucking monster! Why didn't you just kill me too?"

A sly smile lifted his mouth. "There are rumors about twins. Two hearts, one soul. That kind of thing." He chuckled. "I have a very superstitious nature, sister. Don't you remember?"

Superstitious? Greedy, cruel, and callous better described his personality.

"You're an addict. How could you think yourself fit to rule a kingdom?"

"All one needs is a crown, Zali."

Those words told me everything there was to know about Quin Omala. Perhaps once he had been the brother of my heart—a source of joy, my sunshine in the forest of our childhood—but now... he was nothing but a murderer. A thief. And an unrepentant drug addict who had killed his own parents. A lost cause, who I wouldn't waste a single tear over.

I stared him down until he squirmed, his lip curling into a sneer. "For speaking lies against the Regent, for accusing me of murder, I should command that guard over there to put an arrow in your back."

Speaking of an *Arrow*, I thought. "Aren't you curious about where I've been, Quin? Perhaps you should ask if I have any useful information to share."

"You were in the Light Realm and a servant at the disgusting Storm Court."

"I *was* a servant for a time, but then my circumstances changed rather significantly..." I let my words trail off, teasing him.

Quin lurched off the throne and swayed to the edge of the dais before crumpling on the bottom step. He folded his elbows on his knees and craned his neck toward me like an enraged dragon about to strike, both madness and gold fever swirling in his irises.

"Yes?" he hissed. "Tell me what happened."

"The king took a fancy to me, and I slept in his bed every night, soothing his nightmares."

"And no doubt you soothed the ache in his golden cock, too." He chuckled, leaning back on his elbows. "So, the rightful queen of the Earth Realm became Arrowyn Ramiel's whore."

Fury exploded in the base of my spine, but I gritted my teeth and smiled, digging my fingers into the flesh of my outer thigh. "Not precisely."

Chin resting in his palm, Quin tapped his cheek. "Come here, sister."

Hunching my shoulders, I shuffled forward, hoping I looked meek and terrified. "I've been inside Auryinnia Palace, dined with the Zareen. The king killed a man who dared to touch me and even his own guards for trying to hurt me."

"Did he now? Interesting. Perhaps you might be able to help me wrestle the gold trade from that power-mongering bastard's control."

I bit my tongue, holding back the jibe pressing against my lips: *it takes one to know one, you stupid fuck.*

"It's possible," I said. "Tell me something, Quin. When I arrived, Sonail called me the outlaw princess. What lies did you tell to earn me such an unbecoming title?"

"It hardly matters now. Be quiet, Zali, while I consider what to do with you."

Zali. Even if he called me by that name a thousand times, it would never feel like it belonged to me. Another name felt more comfortable. The name that gorgeous, winged asshole had given me.

Picturing Arrow's silver eyes and the sensual smile he saved just for me, I willed tears to form, allowing them to spill down my cheeks.

"Brother," I said, dropping to my knees in front of him and gripping his wrist. I tried to look at him the way Raiden gazed at the Sayeeda, like a pathetic lost puppy. "Please, remember our bond as children. Remember how much we once loved each other."

Delight softened his scowl as I begged, his gaze euphoric with victory. I drew Sonail's little blade from my shirt, aimed for my brother's heart, and thrust hard.

A force caught me from behind, shoving me to the ground before my knife could plunge through leather and hit its corrupted target.

A guard straddled me, his dagger at my throat, and the sound of my brother's crazed laughter echoed through the hall.

"My guards are fast, imbued with fire magic," drawled Quin. "Not even you could get past them. Get up, Zali, before I have him take your head off."

The guard pushed off me, and I stood, my muscles trembling with suppressed fury.

"Well, sister, if you weren't a traitor before, you've certainly proved yourself one today, trying to kill your Regent."

"I think we both know who the traitor in this hall is," I hissed.

I bit my lip, dying to tell him how incompetent his guards were. Not one of them had searched me for weapons before I entered the hall. They'd looked at me and seen a pitiful *girl*, incapable of stealing a weapon. They'd underestimated me, and so had Quin.

"Poor, Zali. You must be disappointed by our family reunion. A little different to the one you imagined, am I right?"

"Not at all. I'm grateful that you've taught me a valuable lesson." I thought of Ari, Ildri, and yes damn it, Arrow *again*. "Thanks to you, I now know that families aren't formed by accidents of birth. They're forged by continual acts of kindness, loyalty, and compassion."

Quinn laughed, and I straightened my spine. "If you find someone who'll hold you when you're at your worst, who'll make you laugh so hard that your tears of pain turn to joy, then *they're* your family. They're the ones you should love with all your might until your last breath. And you, *brother*... well, as it turns out, you were never part of my true family."

He sniffed and twirled his finger in the air. A servant appeared carrying a goblet filled to the brim with golden liquid. "Take the traitor to the central cell in the dungeons," he said to the bearded bear of a guard who had tackled me to the floor.

"The central cell?" The guards' amber eyes goggled at me. "Are you sure that's a—"

Quin snarled. "Have you lost your fucking hearing? You're here to do what I tell you, nothing else. So do it. And while you're at it, tell my counselor to attend me immediately. I have an urgent message to send."

"Sire." The guard bowed low. "As you command."

"Quin, what will you do with me?" I asked.

"I haven't decided yet, Zali. Relax and give me time to enjoy finally having you at my mercy."

As the guard dragged me through a doorway, I glanced over my shoulder. With a sigh, Quin collapsed on the throne, then took deep gulps from his cup of serum.

It wouldn't be hard to kill him, lost in gold delirium as he was. The fire-magic-enhanced guards were another matter, though.

Before Quin had my head cut from my shoulders, I needed to get him alone.

The guards walked me along a narrow hallway lined with more pale, twisted tree trunks. Shafts of afternoon light shone from high windows, burnishing the gnarled roots that buckled the wooden floor. Then we turned down a narrow staircase that stopped several floors beneath the palace and led to a dungeon that smelled of rotting rodents and piss.

Without lighting a torch, the guard unlocked a door and pushed me inside a cell.

"How can you see anything?" I asked. "It's pitch black in here."

"Fire magic. If you behave, we'll light the torches," he growled before stomping away.

I shuffled backward until my back hit a wall, then slid carefully to the ground and hugged my knees to my chest. I took slow breaths and tuned in to my charming new environment, praying my eyes would soon adjust to the darkness.

Nearby, a creature scratched, emitting little squeaks. Water dripped from a pipe, but then, after a minute, I heard the ragged sound of someone else's breathing. A flash of hope made my heart pound faster. Rather than being alone in this stinking shithole, it would be much better to have some company.

"Hello?" I whispered, crawling toward the sound. "Is someone there?" My nose bumped metal, and I swore, gripping the bars tightly and squinting into the black void of the cell next door.

After a moment, a shadow moved in the far corner. Definitely a person.

"Are you all right?" I asked. "Come closer, so I can see you."

A groan rumbled, then with hesitant movements, the shape shuffled forward, a face and thin body forming out of the darkness.

The boy looked young, barely out of adolescence. Short, black hair swept back off a tanned, handsome face, his feline gold-green eyes almost too pretty to belong to a male.

Those eyes flared as they fixed on me, and a guttural cry caught in his throat. He scrambled to the bars between our cells, his grime-coated fingers folding over mine.

I breathed out a curse as my body trembled with the shock of recognition. I knew him. I knew this boy. Had he played in the forest with Quin and me years ago?

I squinted, looking closer, and cogs turned in my head, memories shifting and crunching together until they slid into their rightful places. Like a blade plunged into my gut, horror tore me open.

"Van?" I said in a hoarse whisper, my pulse roaring in my ears. "Is that you?"

The boy smiled, nodding his head as tears made white tracks in his dirty face.

"You remember me, Zali?"

"Yes. Yes, I do. You're my brother," I said, a million memories rushing in at once. "How the hells did this happen?"

"Quin used a Sun Realm mage's spell to steal your memories. They drugged you, then worked magic on your mind. But the spell needed an anchor, someone's face who could unlock your lost memories on sight. Our brother chose me, and then locked me up for safe-keeping."

Fury blazed through me. I would kill Quin slowly and enjoy watching the light leave his gold-fucked eyes, breath by ragged breath.

The pain of what my own brother—the twin who had grown beside me in our mother's womb—had done to my parents, to Van, and to me, eviscerated my heart. Childhood memories rushed back—a happy family, a life of luxury in the Mydorian palace, love and laughter. Then as Quin and I grew into adolescence, his smiles turned to jealous sneers, and we became competitors in a game I'd had no interest in playing. I took Van's face in my hands, cried, and kissed his cheeks in the spaces between the bars. "I'm so sorry. This is all my fault. If I had known what Quin would do... what he was capable of, I would have just handed him the crown."

"No, you wouldn't have. You cared too much about fixing everything that was wrong with our realm—the gold trade, the slaves, and the addicts. You would have fought to make things right with your last breath. Our people know that, too. Not many believe Quin's lies."

Patches of gold marred Van's cheek, and I traced them with my finger. "You're an addict. Did Quin do this to you?"

Van nodded. "He needed me weak, content to lie here dreaming. I'd given up, Zali, but now... listen, I have an idea. Sometimes he lets me out. Like most Mydorians, his guards can't stand him, so he's lonely and has no one to bore with his made-up tales of his wondrous deeds. Over time, during the journeys from here to the hall, I can speak to the guards, begin building a resistance against Quin. We can do this, Zali. Together. We'll crush him."

Stroking his cheek, I said, "For a kid, you're pretty wise and brave."

"I grew up the day our soldiers dragged you before the court, drugged and beaten to within an inch of your life. Quin told everyone you'd had our parents killed and had tried to kill the reaver elves who cloak the city."

"That doesn't make sense. Why would I do that?"

"Anyone with a brain knows you wouldn't. He was projecting his own desires. Some bullshit scheme about controlling the gold."

"And look at where the gold serum has got him," I said, sitting back on my haunches. "Quin's a mess. Almost unrecognizable."

Van dropped his eyes in shame and wriggled away from me.

"It's not your fault, Van. If I was in your position and the serum had any effect on me, I'd definitely take it too."

"It's stopped me from bashing my brains out on a wall, so there is that."

"You can wean yourself off it. Get strong again. After we kick Quin's butt off the throne and into a deep grave, I'll need your help to put things right around here."

"So... about killing Quin. You're not worried about the twin soul myth?"

Slowly, I shook my head. "No. But if it turns out to be true, bury me on top of him, and I'll make sure he stays down there forever."

Van laughed, then crawled into the corner of his cell to retrieve a tiny clay bottle. He poured the contents down the drain in the center of the floor. "Done. No more serum for me. Will you hold my hand while I try to sleep? You look awful yourself. You need to rest."

Grinning at each other, we curled our bodies on either side of the bars and entwined our fingers. Our foreheads were so close we breathed the same air as we tried to relax and fall asleep. It wasn't easy since my mind spun with so many remembered images. My parents, family dinners, conversations with friends, then me in an indigo bedchamber, laughing with a maid who braided my hair. All of them comforting memories, until my face in the mirror changed into Quin's drug-ruined visage.

Just breathe, I told myself as panic tightened my chest. *Just breathe.*

Even though I was a prisoner again and my twin was a psychotic addict who wanted me dead, at least I'd made it home. I could tick that off my list of things I hoped to achieve before I died.

I also had my memories back, one brother who loved and needed me, a kingdom to heal, and hope kindling in my chest. I would cling to that hope like a drowning person bobbing on a single plank of wood in a savage ocean.

I would do everything I could to survive Quin. And if I couldn't, then I would make damn sure that Van did and could rule in my place.

Quin was going down.

Van would rise up.

And me?

Other than those two goals, what wishes and ambitions still flamed inside of me?

As my thoughts grew fuzzy with sleep, I realized what I wanted for myself didn't matter anymore.

"Who cares?" I slurred into the darkness as an answering deep chuckle reverberated off the cell walls, wrapping around my heart and squeezing.

Arrow.

Why couldn't he leave me alone?

Even now, his smirking silver eyes watched me as I tumbled into my dreams, and I wondered... were those eyes a threat or a promise?

Because right now, I could really do with the winged asshole's help.

Chapter 30

ARROW

"All of you... to the throne room. Now," I snapped at Ari, Raiden, and Ildri as we disembarked from our carriages. I pointed at Esen. "Except you."

She bowed, and then without a word dissolved into the night shadows as we marched toward the palace. With my faith in Esen badly shaken after the foundry incident, I couldn't trust my blue-haired guard with any matter concerning Leaf, big or small.

Fury seethed in my gut, like a barely tethered creature that tore through bones and viscera, longing to break free, burn the realm down, and find my Aldara.

Rubbing my aching eyes, I settled on the throne. Then I scanned the line of betrayers who stood before me, their hands clasped in front of their bodies and brows sweating.

I was so fucking tired of this shit. I needed sleep. Food. Something to drink. And to burn the fucking palace to ash, if only to satisfy my need to destroy something.

On the journey from Auryinnia, instead of sleeping, I'd glared at the backs of my eyelids, every muscle strung tight. I was desperate to leave the carriage and hunt for Leaf, and I had to repeat Ari's warning that acting rashly might be the death of her, as if it was a lifeline to sanity. Or perhaps it was a mainline to madness.

Who knew? And who fucking cared, as long as I got Leaf back in my arms as soon as yesterday? Whatever the hells that meant.

Fuck. I was definitely losing it.

A servant darted up the stairs and offered me a goblet of water. One hand gripping the throne's gilded armrest, I drank deeply, tossed the cup aside, then watched it roll down the stairs, stopping at Ari's feet.

"Explain," I said, locking my gaze on her unflinching gold irises. "I'm warning you, don't tarry. As you can imagine, I'm not in a patient mood."

Standing beside his mother, Raiden swallowed repeatedly. Barely able to stop himself from begging for her life, his boots shuffled restlessly over the marble floor. If I was a good man, I'd tell him he needn't worry.

Yes, I was fucking furious with them all, scared witless for Leaf. But everyone in this room had acted with her best interests at heart—perhaps even me in my own twisted way. They wanted her to be happy. And I just wanted her to be by my side at any cost.

Ari cleared her throat. "An ancient gold reaver pact with the human realm holds a cloaking forcefield around their city. Three gold reavers live in Mydorian, constantly renew it, and give their blood to the river, earth, and trees. It's why your soldiers have never been able to find humans in the Sunken Forest. They're hidden."

"The Lost City of Mydorian?" I asked, grinding my teeth together. "And the Zareen knows about this?"

"Of course. Gold reaver elves are linked by blood to the human royal family, and we have always worked to preserve their lineage."

Everything stilled, my lungs, my heart, the very air around me, as my attention honed to Ari's parted lips. "What royal family?"

She raised her chin. "Promise me you'll remain calm."

My hands curled into fists as I sat forward on the throne, no longer slumped and feigning calm. A terrible premonition slid over my skin. Sinking bone deep, it reminded me of the feeling I got during battle when everything was about to change for the worse.

I couldn't speak, so I dipped my head and prayed to the gold I could stop myself from murdering everyone in the room when I heard what Ari said next.

"Leaf's family.... Well, she's the lost Earth Realm Princess, Zali Omala, part reaver elf and destined to take the human throne. I've suspected it for some time. The Zareen, who can sense reaver blood, confirmed it."

For several long moments, a tense silence hummed through the hall while blood roared in my ears. I couldn't move. Could barely breathe. Nausea churned my gut as I forced bile back down my throat.

She had to be joking.

The human royal family had died out centuries ago, or so I'd thought. And what... Leaf was somehow their fucking princess? Impossible.

"Excuse me while I completely lose my shit," I ground out.

"My King," Ari began, stepping closer to the dais.

"Don't you fucking dare *my king* me," I boomed, lightning flashing outside, the energy sizzling along my arms. "Why did the elves keep Mydorian hidden for centuries?"

"A long time ago, my sister, the Zareen fell in love with a human prince. Their union created a female heir born into the weakest of the five realms, a realm where the people had no magic, no protection against the fae of the Light, Sun, Ice, and Crystal Realms. We needed to protect them against *all* of faekind for all time. Using our cloaking magic was the obvious solution."

"But why would you keep this from me?"

"For everyone's safety, Arrowyn. The reaver alliance with the Earth Realm made no difference to Coridon. Or to you and—"

"No difference!" I shot to my feet, leaped from the dais, and stalked a circle around the Sayeeda. "Your loyalty, your life is bonded to *my* service, not the Earth Realm's. *I* rule the Light Realm. *I* govern the Gold Accords. And *your* one and only role is to help *me*. That's it."

Body stiff, she dropped her gaze to her hands. "Of that, I am very aware. Believe me when I tell you that reavers work hard to keep the realms in balance. *All* of them, Arrow. That is our true and eternal interest. Because without that balance, Coridon would fall."

"And yet, with a handful of words, you've destroyed nearly every assumption I've lived by. Your faithfulness. The very order of the realms. And you expect me to believe a Mydorian princess exists, let alone that she could be purchased in a slave market for three gold feathers?"

Raiden's skin was ashen, telling me this was the first he'd heard of this preposterous tale. Ildri's usually pale cheeks were rosy with guilt. When she noticed me staring, she bit her lip, but uttered no words. She was complicit in this betrayal. It hurt me to know that Ari had confided in her closest friend at court, but not her king. Not me.

"We don't know how Zali came to be at the gilt market," said Ari. "If all wasn't well in the Earth Realm, the reavers living there should have got word out to Auryinnia."

"Leaf! Her name is Leaf. I don't want to hear her called anything other than the name I gave her. Is that clear?"

"If you insist. Perhaps I should have made contact with the Mydorian reavers before we sent Leaf home... but the Zareen, who sees all, urged us to let her begin the journey at once."

As growing panic worked its way over Ari's face, deadly silence pulsed between us.

I took her chin between my fingers, pinching cruelly. "What horrors have you sent her back to?"

"If things weren't well in Mydorian, the Zareen would have known."

"Are you certain Leaf is this princess? And if so, does she know it?" I said through gritted teeth.

"I don't think she knows. But, yes, I'm certain of her identity. Only Dust and Stones royal females shave the right sides of their heads. Leaf begged to wear hers that way. Reaver blood only activates in the female line, so unlike her male relatives, gold serum has no effect on her. She passes through reaver gates unaided—"

"But if she's Mydorian, no doubt she saw this royal girl at some point and wanted to emulate her," I said, looking for any explanation other than the one Ari had presented.

"You're not listening. And it doesn't matter if you refuse to believe who Leaf is; the Zareen has confirmed her identity."

"So why didn't you tell Leaf before she left?"

"I worried that if she was captured, under torture she might reveal her identity... and I didn't want her to be in any more danger."

"Captured, Ari? For fuck's sake! Leaf's little adventure ends right now. I'm going to get her."

"Wait... Zali is part reaver elf, so she has the ability to cloak herself. And before she left, I tried to teach her this skill. I gave her a nugget of gold and a spell to chant, telling her they would make her disappear."

My brows rose. "Invisibility is a useful defense."

"Yes, but unfortunately, she didn't quite believe she could do it by herself on demand."

"And with magic, even inherited power, it requires belief to work."

"Exactly. So cloaking may or may not work for her. And—"

"Enough talk. Time to retrieve her."

"*Arrow*! Without me, you can't get into the city. I must go with you and uncloak Mydorian. There is no other way for you to enter."

"Fine. But as soon as you've gotten me into the city, you'll return home. I don't want to risk your safety."

"After what I've told you, Arrowyn, I'm surprised to hear that."

She shouldn't be surprised. I understood why my Sayeeda had helped Leaf escape. Ari wanted Leaf to be happy because she loved her, too. She was just a lot less selfish than me.

Ignoring the disturbing thought that I might love someone other than myself, other than my people, I rolled the ache from my shoulders, then cracked my neck. "Ari, let's go."

"Arrow, you must rest before you fly. Please. You can't know what you'll face in Mydorian, and it would be pointless to arrive in a hostile environment with your power drained. You need a little sleep at least."

Ari searched through the pouch she wore across her body, then offered me the sleeping medicine on the center of her palm.

Fuck, as much as I hated to admit it, she was right. Without sleep, I would be in no shape to convince, let alone *force*, my human to return to Coridon with me.

"Fine. I'll take a small sip," I said, accepting the bottle. "I'll rest for an hour or two. Then we're leaving."

Looking far from satisfied, she nodded. What choice did she have?

I called a servant over. "Send a message to the Zareen. Tell her she needs to contact Mydorian immediately for news on the missing princess and report back to Coridon." The man bowed and hurried away.

Raiden touched my arm. "Traveling on horseback with an escort of soldiers would be the wiser plan."

"When have I pretended to possess wisdom?"

A wry smile flickered on his face. "Fair enough. My mother's role in this matter—"

"I should execute her."

Ari spoke up. "My assistance depends upon your guarantee of our safety—both Ildri's and mine. Exile us if you must, but you can't harm us."

"If that's your price, then I'll gladly pay it. We'll discuss your atonement when I return."

Three sighs of relief stirred the air. They should have known I wouldn't hurt them. They were the family I had chosen. I depended on them all and understood the reasons for their betrayal. I would do anything for Leaf too... except let her leave me.

Raiden had protected Esen because he loved her like a sister.

Ari was bound to me in service, but she was also bound to the Zareen and to her people, the elves. Without the reavers' cooperation, Coridon would fall.

Ildri had always possessed a soft heart. Her cool exterior hid a mother's ferocious desire to protect everyone from harm, especially lost souls like Leaf.

"Ari," I said, walking toward the elevator. "You had better be in my chambers within two hours and not a moment later."

As I entered my apartments, I slugged a shot of the sleeping potion, then stretched out on the floor of the pavilion. I sighed and rested my head on my linked hands, staring up at the mosaics on the domed ceiling.

Winged fae—all past rulers of Coridon—flew across the gruesome tableau, swords piercing their enemies' hearts, wild-eyed muscular horses rearing as they charged across a battlefield of blood and gore.

Nightly, Leaf had viewed those images when I first brought her to live in my apartment. Guilt stabbed my heart as I thought of how they must have terrified her. My little Leaf... who was likely destined to become a queen.

Laughter erupted from me, a harsh sound that echoed in a loop around the dome. Everything about Leaf finally made sense. Her stubborn nature, her fierceness, the way she walked, and held herself. Even her violence.

Of course she was born to be a queen. The stupid thing was... deep down, I had hoped she would be my queen. But I'd bought her, chained her, claimed her as mine because I wanted her, with no thought for her feelings, certain that in time, she'd be content, no, *happy*, by my side.

What an idiot I was.

The knot of guilt tightened in my gut, and I told it to unravel and fuck off. Because I knew I would do it all over again—rip Leaf from that slaver's cage and keep her forever if I could... There was no doubt in my mind.

Helplessly, I laughed again as I thought about what she would do when I flew into her hidden capitol and demanded she return with me to Coridon. It would not go well. What could I offer? How would I frame the idea of her coming home as an attractive proposition?

As I wracked my brain, composing muddled arguments and speeches, the potion dragged me under before I could draft a convincing one.

Someone shook my shoulder and said, "Arrow, wake up."

I lurched into a squat, lightning magic buzzing like armor around my body, my wings lifted for takeoff as I squinted at... Ari.

"Oh, it's you," I said, padding to the edge of the pavilion and sitting down. "Give me a moment to get oriented."

What I meant by that was I needed to get control of the rage and panic that had nearly made me rip Ari's head from her shoulders when I woke and remembered Leaf was gone.

Rubbing sleep from my eyes, I gazed out over the darkened city in the direction I would soon be flying. I couldn't wait to leave, but it felt like I had only closed my eyes a few minutes ago.

"Has it been two hours already?"

"No, My King. Only one." Ari settled beside me and placed her palm over the feather glyph on my arm. "I have news of Leaf."

My boot heels stopped kicking against the stone walls of the pavilion, every muscle freezing. "Tell me."

"First, losing your temper will not improve the situation in any way. It never does. So promise me you will—"

I wrapped my hands around her golden neck, my thumbs pressing into the soft meat under her chin. "I said, *tell me.*"

"A scout has just returned from the Port of Tears," she choked out. "He reported that last night, a human girl matching Leaf's description was sold from the deck of Captain Loligos's ship."

Lightning sheeted the sky, and thunder crashed as my wings slashed above me, the feathers trembling. But rage and terror silenced me as my mouth opened and closed. I couldn't make a sound.

The Sayeeda's expression softened. "Five Earth Realm soldiers took her away on a guarded carriage. According to the rumors, the man who purchased her goes by the title of the King Regent."

"King Regent of *what?*"

"I'm assuming Mydorian."

"Fuck. So a male relative of Leaf's?"

Ari nodded. "Yes. To claim such a title, he would need to be related to her. Six months ago, our resident reavers reported that the heir and her twin brother survived a Sun Realm attack. Unfortunately, both parents were killed and a younger son went missing not long after, now assumed dead."

"Twin?" A cold shiver lashed my spine. "Damn, there are fucking two of her."

But no wonder I felt so connected to Leaf. We were so similar in many ways. Stubborn, determined. Both rulers, wounded by grief and betrayal. Perhaps the gods had given us to each other.

Yes. Leaf was a gift, wrapped in the dual traits of understanding and compassion, who contained the inner fire to withstand my stormy nature and still thrive.

"Reavers believed she disappeared not long after the attack. That's why she was known as the Lost Princess. We doubted she'd survived. The Zareen had little to say on her fate, only that the Earth Realm would have its queen restored after much time and trouble had passed, and that we elves simply had to wait."

I shook my head. "But you knew Leaf was this princess early on?"

"Yes, as soon as I noticed the gold had no effect on her. Loligos's sailor told your soldier that, after the accident, the Earth princess had been imprisoned by her brother as a traitor to the realm but somehow escaped, which is how you found her at the Gilt Market. Slavers captured her."

"Traitor? Leaf may have betrayed me—the man who held her against her will—a thousand times over, but she would never betray her people. Beneath a hard shell, her heart was good and pure. And why would this male yearn to rule over a land in ruins? Mydorian is only rubble and dust."

"You're still not listening, Arrowyn. In the forest, there are ruins, yes. But the city within it still stands, as it has done for centuries."

Abhorrent pictures formed in my mind as I stared past the blinking torchlights of Coridon. A nauseous horror story of the indignities my human might be suffering at this very moment. And I couldn't fucking bear it.

"Lately, communications from the Mydorian reavers to Auryinnia have been stilted, a shift in tone. We elves should have realized something was wrong. Arrow, this is my fault. I should never have let her flee alone."

"What you shouldn't have done was withhold information from me," I said, getting to my feet and holding my hand out for Ari to grasp. "We must go. My Aldara's life is in danger. Get up."

Ari smoothed her tunic as she rose. "Arrow, we should—"

"King Arrowyn," said a voice behind us. "Pardon the interruption, but you'll want to read this immediately."

The guard hurried over and held out a small scroll. I snatched it, tearing it with clumsy fingers as it unraveled. "Who's it from?"

"A raven courier from the Earth Realm."

I scanned the words on the parchment, then flicked my gaze to Ari who hovered next to me. "It's from her brother, the supposed King Regent of Mydorian. He writes to inform me of the city's existence and invites me to visit him. Says his city has run on the illegal gold trade for centuries, and he wishes to discuss establishing legal routes between our lands. He believes I'll be particularly interested in his terms. This doesn't mention Leaf at all."

"Zali," Ari reminded me.

"You can call her whatever you like, but she'll always be Leaf to me."

"Because you can't bear the thought of her being a princess or a queen?"

I scoffed. "I don't care what she is as long as she's mine."

Facing the waiting guard, I said, "Send a lightning courier to this regent prick. Tell him... tell him I shall see him very soon."

"Nothing else, My King?"

"No, I think that should be enough to make him piss himself. It's perfect."

Smirking as the guard's silver head disappeared down the stairs, I lifted Ari into my arms. I clapped my wings together and launched off the pavilion into the sky.

"Arrow," Ari yelled against my ear as the wind howled past us. "Please, think about this. Zali's brother expects a royal visit, which would give you a perfect excuse to take a group of armed attendants with you, as Raiden advised. Plan this properly and—"

"Close your mouth," I said with a laugh. "Or it will soon be full of insects."

Chapter 31

ARROW

Night creatures stirred as Ari and I landed in the Earth Realm forest. Recoiling from the jagged energy of an invisible forcefield, I whipped my wings back and shoved her behind me.

"Arrow, let me go. I'm fine," she said, wobbling on her feet, still dizzy from our rapid flight.

I glanced down at her. "Was that the reavers' cloak?"

"Yes. I'll take us straight through." She shivered, rubbing her bare arms.

The air was much cooler here than in the Light Realm.

I reached out toward the field of translucent energy, drawing back fast as it crackled and burned my fingers. "How do humans with no reaver blood get through this damn thing?"

"Elves gift all Mydorian children with a sigil that grants them access. Listen to me, Arrow, when we're inside the city, I think we should tell the gatekeepers straight away that we've arrived for our audience with the regent."

"*We* won't be doing anything. As soon as we're through the barrier, you'll return to Coridon, and I'll find the regent and fry his fucking brains."

"Don't be stupid," she said, raising her arms and chanting as she led me through the thick veil of magic.

On the other side of it, I groaned, my eyes rolling back as I leaned over my thighs, dry retching from the pain of crossing a magical boundary.

Ari rubbed my back. "You must insist that the regent's sister attend your meeting. Then he'll have to keep Leaf alive, which will at least ensure her immediate safety. If she is dead... well, you'll soon know it."

"Have I told you before how annoying you are when you're right?"

A tall, dark shadow stretched both ways in front of us, likely the city's walls. Squinting, I raised my face to the smoky clouds above, willing them to part so moonlight could illuminate our surroundings.

I grunted when they barely moved. "Interesting."

"Now, do you see why you must take a cautious approach? In the Earth Realm, your powers are much reduced." Ari led me toward metal gates shaped like a giant letter M. "Consider this a game where you must move carefully across the board. Think before you act. In Mydorian, it's quite possible that you may not have the capacity to fry anyone's brains."

"Perhaps I should test that theory on yours," I muttered as two human guards approached us.

I stifled a grunt of laughter as I scanned their thin armor, their pathetic weapons and long guns that I could snap before they even pointed them at me.

"State your business," a guard said, raising a lamp toward us. His close-set eyes flared, and a lump bobbed in his throat. "You're—?"

"King Arrowyn of the Light Realm. I'm here to grant your—hmm, shall we say, regent?—the audience that he has begged for."

The second guard goggled, and the lamp bearer stumbled in his haste to bow before I turned him to ash. I was pleased that my reputation had preceded me.

"Certainly, King Arrowyn."

As we walked through the gates, I flicked my wings out, startling the guard and folding one around Ari's shoulders.

"Please follow me to the steward's quarters," the guard continued. "When he wakes, you will be shown to the best rooms the palace has to offer, apart from the Regent's, of course."

I raised a brow. "Can I not have his? After all, I am a king, and if I'm not mistaken, your regent is merely a man who holds the crown for his sister."

The guard coughed, and I whispered in Ari's ear, "Last chance to obey me and leave."

"I'll be leaving you when I take my last breath," she murmured. "Not a single moment before. Besides, I predict you're going to need my help once we get in there."

"Fine," I reluctantly agreed. "Your schemes got us into this mess. I suppose the least you can do is help me clean it up."

As we moved through the lamp-lit city, I cursed under my breath, astounded that the reavers had kept this place hidden for so long. Most fae believed war decimated Mydorian long before my father's reign, which began three hundred fae years ago.

The glyph on my cheek burned, a good sign that my Aldara still lived. This knowledge helped me bank my rage and prevented me from tearing Mydorian apart stone by stone. The option wasn't completely off the table, of course, but at least for now, it wasn't a mindless compulsion.

We entered a turreted palace of black stone and darkened glass, waking several humans from their beds as we moved through night-quiet halls with the newly awakened steward. He stopped in front of a pair of engraved silver doors on the fifth floor. I estimated at least two more levels ranged above us.

"Your rooms," said the steward with a deep bow. "We have informed the Regent of your arrival. He will grant you an audience in the Great Hall at dawn. Food will be delivered to you shortly, and a servant will direct you to the hall in the morning. Until then, rest well."

Another trembling bow, then he turned to depart. I let him march a fair way down the torch-lit hall before I spoke. "I have heard the joyful news that the regent's sister has returned to him. Tell him her presence is required at our meeting tomorrow. That is not a request. Trade discussions won't occur without her."

The man grimaced and scurried away.

We entered a large sitting room with two open doors on either side that led to separate bed chambers. I gave the opulent red and gold interior a cursory inspection, then turned to Ari. "Get in bed and rest. I'm going to find Leaf."

She flopped over an armchair, her limbs flung out haphazardly. "Absolutely not. You will wait until dawn. It's the safest option. The last thing you want is to be found skulking around the Mydorian palace like a disobedient servant."

"I hardly think I look like a servant," I said, glancing down at my travel armor. "But you're unfortunately right again. So get up. You can cloak me as I search, then I won't be seen."

"Arrow. Please. Lie down. Rest. I understand your urgency to find her. But remember the game we're playing. At present, the element of surprise is your best weapon."

A knock sounded. Ari opened the door, returning with a tray of food—dried fruit, cheese, sliced bread, and goblets of watered-down wine. She sniffed the food, and then the cups.

"Don't eat anything. It's laced with serum. The regent is already working against you, which means he's afraid. Drink the water from the faucet in the bathroom. Then rest. I beg you."

I followed her instructions and tossed and turned on top of the silken sheets until rosy morning light lanced through the gap in the curtains. Then I sprang from the bed and surveyed the city below.

Black and silver streets, accented with gold and wreathed in dark, flowering vines, spread out in a functional geometrical pattern. Beyond the city walls was endless forest. The town was plainer than Coridon, but far from being in decline; it was most definitely thriving.

A snore rustled the air behind me. "Ari, wake up. Hurry."

Rulers in every realm coveted gold reavers. So last night, for safety, I had insisted Ari sleep beside me. Now, she sat up in bed, rubbing her eyes as a single knock thudded against the door. A servant entered, delivered breakfast, then left without a word.

After Ari pronounced the grapes free of serum, we ate them and awaited our summons from Leaf's brother. I paced back and forth across the room, while Ari lectured me about the importance of remaining calm during my meeting with the regent. Not to move against him unless he or his guards harmed Leaf.

Nodding as if I agreed with her, I cracked my knuckles and pictured smashing the pretender's nose to a pulp, praying I wouldn't have to wait long to indulge in the pleasure.

For nearly four hours, I wore tracks in the floor rugs. Then, finally, the steward arrived and led us to the entrance of the hall.

The open doors revealed a large light-filled room, where everything was awash with white and gold, including the twisted tree roots we stepped over.

Once my attention honed on the girl standing on a low dais beside the man I assumed was her prick of a brother, I could absorb nothing else about my surroundings. I could have been stepping over the bones of my dead family, and all I would have seen was her face.

Leaf.

Alive. Unharmed. Mine.

It took everything I had not to immediately swoop down and snatch her from his grasp, his gold-mottled fingers clutching her hand as if they were a united force. My muscles burned to crouch, then leap and take, but the Sayeeda's hand pressed against my clenched fist.

"Breathe, Arrow," she said, and I did my best to comply.

Drawing residual storm particles from the air deep into my lungs and veins, I waited.

"Come closer," said the regent, and Ari and I walked forward like animated statues, burying our feelings, our true natures behind hearts of stone.

I couldn't take my eyes off my human.

Standing with the bearing of a queen, for a split second, her gaze met mine, and the fury I saw in her eyes stopped my heart from beating. My gut twisted and clenched as my lips ached to form words of apology. For what, I wasn't certain.

Perhaps I needed to make amends for everything I had said and done from the moment I met Leaf. Without a doubt, I'd wronged her many times over. And as an idea took shape in my mind, I knew that before I left this hall, I would need to hurt her again.

A sheer metallic tunic flowed over Leaf's bodysuit of tight black leather, the sides made of panels of bright gold metal that molded to the curves of her waist. At first glance, it resembled a warrior's outfit. But then I noticed two tear-shaped slits that ran along the sides of the pants, exposing her outer thighs and knees, rendering her body vulnerable.

The right side of her head was freshly shaved and the remaining hair braided and woven with pieces of twisted gold. It sat high above her head in a crown-like shape that reminded me of a peacock's tail. From her clothes to her gold-painted lips, she looked regal, majestic, and every inch a powerful princess.

But most of all, she looked like my Leaf, my Aldara.

When I shifted my attention to her brother and saw Leaf's features replicated above his padded shoulders, shock faltered my steps. Once handsome, his face had clearly been ravaged by serum addiction.

Now I understood why he wanted greater control of the gold that circulated through Mydorian. His life was ruled by the substance, and I doubted he could survive more than an hour without a dose flowing through his bloodstream.

"Welcome," the regent said as we stopped in front of the dais cradled by a circle of white trees.

It surprised me to see his head shaved in the same fashion as Leaf's, with a crown of rubies and gold slipping low on his sweat-dampened brow.

No bows or smiles were exchanged as he gestured a jeweled hand toward Leaf. "I believe you're already acquainted with my sister, Zali Omala," he drawled, not bothering to use my title.

"Princess," I said, dipping my head slightly. For one glorious moment, her lips parted, revealing the gap in her teeth, and as her eyes met mine, something warm flashed in the deep-green irises.

Silent, she lifted her chin and stared past my shoulders.

"How pleased your people must be, Regent, to have their princess and ruler returned to them," I said, hoping my measured voice hid the barely leashed violence simmering in my blood.

How I longed to rain terror upon this pretender's throne room. Break his every bone. Burn him. And sweep Leaf away from him forever.

"Indeed," the brother replied. "Very pleased."

"And are you happy to be home, Princess?" I asked.

Her nails pierced the flesh on the side of her thigh, the subtle gesture of stress that I never failed to notice. "Yes," she lied in a smooth, soft voice, still staring past me.

"*Bullshit*," I whispered, and Ari cleared her throat loudly.

I dragged my gaze back to the brother. "My Sayeeda tells me your name is Quin."

He gaped and nodded.

"Tell me, Quin, what date has been set for your sister's coronation?"

He squirmed and scowled at my chest plate, while I considered plucking two feathers out and throwing them at his gold-fucked eyes.

"That hasn't been decided," he said. "For the time being, we will rule our kingdom together. Twins, you know? No relationship in the realms is as close and eternal as those who have shared a womb."

Co-rulers. An interesting use of the term. And the twin thing made my skin crawl. I couldn't wait to destroy whatever hold he had over Leaf. I would crush him to a pulp. Gut him. Pull his brains out his nostrils and slowly roast them with lightning. After that I would—

"Arrowyn," he snapped to regain my attention. "Shall we proceed to the antechamber and discuss matters of trade? I imagine you were shocked to learn of Mydorian's existence." He moved toward double doors in the rear wall of the dais.

"No, perhaps moderately surprised," I said, crossing my arms. "Now, whether or not I'm going to step into your antechamber depends on something important."

He turned, raising a single dark brow in the same manner Leaf did when I pissed her off. "Oh? On what?"

"On the value you set upon your sister's life."

"You wish to kill her?" he asked in a hopeful tone.

"No. I want to put her back in her cage in *my* palace. In *my* city."

Still silent, Leaf stared blankly over my shoulder, failing to notice the smile Ari gave her. Anyone well-acquainted with my Sayeeda would know she rarely smiled without purpose, and this particular smile was meant to reassure my Aldara that I was only playing a part.

"What do you mean exactly?" Quin asked.

"I *mean* that I want my property back. And that is the price you must pay to negotiate trade terms with me. Give. Me. Your. Sister. Now!"

Several emotions flashed across his face. Relief, quickly followed by terror when he realized he wouldn't have control over her if she lived in Coridon. Confusion. And finally, pure madness.

"Are you saying you'll only bargain with me if I let you take Zali?"

I nodded slowly, watching Leaf's nails dig harder into her flesh. By the look on her face, she planned to murder me the first chance she got. Fair enough. No doubt I deserved it.

"Why does your sister not speak?" I asked, widening my stance. "What's wrong with her?"

Bright green arrows shot through me as her bitter gaze pierced my heart.

Her lips parted. "I only converse with worthy people," she said coolly. "Slavers don't fall into that category."

Quin snickered, while his sister raised her chin and resumed gazing haughtily past me.

"It is no easy thing to ask of a brother, to hand his sister to a stranger." Quin steepled his fingers under his chin. "I need time to consider your request."

"Consider this; if you give me Zali Omala, I will help you in three ways. I will keep her in my kingdom, away from human sight and interference. I will open gold routes between our cities and, lastly, guarantee you favorable serum prices."

"Will you recognize my claim to the Mydorian throne?"

"I don't see why not. After all, it's in both our interests for you to sit upon it."

"This pleases me. My steward will show you around Mydorian, and we shall reconvene at dusk, giving me time to draw up documents for your perusal."

"No need for a tour. We're still recovering from our journey and will return to our chambers to rest."

"As you wish." The regent smiled smugly.

I took a final long look at Leaf's face—a passive mask of animosity. Then I flicked my gaze over her body, noting the thin line of blood oozing between her fingers and trickling into the leather pants.

Then, without a word, I inclined my head and left the hall. The Sayeeda's soft footsteps kept pace with my boots as they thudded against the white-washed floor.

The doors slammed shut behind us.

Chapter 32

ARROW

Back in our temporary chambers, I resumed wearing tracks in the floor, power shuddering over my skin. "I can't handle this, Ari. Did you see her up there? Trapped by that pathetic leech. What hold does he have over Leaf to keep her so silent? Fuck this! Cloak us. We're going to find her."

"Think for a moment. Before we make a move, we need the regent's answer. If you sign his trade agreement, he may let you walk Leaf out of his hall, and you won't need to resort to bloodshed."

I laughed, flashing my fangs. "Do you think I care? I look forward to removing every drop of blood from his gold-soaked veins, then retching it into the nearest sewer for the city's maggots to feast upon."

"Thank you for reminding me in an unnecessarily vivid manner that you can use your fangs as highly effective weapons outside the bedroom should you wish to do so."

Sighing, I stopped in front of Ari and lifted her chin with my finger. "I just need to find Leaf. Reassure her. Be certain she's unharmed. Then make a plan to eliminate her brother that she finds satisfactory."

"Listen to you, so eager to serve your human."

Ignoring that, I pinched her chin hard, then released her. "Will you help me?"

"Of course. But again, I urge you not to act rashly. The best plan may be to leave her where we find her until we have her brother's answer. But how do you propose we find her chamber?"

I grinned and sniffed the air.

"You can smell her?" Ari asked, her golden eyes wide.

"Yes, her sweet, spicy blood." I breathed deeply, swaying on my feet.

"Arrow." She clicked her fingers. "This isn't the time to swoon like a naiad sighting water in the desert. Snap out of it."

Opening the door, I stuck my head into the hallway, inhaling deeply. "Found her." I seized Ari's hand. "She's below us. Most likely in the dungeons."

"Don't let go of me. The invisibility cloak will be stronger if I'm touching you."

Following Leaf's scent, we moved quickly through hallways and connecting stairwells, finding the palace prison in no time. We traipsed past two humans guarding the main chamber into a torch-lit passage that ran along a line of cells, all but two of them empty.

Stripped of her earlier finery and wearing only a ripped brown shift, my human dozed against the rear wall. Messy braids fell over her shoulders, and the flickering light from a sconce illuminated a patchwork of bruises on her legs. Fury filled me at the sight of her in such a ragged state.

"Leaf," I whispered urgently. "Wake up. It's Arrow."

She jerked awake, scrambled toward the front of the cell, and pushed up onto her feet. "Ari! I'm so glad to see you."

"What about me?" I asked, pressing close to the bars.

Leaf's hand shot through the bars, and she slapped my face. Hiding a grin, I pressed my palm against my cheek. "What was that for?"

"Oh, let me think." The corner of her mouth twisted into a wry smile. "Could it be because you just tried to buy me from my vile brother and make me your slave again?"

"That was a ploy to get you out of here. Do you really think I'd lock up a princess?"

"To be precise, I'm a queen. Or soon to be one, anyway. But yes, I do think you'd imprison me in Coridon again. In a heartbeat."

I thudded my hand over my heart as if I'd been struck by a spear. "Your low opinion wounds me."

"Enough, both of you," Ari scolded. "Argue all you like back in Coridon if it pleases you, but this is not the time to indulge your petty grievances."

Leaf gripped the bars. "Did anyone see you come down here?"

"Not with my reaver's cloak in place." Ari smirked. To demonstrate her skill, she cloaked us for a second, then made us visible again. "If a guard does come down, Leaf, just stare at the wall as if you're alone."

"Step to the back corner of the cell," I told Leaf. "I'll try to blast the door off."

"Your power won't work down here. Quin is allied with the Sun Realm. The cells have been warded by one of their mages."

I clenched my fists, summoning a storm. Blue lightning kindled in my chest, circling my arms, but it sparked and fizzled out when I tried to push it through my fingertips.

Fucking fire mages.

A soft groan drew my attention to the next cell. Within it, a gaping man-child crouched low, as if he couldn't decide whether he wanted to attack me or hide from my sight.

I tipped my head in the prisoner's direction. "That one might inform the guards of our visit. I'll kill him now," I said, already moving to take action.

"Arrow, no!" Leaf's arms reached through the bars, and she dragged me close. "That's Van, my younger brother. Unlike Quin, he's not a vile prick, and I'd very much like for him to stay alive. Is that clear?"

"Yes." I glared at the brother, another fucking gold addict, and he winced, wriggling back into the shadows. "Are you well, Leaf? Did Quin hurt you? If he's caused even the smallest of your bruises, I'll crush his skull under my boot."

"He's feeding me serum, that's all. He doesn't realize it has no effect. His guards haven't been the kindest, but I got most of these bruises on my journey, after I left Auryinnia. Don't you dare kill Quin. That pleasure must be mine, Arrow."

"As you know, I would never withhold a pleasure from you."

"That's not true," she said. "Remember the night you staked me out in the pavilion?"

I laughed and moved closer, my fingers wrapping over hers around the bars. "I wasn't sure if I'd see you up on that dais today."

"Believe me I had no desire to stand humiliated before you again. I've had enough of that to last three lifetimes. But I had no choice. Quin threated to kill Van if I didn't."

"Do you think he's dressed you in less... *illustrious* clothing because he plans to refuse my offer?"

Fire sparked in her green eyes. "Your *offer* to buy me?" She sighed, her fingers loosening beneath mine. "I don't think it means anything other than that Quin is a sadistic bastard who'd take great pleasure in handing me over to the Storm King dressed like a plague-ridden grave digger. But it doesn't matter what he decides if we're going to kill him anyway, right? I hope you two have cooked up a plan."

"Zali, I have to tell you something that will help us," said Ari. "You have gold reaver blood. It runs through the matriarchal line, and the males in your family gain no benefit from it."

"I should be shocked, but that explains quite a few things."

"Yes, you're immune to the serum and can open reaver gates without assistance. You also have the power to cloak yourself."

"By using the nugget you gave me?"

"No. The nugget is unnecessary. With your blood, the chant I taught you is all you require. Either say it in your mind or aloud. Both will work. You must practice cloaking before we make a move against the regent tonight."

"But my parents were human. Will my cloaking powers be strong enough?" Leaf asked Ari.

"I believe so." Ari smiled. "The power of reaver blood in the female line can never be diluted. Your mother must have explained this to you, and if she didn't, would've done so in time."

"When we're with Quin again," I said, "regardless of whether your invisibility cloak is sufficient or not, I'll throw my sword to you. Then Ari will cloak me, and together, we'll take care of any guards in the hall. Meanwhile, you will chop your brother's dissolute head off, followed by his balls, then stuff the withered trinkets down his still-gurgling throat. Finally, wipe your hands on your tunic, and call it a good night's work. What do you think? A solid plan?"

At last, she smiled at me. "It will have to do." She shifted her weight from one foot to the other. "Arrow... Thank you for coming."

"I will always come for you, Leaf. Cry out in pain, and I'll be there. Call my name, and I will raze entire cities to get to you. It will always be this way until desert sand fills my throat and I take my final choked breath. Am I making myself clear?"

Green eyes tracked over my face—eyes, lips, and back again. No. She didn't believe me. But one day, she would. I would die to prove it.

To lighten the mood, I took a deep breath and pasted on a cocky smile. "So, are you going to insist I call you Zali from now on?"

"If I did, it would have to be *Queen* Zali," she said with a teasing grin. "I haven't forgotten that you promised to kill me the next time I escaped from Coridon, Arrow. Is that your plan after you help me get out of here?"

"Did you not hear me just make a dying oath to protect you? The only being I want to kill at present is your fucking asshole twin."

"And that asshole is *my* responsibility," she reminded me, looking away, and then flicking her gaze back to my mouth. "Why are your fangs out? I thought that only happened during..." Her hand waved vaguely between our bodies, but I knew what she meant.

"Sex? Lust? Blood lust has a similar rousing effect."

"How did he steal your memories?" Ari asked.

Van crawled to the front of his cell. "Quin hired a mage from the Sun Realm to work dark magic on Zali's mind, and then, as a backup, had her injected with a drug that can cause amnesia. The fire fae were taking her to their realm for safe-keeping but slavers ambushed them." Van turned to me. "Our brother would have killed you himself, Zali, except he's superstitious and believes that killing his own twin might bring him harm. Since hearing you'd been sold to the Light Realm fae, he's been living in hope that if someone else finished you off, he'd escape the terrible twin-souls' fate his gold-addled mind had conjured."

"Please tell me I can rip his head off," I said, turning to Leaf as storm energy crackled from my fingertips.

Van grimaced. "I hope you're not referring to me. I'm on your side. And a tip... you need to kill Sonail first and the bearded guard, Veznar. They're loyal to Quin. Everyone else hates him. Your people, Zali, are sick of the gold that he floods through the population to keep them weak and compliant. They want reform and I believe would watch our brother fall with glee."

As I nodded my thanks to Van, I gripped my sword pommel.

Ari touched my wrist, stopping me from drawing it. "Arrow, before you rush off to kill Quin, think about what you would deprive Leaf of. This revenge is hers to relish, not yours. Save your fury for dusk. For now, we must return to our rooms and allow our powers time to recharge."

The Sayeeda was right. *Again.*

I pressed my face against the bars of the cell. "Leaf, before I go, kiss me." I grinned but let my gaze show the true intensity of my feelings for her. "If your brother's guard shoves a dagger into my heart tonight, this could be your last chance."

"What a villain, trying to guilt me into it! I think I shall cope without a last kiss from you."

Pain lanced my chest. "Cruel," I murmured. Stepping backward, my wings manifested, flaring above my shoulders like dark shadows of disappointment.

A smile danced over her mouth. "On second thought, how can I resist those wings? Get over here."

"Finally, you admit that you're attracted to me."

"Yes. Annoyingly so. Help me get rid of Quin, and I'll consider admitting a few other things that might interest you."

"An intriguing offer," I said, taking her face between my hands and crushing my lips to hers.

She sighed into my mouth, and we kissed as if the realms were exploding around us and this was the last thing we would ever do. If I could choose my final act, without question, this would be it.

"Leaf," I breathed, breaking away to stare into her eyes, their color as fresh as new grass, even in the dim light of this hellhole. I drank in her features, memorizing every torch-lit curve, familiar shadow, and hollow.

"Excuse me," said the Sayeeda, her voice sounding distant. "We're preparing to enact a murder, not attend a bacchanal at a bathhouse."

With the tip of my fang, I nipped Leaf's lip, then drew back to gaze at her one last time. I flicked her a final smirk that I hoped would give her something else to ponder instead of this dank shithole. Then I sauntered out of the Mydorian prison with Ari grumbling about cloaking spells behind me.

At dusk, we strode into the Earth Realm hall, and I was momentarily mesmerized by the light flickering over the white branches holding the ceiling aloft. But then, as the double doors creaked shut behind us, my worst fears were realized. There was no Leaf standing on the dais beside her gold-swathed prick of a brother.

The back of Ari's fingers brushed mine. "Wait," she whispered.

I released my wings, flaring them above my shoulders. "Fuck that. Where is she?" I boomed, stalking forward, careful not to trip over tree roots as I climbed the stairs onto the dais. Sonail and the bearded guard thrust their swords at my chest. I laughed, swatting them away. "*Where* is your *sister*, Regent?"

Quin rose from his slouch on the throne, his eyes unfocused and movements clumsy. He was practically blinded by serum, which suited me fine. Less dangerous for Leaf, too.

"Have you no sense of occasion, King Arrowyn?" he drawled. "Come. Follow me, and Zali will be along shortly."

Guards opened black diamond-studded doors at the back of the dais, and we walked through onto a rectangular stone balcony. A crowd's roar erupted. Every human in the city seemed to be gathered in the square below us. Hungry mouths gaped open as they screamed, revealing rotten teeth and pale, unhealthy gums.

Quin Omala was starving his people, squandering the crown's money on gold feathers and serum.

A robed servant stood next to a narrow high table. Unrolling a vellum scroll, he nodded at Quin, who raised his arms toward his people.

Silence descended.

"Peasants," he hissed as he beckoned me over with an elaborately plumed quill.

I stared blankly at it for a moment.

"Sign the agreement. You can use a golden feather from your breastplate if you prefer. I presume that's what they're for—so you're never at a loss to put your name to urgent documents. That is, if they even work."

Was he fucking joking? I stifled a sigh. "Oh, they work all right, just not in the way you imagine. Hilarious jokes aside, why would I sign something I haven't read?"

"Well, that answer depends on how badly you want my little sister."

"Little? I thought you were twins."

"One of us had to be born first, and it wasn't your precious Zali."

With deliberate slow movements, I took the quill and twirled it between my thumb and forefingers. "Perhaps I don't value her very much at all, but can't bear someone taking my possession."

Quin's dark brow rose. "Pride walks before a man's spectacular fall."

"The bones of a man cloaked in greed will never be warm," I quipped back.

He laughed like a maniac, wiping his leaking nose. "You entertain me, fae. I'll give you that much, at least. Now sign the trade agreement."

"I will." The quill held aloft, I stepped closer to the table. "As soon as Zali Omala arrives."

"Veznar?" the regent spat out.

The doors swung open, and there she was, my Leaf, dressed in the ceremonial clothing she had worn on the dais this morning, except now the sheer top hung in tatters, and the leather suit was slashed and torn, the edges ragged as if it had been chewed by an animal.

Fury exploded inside me. It took every bit of willpower I possessed, plus another lifetime's reserves, to survey the scene and take careful note of everyone's positions. The two guards, Sonail and Veznar, stood on either side of the regent. He beckoned Leaf forward, and she walked to his side, her expression carefully blank.

I scanned her body. Her fingers were curled loosely against her thighs, not digging into her flesh with worry or fear. Then her hands lifted, and she cupped one over the other in front of her waist, ready to make a grab for my sword when I threw it.

"Behold today's historic occasion," the regent shouted to his people. "The King of Storms and Feathers, Arrowyn Ramiel, will sign a trade agreement with our great city of Mydorian on the proviso that I rule in place of the traitor, Zali Omala. What say you to that, Mydorians?"

A weak cheer rolled over the crowd, petering out like a wave fizzling on a sandy shore. In the undercurrent, people booed and muttered curses, but Quin ignored them and beckoned me closer.

"Very well," I said, moving forward, the quill poised between the fingers of my left hand.

As I pressed the tip against the parchment, angling my face slightly toward Ari, the regent's expression remained clear and optimistic. The fool was clueless. My skin tingled as the cloaking spell slithered over me.

"I'm right-handed, you stupid prick," I whispered as I drew my sword and with four quick movements cut the regent's favorite guards from groin to neck.

Quin screamed, and as I looked up from the spilling entrails, Leaf disappeared as I tossed her my sword.

In what was probably the fastest move he'd ever made, the regent's arms wrapped around thin air, then he threw himself sideways off the balcony, taking an invisible Leaf with him.

"No!" I roared, shooting into the sky and out from the cover of Ari's cloaking spell.

Chapter 33

LEAF

Held in the iron grip of Quin's arms, I slid down a length of canvas that was fixed to the wall beneath the balcony.

It seemed my brother had made preparations to throw me over, perhaps to get me away from Arrow if his plans went awry, which, of course, they had done. Quite badly.

Well, fine. I was also prepared. Prepared to kill Quin if it would free our people from the rule of a gold-addicted tyrant. I wouldn't go down without a fight.

We hit the ground on the left side of the crowd in the town square, their bodies parting like the tide from the beach as Quin dropped me. We both scrambled to our feet, and I whipped Arrow's sword up, then slashed it down. Quin blocked it with his blade, the metal clanging together as the force of the blow reverberated down my spine.

Despite me shouting the reaver chant like a woman possessed, my damned invisibility cloak flickered on and off, not holding for more than a few seconds at a time.

We fought back and forth, and Quin's eyes blazed with ferocious energy, the brightest they had looked since my return. We clashed again, the sound of metal grinding on metal ringing out before we pushed apart, circling each other as the crowd chanted.

The smell of sweat tinged the air, and the energy of the Mydorian's excitement sizzled along my skin, a field of power urging me to move faster, strike harder. I thought I heard the word *Zali* chanted on repeat. But that was probably just my imagination working to spur me on.

Before, on the balcony, it was clear to me that Quin's veins were serum-flooded. Practically cross-eyed with the drug, he could hardly hold the crown on his head, let alone raise our father's sword above his shoulders. Somehow, he had gained strength, and he was now faster, more determined to take me down.

When I got up close and saw flames leaping in his eyes, I knew exactly what he had done. The bastard was using fire magic to fight me.

He spat on the ground near my boot, emitting a pleased chuckle, as if that scored him a point. "A gold feather for your thoughts, sister. I'm certain they are fascinating."

"You wouldn't care for them, Quin. They'd injure your pride. And everyone knows how you handle such wounds... with the poise of a deranged child."

Hate twisted his features as he attacked. I let him get close, stepping aside at the last moment, and he screamed like a banshee as he spun on his heel, and our swords swung and clashed, swung and clashed, over and again.

Years of combat training fired my muscle memory of attack angles, each one perfectly matched to take advantage of Quin's weaknesses. This fight was a familiar dance, albeit a deadly one. My brother and I had spent years doing exactly this under the persistent tutelage of instructors and our parents, me whipping his ass and Quin exerting himself as little as possible.

Well, he would pay for his laziness today.

As I realized I could predict Quin's every move, each angle he would choose to strike from before he even shifted his grip on his sword, renewed confidence strengthened my limbs. But unfortunately, fire magic elevated his efforts above his skill level, making him swifter, tougher, and I gritted my teeth each time our blades ground together.

Coated in a slippery layer of sweat, my arms shook as I dodged his swings again and again until his blade finally caught my bare shoulder. I spun out of the blow and swore as dizziness crashed over me and blood trickled down my arm. I felt no pain, only the numbness of ice-cold fury filling my veins.

I wouldn't let Quin win. For Van and every single Mydorian, I just couldn't.

Damn the fucking gold trade. Damn the raiders and every idiotic ruler who preferred their subjects sick and oppressed instead of hale and happy. And most of all, damn me for whatever I'd done to make my stupid brother need to subjugate and conquer me at the cost of our kingdom.

With a roar, I surged forward, hacking, feinting, kicking, thrusting, using every dirty trick I could think of. Yes, the fire magic enhanced Quin's skills, made his movements graceful and nimble, but I fought with the fiery passion to protect everything I loved—freedom for Mydorians and myself.

And I was stronger than him. I had always been strong, even at my lowest point, when I was caged like a bird in Arrow's pavilion, hanging off my gold chain at ridiculous angles, building muscles and endurance.

I could beat Quin.

I *would* beat him.

There was no other option.

The sky turned slate gray, and thunder growled above, the sound vibrating through the air and drowning out the noise of the crowd and the cries of three falcons as they flew overhead.

Curse the Storm King. I felt him above me. Felt his need, his desire to save me from Quin, as if it was a current that burned through my bones, distracting me.

Arrow needed a job to do. Right now.

I looked up and met his silvery gaze as he hovered above. "*Van!*" was all I said, certain that one long screeched syllable would be enough for Arrow to know what he needed to do.

For a moment, he frowned, fighting his need to stay and protect me. His wings beat the air hard, up and down, then he flew to the balcony, swooped, and snatched Ari into his arms. They disappeared through the doors of the Great Hall.

Good. At least now I could concentrate without worrying about them both.

"Auron khaban ana," I chanted aloud, spinning, and then slashing wildly at my brother.

Thanks to my shoulder wound, I needed two hands to hold the sword, which shortened but fortified my strikes.

After a while, I gave up trying to keep the cloak in place. It barely worked, and I needed to focus on each breath and every move I made. My vision blurred, and I wiped sweat from my eyes. Then finally, Quin stumbled, his sword leaving an opening that my blade cut into, blood darkening his leathers over his thigh.

"You should have spent more time practicing, Quin..." I grunted and lunged, my blade tearing his leather bracer. "Not... drinking dust-damned serum and courting the favor of dark magicians."

Slashing my blade, I kept him moving backward, pushing him into the crowd as he tried to defend himself. He cut the side of my leg open with one savage thrust. The Mydorians shoved him forward, as if they wanted him to fail.

"Oh, do you think so, Zali?" He flicked his hand out and magic blinded me. "Some of us prefer to utilize easier methods."

Pain slammed across my forearm, and when the magic cleared, my sword was gone.

Thrown backward from the force of the energy he'd released, Quin's body was spread out on a patch of grass a short distance away. On the ground beside him, rested Arrow's beautiful sword.

Quin looked over his shoulder, his hand grappling for the blade, then he threw it into the crowd, not caring on who or where it landed.

Shit. How could I win this fight without a weapon? This was over. *I* was over. Raising my fists in front of my face, I looked at the sky. Thank the gods, Arrow had returned at lightning speed. Back-lit by silvery clouds, he hung in the air like an avenging angel, his wings slowly stirring the breeze. He grinned and dropped a dagger, and I caught it by its golden hilt. Auryinnian silver, the strongest material in the realms, flashed in my fist like a bolt of lightning.

"Good catch," he mouthed.

"Good throw," I whispered back, widening my stance and getting a good grip on the dagger.

Screaming, Quin launched to his feet, his limbs blurring as he charged toward me, spit flying from his mouth, like a rabid beast. Crouching slightly, every muscle tense, I waited for the right moment, my world, my whole life narrowing to this second. And then I leaped into the air.

Propelling myself forward on the steam of murderous fury, I sank Arrow's knife through leather and plunged it into my twin brother's heart. Once, twice as I roared, twisting the blade to be sure.

Releasing a tortured moan, I wrapped my arms around him as we fell to the ground, our limbs entwined.

"Quin!" The breath whooshed out of me, and I heard Arrow speak as if from underwater, barking at the crowd to *move*. To give us space.

My brother's breath rasped against my cheek.

I leaned over him. "It's all right," I lied. "I've got you."

"Zali... I'm so cold. Don't leave... please."

"I won't. I promise. I'll stay right here."

Cradling his head, I brushed hair the same shade as mine from his eyes and let my tears fall and merge with the blood pulsing from his chest.

I didn't cry because of what he'd done to me. I cried for what we had once been—brother and sister, twin hearts, rambling through the forest for days on end, so happy that if we had died jumping off those cliffs into the river, we would have been at peace with our lives ending then. Because we were together.

My visions hadn't been wrong. I was sure of it. Once, he had loved me. And that version of Quin, I swore to always remember, the brother with clear green eyes, smiling at me through a riot of vines and leaves in the forest.

"Zali?" He coughed, blood spurting from his mouth. "Remember... our tree?"

"The white ash? Of course."

"Mother always told us... don't jump from it. Too high. But we... never listened."

"No. We never did."

He touched my chest with shaking fingers. "Twin souls. Are you worried you might die, too?"

"No. And if I do, our people have the gold reavers and Van to set them on the right course. All is as it should be, brother. No need to worry. You can rest now."

"Yes... rest. So tired." Even as he took his last breath, his hand patted his pockets, searching for his vial of serum.

"You don't need that anymore, Quin." Instead of the vial, I pressed my lips to his mouth. "Sleep well, brother," I whispered and watched the last spark of life in his half-closed eyes extinguish.

Van appeared, crouching at my side, and I dragged him into my arms as we sobbed together.

"It's all right, Zali. He can't hurt you, can't hurt anyone now." Van kissed my cheek, then rose and scanned the crowd, his gold-green gaze intense. "Look at your princess. Then look at what greed for power and gold addiction has done to her twin. Quin Omala was no regent of the people. No caretaker."

Still cradling my twin's dead body on the ground, I watched my younger brother with awe and tried to swallow my tears.

"Quin was a usurper who conspired with the Sun Realm," Van continued, "used dark magic to steal his sister's memories, sold her to the fire fae, and locked me in a cell. Quin Omala was the traitor, not the girl who killed him to free you. Will you stand with her?"

As the sun set behind the city walls, the crowd roared and stamped the ground, the sound vibrating along the backs of my legs. Van held his hand out, and I took it and rose.

"Behold," he said. "Zali Omala, the lost princess of Mydorian. Your future queen."

Squeezing Van's fingers, I forced a smile and thanked the Mydorians, promising to strive to restore our city to the thriving capital it had once been and its residents back to health and happiness. Not easy tasks, but I vowed to dedicate my life to them.

My gaze searched the crowd for Arrow, and I found him standing beside Ari, his fists clenched and body poised to surge forward at the slightest hint of trouble. Staring into his eyes, I poured my soul into his, hoping he would receive my message.

I needed him.

Now.

Arrow's lips parted, then he moved so fast his body blurred, catching me just as my limbs folded in on themselves.

"My Leaf," he whispered, kissing the top of my head. "Are you all right? Please... I need to know that you're going to be all right."

I nodded, and he squeezed me against his chest, probably bending a few bones out of shape in the process. I coughed, and his grip loosened.

"Sorry," he rasped.

My throat burned as I breathed slowly, deeply, determined not to shed any more tears. None for Quin. And certainly none for myself.

Arrow picked me up, his gaze trailing my face, my arms, inspecting the blood, the entire horrible mess of me. "The hardest fucking thing I've ever done was stand by and let him hurt you."

"Technically, you weren't standing," I slurred. "Not on the ground, anyway."

"Must you always have the last word?" He laughed, then asked a question I couldn't answer. "Where's the closest bathroom?"

"Second floor bathhouse," Van answered. "Head east. I'll have clean clothes delivered there shortly."

Holding me close, Arrow shot into the fiery pink sky, through an open palace window. Then he ran, opening door after door until he found the bathhouse and the largest tub within it. He lit torches with lightning magic, then cradled me gently on his lap as the bath filled with water. His wings wrapped around my shaking, blood-splattered body.

After a while, Ari entered, clean clothes and healing supplies in her arms. "You scared me out there, Leaf. When your cloak wouldn't hold, I thought you were finished."

"Me too," I said. "But fortunately, I'm too stubborn to die."

She chuckled, threading a needle. "Indeed you are."

Arrow took it from her. "Let me do it," he said, his voice a low command.

She bowed and left without another word.

While Arrow undressed me, he asked about my memories, what made them return and how much of my life in Mydorian I remembered. As I told him, I stroked the silky edge of a purple-black feather.

"Since you've been in Mydorian, your wings are on display. You normally keep them hidden. What's going on?" I asked, a tremble of suppressed laughter in my voice.

A sound, closer to a growl than a chuckle, rumbled in his chest. "Let's just say I'm feeling very protective of you. It's taking everything I've got to stop myself from sweeping you up, shooting through the glass ceiling, and getting you as far away from this place as possible."

"I can't leave," I whispered.

He heaved a long sigh, then cleaned my cuts and stitched the deepest ones with great care. I ground my teeth together and blinked repeatedly.

"It's all right to cry, Leaf. You've been through a lot, too damn much. Crying isn't a weakness."

"Did you cry when you lost your family?"

He bowed his head and kept working on my cuts.

"Thought so. Of course you didn't."

"But I may have roared and shouted excessively for far too many days and nights," he said, lowering me into the tub. "However, I *would* cry if I lost you. If you had died tonight, Mydorian would be awash with my tears, and not long after, ablaze with my fury."

Warm water soothed my body, but at his words, my muscles drew tight again. I waited for him to say more, every nerve abuzz, as if a sparkle of fireflies flew through my veins, igniting hope.

He took a cloth and washed blood from my arms, then drew a sharp breath. "You've taught me that caring for someone is worth the pain and risk of possibly losing them. And that to love someone isn't a weakness but an act of bravery, for which the rewards are endless."

I stared at him, shocked by his confession. Was the Storm King trying to tell me he'd developed *feelings* for me? And if so, what was I going to do about it?

Broad shoulders shrugged as a shiver ran along his dark wings. "And I've learned that I feel physically unwell when I cannot see you and keep you safe."

"Now you sound like a stalker."

He chuckled. "If so, I feel no shame, only gratitude that I am here, caring for you now. Let go of the pain, Leaf. It's safe to break apart while I'm holding you. I've got you."

As I ducked my head under the water, I did what the storm king urged and let my tears fall again. While my body shook, I cried for the loss of my family. For the brother who grew to hate me because he was born two minutes before me, yet could never inherit a throne.

As Arrow rocked me, his voice rumbling against my ear, I sobbed for the dissolution of old hopes and dreams until, finally, I smiled with gratitude for what was left.

Van. A land of free people that I belonged to. And for the man who held me in his arms—Arrowyn—the enemy who had bought me, freed me from a cage only to lock me up again. My lover, who I had sworn to hate forever. The king I loved with every fragment of my broken heart.

"Thank you," I said, smiling as he wiped my tears.

He kissed my forehead, my cheeks, and assured me everything would be all right, that he would never let anything bad happen to me. Never, he swore. Never again.

Ignoring the clothes Ari had delivered, he wrapped me in his cloak and carried me to the chambers the Mydorian steward had assigned him. As if I was made of delicate crystal instead of dust and stone and grit, he laid me in the bed and tucked the covers around me.

As he sat beside me, his lips curved in a tentative smile. "I suppose now is as good a time as any for me to grovel."

Grinning, I smoothed the covers over my stomach. "Yes, it's a fine time for groveling."

"As you wish." He drew a deep breath. "Leaf, I am sorry for every pain I caused you, every fear I ignited in your heart, and every hope I dashed. Can you forgive me?"

"Are you apologizing because I'll rule a realm that you hope to remain on good terms with?"

He loosed a hard breath, his big shoulders heaving. "No! I say it because it is true. Because I can't bear for you to hate me. I've never begged for anything in my life. Not even when my family died did I beg the gods for the pain to ease. I wanted to endure it. Pay the price for surviving when they didn't. But if it will help my case, I would fall to my knees for you a million times over, Leaf."

"A million? If you plan to achieve this before sunrise, you'd better get started."

He knelt beside the bed, clasping my fingers between his steepled hands as if in prayer. "Zali Omala, Queen of Mydorian, my Aldara, my vicious, most precious Leaf, I beg forgiveness for my past mistakes and plead with you to return to Coridon with me as my—"

"Arrow, I can't leave here. I have a kingdom to set in order and Van to take care of. The time has come for you to set me free."

He swallowed. "But when I picture leaving you... I cannot... I can't see myself doing it."

"Arrow, letting me go is the least you owe me. Then when I return to you, you'll know I did so willingly, not out of obligation or fear."

"Fear? I don't think you were ever truly afraid of me."

"I'm afraid now," I said.

A dark gold brow rose. "Why is that?" he whispered.

"I'm afraid you're never going to kiss me again."

He laughed and got to his feet, flinging his clothes off before sliding into bed beside me. Slowly, we worshiped each other's bodies, each tender touch expressing what we couldn't bear to say aloud, as we dozed on and off throughout the night.

The next day, we slept through dawn and rose after lunch to inspect the palace, the city, and reassure Mydorians that peace and order would be restored, and that the Storm Court would stand with us as our allies.

For three days, Arrow remained by my side and on his best behavior, begging, cajoling, treating me like his queen. But on the morning of the fourth day, Raiden arrived with Arrow's black stallion, Yanar, in tow and whisked the Storm King away to discuss urgent matters.

Hours later, when Arrow returned, his silver gaze was guarded. By the afternoon, he'd worked himself into an agitated state and declared he needed to leave immediately and deal with disturbing news regarding the Sun Realm.

Not even four days prior, I'd begged the Storm King to set me free, and now, when the time came, it was me who couldn't bear to part with *him*.

My heart breaking, I rode with him into the forest, Raiden trailing behind us.

Not far past the reaver veil, Arrow gestured for his friend to continue riding as he tugged my horse's reins and pulled me close. He kissed me like a man leaving for battle, as if he never expected to lay eyes on me again.

"Promise me you'll take care of yourself," he said, removing his feather-embroidered cloak and wrapping it around my shoulders. "Keep this, then I'll always be able to keep you warm."

My aching heart dropped down to my stomach. "I'm the one who should be worrying. Can't you fly home instead of traveling on horseback?"

"Raiden and I have meetings along the way, and although I've offered many times, he has never once let me carry him while I fly."

I laughed at his wry smile. "That sounds like Raiden. But you'll return for my coronation soon, won't you?"

"Of course, I wouldn't miss it for all the gold in the realms. And remember, Leaf, if you ever need me, I will come. I'll take to the air and fly through blood and ash to get to you. Remember who you are—my winged gift, forever my Aldara."

In bed the night before, no matter how many times I'd asked, he'd refused to drink from me. I longed to be as close as possible to him, to connect, but he believed I needed my strength to heal the wounds of my body and heart and didn't dare weaken me.

But now, bidding him goodbye, I wouldn't take no for an answer.

"Renew the Aldara bond before you leave. Drink from me," I urged. His silver gaze flashed over me. "Just a little. Please, Arrow. Before you go, I need to feel our connection again. Nothing would make me happier. If you don't, I vow to return to my rooms, draw my blood myself, and then send it to you in a vial, just to torture you."

He sighed and tugged me closer, nuzzling my hair. The horse shifted restlessly beneath me as Arrow's teeth nipped my ear. I inclined my head and offered my throat. "Please."

"Not there. A smaller vein. It's safer." He raised my wrist and kissed it softly, his mouth opening, moist and teasing. I cried out as he sank his fangs in, moaned as he drew on the vein slightly, once, twice, before his tongue sealed the flow of blood.

"Arrow!" I chided. "Take more."

"Has anyone told you what a greedy, violent little thing, you are?"

"It takes one to know one."

"Is that another of your quaint human sayings?"

"Yes, did it offend you?"

"Not at all. I like everything you do with your mouth."

I laughed, and he licked blood from his lips, giving me a wicked grin.

Arrow urged Yanar into motion, and in four heavy heartbeats, the trees had opened up and swallowed them whole.

Then I was alone, staring at the forest, deep within the Land of Dust and Stones. The exact place that until this very moment, I'd always thought I belonged in.

Chapter 34

LEAF

Mydorian coronations took time to arrange. Bound by ancient reaver traditions, the elves would only travel from Auryinnia at the most auspicious time.

Not only did the stars and planets need to be in perfect alignment, but the position of each grain of sand, cloud, and shadow throughout the lands seemed to matter, too.

This morning, with a relieved smile, Ari informed me that the Zareen had declared the conditions to crown me would be favorable in two weeks' time. Even though I was beyond tired of anticipating the coronation, I smiled back, grateful she'd remained in Mydorian to support Van and me as we adjusted to our new roles.

Two weeks was too long to wait. The sooner it happened, the better, because then I would see Arrow again.

"Another letter from Coridon, sister," said Van, catching up to me as I walked along the river with three ladies from the court.

"Who is it this time?" I asked, shading my eyes from the sun and feigning disinterest as I let my friends walk ahead.

He smirked, offering me the tiny scroll sealed with the Storm Court's insignia, two lightning bolts on a background of floating feathers. "There's only one way to find out. Hurry up and open the damn thing."

Holding my breath, I snatched the scroll and unraveled it, scanning the signature. I swallowed my disappointment. Stormur again.

Three weeks had passed since Arrow left Mydorian, and in that time, he'd only written to me twice, both letters extremely unsatisfying.

I longed to read poetic declarations of love and devotion. And instead, he wrote long descriptions of the weather and repeatedly asked me to allow his Sayeeda to return to Coridon before the coronation.

That decision was beyond my control. No one, other than Arrow, could tell Ari what to do. If she wasn't responding to his requests, then he should have realized he would only have her back in Coridon when she was good and ready to leave here.

Arrow's letters felt wrong. Off. In fact, they didn't sound like him at all. Not just the lack of frequency, but their content and tone told me he regretted declaring his affections and wished he could retract the words he had spoken.

But Ari saw no issues. Tensions still ran high between the Sun and Light Realms. And she assured me that Arrow would write little of importance, fearing fire fae might intercept the missives and use them against me.

I couldn't wait to see him down on his knees, begging forgiveness for making me worry that his feelings had changed. And I couldn't wait another two weeks for him to do it.

For dust's sake, the man had wings. Why hadn't he flown to Mydorian for a sleepless night of fun?

I stopped walking and spun in a circle, a thrilling idea taking shape in my mind.

"Van," I said, linking our arms and strolling forward. "Everything is progressing well in Mydorian, is it not?"

"Indeed. Our people's stomachs are full, and they wear smiles again, instead of grimaces of fear."

I scanned his handsome face, noting that color and fullness had returned to his cheeks. "And you're well and not tempted to take a dose of serum?"

"Absolutely not. Thanks to you and Ari, I never will again."

"Excellent! Conditions are perfect."

"For what?"

Grinning, I said, "Will you ask the scribe to send a letter to King Arrowyn? Tell him not to leave his city, a female envoy from Mydorian is coming to visit, leaving today. Be sure he underlines the word *female*."

"Zali, you're not serious. You can't leave the city now."

"It will be fine. I'll go alone, cloaked, and sneak into Coridon with ease. Don't look so worried. I know you'll take good care of everything while I'm gone. I'm bored and need an adventure. I'll only be away for a week at the most, I promise, then I'll return. If I'm needed, Arrow can fly me back within hours."

"It isn't safe!"

"I've worked hard to improve my cloaking skills. If I can't be seen, I can't be hurt."

"When will you stop being so reckless, Zali?" he said, raking a hand through his dark curls.

I laughed. "Probably never." Tugging on his arm, I swung us to face the palace. "After you've had the letter sent, come and talk to me while I pack."

The hardest part of leaving had been getting away from Van, Ari, and several worried counselors. But three days after my conversation with my brother, my white mare, Luna, and I were traveling across the desert near the Auryinnia Mountains.

The swift ride to the port and journey on a large fishing boat had been uneventful, and now, excitement bubbled in my veins, and I could barely keep my seat in the saddle. Because before long, I would be back in Coridon and engaging in my favorite activity—torturing Arrow in his crescent-shaped bed.

Smiling at the thought, I pulled Luna to a stop, wiped sweat from my face, then gulped water from my pouch. In the distance, a dust storm rolled toward me over the desert. Inside it, two midnight horses pulled a carriage so black it seemed to suck the red and gold hues from the dunes.

Since I didn't recognize the armor of the five riders who galloped around the carriage, I prepared to draw a cloak of invisibility around my shoulders. Then I noticed blue hair escaping from beneath the first rider's helmet, and my heart leaped into my mouth.

Esen.

Had something happened to Arrow?

She rose in the stirrups and waved as I nudged Luna into a trot.

As I got closer, I studied Esen's face, looking for signs of sorrow. Her expression was serious, but not sad.

"Is Arrow all right?" I asked the moment her steed wheeled in front of mine.

"Yes, he's fine. But very soon, *Leaf*, I can promise that *you* won't be."

Fuck. I summoned my cloak, and a crimson-haired fae pulled up beside Esen and laughed at my efforts, twin flames burning in his black eyes. The usual gentle tug I felt as the cloak's forcefield settled around my body didn't happen.

Nothing happened.

I glared at the Sun Realm fae. "Your magic is blocking me."

A smirk spread over his face, then he nodded. "Zali Omala of the Hidden City of Mydorian, by order of Arrowyn Ramiel, the King of Storms and Feathers, you are under arrest. You're coming with us."

"You're lying! Under arrest for what?"

I stared at Esen as another horse pulled alongside hers. The fae removed his helmet, and dark chestnut hair tumbled over his shoulders.

Raiden.

He smiled, brown eyes crinkling with malicious glee and not a hint of his usual kind humor.

My heart stampeded against my ribs, nausea, then fury spinning through my head.

How?

How was this possible?

I wracked my brain, thinking of Arrow's stiff letters. The way his demeanor had changed toward me the day Raiden appeared in Mydorian with Yanar, bearing bad news about the Sun Realm. And after their meeting, the way he couldn't wait to return to Coridon.

From that moment, Arrow had been drawing away from me, and I'd been too stupid, too besotted to see it.

So it seemed there was only one explanation. What Esen said had to be true. The Storm King wanted rid of me.

I drew my sword.

As my vision narrowed and darkened, my last painful thought was of that lying, betraying, silver-eyed asshole, Arrow, who I would never, *ever* forgive.

Not even after I had cut out his rotten heart.

Leaf and Arrow's story continues in book 2, **King of Fire and Flames!** ***Check out the audiobook.***

Acknowledgements

Thank you for reading Leaf and Arrow's story! I hope you enjoyed it.

I absolutely love hearing from readers, and I'm so grateful for every lovely review I've received, no matter how brief. Thank you so much for taking the time to recommend my books to other readers. Your support and enthusiasm is what me keeps writing stories!

Thank you to Saint Jupiter for another gorgeous cover and for being such a pleasure to work with!

And massive thanks to my amazing beta readers Rosemary, Ken, Amelie, and Saskia, to my wonderful ARC readers, and also to Erin at The Word Faery for your perfect feedback!

Until next time,

Juno

Also By Juno Heart

If you enjoyed King of Storms and Feathers, check out the audiobook and further books in the series. Also, the gorgeous color artwork of Leaf and Arrow appears in the hardcover edition and the black and white version is in the special fae king paperback and symbol paperback.

In the meantime, check out the Black Blood Fae series, fated mates, enemies-to-lovers stories that are a little lighter and not as steamy as the Courts of the Star Fae Realms books, but packed with swoony angst and bantery humor!

Book 1: Prince of Never
Book 2: King of Always
Book 3: King of Merits
Book 4: Prince of Then, the prequel

The series is complete and ready to binge in Kindle Unlimited!

About the Author

Juno Heart writes enemies-to-lovers fantasy romances about arrogant fae heroes and the feisty mortal girls that bring them to their knees.

When she's not writing, she's probably busy herding her cat and dog around the house, spilling coffee on her keyboard, or searching local forests and alleyways for portals into another realm.

Join Juno's newsletter for new release and special deal alerts!

Email: juno@junoheartfaeromance.com

Made in the USA
Coppell, TX
20 June 2024

33709217R00246